EMPIRE OF SHADOWS

BOOK THREE OF THE CORAIDIC SAGAS

ALICIA WANSTALL-BURKE

Cover art by Pen Astridge
Edited by AJ Spedding
Map by Alicia Wanstall-Burke

ISBN: 978-0-6484478-5-6
Imprint: Independently published

ALSO BY ALICIA WANSTALL-BURKE

The Coraidic Sagas
Blood of Heirs
Legacy of Ghosts

For Graham,
for catching me when I fell.

In loving memory of Aiki Flinthart,
who taught Lidan to fight like a girl.

Dorfa

Redona
City

Lake Lith

The Woadler

Burd

Shartridor

Fort
Dowa

Bata

Iscrol

Grey
Cliff

Arin

Ravens

River Arrx

Port Hadeen

Wolban

Syod Archipelago

Marsaw

Na

Daylin

The High Tund

pire

Marlow

·Harben

Orhia

odwin

·Usmein

anor

Vixorcrest

·Laliva

The Ruken

ja

·Kederen

The Alapa

The Malapa

Fracture Pass

Jungle Monster

The South Lands

Tolak

Jungle River

The Black Teeth

"Evil is always unspectacular,
and always human,
and shares our bed and eats at our table."
W.H. Auden, Collected Poems

PROLOGUE

Blinding white light.

A horse snorted and a hoof stamped against hard ground, the vibration felt in the bones of a swollen face.

'What's this then?' a voice asked with all the weight of time and mountains.

There was no reply from burning, bruised lips. Distant pain. A shadow of discomfort. A memory needling at the edge of perception.

The voice grunted, derisive. 'You're not done, boy.'

A groan escaped. Blood, tangy and harsh, slipped from the corner of a mouth across icy skin.

'You're not even close to done.'

Leather creaked.

'Send him back.'

A hoof slammed into reality, snapping it clean, opening it to possibility, manipulation, and all of time. In a single frozen heartbeat, a body plummeted through realms beyond imagination, pulled from the white, drawn, stretched, reformed, pushed back toward warmth and pain and fleeting, fractured hope.

Voices across immeasurable distance. Hard, callous laughter.

Snide, foul jibes.

Rough hands, pulling, poking, shoving. Stone scraped across skin, leaving hot stinging trails as their weight lifted.

Breath.

Warmth.

Agony.

Life.

The smallest sliver of daylight.

A laugh. Familiar. Soul destroying.

No... He couldn't quite grasp why that voice sparked a flame of hate, but it caught on something deep within. There was no memory to attach to the sensation, no recollection of its source, just a bone deep knowledge that this voice was to be feared, loathed.

'He's breathing?' asked the familiar voice, pitch rising in surprise. 'Someone's looking out for the fool. Get him up.'

Hands grasped at aching limbs and dragged them free of their confinement. Darkness and sweet, painless oblivion called, tempting from the edge of the agony, but the tiny fluttering flame of rancour burned brighter, a fire that should have guttered with the spark of life long ago.

Igniting in the depths of a heart that should not beat at all, it flared with a hiss to chase back creeping death. A thud, and another; a rhythmic drumming awakening a corpse. The fibres of his being quickened, called back by the thumping siren song.

They were not finished yet. There was more work to do.

He was not finished yet.

CHAPTER ONE

Anywhere but the South Lands

Sellan slammed into the ground, the air punched from her lungs by an impact she hadn't seen coming. She'd intended to land with grace, materialising above the earth and stepping lightly down with no more than the whisper of a falling feather. Instead, she lay wheezing in the dirt, her chest searing, limbs trembling and at least one rib cracked. She moaned and rolled onto her back, sucking air between her teeth and squeezing her eyes shut.

'Fuuuuuck,' she managed to breathe. For a moment she stiffened, listened carefully, wondered if anyone had heard her profanity, then promptly remembered she didn't care. Her masks and pretences had been stripped away, some taken, others thrown, all of them gone now. At this moment, she was precisely whoever she might like to be, not what was required or expected.

She opened her eyes slowly and blinked up at the sky.

Stars. Inky, blue-black darkness. The last crescent of the moon bright sliver against a halo of cloud.

How long had she been travelling? It had been morning when she'd vanished from that foul little riverside village south of the Ice Towers, the sun barely halfway to midday. Yet here, where she'd fallen, it was well after sunset.

Where *had* she fallen?

She arched her back and rolled onto her stomach again, cursing the burning stab in her side and the sudden white-hot bloom of pain in her shoulder, and levered herself up onto one elbow. Lights twinkled in the distance, growing in number as her vision cleared.

A town. Bigger than a village, but not a city as far as she could tell. Unless there was a spectacularly high wall blocking her line of sight. The highest lights shone from windows no more than three storeys from the ground.

She grunted and swore, dragging herself to her feet. This was unfortunate. Actually, it was downright infuriating. This was not where she had intended to land.

Staggering forward, she scanned through her body. Her legs and their associated joints seemed to have survived the fall, though they trembled with each tiny step. Pain lanced through her chest, one shoulder unwilling to respond to her commands as it should. She fingered the joint and hissed, biting down on a wave of nausea. There was an unreasonable gap between the top of her arm and the cap of bone at the end of her shoulder, on the same side as her snarling ribs. Her body wasn't going to put *that* to rights on its own, not after the massive volume of magic she'd expelled to get here. This wrong would have to be corrected by the hands of a healer, and quickly, in case her power decided to set things where they didn't belong.

It had been many years since her body had healed itself by magic. Thanie had held it back, like a dam banking up a river. Fast-healing wounds would only draw unwanted attention to something they were trying very hard to hide. Now that wall was gone; vaporised under the sheer weight of what it had taken to get Sellan from that steaming hot shithole of a settlement to the much cooler climes of this, she assumed, northern town. Her power was weak but it would return, and when it did, there would be nothing to stand in its way.

Just as there was nothing standing in her way now. No rules, no expectations, no fallacies to maintain, no more fucks to be given for anyone but herself. She moved toward the blinking lights of the town, stronger, more sure-footed with each step, ignoring the pain and the dryness in her mouth. Dawn would break eventually, and the day to come was hers to do with as she pleased.

Sellan smiled; a slow, creeping thing that twitched the top of her lip as if it so desperately wanted to become a sneer.

For the first time in almost twenty years, she was free.

Chapter Two

North of the Ice Towers

A defensive wall loomed from the darkness, its height marked by flickering torches and lamps, back lit by the dim glow of the town it sought to protect. Sellan slipped into the shadows of a roadside copse of trees, her gaze wandering southward along the wall to where it vanished into the night. She cocked an eyebrow at it.

She knew this wall.

For the first fifteen years of her life, she'd passed through its gates, wandered the market squares and streets within its boundary, and glanced over her shoulder at it when she left for the capital and the Academy.

This wall encircled Baleanon—the place of her birth.

She cursed and spat in the dirt, glaring at the town as if it had personally insulted her with its presence. In a way, it had. It wasn't supposed to be here because *she* wasn't supposed to be here. She'd landed within the Woaden Empire's expansive borders, but this was not where she'd intended to arrive. It was entirely possible that thinking of *home* while transporting across a vast distance of space had led to this cock up, but she'd never admit it aloud. Sellan sighed and cradled her injured arm against her chest as best she could.

This wasn't the plan, but it would have to do. She could work with this. She hoped.

The gravel road crunched beneath her shoes and she limped slowly to the gate, emerging into the faint circle of light reaching out from the parapet. Goosebumps prickled across her skin and she licked at dry lips, suddenly and infuriatingly nervous. What in the depths of the Underworld was she going to say? Open up? Knock knock?

Instead, she coughed, clearing her throat and squinting up at the gate-house set above the lintel. Nothing happened. Sellan ground her teeth and stifled a snarl. It was cold out here and her shoulder burned with a furious inner fire that did nothing to warm her. Her flowing, lightweight dress wasn't made for the much milder northern summer but rather the humid, sweaty nightmare of the South Lands. By the gods she was glad to be rid of that place, though she'd kill for a shawl to cover her arms. She coughed again, louder this time, and watched the glowing door of the gatehouse. It had either been abandoned or was manned by the most incompetent guards in the Empire.

She limped closer and banged her fist against the timbers, shaking them enough to rattle the chains on the other side of the locks.

'Hello?' she called, her voice crackling from lack of use.

A shadow appeared above, peering over the rampart. 'Who's this then?'

Swallowing, Sellan considered her options. Best to play this close and careful, as much as it went against her baser instincts. She had no way of knowing what waited on the other side of the gate after so many years of absence. Dropping any hint of an education from her accent, she blinked up at the guard. 'A traveller.'

'Iss'a bit late to be out and about, ain't it?' the man called, as if her being abroad at this hour was either the most impressive or ludicrous thing he'd ever encountered.

Wincing a little more obviously and shifting uncomfortably on her feet, she gestured back down the road. 'Came to grief a few hours back. The cart broke apart and the horses bolted.'

'You alone?'

Does it look like I have a fucking entourage? Sellan bit down on the thought before it became a tirade. Losing her temper would be unwise. It would do nothing but piss the guard off and almost guarantee she'd spend the night outside the walls. She took a deep breath, let it go and looked back at the silhouette. 'Yes. I'm alone. I got hurt bad and need aid.'

'Seems odd...' the man ventured.

Fury rose in Sellan like a dark tide, slow but strong, filling her from the soles of her feet to the crown of her head. She was cold, she was in pain, she was hungry, and her patience was a thin misty veil vanishing rapidly into the pull of the wind. Her slight smile fell flat but she kept her frustration as far from her voice as she could manage, fighting the urge to glower at the guard, knowing full well that he was as common as horse shit and well beneath her station.

'What's your name?' she asked, her gentle question floating up through the cool night air.

The man appeared to shuffle his feet and glanced over his shoulder. He was alone then, looking for back up in case things went awry. 'Uffran.'

'Please, Uffran,' she pleaded. That left a bitter taste on her tongue. It had been many years since she'd begged for anything; so long in fact that she really couldn't remember the last time she'd sunk so low. 'Just for the night. I've no weapons or companions. I mean, look at me. I'm no threat!'

He seemed to consider, and though shadow obscured his face, she imagined his beetling brows as he studied her carefully. Her leg started to shake then, muscles fatiguing, strength waning. She looked down at herself.

She was a sight.

Filthy with mud from the hem of her dress to her knees and damp from the dewy grass in the fields, the cold seeped through holes torn in the fabric while clambering over stacked stone boundary fences. That was one thing the South Lands didn't have: boundary fences. At least not in the wide, open spaces of the ranges. Here every man and his dog had marked out a patch of land and bordered it with a bloody fence, as if they were each tiny kingdoms with their own tiny kings. It made trekking cross-country directly toward the town quite a chore, dragging on for hours until she'd fallen from the top of one rough-hewn construction into a ditch and stumbled out onto the road. The gods only knew what her face looked like after such an embarrassing tumble. What she could see of her dark red hair swirled in wild disarray, knotted and unable to be bound thanks to her single functioning hand.

At least she *looked* like she'd been in a cart accident and staggered across the wilds to get here. She glanced back at the top of the gate and realised Uffran was gone.

Fuck. She shut her eyes, pursed her lips and released a sigh. She'd never had a problem with cursing, but the words poured out of her tonight, such was her frustration with how terribly things had gone. Not just arriving here, of all places, but back in that Tolak village. If she ever caught Lidan or Marrit swearing like this—

A pain shot through her chest, her heart clenching. She staggered, gasping sharply. Somewhere beyond the gate, chains clanked and clattered, someone muttering something incomprehensible. She barely heard them over the thud of her pulse.

Lidan and Marrit. Her daughters. Her only children.

She wouldn't hear them swear or laugh or cry. She wouldn't see them either, because they were an entire world away. *She* had done that. Left them and run, or flown, or vanished. It didn't matter how she'd done it. They were there and she was here, and there was exactly nothing she could do about that now. She'd made her choice. Blinking hard and lifting her chin, she crushed the pain down into a dark place where it might, in time, rot away.

The gate eased open, the guard called Uffran putting his shoulder into shifting the weight. He let up once there was enough space for her to slip through and stood there puffing. With a nod, he invited her in and shut the gate tight, hefting an oil lamp to light their way.

'Boss says I'm to see ya to an inn or what not. Can't have you wander'n round town on your own.' Uffran swung the lamp to indicate the broad street ahead. It was the same as she remembered—paved for the most part with wide, flat stones, and deep drains at the sides to collect storm water. Houses and buildings loomed on either side, columns at the front lit by hanging lamps, the baked clay tiles of the roofs obscured by the night.

Off down the side streets lay everything from market squares and a river port to poorly maintained slum dwellings for the most common folk, just as it was in every town she'd ever been to in the Empire. The wealthy and high-born lived cleanly, with heating under their floors and fountains in their gardens, while the rest... Well, Sellan had no idea how the rest lived and rather thought she didn't care to. Unless things went spectacularly wrong, she'd never have any need to find out. She glanced around with wide eyes, a show for Uffran, playing at astonishment at the scale of the buildings.

'You from round here?' He huffed as they walked, not exactly fit or trim for a guard, carrying a paunch at his midsection that stuck out over his belt. He might have been in his fifties, or at the later end of that decade—it was hard to tell just by looking. His helmet sat awkwardly, cheek guards angled out at the sides as though his face had grown wider over the years and his helm hadn't been adjusted to suit. He was a perfect example of why, if the Empire wasn't careful, the black-blooded Free Nations would one day overrun these outlying towns under the power of sheer complacency and dumb luck.

Sellan shook her head and hugged her dislocated arm a little tighter. 'Not really. Been travelling.'

It wasn't a lie, but it wasn't the truth either. She didn't fear this man, or she wouldn't be following him down a maze of ever deteriorating streets into the less reputable parts of Baleanon. For now it was best that her past remain outside the realms of common knowledge. At least until she knew what kind of welcome awaited her.

'Here's you.' Uffran pulled up and waved toward the door of a reasonably grotty looking inn on a side street paved with uneven dirt and patches of mud. Music jangled from inside, pipes played badly and singing that might put a pained cat to shame echoing out the door and against the buildings opposite. The sign above the entry was obscured by grime and years of neglect, but the name *The Scythe and Shears* was still clear enough. A farmer's pub, then. 'They don't mind take'n folk from abroad, as long as you've coin to pay.'

He turned before she could say more than a half-hearted thank you, and left her standing in the street clutching her arm.

Well. This was fucking stupid.

Sellan squinted up as a light drizzle began drifting lazily out of the sky. She hadn't noticed the heavier clouds roll in, but then it was dark, so it was unlikely she would have. Just about as unlikely as her getting anywhere in that inn. She had nothing but the clothes on her back and they were in terrible condition. She had no coin or valuables to trade either, so she couldn't afford a room, or food, or even a drink. Had her shoulder been in one functional piece, she might have traded work for board, though she loathed to think of it. And there was no money to pay a medic or medius mage to fix her shoulder so she *could* work. In any case, she'd survived thirty-five years without putting in a full day's manual labour. She wasn't about to change that now.

9

However, all this left her in a tight spot with no possibility of wriggling away from the reality of her situation.

With a grunt, she turned back toward the main street and limped along in the shadows of the buildings. Rain washed across the stones of the road, growing heavier as she hurried across an empty plaza and slipped clumsily around the margins of a massive fountain. She'd thrown coins in there as a child, but even in her current state of need she wasn't going swimming to see if there were any at the bottom of the black water.

The buildings grew as she made her way through town, the street-facing columns higher and grander, the distance between each doorway longer as the places behind the walls became ever more palatial. There was hardly anyone about, save for a few stray dogs and an extraordinarily unimpressed cat who had anticipated the change in the weather about as well as she had. It glared with narrowed yellow eyes as she limped past, rain dripping from its soaked fur. Sellan glared back, daring it to comment on how she must look like a drowned rat.

The final corner she had to navigate came into view and she paused under the shelter of an eave. Water gurgled through the drains, here capped by stone to keep them hidden from high-born eyes. Light shimmered through the rain, sparkling halos of droplets encircling each lamp. The only other sign of life in the plaza was a lone figure sheltering under a narrow awning, hardly protected at all from the weather, cloaked in darkness and shadow. Sellan recoiled. Had the proper way of things altered so greatly that the city guard no longer cleared such folk from the better parts of town? Though she couldn't see the figure's face, she felt their gaze, deciding without hesitation to ignore it completely.

At the far end of the street stood the grandest building in the entire town, an immense thing on a foundation high enough to warrant three flights of terraced steps and a guard of two smartly dressed soldiers standing in the lit porch behind the columns. At either side of the road, facing each other across a grand square, stood two enormous homes, both of which she would recognise until the day she died. The slightly smaller of the two—and she would always emphasise just how slight the difference was—stood to the left, and she limped across the rain-soaked square toward it.

Sellan looked down at herself again. This wasn't exactly how she'd imagined this day, the few times she'd thought of it at all, but she was left with no other choice. For some reason, the Dead Sisters had decided she needed to be here. Who was she to dispute fate?

Each step tore at her ribs and her fingers were numb, but she made the porch above the slick stone steps and gently let her injured arm hang at her side. She pulled down hard on a cord hanging by the door, and waited. Unlike the gate guard, the man on the other side of this entryway was not slow in attending the bell. Within moments the door swung open, and warmth exhaled out over Sellan's icy skin.

'What in the—' He was a short man, not much taller than Sellan's shoulder, with white hair around a shining bald patch. His round face contorted at the sight of her, pinching inward with disgust. 'Are you mad? The slave door is round *there*!'

He jabbed his finger off to the left and made a swift move to slam the door in her face. The panel swung hard and Sellan's good hand met it with a wet slap, stopping it dead.

The man started and glared. 'What do you think you're doing?'

At this point, she wasn't entirely sure, but she was at the end of her rope and about done with pretending. Her injured arm hung useless at her side, agonising as her muscles stretched in ways they were never meant to, and her body shook as she forced her remaining strength into holding the door open despite the man pushing at it from the other side.

'I'd speak to Lady Mediia, if she's in,' Sellan said through chattering teeth.

'At this hour? Of course she's in, but she's not about to receive the likes of you!' he spat.

'Really, Paud? Are you sure?'

He baulked and narrowed his eyes. 'How do you...'

He didn't use that name in public and few people knew it outside this house. It was his birth name, given to him before he'd been taken as a slave from one of the northern colonies, not the name he'd been given by his first owner.

'I'm actually surprised you're still alive. I'd have thought all those midnight tipples in the cellar would have done you in by now. Perhaps it pickled you.' A mocking smile crept across her lips. She'd held onto it for so long, she couldn't help but let it out. The look on his face was priceless. Clearly, he thought his theft from his master's cellar had gone unnoticed, but she'd seen it on her rare visits home from the Academy.

'Who are you?' Paud hissed. His round face brightened to red, flushing all the way back through his white hair. 'Name yourself!'

'Sellan Parben, daughter of House Corvent of the Burikanii.' The name fell from her like a discarded veil, words she'd sworn never to speak again. 'Now if you would be *ever* so kind as to tell my mother I'm home, I could use a fucking drink.'

CHAPTER THREE

Baleanon, the Woaden Empire

Paud hurried away into the house, leaving the door swinging. Sellan blinked in disbelief, stepped across the threshold, and stood dripping rainwater onto the entryway floor. He hadn't even disputed her assertion. He'd just run off, presumably to find someone else to deal with her.

The stone floor, inlaid with mosaic tiles had been refreshed with new colour since she'd last been here. At the far end of the entry hall stood a long atrium with a lush garden and splashing fountains, rain falling through the open roof and glistening on the leaves of fruit trees and trimmed shrubs. Across the garden, deep in the main part of the house, someone began shouting, demanding an explanation. Footsteps hurried toward her, the voices echoing, growing clearer.

She carefully took hold of her elbow and eased her injured arm up against her chest, relieving some of the pain but not enough. Weakness trembled in her knees and Sellan cursed herself. What a way to come home after some twenty years. The sound of hissed whispers and bustling footsteps stopped, and she looked up into a much older version of a face she knew too well.

A woman who had once been her own height gaped in wide-eyed shock, her once dark red hair now streaked with silver, the once firm, smooth skin of her face and neck creased with age. Sellan had grown taller since she'd last seen Lady Mediia Parben, but her mother still seemed to have shrunk. She was thin, but not gaunt, and her mouth snapped shut.

Paud stood at Lady Mediia's shoulder and lifted his hand toward Sellan. His fingers trembled and his lips moved as if he wanted to speak but couldn't find the words. What could he say? They had probably assumed she was dead, perhaps even hoped she was, and that was exactly how she'd have preferred it to stay. Sadly, that was a luxury Sellan could no longer afford.

'Mother,' Sellan said, heart thudding, her mouth still dry for some odd reason. Was she nervous? Why was she nervous? She didn't *get* nervous... But this was her mother, and the woman had ever been hard to read.

Mediia gave Paud a slight nod and he took off into an unseen part of the house.

Sellan's stomach lurched. *Oh shit...*

Had he been sent to fetch the local mage representatives from the Congress? Would her mother hand her in just like that, without a word of greeting or a question of why or how she could possibly be here?

'Mother, I—'

Lady Mediia put a single finger across her lips to silence her daughter. Then she turned, gesturing at Sellan to follow.

The house was silent, save for the whisper of rain on the roof tiles and the paved pathways in the garden. They walked quietly around the colonnaded portico at the edge of the atrium, the open roof to their left and doorways leading to reception rooms and guest chambers to the right. At the far end of the garden, Sellan's mother led her up a short flight of steps and along a hallway decorated liberally with wall paintings, hangings and busts, to a sitting room. They were alone, and the older woman shut the door.

A fire crackled and popped in a hearth, a collection of day beds and lounges arranged nearby. Beside one, a bound volume of parchment with quill and ink had been set aside on a small table. Though the book's green leather cover lay shut, Sellan recognised it as one of her mother's ledgers.

She stood still and waited, shivering, clutching her arm. Was Paud about to burst through the door with a troop of soldiers brandishing swords? Or would a mage from the Baleanon Congress office sweep through in a swirl of robes and declare her an enemy of the state? She'd made a colossal mistake coming here. Surely she'd be dead by sun—

Mediia appeared in her field of vision and scattered the spiral of rambling thoughts. Her mother's hand reached up, and between two perfectly manicured fingers, lifted a matted, rain-soaked lock of hair away from

Sellan's face. Mediia's eyebrows rose just a little, then she let the lock of hair fall, turning away and indicating to a seat near the fire.

'You look terrible,' Mediia announced.

Sellan rolled her eyes. 'It's nice to see you too, Mother.'

'And I see you haven't lost that acerbic little attitude you picked up at the Academy.'

'It's good to know some things don't change, isn't it?' she shot back.

Mediia sat and waved at the empty seat again. Sellan remained where she was.

'Fine.' Mediia sniffed, rearranging the layers of her stola and leaning back against the cushions. 'You're too filthy to sit down in any case. I thought I'd be polite.' She folded her hands in her lap. 'So, you're not dead. That is something of a… surprise.'

Sellan stared at her mother for a moment, then glanced at the roof, as if the Dead Sisters of Fate were watching through the rafters. *Why did I come here? Why did you bring me here?* 'No, I'm not dead. Yet.'

Mediia feigned bewilderment. 'Are you planning on it?'

'Not if I can help it.' Sellan shuffled her feet and her grip on her arm slipped, dropping her elbow slightly and jolting the muscles and tendons barely holding at her shoulder. Hot barbs of pain dug deep, a groan escaping as she jammed her teeth into the back of her lip.

'That doesn't look at all pleasant, dear.' That was about as close to sympathy as she would get from Lady Mediia. The woman wasn't exactly cold, rather more acidic, as if letting her guard down might expose her to some sort of emotional injury. Sellan had learned that trick from the best.

The door opened behind her and Paud bustled in. 'My lady, Eddark will be along shortly. He was just returning when I sent out the messenger.'

'Very good.' Mediia nodded and Paud disappeared again.

'Eddark?' asked Sellan, ignoring the sweat breaking across her brow despite the chill of her soaked dress. Shivers trembled down her limbs, no matter how she contracted the muscles to try and stop them. Dark spots bloomed in her vision before she blinked it clear. 'The slave boy?'

'The very same,' Mediia replied. 'Although, much like yourself, he's no longer a child.' She got up and collected a thin blanket from a nearby lounge, tossing it over the single odd-shaped chair with a very short back, a seat that looked like a cup that had been cut in half down the middle, and four elaborately carved legs. Probably some new fashion from the capital. The blanket obscured a plump cushion and Lady Mediia jabbed her finger at it. 'Sit, before you fall over and break something else.'

Sellan did as ordered, and a man slipped through the door with a leather case in one hand.

'M'lady,' he said with a nod at Mediia.

'Eddark.' Mediia eased back into her seat and gestured to Sellan. 'You remember my daughter, Lady Sellan?'

To Eddark's credit, his shock lingered for only the briefest of moments before vanishing behind a polite smile. 'Of course.'

He gave Sellan a slight bow, as if her sudden appearance in her parents' house was nothing out of the ordinary. Sellan knew better. Not only had she been declared derramentis and ear-marked for the eastern front the year she'd turned fifteen, she'd disappeared completely, choosing the life of a fugitive rather than face such a death sentence.

She *should* be dead.

If discovered, she could very well be arrested and executed within days. The only thing standing between her and that fate were the people in this house and their ability to keep their mouths shut. Fortunately, if things were as they had been when she was a child, then the slave-staff her mother kept were experts at secret keeping. In fact, they prided themselves on it, and she kept them well rewarded for their efforts. Unless Mediia gave them licence to speak, Sellan doubted the news would reach beyond the walls of this compound.

'Sellan has been abroad and seems to have injured herself. Could you see that she's put to rights?'

'As you wish, m'lady.' Eddark put his leather case on the ground by Sellan's feet and knelt beside her knees. His large hands reached for her wounded shoulder, and she instinctively flinched back. This was going to hurt something cruel and she wasn't at all sure she wanted to go through it while her mother stared from across the room. There was sympathy in Eddark's deep brown eyes, and a wry smile on his lips. She did recognise him. He'd had a mop of dark blond curls the last time she'd seen him...

'Sellan?' Mediia drew her attention and Eddark set to work, rummaging through his case, retrieving this item and that, then arranging them on a nearby table. Her mother nodded at the dislocated joint. 'Why has that not corrected itself?'

She would have shrugged had her arm not been hanging from its socket. 'Not enough magic left, I suppose. I used almost all of it to get here.'

The ghosts of screams hit hard, tearing through the calm of the room, piercing her ears—Thanie begging her to stop, Lidan demanding answers, that pissant Orthian boy firing shots, forcing her to expose herself, forcing her to flee and abandon the life she'd managed to make for herself, as much as she'd hated it.

'Is that so…' Mediia left the statement hanging and Sellan let it go. She wasn't ready to explain herself. Had she the funds to pay for a healer, she wouldn't be here. She wouldn't have even come to this part of town. As soon as she was able, she'd be in the wind. She had no intention of staying.

A thin metal bowl settled in her lap. She glanced down, then straight at Eddark. 'What's that for?'

'Just in case.' A grin tugged at his mouth but he held it back.

'No, I'm serious,' Sellan countered, the pitch of her voice rising despite herself, her heart rate climbing, sweat prickling on her skin. Eddark put one hand on her upper arm and took her wrist in the other, carefully manoeuvring her forearm around toward him. 'What is it for?!'

Eddark didn't answer, his eyes trained on her arm.

'Your father should be back soon,' Mediia put in, as if she and Sellan were casually chatting over tea.

'Where is he?' she asked quickly, glancing around the room, wondering why she hadn't noticed his absence before now.

Mediia waved a hand dismissively and clicked her tongue. 'I'm sure I have no idea, but he's usually stumbling in by now.'

With a wriggle and pop, her arm bone slipped back under the cap of her shoulder.

Pain exploded from the joint and Sellan threw up.

'Told you,' Eddark muttered, not even trying to keep the humour from his voice as she gagged and retched, face down in the bowl, coughing violently. 'Just in case.'

There wasn't much to vomit out, apart from the sparse remains of her breakfast and some acidic bile, but out it came, her whole body shivering with shock and rolling waves of nauseating pain. Glaring at Eddark and wiping spit from her lips, she wanted nothing more than to slap the smirk off his face.

'Thank you *so* much,' she hissed. Eddark winked at her, and she fought the urge to fling the bowl at him.

'Anything else amiss?' he asked. Carefully, he took the bowl from her trembling hand and covered it with a cloth.

She looked away and glowered at a distant wall, staring daggers at a bust of one of her ancestors. There were other injuries, hidden under her ruined clothes, but she'd rather suffer than let him get his hands on the rest of her.

'Sellan,' her mother scolded, and she snapped her gaze back to Mediia.

'I'm quite well, thank you.' The words were barely audible through her clenched jaw.

'You used to be a better liar, child.'

'I'm not a child!' she snarled.

'Then do stop acting like one,' said Mediia, rolling her eyes.

Eddark sat back on his heels and waited, unwrapping a length of bandage that she assumed would become a sling. 'Did you fall on that side?'

'Yes?'

'How are your ribs?'

'Fine.'

'Cough then,' he ordered. Sellan baulked, taken aback by the man's gall. For a slave, he had some balls to talk to her like that. Her two-decade absence aside, she was still the eldest daughter of his owner, and niece to the Lord of Baleanon. Yet her mother made no move to chastise him. In fact, Mediia looked at Sellan as if she expected her to comply with Eddark's ridiculous direction.

'I will do no such thing—' she began.

'Sellan Abrial Parben, you will do as the man requires!' Lady Mediia's command echoed against the ceiling, jolting through Sellan like lightning. Silence filled the space left behind and Sellan ground her teeth.

Nothing had changed. In her mother's eyes, she was still a rebellious teenager who refused to do *as* told, *when* told. How could so many years pass, so many things happen in her wild and unconventional life, and still she was reduced to cowering in the presence of this woman? Her eyes stung and she glanced fleetingly at Eddark.

'I might have cracked a rib,' she said quietly. 'It hurts to breathe too deeply. I've heard that's what that might mean.' She hadn't ever experienced it, but she'd listened to both her girls prattle on about this healing procedure and that, absorbing at least some of what they knew despite herself.

Eddark moved around behind her and started manipulating her back with his fingers, taking care to notice each hiss and flinch and snarled curse. 'Breathe in as deep as you can?'

Sellan narrowed her eyes at Lady Mediia, who artfully focused her attention on the ledger, leafing through pages of parchment and pausing to scan lines of text, offering no mercy or salvation to her daughter. And Eddark, the man she had once known as a thin, ratty little kitchen boy, seemed unwilling to relent, leaning over her shoulder and watching her face.

Oh for fuck's sake. Fine…

She took a deep breath and gasped at the spear of agony that cut through her chest. Her good hand gripped the arm of the strange, half-cup chair and she shivered again. This was ludicrous. 'Surely you've got something for pain in that bag of yours?'

He came back around the chair and shrugged. 'Might do.'

'Are you going to stand for this, Mother? I mean, really! Is he a slave or not? What kind of house are you running—'

'Eddark was freed when he reached manhood. He's not been a slave for many years.' Mediia's pale green gaze met Sellan's and she bit her tongue. 'He is an employee, and a loyal one, though we tend to keep that small fact to ourselves.'

'An *employee*?'

What had happened here in the years since she'd been gone? High-born families didn't have employees! They had slaves who were grateful not to sleep on the streets and were rewarded for their ongoing service and loyalty by not being sold into a salt mine. That service and loyalty often resulted in freedom, but they certainly didn't become employees after the fact. Such a notion was preposterous. Yet here she was, staring in unveiled shock as she realised her mother was not joking, and was indeed *paying* this man for his work.

'Of course, you'd never admit it in polite company, would you, Mother?' Sellan challenged.

'Oh no, but there are many things that go on in this house that aren't spoken of in polite company.' She gave them a stiff smile and went back to her ledger.

'Here,' Eddark said, pressing a cup into Sellan's good hand. 'Drink this while I sling your arm. You've bruised those ribs, maybe cracked one, but it's not broken all the way through. You'll need to rest until it heals. There's not much to be done for them, I'm afraid.'

Marrit's endless chatter echoed in her mind, a blurred and dismissed moment that she suddenly wished was clearer, easier to hold on to, a moment she could burn into her memory. 'So I've heard.'

'Will that be all, m'lady?' Eddark asked Mediia, packing his bag and leaving a stoppered bottle of dark liquid on the table beside Sellan.

'Yes, thank you, Eddark. I'll send Paud up to fetch you if we need anything more tonight.'

He inclined his head. 'I'll check that shoulder before I leave for my rounds tomorrow.' He put his finger on the top of the bottle and waited for Sellan to look up. 'For the pain. No more than a thimble full, three times a day.'

She nodded and he left, shuffling out the door as someone else staggered through it.

'Eddy!' a man's voice boomed.

'Sir,' Eddark replied, and Sellan turned as he vanished into the hall beyond, leaving a rain-soaked figure standing in the same place she'd been, dripping into the same barely dried puddles she'd left on the floor.

'Well, Mediia, what's the matter with you, then?' The words slurred, inhibited by drink, and the man stepped into the light, wavering slightly. 'Who's this? New slave?'

He grunted in a manner that turned Sellan's stomach, his flinty grey eyes roving over her form as he raked his teeth across his bottom lip. He had very short, dark hair, and trimmed sideburns that melted into the stubble on his face. At least as tall as Sellan, she remembered him towering over her as a child, hard hands and a loud, coarse voice that rumbled in her ear whenever he got home from wherever he disappeared to each evening.

'No, Warrin; not a slave.' Was that a hint of amusement in her mother's voice?

'Who then? She's a right mess.' Rook Warrin Parben glanced at his wife, somewhat miffed. Grinding her teeth against the pain, Sellan stood, drawing herself to her full height and staring him down as she lifted her chin.

'Your daughter,' Mediia replied.

Warrin blanched, staggered, then barked a laugh. 'Well, fuck!'

CHAPTER FOUR

Tingalla, Tolak Range, the South Lands

The fresh black ink etched around her forearm stung with incandescent fury. Lidan balled her hand into a fist, the burn crawling across her skin then fading as she released her fingers. Each time she submitted to the needles she wondered why she did it to herself. Then time dulled the pain, as it did the memory, until once more she sat patiently beside the tattana master and let him pierce her skin again.

Lidan would have preferred this tattana to be a choice, something she'd designed or been gifted to celebrate an accomplishment, but it wasn't. It was another mourning band, another black ring around her arm to mark a passing, no more than a finger's breadth from the band she wore for her sister.

Her nostrils flared and she bit her lip to stop it quivering.

This one was for Loge.

She looked away from the angry new ink, away from the irritated skin around it. It wasn't the only hurt she carried. Her left shoulder stabbed cruelly each time she shifted the wrong way or moved too quickly. Cuts marked her left side from her forehead to her ankle, the bruises on her face and around her collar still darkening, not yet old enough to yellow at the edges, fresh enough to remind her of the battle she'd fought and survived while others had not.

Her good hand wrapped around the neck of a wine urn, reaching for its embrace and finding it cold. She'd only just finished the last, but she filled her cup to the brim again, watching the dark liquid spill out. Oblivion hid in those fathomless red depths. It was elusive, but she would find it eventually. She just had to keep looking.

Outside, people sang while others laughed. The scent of bonfire smoke wafted through the doorway of her quarters, the thudding beat of drums and the high trill of pipes carried on the lazy breeze despite the distance from here to the common. Out there was drinking and feasting, mourning and celebration, all tangled up in one humid evening. The sun had sunk beyond the western horizon, the sky still clinging to the stain of its lingering light; blushing pink and deepening mauve painting the midsummer sky.

Tonight should have been about thanking the ancestors for the year that had passed; a celebration of the rains and the harvests and the hunts, a farewell to the warmth that would fade into brittle, frigid darkness as the dry season crawled across the South Lands. But it was a memorial as well. Tolak rangers had been lost recovering her brother and sister from the Namjin and Marsaw raiders. Rangers had given their lives, and their bodies had not returned to be buried or burned. There had to be a ceremony to mark their passing and the daari, her father, had decreed the midsummer feast would serve as such.

Feasting and drinking also served to distract the clan from the barefaced fact that their dana, *her* mother, had vanished into thin air the previous morning. The dana's companion, who they'd all assumed to be an aged crone, had turned out to be a much younger woman concealed by a glamour of magic. Sellan and Thanie had spent *years* among the clan, sheltered by the dana's position as Daari Erlon's first wife and the mother of his eldest child. They'd used those titles to hide from what they'd done— the awful truth of a massacre they'd wrought on a northern town and what they'd turned the corpses of those unfortunate souls into.

The same hands that had borne Lidan into the world had made monsters. The ngaru.

The same hands that had nurtured and hurt her had dealt death with impunity. That rot tainted Lidan now. She couldn't look her father in the eye, nor the rangers she'd spent the past four years travelling and training with. Her mother was the reason so many clan's people were dead or grievously wounded and traumatised. Her mother was the reason the ngaru existed—the *sole* reason—and it gnawed at her conscience with jagged, bloody teeth.

The single comfort was that the scourge of the ngaru was finite. There were only so many in the world to begin with and those numbers had begun to dwindle. It might have been a greater comfort had Lidan known there would never be any more, but the words of the woman once known as the Crone echoed in her mind.

Sellan would begin again, if given the chance. There would be another army of dead things, and this time, she would seek to finish what she'd begun all those years ago. She would murder and violate until she had a legion to control, to unleash upon her enemies, all to prove a point.

Lidan couldn't face any of it. She couldn't bear the stares and the whispers as tales and rumours swept through Tingalla. She'd survived what remained of the previous day by ignoring the worst of it, collapsing into bed before the sun went down. Then morning came with a crushing weight of melancholy and a searing pain even Marrit's strongest draughts couldn't quell. She hadn't left her dark little hut all day. Even the tattana master had come to her.

Instead, she sat alone while Vee replenished the wine urns, pulling excruciating memories of Loge from the wound where she'd stuffed them. She should have left it alone, but she couldn't. She picked at it; searching, hunting for an unnamed thing she knew she was missing. Each time the vision of his face faded, she reached for the scar and scratched until it bled. She didn't care that it hurt, because when it hurt, it meant he was still there.

'What are you doing?'

Her gaze rose from the ripples in her wine to the silhouette in the doorway. 'Nothing,' she replied. She lifted the cup and took a long, slurping draw.

'That's fairly obvious,' he said, his accent heavy with a northern roll that marked him as foreign. 'Why are you doing it in here, on your own? Aren't your people setting fire to things to celebrate midsummer?'

'They are.' Lidan nodded, blinking slowly and sucking wine from her teeth. 'I don't want to go out there anymore.'

Ranoth stepped inside the doorway and the light from the candles fell across his face. His brow furrowed as he narrowed his eyes. 'You're fucking shit-faced.'

'Yup,' she agreed and tapped the base of her cup against the rim of the urn. It made a sort of hollow sound she chose to ignore. Her stomach growled. 'You're not having any though.'

'Doesn't sound like there's much left.'

Lidan rolled her eyes and the room tilted. Good thing she was sitting down. Her tattana began to sting again and she flexed her fingers. 'Did you come here to scold me, or do you have something to say?'

'I came to see how you were...' Ran's bright blue eyes were almost pale grey in the candlelight, absent of the shimmering iridescence they sometimes held. Had his magic returned since his battle with Sellan? Lidan's chest tightened, and she doused the memory with another mouthful of wine.

She shrugged. 'You've seen me now.'

He leaned forward and grasped the back of the chair opposite. His knuckles paled a little and a muscle in his jaw jumped as he ground his teeth. He let out a sigh. 'I know this hurts. I've lost people I care about, I know how that burns—'

'Oh, you do?' she snapped. 'Lost your mother? Lost your friends?'

She wished there had been more anger in those words but they were flat, muted by drink and a lack of fucks to give. He'd slithered into her father's trust with a half-truth about why he'd travelled so far from his northern homeland, and there was a good chance he'd try the same ruse to gain her trust now. He'd conveniently failed to mention that he was a high-born prince or some such, leaving out the part about his magical abilities and keeping suspiciously silent about the reasons he and his companions were hunting Sellan and the Crone. It had all come spilling out after they returned from rescuing her siblings, but even then she sensed he held something back.

'Yes, actually.'

That pulled her up. Lidan glanced at him, registering the pain in the lines of his face and the tension in his shoulders.

'My mother... She could be dead, I don't know. Brit was the last person I know to see her alive. That was years ago. He says my father is on a rampage and—look, fuck that, it doesn't matter.' He pushed back from the chair and sliced his hand through the air. 'You're sitting here getting fucked up in your own misery and I know how that is. Drowning your sorrow won't make it go away, Liddy.' Ran's truth angled hard into her chest and pain lanced away as if he'd struck her, sparking her anger again.

'You don't know me!' she snarled, glaring and digging her nails into the table. 'Don't you dare presume to judge me!'

Ran threw his hands out, exasperated. 'I *don't* know you. I don't. But I was there. I *saw* it. Do you remember me carrying you?'

Silence.

She didn't remember. That part was buried under a landslide of sorrow.

'Do you remember how we got back?' he continued, ignorant of the fresh tears brimming in her eyes. 'I carried you because you couldn't walk. You couldn't speak. You could barely fucking breathe. I carried you because you broke. You broke and it was near on the worst thing I've ever fucking seen. I don't know you, but I've seen you raw. I've seen you peeled back and bleeding out all you have, bare before the sun, and I *will* judge you. Do you know what I saw, when all that was laid bare? Not bone and blood and sinew and grief. I saw steel. I saw iron. I saw a red fucking dawn, and if you lay down now then what good is any of that but for scrap?'

'I'm not laying down,' she muttered, unable to look at him.

'You are.' His words rumbled toward her, all ugly, inescapable truth. She hated him for it. 'And I know it feels right and proper and all that shit, but it's not. You know he wouldn't want you to walk that path.'

She didn't reply or counter. Just let silence fill the void as her throat contracted. It was all too much too soon. It was all too heavy and immense, too fathomless for her to see beyond. Too hopeless.

'Have the nightmares started yet?'

'Yes,' she murmured.

'The sweats and the nausea?'

Lidan nodded, her mouth suddenly dry.

'Thought so,' Ran whispered. She didn't elaborate and he didn't ask.

She didn't want to tell him she'd woken up screaming the last three nights. How her throat burned as she sat bolt upright, desperate for air, as if she'd been held underwater for an eternity. Vee had been there, a comforting hand in the dark. Apart from today, she'd hardly left Lidan's side—a silent presence, as close to a shadow as another person could be. The tine had been needed to help prepare the feast, only reluctantly leaving Lidan to her own devices. She'd been glad to be alone for a while, but as Ran's appearance cut through her drunken, foggy thoughts, she wondered if sending the girl away had been a mistake.

'You can let this beast eat you alive, or you can tame it and make it your own.' Ran leaned forward and put his hands flat on the table, pinning her with a look she couldn't escape.

They'd known each other for a handful of days, yet they'd been through a fire together. Somehow that counted for something. She'd hated him when he arrived, been suspicious and cautious of his reasons for remaining with her people, and rightly so. He had an agenda she couldn't see for all her attempts to unravel it. But despite all that, this pale northern prince with weird blue eyes had helped her save her siblings, had fought at her side when it mattered and dragged her grief-stricken body from the aftermath. That day had welded them together in a way she wished she could ignore, but for all her trying, could not.

He reached over and took the wine cup. She made no move to snatch it back. 'Get changed.'

'What?' Lidan scowled as he drained her wine.

'I'm not leaving you in here. I know where this goes and it's nowhere good. So, get changed. We're going out.'

Ran waited beyond the door while Lidan fumbled around, searching for something presentable to wear, tossing a shirt, a thigh length embroidered tunic and a clean pair of trousers on the bed. It wasn't the best outfit she'd ever thrown together, but it would do. Her mother's distaste at her lack of care echoed through the cavern of her mind and she crushed it under the heel of her boot. This was the best she could manage right now.

People could judge if they liked, but they should be thankful she'd put on clean clothes at all. She'd have happily stayed in her room, curled up in one of Loge's spare shirts, drinking herself unconscious if Ran had given her any other choice. He was stubborn though, as unlikely as she was to give over without a fight. It was easier to bend before such force than resist it. She just didn't have the energy for it.

Reaching for the hem of her shirt, the sling caught her injured arm, pain biting at her neck as the limb snapped back against her chest. She arched away from the knives driving into her body and sucked a sharp breath through her teeth.

'Fuck you,' she snarled, cursing all the little ways the wounds reminded her of her weakness. With a sigh, she stared at the fresh clothing, dread crawling across her skin. There was only one thing for it. 'Ran?'

'You all right?' He leaned into the doorway, wide eyes scanning for danger.

Lidan swallowed the bitter taste of helplessness. 'I need help.'

His gaze fell to the sling, then to the clothes she'd laid out, then shot straight back to her face. 'Oh.'

'Sorry...'

'No, no.' He cleared his throat and came back through the door, stepping up to untie the sling from the back of her neck. Pressure shifted in the close air of the hut, brushing across Lidan's perception and Ran snorted an unexpected laugh.

'What did she say?' Lidan asked, her skin prickling as magic washed over her like icy breath.

'She said she never thought she'd see the day I played the nursemaid. Now, hold your arm close for a minute,' Ran instructed, before he let the sling fall loose and slid the fabric out from under her elbow. Lidan couldn't be sure she'd ever get used to the whispering of Ran's ghost, a conversation she could sense but not understand. There was no way to know when the dead girl was with him or not, coming and going as she pleased, sometimes gone for days at a time. 'Can you manage those buttons?'

Lidan shook her head and he set to the task without comment, releasing the fastenings of her shirt until she slipped her good arm free and let him carefully peel the left sleeve away from her angry shoulder. Their eyes didn't meet as he shook out the clean shirt and retraced his steps, feeding her wounded limb through and moving to fasten the closures. She set her jaw against the pain and tried to stop the nauseating tremors rolling through her body.

Ran turned and stared at the trousers and tunic and Lidan swallowed a knot of embarrassment. 'These are fine,' she muttered, brushing down the pants she already wore.

'You sure—'

'Yep.'

'Not a problem.' He cleared his throat again. 'Sit down. Where's your—oh, here it is.' He darted to a small table and collected a brush, setting about combing the knots from the unruly black bird's nest of her hair without further comment.

'Have you done this before?' Lidan frowned suspiciously as his fingers sectioned through the lengths and eased out the tangles.

'Not in a long time…' he murmured. He worked in silence for a while, and she wondered where his thoughts had wandered. 'My sisters had hair down to their arses and they'd scream bloody murder every time their nurses brushed it. They're twins—easy enough to tell apart but they've got these mad, wavy curls that never behave. A bit like mine, but thicker.'

Lidan closed her eyes and released a breath, letting go the tension in her shoulders, Ran's story filling her mind as he worked on the braids. Part of her rebelled against it, insisting his display of friendship was nothing more than a way to ingratiate himself. Another stronger part of her craved the easy conversation and the lack of a need to do anything but listen. It was nice to just listen, after what felt like years screaming without being heard.

'Anyway, Eboni could be reasoned with, but Nerola was so bad the maids wouldn't go near her for fear of being accused of torture. Gods, she made a racket. One day—I don't know where our parents were, but Ma wasn't to be found—I coaxed Nerola out with bribes and brushed it myself. Course, after that she'd only let me do it. *Then* I had to learn all these braids and styles and fuck me, the pins it took to hold it in place. I swore if I never saw another of those bloody things again it would be too soon.'

His hands ceased their weaving and Lidan reached up to find he'd tied the ends off with a length of string.

'When did you last see them?' she asked quietly, shuffling around to look at his face. He stared out the window, eyes trained on the twilight, memories dancing where she couldn't see them spin.

'Years ago…' Ran shrugged, running a hand through his hair and casting around. 'Need anything else?'

Lidan shook her head. 'There's not much point taking my knives. I can't use them like this.' She gestured at the re-slung arm and Ran nodded.

'Maybe stay close to me and the others then, just in case someone gets any funny ideas.'

'Ideas?' The pitch of her voice rose, her fears given life by his words. What if someone took offence at her being at the feast? What if they blamed her by proxy for the death of a loved one who'd been taken by the ngaru? Was it even common knowledge her mother had made the creatures, or was that still a closely held secret? Her thoughts spiralled and before she knew what was happening, Ran led her to the door by her uninjured arm and guided her out into the cool, fresh air of the evening. 'Wait, what if—'

'No time for "what if".' His demeanour shifted and a glint of mischief twinkled in his eye. It only barely hid the gleam of sorrow pooling beneath. He too had shadows to drown in the bottom of a tankard. 'Only time for "what now", and now, we drink.'

Lidan groaned. It was going to be a long night.

Chapter Five

Tingalla, Tolak Range, the South Lands

They walked together through the village, sounds and scents becoming clearer as they approached the common, the cooler air drawing back the haze of Lidan's drunkenness. She watched Ran from the corner of her eye, his hand on her elbow for support as she limped along, noticing that he did not. Any injuries he'd carried home from the western tablelands seemed to have disappeared.

He'd been hit by the very same wave of cruel water, displaced by the falling rock of the gorge wall. She might not recall the journey back to where the others waited with Lucija and Ehran, but she remembered the look of his face when he'd held her back from clawing the stones in search of Loge. It would have been a vain search, a hopeless endeavour—she saw that now. Ran had been as cut and bruised, as bloody and as filthy as Lidan, yet it was impossible to tell by looking at him now. He lacked even the shadow of a bruise, moving with comfort and certainty that her body struggled to regain. Was it the magic? Had it healed him in the mere days since the battle?

'Aren't you sore?' she ventured, heartily sick of wondering and too tired to care if he took offence at her question. He had, after all, just undressed her, so what else remained between them but a false sense of polite decorum? Surely they were beyond that now, after everything the past few days had thrown at them.

Ran shrugged a shoulder. 'A little. It's deeper, under the surface. I'm tired and I'm aching. The fatigue is in my bones.' He stopped and lifted his hand, splaying his fingers wide. They trembled so slightly she barely saw it. 'I've had the shakes for days. Eian and Zarad have it too.'

Lidan nodded as if that answered her question and they continued on, breaking into the common and the commotion of the feast. The large pavilion tent erected for her sister Bridie's matching had been put up to one side, long tables standing beneath, surrounded by chairs. Most folk crowded around the roaring bonfire in the centre of the open space, clustered in groups with all manner of wooden benches and other makeshift seats for those not keen or able to stand. The area under the pavilion was reserved for the families of the daaris—Erlon Tolak and Horice Daylin— with several tables and tents set closer to the hall, groaning with roasted meat platters and bordered by barrels of ale and large stacks of wine urns. Apprehension gripped Lidan as a few people looked her way, some nodding in recognition, others staring at her with unabashed curiosity, then at Ran. A couple of wary parents herded excited children from their path. Ran didn't seem to notice or care.

'They're all staring,' Lidan hissed under her breath.

'Let them.' Determination set his lips in a hard line. 'They don't understand what happened. Most don't even know the whole story. They're ignorant, that's all.'

'I don't like it,' she muttered as he guided her behind a group of laughing rangers she didn't recognise.

'You'll get used to it.'

'Did you?' She glanced at him, surprised. From what she'd gleaned from the barrage of spite he and her mother had shouted at each other, it didn't sound as though Ran's people were particularly fond of magic-users.

He shook his head, dark hair falling across his eyes. 'No. Never got the chance.' He shot her a sympathetic look. 'I doubt you're the one they're staring at. They're probably gawking at me.'

Lidan realised he was right. Some folk gave her consideration, but most stared straight at Ran. He was the oddity here, not her. She looked a sight, and it had been her mother who fought him and disappeared in front of half of Tingalla, but Lidan wasn't the focus of their curiosity—Ran was.

They shuffled between clusters of revellers, Ran leading her by the hand and shoving a man aside so she could pass without knocking her arm. They emerged before the pavilion and Lidan let go a sigh of relief to be free of the pressing crowd. Then something heavy slammed into her leg.

'Oh fuck,' she gasped and staggered back, Ran whipping around to find the source of her outburst.

'Liddy!' the heavy object on her leg squealed, a mess of curls and two thin arms wrapped tightly around her thigh. A bright, round face looked up and beamed at her. 'You're here!'

'Lucija! You scared the breath out of me!' Lidan's heart thumped hard, shock and fatigue and all that wine swirling together, her vision swimming.

'Lucy, get off your sister!' Farah's reprimand echoed against the roof of the tent. Her father's fourth wife wove through the gathering and slipped her arms around Lidan, planting a gentle kiss on the unblemished side of her forehead. 'It's wonderful to see you up and about.'

'How's Ehran?' Lidan asked.

Farrah waved a hand and reached to weave sprigs of sun-gem flowers into Lidan's hair. 'Doesn't like to be alone and has taken to sleeping in my bed or with any sister he can cajole into agreeing, but he's all right. Come, your father will want to see you.'

Farah peeled her reluctant daughter away from Lidan's leg and led them both toward a table, the heady scent of the blossoms recalling midsummer's past. Erlon sat with Horice, deep in conversation, surrounded by their wives and the eldest of their children. Bridie smiled and waved across a table, flower garlands and greenery perfuming the air, her new husband, Harran, at her side.

Lidan hid her confusion under a weary smile. She'd expected the Daylin, along with her sister, to have departed for their clan lands on the coast by now. Although, with everything that had happened and midsummer upon them, perhaps it made more sense for their allies to remain and discuss a response to Yorrell Namjin and Merk Marsaw's incursion on Tolak territory.

'Look who Lucy found in the crowd,' Farah said to Erlon, and the big man glanced up quickly.

'Liddy.' Her name was barely more than a whisper on her father's lips as he stood and shuffled around from behind the table. He reached to wrap her in a tight hug, and she flinched away. It was a minute thing, a move so fast others hadn't noticed, but Erlon paused, looking her up and down. Only then did he register the sling and the bruises, as if he'd forgotten the extent of her injuries. 'Is it any better?'

She shook her head slowly. 'Not by much.'

'Come and sit.' Erlon's broad, muscled bulk created a clearing in the crowd, people flowing around him like a strong current past a boulder. Lidan sheltered in the calm, scanning the length of the table and realising there was not a seat to be had. Someone coughed behind them. They turned and found Ran patiently waiting a few paces away.

'We've an empty seat up our end, sir, should Lidan wish to sit with us?' Ran indicated to the far end of the tent, closest to the hall and the ale barrels.

Erlon spared Lidan a cautious glance. Did he doubt Ran, or want to keep his eldest within sight? As much as the daari was surely grateful to the northerner for assisting in recovering his children, Lidan wondered if the revelations of the previous day had given her father reason to question Ran's motives. Still, there was little harm to be done sitting with him and his friends for an evening, so Lidan nodded, careful not to move her neck with too much force.

With a sigh and a gentle squeeze to her uninjured shoulder, the daari let her go, silence filling her wake. Those seated near her father watched as she left, and again she wondered if they were studying her or Ran. What were they thinking? What questions rose in their minds that they didn't dare speak? Perhaps together she and Ran were enough of a curiosity to draw attention. Or perhaps they simply had no idea what to say.

Aelish's gleaming blonde hair came into view from where she stood nursing a tankard at Brit's shoulder. The tall man's arm curled around the small of the trader's back, an intimate gesture that Lidan realised was to support the woman as she wavered slightly on her feet.

'You need to sit down,' Brit scolded as they drew near.

Aelish replied with a sharp shake of her head. 'I'm *fine*,' she growled through her teeth. While Brit had helped evacuate the children from the battleground in the gorge, Aelish remained with Lidan and the others to fight the raiders. She could only guess at the unseen wounds the woman carried, but the stubborn set of Aelish's jaw told her the trader wouldn't allow them to bring her down. At their approach, both trader and watcher inclined their heads, dark circles under their eyes speaking to their exhaustion.

'You made it out, princess?' Brit asked, giving her the northern title she wasn't sure she liked or deserved.

'I wasn't given a whole lot of choice,' Lidan replied dryly, smirking in Ran's direction.

Brit barked a laugh. 'Our Ran ain't an easy one to refuse, I'll grant you that.'

'Shut it, you two.' Ran rolled his eyes. 'I'll get some drinks. Set yourself down there. Don't let her out of your sight.' He pointed at a chair beside Eian and Zarad, then vanished into the crowded darkness.

The young men sat quietly, cups in hand; Eian with one of his thickly muscled arms slung along the top of Zarad's chair, while Zarad cradled a hand wrapped in a bandage. Lidan settled beside them, wincing as she eased into the seat and Eian pushed a platter across the table toward her.

'Have you eaten?' he asked.

'No, I—' Suddenly starving, she picked a slice of meat and bit into it, taking a moment to savour the flavour of herbs. At the back of Eian's neck a raw burn glowed flame red, a perfect print of his lover's hand, gleaming with the sheen of an ointment or salve, likely something her sister Marrit had found in her trunks of healing supplies. 'How's your neck? It hasn't healed on its own?'

'Nah,' Eian shrugged. He'd sprouted the beginnings of a fair beard since his arrival. Evidently, he'd given up trying to maintain a clean shave. 'The power hasn't come back just yet.'

She turned to Zarad. 'And your hand?'

'It's getting there slowly. We're both too depleted to heal faster than a normal person.' The redhead looked down and flexed his fingers. 'It took everything we had...'

The memory of blue light cracking through the stone of the gorge bit into Lidan's heart and she shuddered, blinking away threatening tears. The final act of the battle had been necessary but cost so much she wondered if they couldn't have found another way.

A trio of wine urns plonked onto the table, followed by an empty cup and a tankard brimming with ale. Ran handed her the cup and set about filling it, Brit leaning forward to pour out more wine for those drinking it, and they settled into a moment of comfortable silence.

Musicians played nearby, thumping drums and whistling through pipes. The sound drew Lidan in, folk moving with the beat and swaying to the tune. Embers soared into the darkness, the orange glow broken by dancing shadows, smoke billowing as more logs fed the hungry flames. It was mesmerising, the warmth of the night and the wine sinking into Lidan's hurts until they were a dull ache, a faded memory that would return by morning to remind her of what she'd lost.

A high voice intoned a chant, taken up by the gathered clan, carried through the crowd. She knew the words from funerals she'd attended, called by the tale-keepers and repeated by the gathered. She didn't join their ranks, the northerners by her side ignorant of the language and unable to repeat it. They spoke in hushed tones, Brit finally convincing Aelish to take a seat and rest her legs, while he perched on the edge of the table.

Lidan leaned toward where Ran sat beside her. 'I thought Eian and Zarad would have healed like you.'

He glanced into his tankard, swirling the liquid gently. 'I did too. From what they've said, it took a fair whack of magic to crack the cliff—much more than either of them thought it would. None of us were in peak condition before we got to the gorge. It wore us all thin. I'd planned to head off soon, today ideally, but they're not in a fit state to travel. Neither is Aelish, though she won't admit it.'

A cold shudder washed over Lidan.

They were leaving?

Of course they were. They had what they'd come for, or at least half of it. Thanie remained locked in Tingalla's small cell block, carved into the cliff under one of the sentry towers. Ran had made clear his intentions to take her back to his homeland to face justice, so why did his plan now fill Lidan with dread?

'My father said you can stay for as long as you need. There's no rush.' Even as she said it, she knew she clutched at excuses.

'Oh, but there is.' Ran's eyes locked with hers. 'The Pass will close if we stay much longer, if it's still traversable at all after the damage we did coming through. It'll take at least a fortnight to get there and see what we're up against.'

'It's midsummer,' Lidan reasoned. 'It's going to be warm up there for a month or so, surely?'

He took a long draw on his drink, looking back at the fire. 'You'd think so, but that witch in the dungeon left a spell in the Pass that's making the air colder. More favourable to the ice serpents, more unpredictable for travellers. I don't want to run the risk of being stuck down here until next summer with her languishing in a cell.'

An icy hand of fear traced its fingertips down the length of her back. Once Ran and his companions departed, the threat of Thanie's magic left with them, as did the only distraction she had from the emptiness awaiting her in Hummel. Their leaving was the end of the tale, the final verse of the song. It closed a door on this whole mess, and as much as she wanted to see that end, she dreaded the finality.

Ran stood and checked the wine urns, collecting the empties and the tankards and carrying them away to retrieve more, leaving her alone with her whirling thoughts. What would she do once this was all said and done? What role did she have among her people? She was no longer the heir. Was she still required as a witness of the blood? Her father had given her the title out of necessity, but she hardly thought it carried much weight or responsibility once the family returned to the safety of Hummel. Her father had said as much the night before Merk Marsaw stole Lucija and Ehran from their beds. Her brother no longer needed a protector and Lidan was no longer a ranger's apprentice, her role stripped as punishment for killing another ranger. Her future would be exactly as her mother had predicted— matched to a man she didn't know for a political purpose as changeable as the wind.

Any hope of something else, of some other fate or path, had been ripped away.

Caught by the need to move, Lidan stood and limped to the eave of the tent as Eian and Brit haggled over the finer point of a debate she had only loosely followed, the volume of their voices rising with the aid of drink. It felt good to stretch. Her hips ached, as did her knees for some unknown reason. She drew a deep breath and let it fill her, releasing it slowly in the hope it might take with it some of the anxiety tightening her chest.

It didn't.

Scanning the gathering, she found Ran at the food tent, distracted by his quest to acquire more ale and wine. The hall stood behind him, a large structure of stone, clay and thatch silent in the gloom, its windows portals of light in the deepening dark. Beyond that, illuminated by torches, stood a tower built of the same stone. It stretched up from the height of the wall, several feet above the timber palisade, a steady presence gazing across Tingalla and the river lands far below.

Somewhere, under the base of that tower, was Thanie's cell.

An inexplicable urge seized Lidan and she hurried into the shadows behind a collection of sleeping quarters. Abandoned by folk enjoying the midsummer feast, the Daylin clan's quarters were quiet, and she moved unchallenged to the base of the settlement's wall. Stairs rose before her, leading to the palisade and the tower's only entrance. She had to go up to go down, climbing before she could descend to the cells cut into the cliff below her feet. Could she manage it? Could she drag her wounded, weakened body down to confront the woman confined there?

She would.

She had to.

She had questions, and she would have the answers before it was too late to ask.

Chapter Six

Lidan paused to catch her breath at the top of the stairs, clutching her throbbing arm and cursing. What was she thinking? She didn't even have the key to the bloody door!

Cells were one of the few places her people bothered with keys, locking them with complicated mechanisms of interconnected hardwood bolts and tumbler pins that responded to a length of timber carved with an exact, unique combination of prongs. The door might have been unlocked for her the day before, but it would sure as shit be shut tight now. Was the key up here somewhere, or did her father's chief ranger have it safely in his care?

There was a good chance she'd climbed all the way up here for no reason, for no benefit and—

Someone coughed and she froze, taking refuge in the shadowy doorway to the stairs. A small shelter stood off to her left, a sort of timber awning lit by a glowing brazier and a torch. It jutted out where the wall met the tower, a cover for rangers patrolling the rampart. A guard hunched in the gloom.

'Fuck.' Lidan clenched her jaw to quell the sting slicing through her shoulder. The awning had been hastily built since she'd been here last and now she had to negotiate the shelter and its inhabitant to access the stairs to the cells. So much for sneaking in unnoticed. With any luck, the poor soul stuck up here missing the feast would have the key. But would they give it to her?

She stepped from the shadow and squared her shoulders as best she could, lifting her chin as her mother had taught her—grace, elegance, and strength. Not to be fucked with. That was the expression she tried to paint on her face; a *do not question me or you will face the wrath of my status* kind of look. Her mother had worn it well. Lidan had sworn she never would. Yet she clung to the woman's unwanted lessons as a child clutches a comforting blanket.

At the edge of the awning, she cleared her throat. The ranger's gaze snapped up, hand reaching for his flint axe.

'Who's in charge up here?' Lidan demanded, cringing. The voice echoing back sounded so much like the missing dana she felt a little sick. This was a performance, she reminded herself—a show for the guard, a way to get what she needed, a mask she would discard as soon as her need was filled.

'Er, um, well Jonnoh is, but he's round at the other—'

'I need to speak with the prisoner,' she interrupted sharply.

The young man blanched and looked her up and down. 'Not sure I can—'

'I don't have time to wait for this "Jonnoh". Just unlock the door and I'll manage the rest on my own. No need to leave your post.'

He scratched at his ear, stood and cast around the shelter as if someone might appear to make the decision for him. Lidan didn't recognise him, so he probably wasn't from Hummel, and if he hadn't recognised her outright, he'd certainly registered her tone and carriage as that of an authority. Apparently, the *don't fuck with me* face worked.

'I'm really not sure…'

Lidan stepped under the awning and gave the guard a cool, steady look. 'Do you know who I am?'

His nervous twitching ceased. 'Yes, Witness.'

He wouldn't have been *her* first choice to guard the tower—too easily influenced by fear, too quick to take new orders from someone who looked like they were in charge without any instruction to do so. He was more dangerous than useful. The senior rangers had probably left this younger man—barely past his apprenticeship, if he had completed it at all—in charge so they could enjoy the feast.

'Then find the key and let me pass. If anyone questions you, they'll answer to me, understood?' Her expression softened, just as her mother's would have. Strike hard, then relent—reel them in, make them feel safe. 'I won't get you in trouble… Sorry, what was your name?'

'Wiley,' he murmured.

'You have my word, Wiley.' Lidan gestured to the tower. 'Open the door.'

Slowly, without taking his eyes from hers, he lifted a loop of leather from around his neck. On it hung a length of timber about as long as her hand and no thicker than the width of two fingers. A series of prongs jutted from one end, uneven timber teeth matching exactly with the tumbling pins inside the lock. Wiley slipped the key into a concealed slot in the door and lifted, setting in motion a clunking chain of movements within. Then the young guard pulled back on the handle and stood aside.

She nodded as she stepped past, but he didn't meet her gaze, staring at the ground and handing her a torch. The door shut with a swift thud and the locking pins dropped back into place as Wiley removed the key.

Lidan shuddered.

That had come far too easily. She'd flat out manipulated the man into following her orders. He hadn't done it because he wanted to or out of any sense of loyalty. He'd done it because he was afraid; afraid of what she might do or say, afraid of the punishment disobedience would bring. She hadn't even threatened him. With nothing more than a shift in her tone and a look down her nose, he'd succumbed.

She began the decent of the winding timber stairs, disgusted at how thrillingly addictive that moment of power had been. The smallest taste of simply getting what she wanted without question left her tingling with exhilaration.

The stairs became stone, and she continued down, wondering if it had been the same for her mother. Had Sellan one day found she could move those around her with a word and a look, realising in those small seconds she had within her grasp a power denied, if not outright forbidden? Had it been a struggle, a war between right and wrong? A slow decent, as jarring and painful as Lidan's journey down these stairs, to a point from which she could no longer return? Or had the manipulation of others come to Sellan as naturally and as easily as breath?

Thanie may have the answers, but Lidan wasn't sure she wanted them. For now, she wanted to imagine she and her mother weren't cut from the same cloth. Was it somehow better if her mother's behaviour was as much instinct as a snake devouring a little thorn-tail hopping rat? Lidan *chose* to bend Wiley to her will, knowing exactly what she was doing. And it disgusted her.

She found herself at the door to Thanie's cell, the long, cool tunnel stretching out behind her, the echo of her uneven footsteps long gone. What she'd done to Wiley wasn't even close to criminal. Frowned upon at best. It was nothing. He would be fine. She'd be back before anyone noticed she was gone, and no one would know any different. She was fussing over nothing, over-working a problem that didn't exist.

It was nothing.

She tapped her fingers anxiously on her thigh and watched the light from the flickering torch dance across the door. The small viewing hatch hung open, the shutter on the cell's window slightly ajar, permitting the slightest breath of fresh air to swirl through.

'Are you coming in or are you going to stand out there all night?' Thanie's disembodied voice asked, and Lidan started at the sudden sound.

Her hand hesitated over the largest latch on the door. Ask anyone in the common if this was a good idea and to a person they would say she was mad. They'd say there was nothing gained from digging around in a wound that would, given time, begin to heal, but had yet only barely ceased to bleed.

Ignoring reason, she grabbed at the latches and snapped them aside, working quickly before she could question herself, fumbling the torch and dropping it as she fought to pull a bolt down from a slot in the roof. Pain burst from her shoulder, and she swore as she shoved the door inward.

The thick timber of the torch handle scraped loudly on the floor as she collected it and stepped across the threshold, kicking the door shut with the heel of her boot. Light washed into the cell, lurching and unsteady, illuminating the sorry figure of Thanie crouched in a corner. Had she moved at all since Lidan had last seen her?

The woman held a hand before her eyes, shielding them from the sudden glare, her face crumpled in a grimace. A little jolt of surprise ran through Lidan, still shocked by the woman's appearance.

In her mind, Thanie remained the Crone—an aged woman who had long defied disease and infirmity. In reality, the woman looked no more than a few years Sellan's senior, her dark hair streaked only with a little grey, her lips fuller and her skin furrowed with fewer creases and wrinkles. The magic that hid the real Thanie from view for eighteen years was a mystery to Lidan—one neither Ran nor his companions could explain—and it awed and terrified her.

Thanie slowly lowered her hand, blinking as her eyes adjusted to the light. 'You look like you've been beaten half to death.'

'Thank you?' Lidan frowned and winced.

'Got any food?'

'Ah, no—'

'Then what are you doing here?' It was as if nothing had changed. Lidan was once again a small, skinny girl with a cruel mother and a dismissive father, caught off-guard by the older woman's whip-fast questions. There was no hint of remorse or regret in Thanie's tone, no sign that her imprisonment had diminished the strength of her spirit. Thanie's eyes narrowed. 'They don't know you're down here, do they?'

Lidan cleared her throat, glanced around for the stool and dragged it free of the dark corner in which it hid. She sat with a sigh and dropped the torch on the ground between them, her arms too sore and too tired to hold it up any longer. 'So what if they don't?'

Thanie shrugged. 'Curious… Wondering what you're planning to do to me.'

'Why would I—'

The older woman regarded Lidan with a flat look and the remainder of her response evaporated. 'There are very few reasons why you'd sneak down here without the company or knowledge of others, and even fewer that bode well for me. I doubt you're here to set me free.'

'You'd be right on that score,' Lidan said. The desire that had driven her up onto the wall, past the gullible guard and down the tower steps began to wane, abandoning her like receding flood waters. Where once she'd been inundated with a need to speak to Thanie, a need to demand answers, she now sat shivering and empty on a bleak shore.

'You could be set on delivering my sentence before that boy can drag me back home, but I see no weapons.' Thanie frowned, stern eyes scanning Lidan's face. 'Do you even know why you came down here?'

Lidan began to pick at the fabric of her trousers, nervous energy itching through her fingers. 'I thought I did, but… I can't feel the ground anymore. I don't know where I stand.'

'What happened to you out there?'

'You know what happened,' Lidan snapped, scowling at the older woman, poisoned by pain and weariness. 'You heard and you saw.'

43

'Oh, I know what you did and where you went, but what actually happened to *you*? That I can't see.' Leaning forward, Thanie aimed a finger at Lidan, her nails chewed down, the quicks darkened with dried blood. 'Something's changed in you.'

Lidan stared across the cell, her heart thudding hard. 'I don't know who I am anymore,' she blurted. 'I don't know what to do now. I can't see my path anymore.'

Eyes the colour of storm clouds stared back, unmoved. The pause settled and dragged. Lidan's skin began to crawl.

'I once knew a girl who was certain of who she was. She knew who her parents were, where she belonged in society. She knew her future, knew the story not yet written, knew what it held for her. She knew exactly where she was going. Until one day, she didn't. One day, it all fell apart. Everything she knew was ripped away and she was adrift, all hope lost. She changed so deeply then, so fundamentally, that she hardly recognised the person looking back from her reflection.' Thanie tilted her head slightly. 'It was a terrible, tragic thing to watch, knowing there wasn't a single thing I could do about it.'

Lidan opened her hands, fingers tensed into frustrated claws. 'You could have helped me!'

'Who said I was talking about you?'

CHAPTER SEVEN

Tingalla, Tolak Range, the South Lands

Silence stretched between them, Lidan too stunned for words.

'What?' she finally whispered.

'It could be your story, true enough, but it could easily be your mother's.'

The room seemed to tilt, walls leaning in, heavy wet stone looming toward Lidan, pressing down until there was barely enough air to fill her chest.

'It could be *my* story…' Thanie continued, her voice a hoarse rasp, thick with memory.

Were the three of them so similar their tales could be told without differentiation? No. Lidan couldn't believe that. Wouldn't. She was nothing like her mother. They shared blood, perhaps they even shared traits, but she was *not* her mother. Nor was she the Crone. These women were broken, consumed by hateful shadows, driven by a deep darkness to murder and mutilate innocents for their own ends.

She shook her head vigorously. 'I'm nothing like her. Or you.'

'Oh? I doubt that.' Thanie gave a morbid little chuckle, and goosebumps rushed across Lidan's skin. 'There's so much of her in you it hurts to behold. There's so much of *us* in you I can hardly bear to look at you. But there's one marked difference, I'll give you that. We went to war to take back what we'd lost. I failed, as did Sellan, but she won't give up. She doesn't know how. Whereas you… You've just taken the poison and you're waiting to die.'

'I am not!'

'Aren't you?' Thanie crawled to her feet and Lidan stood sharply, ignoring the jab of pain in her side and knocking the stool back. The bang and clatter of timber on stone slapped hard against the cell walls and Lidan flinched. They stood face to face for the first time since Thanie's transformation. Fury burned in the witch's eyes, her lips forced into a fierce line, her weariness only betrayed by the quiver of her chin and the tremor of her hands.

Taller now her hunch had vanished, Lidan had to look up slightly to meet Thanie's eyes, just enough that glaring back became uncomfortable after more than a few seconds. Lidan fought the urge to stagger away from the furnace of Thanie's gaze. Even the smallest step was a failure, a defeat, conceding ground she wouldn't give.

'You are many things, Lidan Tolak, but you are not this snivelling wreck I see before me.'

Snivelling? Lidan set her jaw and glowered, her own hand beginning to shake as she balled her fingers into a fist. Maybe she should have brought her knives. 'You have *no* right to judge me. You have no idea what I've been through.'

'I do, Lidan. *That* is my point. You're not the only one to lose their way, not the only one to sacrifice things you loved.' Tears glistened in Thanie's eyes, furiously blinked away before they could fall. 'No idea who you are anymore? Can't feel the ground? Lost your path? Tell me another sob story. The Dead Sisters know I've got the time!'

'How *dare* you?' Rage rose in Lidan, a banked fire fed by every word Thanie threw at her.

The older woman began to pace; a shivering limp, no steadier than Lidan's own gait. 'What are you going to do? You're listless and weaponless. Lost.' Thanie's lip curled in disgust. 'You're right. I can see it now. I barely recognise you. Maybe she was right, maybe you haven't got it in you—'

'Haven't got what? Fury? Strength? I survived you two, didn't I?' The rage boiled now, a rumbling force welling in Lidan's chest, warming her limbs, tingling across her skin, flame in her bones. 'I survived my father's whims and those fucking *things* you made. I've been beaten and wounded and lied to. How *dare* you!'

Thanie threw her arms wide. 'And yet here you are, teary-eyed, telling me you're lost. Telling me you don't know who you are.'

She shouldn't have come here. This was a mistake. She didn't need to hear this. She didn't *want* to hear this. 'I don't know—'

'You've come to me, of all people, to tell you what to do next? Here's an idea—don't execute me. Don't send me back with that Orthian boy. I can help you, if you've a mind to listen. Does that sound sane to you? Does that sound like wise counsel?'

'No—'

'Well then listen to *this*—' Thanie shoved her palm into Lidan's chest, just above her heart, and the young woman stumbled back. '—and heed what it says. Years ago, I told you to find your own path. I told you to look beyond what they wanted and the story they said was your future, because I knew it wasn't going to be there. Someone, someday, was going to take it from you, just as they did your mother and I. You had to decide what you wanted—which story you wanted to tell—his, or hers. Ruthless ruler or loyal servant? Except you're *neither* of those things, Lidan. Your story wasn't written for you. They tried, but fates are fickle like that. I should know. Mine was left behind in the burning wreckage I fled twenty years ago. I had to find a new path, a new story. The one written in *my* blood.'

Heart hammering, Lidan weathered Thanie's storm, let it lash her like wind-driven rain, all the pain she'd shoved away bubbling up. She'd lost her anchor when Loge vanished under that pile of unforgiving rock. She'd lost her path when she'd killed Owin and been stripped of her apprentice-ship. Forced into a role protecting her brother, then had that taken when it suited her father. She'd been betrayed and humiliated by her mother's lies. Each beating, each hit wearing her down until she had nothing left but a broken body and a shattered heart.

'You don't know who you are anymore?' Thanie continued, her hands stabbing and slashing at the air as she paced, punctuating her words. 'Good! I don't care who you were. I want to know who you're going to be. That's far more interesting and important than all this shit about being a usurped heir or a lover in mourning. Those are *part*, not the entire sum, of who you are. They do not define you, and neither should anything else. You've lost much, but in the emptiness left behind you must find *yourself.*'

Lidan glared as the tirade soaked through her skin and settled in her soul. How dare she. How dare she bring it all back. How dare she force Lidan to see. No… She wouldn't concede. She wouldn't give in. Lidan clung to her rage, trembling as if the woman's anger were a whirling gale and she nothing but a brittle leaf caught in its grip.

How dare she.

How dare she be right.

She was fucking right and Lidan hated her for it.

'So, who are you?' Thanie finally asked.

Lidan licked dry lips and set her jaw once more. She lifted her chin and straightened her back. Leaning into the pain in her shoulder and breathing through the urge to crumble under its will, she opened her mouth to speak.

'Ah,' Thanie lifted a finger and held it steady. Wait, that gesture said. Wait, and see. Do not rush this.

Lidan calmed as she stood in the thrall of the woman's gaze, captivated now, unafraid. The terror she once felt in the presence of the Crone, the revulsion and confusion, ebbed away, seeping through the soles of her boots and into the stone beneath. Her breathing steadied. Her heartbeat slowed. Finally, she found the emptiness, felt about its edges as she might the gap left by a lost tooth; tentative, wary, yet curious.

The raised finger Thanie held between them lowered until the very tip pressed against the centre of Lidan's chest. She didn't flinch away. An odd, unfamiliar calm washed through her limbs, skin prickling, her mouth dry and tacky.

'There,' said Thanie in a crackling whisper. 'That's where you'll find her.'

'Who?'

Grey eyes that seemed to see further than the realms of the living, through skin and bone and stone, met her gaze. 'The woman you'll become.'

A careful hand reached up to Lidan's hair and drew from the braid a sprig of blossoms, gently unravelling it from the jet strands. Spherical yellow flowers bobbed alongside long, thin leaves as Thanie twirled the delicate twig between her fingers. All their fury fled the cell, taken on a weak breath of breeze, dispersed into the night beyond the window. Years of unspoken truths, hidden rather than revealed, the binding force that held together a wall of tension and hate, vanished.

'These things always make me sneeze,' Thanie said. Whip-fast she reached and caught Lidan's damaged shoulder in one hand, shoving the sprig of blossoms against the broken bone of her collar with the other.

Lidan screamed and jerked, pain exploding from the bones, ripping down her arm and up her neck, muscles snapping tight. The woman's grip tightened; her face warped in a fierce grimace. Teeth grinding, Lidan crumbled under the pressure, bending beneath the force of the agony tearing down her left side, pulling back from the talon-grip of Thanie's hands as they dug into her bruised flesh.

A scream tore from her once more, and her legs went out from under her. Thanie followed her down, pressing the flowers harder against her collar. Blinding agony burst from the point of the break, spearing outward along lightning lines. Thanie's arms shook with the effort, holding Lidan still as she began to thrash, screaming and crying wordless nonsense.

What the *fuck* was she doing?

Lidan's shoulder burned, consumed by wild heat pulsing away from the broken bone and coursing down her arm and side. Her ribs throbbed, her teeth ached, her inner ear screamed as if someone had shoved a knitting needle through her skull. The muscles of her neck were hard as stone, contracting tighter than they were ever meant to in an effort to wrench away from the blazing torment of Thanie's hands.

Sweat beaded on the woman's brow, her lips trembled as her body shook. With one final shove Thanie let go, staggering back as Lidan collapsed.

Cool stone embraced her, relief washing through her limbs as the pain subsided. The fire burned down to a smoulder, the ache fading as the cold crept up to greet her. Her breath shuddered as her eyes eased open. Across the cell Thanie collapsed against the wall, paler than Lidan had ever seen her, hands shaking.

'What the fuck was that?' Lidan demanded, her voice a ragged mess, torn by savage screams.

Thanie lifted a desiccated twig between her fingers, barely visible in the wan light of the torch. Blossoms once the colour of the midsummer sun were now blackened ruins, charred to ash and crumbling as Lidan watched. The sprig, once bouncing with the energy it retained from its tree of growth, was crisp, hard, and about as lifeless as a rock.

'No need to thank me,' Thanie snarled. She dropped the scorched twig and slid down the wall, folding up on the floor and curling into the corner. Shivers wracked through the woman as if the room were carved of ice.

Lidan walked tentative fingers up to her shoulder, her neck relaxing as she pressed against skin that had not a few minutes ago been stained deep purple with bruises. The nauseating pain had vanished, leaving nothing more than an aching stiffness in her joints.

She slipped her arm free of the sling, carefully holding the top of her shoulder as she swung her arm back and forth. Shifting her shirt away, at her collar, where the bone had broken and bruises had bloomed, a faint scar remained, a vague shadow of the blossom sprig etched into her skin. Where the incandescent heat of Thanie's hand had been, pale lines splayed out like forks of lightning in her light brown skin.

'Thanie?' Lidan murmured. The woman looked up from where she sheltered behind her knees, tucked in behind her arms. 'What did you do?'

'I fixed it.' She coughed; a wet bark that rattled in her chest. 'Might have gone a bit too hard, though.'

Lidan rubbed at her shoulder, probing the smooth lines of the strange scars. It wasn't possible. It had to be a trick. 'I mean it. What did you do? When will it wear off?'

A sharp laugh echoed against the walls.

'It won't unless you snap it again.' She caught Lidan with a serious look and she knew then there was no trick here. 'I'm not one to show off, Liddy. I hid who I was for your entire life and now I don't have to. I healed it.'

If not a trick, then surely this was a bribe. The woman wanted something, and it didn't take much to figure at what. Lidan narrowed her eyes. 'Why?'

Thanie jerked upright, an open hand extended toward Lidan. 'I can break it again if you like?'

'No,' she replied quickly, scooting backward.

'Didn't think so.' Thanie smirked and curled back into the corner, pulling her single thin blanket over her legs and flicking a corner over her shoulder.

'Um… Thank you,' Lidan said. She found her feet, easing upright against the wishes of her remaining bruises.

Thanie's eyes slid closed, and she sighed. 'Think on what I said, girlie.'

Lifting the sling from around her neck, Lidan balled the fabric up and went to the door. She expected another pearl of wisdom or witty comment to follow her into the tunnel, but only the soft sound of sleeping breath filled the air beneath the sound of her locking the door.

Lidan swallowed a little knot of emotion. Her mind buzzed with confusion, her fingers worrying at her shoulder as if she might find the pain again if she just pressed hard enough. Climbing the stairs out of the tunnel and to the top of the wall seemed easier now her shoulder didn't scream in protest at every step. Within moments she reached the landing and tapped on the door.

'A moment, Witness,' Wiley replied. He scuffled around, banging into something and knocking something else to the ground. He swore and fumbled with the key, jiggling it in the lock until it released the pins and the door swung open.

'Thank you, Wiley,' Lidan said in the same aloof tone as before. He glanced into the darkness of the tower stairwell, consumed again with shadow as she handed him the torch. 'The prisoner is secure, though I won't be offended if you feel the need to check.'

She didn't wait to see if he did. She hurried into the night, keen to get off the wall and away from the tower before someone noticed her. Her fingers squeezed the balled-up sling and she glanced down at it. How was she going to explain this? No one just *recovered* from a broken bone overnight. Perhaps it was best if her miraculous rehabilitation remained a secret. No one need know.

She stepped down from the final stair and walked straight into Ran's chest.

'Ooof,' he gasped, stumbling back as Lidan staggered, holding her arm close. 'What in the name of the gods are you doing here?'

'I could ask you the same thing,' she shot back in an accusatory whisper, glancing around. Had anyone seen them? Anyone who might feel the need to tell her father where she'd been? There were many awkward questions she'd rather avoid for now.

'I was looking for you!' Ran brushed at his shirt and trousers as if she'd thrown a handful of sand at him. 'What were you—where is your sling?' His eyes widened before they narrowed, thoughts cascading through his mind as she watched, calculations and assumptions piling together to form conclusions. Best she put a stop to that before it got out of hand.

'I needed some air and the wall blocks most of the breeze.' She gestured with a nod at the top of the parapet. 'It's cooler up there.'

'Right,' he said slowly, not even attempting to disguise his scepticism. His eyes flicked from her face to the arm she held tight to her chest. He didn't believe her. 'And the sling? Did you lose that over the edge of the wall?'

'No! Don't be stupid.' Lidan lifted the ball of fabric and let it fall open from her hand, waving it like a flag. 'It's here. I took it off to cool down.'

He raised an eyebrow, and she just knew he was hunting for a hole to wriggle though her lie. She wasn't about to give him the chance. He wouldn't approve of her visit to Thanie and she had things she needed to think about.

'I'm tired,' Lidan said matter-of-factly, glancing off into the distance. 'If anyone asks, I'm going to bed.'

Lidan took a step and Ran snatched at her upper arm. With a hard jolt she snapped to a stop and met his gaze, glaring as his grip tightened.

'What were you doing up there? Did you go to see *her*?' he demanded through gritted teeth. Another hand came up to seize her other arm, tight as a vice. Jerking in his grasp, Lidan tried to break free, but he held fast and shoved her back against the wall. 'Tell me what she said!'

Dark spots erupted in her vision and Lidan gasped. Healed bones she may have, but the muscles and skin were still swollen, damaged beneath the seemingly unblemished exterior. Her heart hammered and she glared at Ran's furious face, ramming her teeth down on the back of her lip to distract from the pain.

Blinded by rage, his arms shook and sweat broke across his brow. The strong stench of ale rolled off his skin and she caught the faintest hint of panic. He was frightened, lashing out like only a coward could.

Lidan met his hard eyes with a stony look of her own, forcing her fear down, dropping her tone dangerously low. 'Go on, Ranoth. Hit me. What's one more bruise?'

He baulked and blinked, then released her and stepped back. His lips moved but the words to explain what he'd just done fled into the night. Instead, he staggered, rubbing at his wrist. Lidan's skin burned where he'd touched her, a fiery brand no one could see.

'I'm sorry,' Ran murmured. His eyes darted, never falling on one thing for more than a heartbeat. Lidan frowned. He stepped away, ashen, seemingly lost. 'I'm sorry. Did I hurt you?'

She glanced down then shook her head, feeding him a lie if only to slip away. 'No, I'm fine.'

'I can walk you back—'

'I know the way,' she snapped, and he flinched as though he'd been slapped. He knew she was lying. He saw the fear in her eyes as clearly as she felt it, growing colder as they stood in the broken light of the wall torches and the bonfire in the common.

'Until tomorrow then...' Ran gave her a stiff bow.

A curt nod was all Lidan could manage, and she stepped back, well out of range of his hands and the eyes that might see how she shivered under her shirt, away from the gaze that might notice the tremble of her hands or the way her chin quivered. 'Goodnight, Ran.'

Chapter Eight

Tingalla, Tolak Range, the South Lands

'What the fuck was *that*?' Iridia stormed from the shadows.

Ran glanced away, not only because she shone as brightly as a full moon, but for shame. 'I have no idea.'

'Well you better think of something, because "you went to speak to my pet witch" isn't going to cut it.' Folding her arms, Iridia scowled, her translucent form ablaze with rage.

'I said I don't know!' His fingers scraped back through his hair in frustration, his gaze drawn to the sky, starlight dancing across his vision. Exhaustion slammed into him and he staggered back another step, head swimming with a toxic mix of emotion and too much drink. 'We need to get out of here,' he muttered. 'The longer we stay, the more chance there is of something going wrong.'

Iridia had remained distant since his fight with Lidan's mother. The shock of it and the power he'd expelled battling the woman had wounded him so deeply that Iridia's connection seemed weaker than ever—a thin gossamer string, no thicker than a spider's thread, holding them together through the tempest. She hadn't appeared until he'd found Lidan and brought her to the feast, drawn to the one person who might understand what he was thinking. Even then, he was alone.

It should have done Lidan some good to be out in the fresh air with company. It had helped when he arrived at the Keep and fell into a pit of wallowing self-hate. When he discovered Lidan had disappeared, he'd assumed she'd gone to the privy or to speak with her family. Time proved both assumptions wrong, and Iridia returned as he wandered the crowd, questions on her lips along with the suggestion Lidan may have snuck away to speak to the captive in the tower.

She wouldn't be there, Ran told her. Lidan was in bed, or visiting the stables, or whatever these people did when they wanted to be alone. Running into the southerner at the foot of the stairs had not been on his list of expectations, nor had he thought to boil over with anxious rage, demanding to know what she'd been doing or saying to the witch.

Regret and embarrassment washed through him, and he slumped onto the lowest step, resting his spinning head against the rough-cut timbers of the wall. A frown framed Iridia's iridescent eyes and she drifted to sit at his side. It still perplexed him that she moved easily through solid objects one moment, then interacted with them at will, as if her body were as corporeal as his own. There was the slightest tug on his magic whenever she did, taxing just a little to bring herself further into this world.

'I'll speak with Lidan in the morning,' he conceded, ravaged by weariness.

They were all broken, worn out and stretched thin. Brit had taken to mothering them, especially Aelish, who despite protesting that she could do everything herself, leaned against the tall man's arm and closed her eyes when she thought no one was watching. Eian and Zarad had formed a little coterie of quiet care, moving without words, tending each other with a familiarity and comfort Ran both envied and adored. They simply knew each other down to the ground, and it held them together while they healed.

Ran was adrift, wandering and uncertain, while the path ahead stared him in the face. As much as he wanted to depart for Orthia, taking the witch to her doom at the hands of the Duke's Justice, he hesitated. He couldn't yet say why.

Iridia gave him a stern, unyielding look that solidified the shame in his gut. 'Aelish will have your balls if she finds out.'

He grimaced. 'That she will. I'd deserve it too.'

An apology might not be enough. Lidan would be well within her rights to expose his outburst to her father and never speak to him again. Not that he'd have to worry about that—he'd probably be dead.

They watched the night together, little green tree dragons chirping as they dove to catch insects congregating in the torchlight. Dragons of any kind were such a rare sight in the north, hunted close to extinction for their skins and for fear. Revelling in the cool breeze cutting the close, humid air, Ran drew a deep breath thick with the heady scent of approaching rain.

'Are you going to ask her?' the ghost finally ventured.

'Who?' he asked. She twitched her head toward the tower. 'The witch?'

Iridia nodded as whooping laughter and singing echoed between the buildings. Somewhere in the distance, lightning flashed against a bank of cloud. When he couldn't find Lidan, he'd thought to speak with the witch, perhaps just to prove Iridia wrong. Those plans had been thrown off course on discovering Lidan on the stairs.

Ran shrugged, turning to face Iridia along the length of the step. 'I'm not sure where to start, to be honest.'

'How about, "what did you mean when you said Iridia had to choose?".' That's what she said, wasn't it? That I had to choose where I was going—here or the place beyond. This realm or that of the Dark Rider.' They shared a moment, eyes locked.

'What would you choose?' he asked. His heart gave a heavy, anxious thud and heat rose in his cheeks.

Her gaze didn't leave his face. 'That depends on the cost.'

'The cost?' His brows drew together and Iridia released a deep sigh.

'There's always a cost, Ran. The gods give nothing for free. You suffer whenever you use your magic. The witches would have paid dearly for the power to create the dradur. Even now, you can see it in Thanie's face. She's not much older than the other one but she wears the toll of maintaining that disguise in her skin.' Iridia lifted her hands in a helpless sort of gesture and let them fall into her lap. 'There may well be a way to bring me back, to break me free of the place between, but at what cost? What must we pay for that? I can't say which I'd choose without knowing the price.'

Ran watched her intently, his throat tightening. 'If the cost were nil, if there was nothing to pay, what would you choose?'

'You know the answer to that,' Iridia said softly.

An effortless silence settled between them.

There was no missing the dark, gaping tear across Iridia's throat—the old wound that ended her life before Ran was born. But beyond that, she was all savage wit and fury, then a quicksilver switch to childlike wonder and infectious laughter. He never knew which he'd face on any given day and her unpredictability had become his shelter. He reached for it when the world confused or hurt him, sought it when faced with the unfamiliar and unsettling. She wasn't there to fix him or save him. She'd made that abundantly clear in his escape from Usmein. She'd let him make his own mistakes, and in so doing, had become a constant he wasn't sure he could live without. The idea they couldn't remain like this forever turned his stomach. It had done all night.

It was the last thing he'd expected the witch to say when he'd confronted her. Denial and manipulation, yes. Much the same as Lidan's mother tried when challenged, but Thanie showed no such resistance. She'd calmly accepted her discovery, as if she'd known one day her past would chase her down. She hadn't seemed at all surprised when it finally did. It was Ran who'd been stunned by the things she knew and could perceive. She could sense Iridia much more clearly than Lidan and Aelish, even hear her voice, though she couldn't see her. And she'd told them Iridia would have to choose between this life and the next. She hadn't told him how, or even really why. She'd simply dropped a question in his lap that he couldn't answer.

How could Iridia stay?

His reaction to the thought of losing her was as unnerving as the idea itself. Up all night, tossing and turning, staring at the ceiling despite his exhaustion and bone deep aches. Something had shifted in the dark, unseen places within him. At his core, something had changed. The path he'd thought to walk didn't seem to lead where he wanted to go.

'Well?' Iridia pressed, breaking through his thoughts and drawing him back to the present. 'You going in or not?'

Ran stood and looked up the stairs, contemplating his options. The witch wasn't going anywhere, and he trusted Lidan enough to know the woman wasn't missing from her cell. Lidan was as much a victim of the witch's lies as he or Iridia—she had no reason to fashion an escape. But had she gone to the cell to do Thanie harm? Had Lidan taken out her rage on the older woman? He glanced out toward the buildings, tracing Lidan's footsteps. There was no evidence of blood, no sign of a struggle…

Realisation crawled up from his belly and he froze.

Lidan's arm.

She hadn't been wearing the sling. He knew how painful a broken collarbone could be. There was no way she'd taken it off on her own, no way she'd done it just to cool down. The pain simply wasn't worth the reward.

'No, that's not who we need to speak to.' He stepped from the shadows of the wall into the hot, noisy night.

'What? Where are you going?' Iridia shouted after him, hurrying to keep up.

Ran cut around the back of the hall's kitchens, avoiding the midden and the compost pile and angling toward Lidan's quarters. 'Her arm. Something happened to her arm.'

'She broke it. You were there!' Perhaps Iridia hadn't noticed. Perhaps she believed Lidan's story, but Ran was having none of it.

He shook his head. 'No, something happened in the witch's cell.'

Lidan's quarters came into view; a small, thatched hut set amongst a dozen just like it, surrounded by a maze of boardwalk paths that kept folk out of the mud during torrential summer downpours. The door was lit by a flickering torch and two more fat tree dragons sat under the eave, snatching moths with long, sticky tongues.

Iridia darted in front of him and held out her hands. He didn't stop moving. Her arms flexed and an invisible force shoved him back. Drawing on his power, she turned it against him with a gut-wrenching thud. He stumbled back, breathless and gasping, clutching at his stomach and blinking hard. His lungs screamed for air and he dragged a breath in as deep as he could, reeling from the impact.

'What?!' he wheezed at Iridia, blocking the path with outstretched arms, palms open toward him.

'If you storm in there with a head of steam, she'll kill you as soon as look at you.'

'I wasn't—'

'Shut up and listen to me!' she snapped. 'You hurt her just now. You frightened her. Did you see that, Ran? Did you see the fear? You made her feel like prey. If you corner her in that room, injured or not she will fight you and she will kill you. Don't you remember what it was to run from a hunter?'

Barely able to catch his breath let alone speak, Ran waved a hand, surrendering with a defeated shrug. It seemed he could do nothing right today.

Slowly Iridia lowered her arms and his breath returned, invisible bands loosening from around his chest until his lungs once again filled with air. He eyed the ghost warily. Either she was developing power within herself, or she was becoming more adept at drawing his magic away for her own ends. He didn't understand how either of those things were possible, but he heartily disliked being on the receiving end.

Four steps brought him level with Iridia. Four slow, cautious steps.

'What's gotten into you today?' she whispered.

'I could ask the same of you,' Ranoth replied, incredulous.

'You're wound tighter than a drunk bard's lute and fit to snap.' Genuine concern creased her brow. She lifted a hand toward his face, then seemed to think better of it. 'Should you do this now? You still need her, Ran. *We* still need her. We can't afford to lose her support.'

He sighed and shook his head. 'I know, I just... I'm tired.'

'Tired?'

'Yes, tired. I didn't sleep all that well.'

'I know.' Her reply took him by surprise. She'd been watching him then, from the edge of the night. He knew what this was now, the fuel beneath this fire, and hated it. Iridia nodded reluctantly. 'Be careful. Just, don't scare her off.'

CHAPTER NINE

Tingalla, Tolak Range, the South Lands

'Come in,' came the answer when he finally hammered his fist on the door.

Pushing it aside, he stepped through to see Lidan crouched by the fire, stirring the coals beneath a pot. The strong fragrance of flowers filled the room and she stood slowly, eyeing him as he eased the door shut. She wore a snug-fitting sleeveless shirt and a loose pair of linen trousers that weren't the same pair she'd worn at the feast. Somehow, she'd managed to change.

Lidan didn't move to hang the thick timber fire-stick on its hook by the hearth, instead weighing it slightly in her hand. It was a subtle movement, but one he paid heed as she watched him across the room. A meal stood cooling on a tray, perhaps brought by one of the slaves who attended the daari's family.

'You didn't go back to the feast?' Lidan asked, casually stepping away from the hearth.

'No.' Nervous fingertips rubbed at sweaty palms, and he smoothed his hands down the sides of his trousers. 'I think I've had enough ale for one night. Not feeling the best.'

In truth, he'd only had a handful of tankards. He'd been too distracted by his own thoughts and the prying glances of the clan-folk to want for more. That wasn't usually enough to relieve him of his senses, but so far tonight he hadn't made the best decisions. Perhaps he really wasn't in his right mind.

Nodding, Lidan shifted awkwardly. She wanted him to go, that much was clear. She wasn't interested in talking. Fine. He'd get this done and leave her alone. Ran sighed and took two steps forward. 'Look, I just wanted—'

For someone as injured as Lidan, she moved with surprising speed, darting past the table like a cat and whipping the fire-stick up, arm extended, levelling the charred point dangerously close to the soft flesh of his throat.

Ran's hands came up in surrender. 'I'm unarmed.'

'I can see that,' she muttered, looking him up and down as if she expected him to draw a weapon at any moment. 'What do you want?'

'To say I'm sorry. I was out of line—'

Lidan snorted. 'No shit. I've got nothing to say to you.' Anger flared in her eyes, firelight reflected in the glimmering green.

Told you so, the ghost whispered from a shadow drenched corner.

Please don't, Ran begged. He didn't need any distractions.

'Is she here?' Lidan demanded. One eye narrowed to a pained twitch, and she glanced around the room without shifting her stance.

With a nod, Ran lowered his hands. 'Yes, Iridia is here.'

'Did she see what you did?'

'Oh yes. She's already given me an earful.'

He shifted sideways and Lidan spun, mirroring his step and swiping the fire-stick down to whack the outside of his thigh. He blocked the blow with his forearm and Lidan advanced, attacking as though the fire-stick were a sword. Blows rained down and Ran scrambled, blocking and parrying with his bare hands, absorbing each stinging hit with a pained grunt. Finally, he smacked the stick away and lunged with a jabbing punch, Lidan shifting aside mere seconds before his fist would have connected with her face.

The fire-stick struck, swung backhanded into his side. Ran roared, doubling over and clutching at his waist. 'I said I was *unarmed!*'

'I don't *care*,' Lidan growled. Breathing heavily, she pushed the end of the poker up under his chin, forcing him to stand. Apparently, she'd had some practise with that sword she'd lost out in the gorge. Not that she needed the aid of steel. She managed just fine with a re-purposed tree branch.

'*And* I said I was sorry.' He wouldn't plead for forgiveness. He'd only grabbed her arms. It wasn't like he'd hit her or attacked her with a fucking stick.

Another dark laugh. 'My father told me once that sorry is meaningless; a word used as a bandage by children and those who should know better. It fixes nothing.'

'Don't you think you're over-reacting a bit?' he suggested, furiously rubbing the rising welt beneath his shirt.

Oh, you've done it now... Iridia's observation did nothing to help things and his heart hammered a little harder.

'Over-*reacting*?' Lidan repeated, the pitch of her voice rising. 'Look at my arms! I can almost see your fingerprints in those bruises!'

Ran glanced at where he'd grabbed her, the skin gleaming in the firelight. What might have begun as a bright hand mark had begun to purple, dark lines left where he'd squeezed her. The handprint was clear, a mirror to the width of his fingers and the breadth of his palm.

A wave of nauseating guilt crashed over him. 'I swear, I didn't mean it.' Now he began to plead, the severity of what he'd done slowly dawning. He might as well have smacked her across the face for all the damage he'd inflicted. There were bruises forming that he couldn't see, wounds below the surface that he might not be able to mend. 'I snapped. I'm tired and I—'

'I do *not* have time for your excuses!' Her voice shook, tears pooling in her eyes; shimmering wells of anger and sorrow, sparkling with a morbid kind of beauty he wished he didn't have to see. 'I am sick to death of excuses, from everyone, including you.'

Iridia said nothing and he wondered if she was still there. Instead of glancing at the dark corner, he set his jaw and met Lidan's gaze. 'Fine. I won't bother you again.' The sharp end of the fire-stick began to shake, Lidan's arm trembling with fatigue as a muscle jumped in her neck. Mysteriously healed or not, she'd been weakened by her injuries. She wouldn't last much longer holding the heavy length of hardwood like that. 'I wanted to see how your shoulder was.'

She blanched at that.

'Need help getting the sling back on?' he continued.

Lidan's eyes betrayed her, darting sideways, then back to his face. He followed her glance and spotted the sling, tossed in a crumpled heap on the bed.

'I can manage.' The fire-stick shook a little more.

'I've got about as much time for your lies as you do for my excuses,' Ran countered. 'What happened in the cell, Lidan? What did she do?'

'Nothing—'

'Bullshit!' he snapped.

Ran, Iridia warned, pushing a sense of caution toward him, the pressure pulling him away from Lidan. He ignored the ghost.

'You broke that bone *four* days ago. A few hours past you could barely move your head for the pain. I had to dress you, for fuck's sake, and now you're walking around as if it never happened at all!' Ran nodded sharply at her arm. 'You want to talk about bruises? What happened to the great fucking mess of black and blue you had there this afternoon?'

Lidan glowered at him. 'I. Don't. Know,' she ground out, as if the very words were squeezed from a stone.

'What did she do, Lidan?' His voice softened; his fury doused by creeping curiosity. If she didn't know what the witch had done…

'She took a sprig of flowers from my hair and did something with her magic.' The fire-stick dropped away, the point resting on the floor as fatigue won the battle for control of Lidan's arm. She didn't put it aside. Ran made no attempt to move lest she find a renewed strength and hit him again. He didn't want to give her another reason to defend herself tonight.

Something moved in the corner of the room and Iridia materialised from the gloom, a curious tilt to her head. Lidan pointed to the table and Ran noticed a small collection of twigs adorned with long, thin leaves and yellow, ball-shaped flowers. Their perfume was strong, filling the room, and he realised it was their scent he'd caught when he walked in.

Lidan shrugged and defeat dropped a weight on her shoulders, diminishing her stature. 'I don't know why I went to the cell. I thought… I thought she might have answers that could help me figure out what to do next.'

'Really?' Ran frowned and glanced at Iridia, who shrugged and settled on the bed in her odd little way. 'Why go to her for advice?'

'Who knows,' Lidan conceded and slumped into a chair in front of the fire. Her hands worried at the surface of the fire-stick, as if seeking comfort in its strength as she stared at the flames. 'She isn't like everyone else. She never was. For all the evil she did and allowed to be done, she protected me in her own way. She shielded me from my mother and redirected her fury. She even tried to show me what my mother really was, but I couldn't see the whole of that truth. Perhaps I didn't want to.'

'Can I?' He pointed at the chair opposite and Lidan nodded, dark circles under her eyes drawing her face into a gaunt mask. It took a while longer, but she finally relaxed the muscles of her neck and shoulders. She was so incredibly tense, so close to breaking that he found he couldn't fault her reaction to his outburst. As strung out as he was, she'd lost her mother and her closest friend in the space of a few days. She'd almost lost two of her siblings and wrecked half her body just to get them back. It was a miracle Lidan managed to pull herself out of bed that morning. 'Did she have the answers you needed?'

Lidan shook her head, this time without a wince of pain. What *had* the witch done? 'By the time I got there I barely knew what I wanted to ask, or why.'

'What did you talk about then?' he pressed, desperate to reach the moment Thanie had somehow healed Lidan but wary of forcing his will on her again. Iridia slipped silently across the room and curled up at his feet, staring into the flames as Lidan did, her knees drawn up under her chin.

'I wanted to know what I should do next. I needed to know where my path led now. Needed some hope, I suppose.' Lidan paused, pulling back from a wound she didn't want to reveal. 'Now everything has changed.'

'What did she tell you?'

Their eyes met and she held his gaze for a long, heavy minute. 'She said the path I had thought to walk was gone. I need to forge one of my own.'

'That's a bit vague,' Ran said with a scowl.

'I know. Not exactly helpful, but there you go.' She shifted in the chair, restless, and Iridia glanced up. 'Then she did the... the thing.' Lidan waved a hand toward her collar, obviously flummoxed.

'The thing?' Curiosity had him well within its grip now. He leaned forward, elbows pressing into the top of his knees.

'With the flowers.' Lidan looked at him as if he should know exactly what she meant.

'I don't—' Ran began.

'She used the flowers to heal the bone!' Lidan shouted the answer and his brows shot up, skin tingling. The burn of ice-cold breath made him shiver as Iridia moved, shifting through his leg a little as she turned to Lidan.

'She *what?*' It was all Ran could manage through his confusion. He looked quickly down at Iridia, heedless of what Lidan thought of him glancing at empty air.

The ghost shook her head, eyes wide with surprise. *I have no idea what she's talking about.*

You never saw the witches do anything like this?

No. Neither of them. They were more interested in harming than healing.

He registered the anxiety in Lidan's eyes. She'd have felt that conversation even if she couldn't hear it. 'I've never heard of such a thing, and neither has Iridia.'

'Excuse me?'

Shaking his head, he struggled to find the words to explain. 'I've never seen magic heal outside a magic-weaver's own body. I can't even begin to think how it could—'

Transfer of power, Iridia said suddenly, halting Ran's galloping thoughts. *You can transfer magic from one person to another, yes?*

He replied with a nod, painfully aware of the disturbed look Lidan levelled at him, one brow raised, her gaze flicking between his face and the empty space where Iridia sat.

What about power transfer to an animal? Or anything that's alive?

I suppose, Ran acknowledged.

The ghost stood and approached the table, pointing to the abandoned flowers. *These are still alive, yes?*

'What is she saying? I know she's speaking to you.' Lidan's eyes narrowed and Ran realised he'd have to start translating.

'She's talking about transfer of power and asking if the flowers are alive.' He looked back at Iridia, confused. *I'm not sure if cut flowers can be considered alive? And I've never seen transfer of power to an animal. I'm not sure why anyone would want to. Or if animals even have magic.*

Iridia rolled her eyes. *Everything has a little magic, Ran. Just not as much as you!*

Lidan stood and picked up a sprig of blossoms. Using her thumbnail as a knife she scraped back a strip of thin bark from the stem. 'It's still green, so there's life in it.'

Magic can heal and it can move from one being to another. Magic can give life to something that has none. How else could dradur be made? Iridia shrugged. *Could it not, in theory, take life from one thing and give it to another, even just to heal a broken bone?*

Ran sat very still as he relayed Iridia's words, watching Lidan's sceptical, pursed lips relax into an expression of bemused wonder. His heart beat a little faster, his skin prickling with fear and excitement. How could this be true? How had he not known this? He'd been at the Keep for four years and not once had he seen anyone use magic to heal another person. How many lives could have been saved after the dradur attack if they had?

'The ngaru were made like that,' Lidan said suddenly, cutting across his thoughts.

'Sorry?'

'A few months back, before we left Hummel to travel here, I had dreams. I saw someone working on a body, sewing weapons to its limbs.' Lidan shuddered with revulsion and Iridia recoiled from the thought with a grimace. 'Thanie sent me those dreams to show me what my mother had done. I saw them use magic to bring the body back to life. Is that what Iridia means?'

Ran nodded, translating the ghost's response, feeling for a moment like a transfer point rather than a participant in the discussion. 'So Thanie used the same sort of magic as when they made the dradur. What happened to the flowers?'

'They died. Burned up, actually. The flowers turned to ash, and I was left with this.' Lidan tugged her shirt aside, revealing a spiderweb of pale scars running out from the centre of her left collar bone. Along the bone itself, the impression of the flowers, their cut stem and leaves had been burned into her skin.

A lengthy silence followed as the three of them fell into thought. Of what Ran knew of power transfer, it only worked if the magic was volunteered, but he'd only ever seen it taken as a loan, not given. Even when he'd killed the Woaden mage in Usmein all those years ago, he'd done it by drawing away her power, not by forcing his own on her. It hadn't ever occurred to him that it might be possible.

'How... how did it feel? Was Thanie weakened by it?' he asked, careful to absorb every word.

'As though she'd set me on fire. I'm surprised no one heard me scream-ing. Once it was over, the pain vanished.' Lidan worked the shoulder as if to prove her point. 'It's stiff and I'll need to train hard to bring it back to fighting strength, but it's not broken anymore. I asked if it would wear off and she said it wouldn't. She was tired afterward, like she'd been awake for days. She seemed peaceful though. It's an odd thing to say, but it was a content kind of weariness. She kind of just curled up and went to sleep.'

Possibility swarmed Ran's mind, brushing back the lingering, dull ache of a headache and fatigue that begged him to go to bed. A single glance at Iridia told him the same idea had occurred to her. There was nothing either of them could do about it tonight. He had no idea what time it was, the night running away from him. If he wanted any chance at rest, he had to take it now.

'I need to think about this some more.' Pushing himself out of the chair, he stood before Lidan and paused to look at her shoulder again. 'I still don't... Never mind. Let me see if I can think this through. It makes sense that it's possible, but I can't fathom that I spent four years in a keep full of magic-weavers and never once came across this practice.'

'Not once?' Lidan frowned. 'You *never* learned this?'

'No, I've never seen it before. But I'll figure it out. We need to know what she's playing at.'

'I'm not sure I understand...'

'I don't trust her, for obvious reasons. She's worked magic on you that I can't explain, and it isn't the first thing she's done that goes beyond my understanding of magic. I can't explain how she hid your mother's thau-malux, or how she disguised herself. I certainly can't explain how your mother was able to escape, other than she stole Thanie's magic to do it.' He sighed and rubbed at the outcrop of stubble on his chin as he thought. 'It stands to reason she knows far more about our powers than Eian, Zarad and I combined, which is troubling to say the least.'

It wasn't just troubling—it was terrifying. How could he hope to restrain someone like that on a journey the length of theirs? Could the three of them contain Thanie, or would she break away at the first chance she got? Then there was opportunity bubbling at the edge of his mind, hinting at him to come closer.

'Will you be all right here tonight? If you want someone to stay nearby, I can camp on the floor or—'

Lidan shook her head. 'No, I'm fine. Vee will be back sooner or later. She rarely leaves me for too long.'

'I am sorry, by the way. For what I did.' He shifted his feet, uncertainty trembling in his bones. 'It won't happen again.'

'I know,' Lidan said.

Ran glanced at her and his breath caught. For a moment he couldn't move, trapped by her uncompromising stare, and knew without doubt that she was right. Should he make such a mistake again, he would not survive to tell of it.

With a nod he stepped toward the door, Iridia fading from his sight but maintaining her presence just beyond the walls of the hut. At the threshold, he turned back, his hand on the latch, a single persistent thought biting at him. 'Did Thanie say anything else, before you left?'

Lidan's bright green eyes met his. 'She said she could help us.'

'She said what?' A chill shivered through Ran, despite the warm air and the heat from the fire. He'd not expected that.

'She said she could help us, if we had a mind to listen.'

'And do you?'

'I don't trust her any more than you do, but she knows things, Ran. She's proven that many times over. I'm not sure she's entirely as she appears to be, or what we've assumed she is.' Lidan gave him a small sad smile, the same he'd seen so many times since meeting her. 'Does she deserve it? No. Will we regret it if we don't? I'd bet my life on it.'

CHAPTER TEN

Tingalla, Tolak Range, the South Lands

He'd played with the idea for the best part of two days, yet could see no other way. Wondered if he was mad to even consider it, to even float it in his own mind. But it flitted here and there, interrupting other threads of thought, cutting them away before he could snatch them back again.

The magic-weaver had been clear. She could help him and Lidan if they gave her a chance.

But what did that mean? What would it cost?

Ran put his water skin down and wiped a sweaty hand across his brow. His clothes were soaked and his skin prickled, muscles singing from exertion. He'd been bored enough to join some of the rangers practising close combat, and two of them continued as he took the chance to rest. Exercise gave him uninterrupted time to think, or at least an empty space to pour his thoughts into, a place for them to coalesce into answers. Some people liked to read, others to paint, others rode or took a walk. He preferred to punch things.

'Ran?' Aelish asked in a low, weary whisper. He turned to find her on a bench in the shade, watching the rangers as they trained. Her sturdy northern riding clothes had been abandoned for a light gown that wrapped around her waist but hung loose from her frame. He had to admit, it looked a damn sight more comfortable in this heat than thick trousers and a leather jerkin.

'You all right?' he wondered, moving to lean against the support post of an awning jutting from the compound's wall—a shelter for water barrels and storage crates.

Aelish nodded, then glanced away. She was visibly exhausted, the brightness of her eyes still dulled five days after the battle in the gorge, her skin much paler than it should have been. There was an awkwardness to her glance, narrowing her eyes against the light of the setting sun. Insects whirred in the air and the scent of cooking meat wafted from the hall's kitchen. The hour grew late, yet she just sat there, the bold northern trader looking drained and careworn.

'The boys and I have been talking...'

Oh shit. Here it comes.

She brought her gaze around to study him. 'Have you changed your mind?'

With a sigh, Ran dropped onto the bench beside her. 'Look, I'd always planned to take her to Usmein—'

'You're still set on that then? Even after everything we talked about?'

His finger traced the stitching of his trouser seam. Aelish had taken up Brit's cause, convinced that returning to Usmein was folly. Of course, upon hearing the fullness of the plan Ran had for the Woaden magic-weaver, Eian had thrown a merry fit, and Zarad had glared in silent judgement, an expression that reminded Ran so much of Sasha he decided he never wanted to see it again. None of his companions agreed that taking the witch back to face his father's Justice was wise, and their concern had gnawed at him ever since.

Ran watched Aelish for a moment, then licked salty sweat from his lips. 'I've thought about what you said, and I haven't made a decision yet.'

'Ran,' Aelish murmured and shook her head. 'I know this isn't what you wanted, but we can't stay here forever. At least, *I* can't. I need to go home, and so do Eian and Zarad.'

'And Brit?' he asked, almost sure he didn't want the answer.

She shrugged and looked at the ground, scuffing the dirt with the heel of her boot. 'He's torn. He wants to do as your mother commanded, but... He'd like to come back to Isord with me. What he won't do is leave you here on the promise that you're staying, only to have you pack up the witch and make a break for Orthia on your own. He'd follow you into the Under-world if he thought it would keep you safe.'

Ran was sure he'd explained the plan to both Eian and Zarad before now. But on reflection, he wondered if he'd only told them they were hunting the witches with the intention of killing them, not escorting them halfway across the world into hostile territory. Obviously, the idea of returning to Usmein, or anywhere else in Orthia other than the Keep didn't sit well with the couple. Nor did it rest easy with Brit, who was adamant he had a duty to fulfil in taking Ran to safety, somewhere far from where the duke's soldiers might find him.

Annoyingly, Ran had come to realise the lot of them were right. It was indeed foolish to travel across Orthia, four magic-users in a party of six. If they were discovered, they'd be dead by the following dawn. But the deeper dangers of his original plan had been revealed when Lidan emerged from the witch's cell healed of her injury. Thanie was something else, something he couldn't explain or measure. She was not what he'd expected to find, and he was less certain now that simple shackles and ropes could restrain her.

Of course, this left him in the unenviable position of having to admit that he was wrong and make a decision on what to do with the witch he had exposed as a liar and a fraud. He couldn't leave her confined here, nor could he let her go. Did the southerners' laws allow for execution as a punishment? Surely that was the only option now. Leaving Thanie to rot in a cell seemed as misguided as releasing her. Her powers would return eventually, and doors and bars would offer little resistance.

Lingering in the background was the none too insignificant prospect of the witch's offer to help, and the idea he had been toying with all day like a loose tooth. 'Aelish, I know you need answers and I promise you'll have them—'

'When?' There was no malice in her voice, no anger. She was just done; too tired to put up with his twisted reasoning and stalling for time.

Ran turned toward her, narrowing the space between them. 'What's wrong? Has something happened? Has someone—'

'Nothing. I just need to know. Brit needs to know. We need to... *I* need to know if you're going to drag him off on some ill-conceived quest into danger. I need to know so I can prepare myself for that.' The words spun out, tears pooling in her eyes. Instinct told him to recoil from the sharp, ragged edges of her splintering emotions. Where was this coming from? 'I've only known him a few weeks, maybe a moon, but by the White Woman if you take him away from me—'

He touched her arm and cut through the storm. 'No.'

Aelish scowled, trying to understand. 'No, what?'

'No, I'm not taking him away from you.'

'But he said—'

'Ignore what he said. He's a big idiot but he'll listen.' The thought that his companions might abandon him to his poor decisions and their consequences hit hard. He'd already put them in more danger than he had any right to, already made choices that resulted in other people's pain. Could he ask more of them? Would they be stupid enough to follow him? He doubted it. He wasn't ready to move, but he had to give Aelish something before she spiralled.

She wasn't simply tired from the exertion of the fight, she was exhausted by worry, tying herself in knots about her future and what would happen when Ran made his choice. A self-centred bastard he might be, but he couldn't let his friends tear themselves apart for his sake. He just hadn't expected this simple thing to matter so much to Aelish, or for the prospect of being separated from Brit to elicit such a reaction.

'I won't stop him going with you, Aelish. I won't pull you apart. The only thing left to decide is what I'm doing with myself and the witch. For that, I need a little more time. Can you give me that?'

Relief eased the tension in her shoulders, and she nodded, her lip trembling as a tear slipped down her cheek. 'I can.'

It wasn't much, but it would be enough. He'd delayed as long as he could. The time had come to move a piece on the board, consequences be damned. If he failed, if it was all a monumental mistake, then so be it.

Rounding a corner, Ran spied Lidan waiting at the base of the tower stairs. She'd received his message, whispered over dinner by a slave assigned to the care of the northerners. Despite their altercation two nights ago, she'd come.

Her ever-faithful attendant stood with her, Lidan showing the young woman how to wield one of her long, curved knives as the sun set. He'd seen the weapons before but never up close—she rarely removed them from their sheaths unless needed. They seemed a fine pair of blades, strikingly unusual in a society that still favoured stone, bone, and timber, with only a smattering of bronze and steel among the most powerful and wealthy.

You're sure about this? Iridia asked from a hidden corner of his mind.

No, but I have to ask. I have to know. I refuse to waste time wondering.

Learned your lesson then?

What? He stopped himself from rounding on a woman who wasn't there and kept walking. *What's that supposed to mean?*

You wasted time refusing to open that scroll your tutor gave you...

Yeah, well... that's the curse of the young and the stupid, isn't it? We think we know everything until we don't.

Iridia snorted a laugh and eased back, leaving him in silence as he arrived beside Lidan and her attendant. 'Ready?' he asked.

'Not really. It's our best chance at answers, though.' Lidan shrugged and glanced at the tower. 'Vee has spoken to Wiley. He should be ready.'

Ran nodded at the slave-girl. 'My thanks.'

'She's not taking the fall for this if it fails,' Lidan warned, returning her knife to its sheath with a sharp click.

'I wouldn't—'

'Just be sure it *doesn't* fail. That's is your father these days, all I ask.' She fixed him with a steely look as Vee climbed the stairs.

'Are we likely to be interrupted?'

Lidan threw a glance at the hall, adjusting her belt and checking the ties on a leather bracer at her wrist. 'No, my father is up to his neck in talk of war with Namjin and Marsaw. Siman is with him, and almost every other ranger of rank who isn't watching the river and the tablelands. No one is paying attention to this side of the wall.' She pointed north-west. 'The danger is out there.'

Stepping closer, Ran lowered his voice. Neither of them wanted this getting out of hand, or to be discovered before they had a chance to get what they wanted. 'If it comes to it, are you ready to do what needs to be done? I can't promise I can stop her on my own.'

She nodded, chewing at her lip. 'If it comes to it, yes. I'm not as strong as I was, but I can do it.'

Ran put a gentle hand on her shoulder, pleased she didn't flinch away. 'Let's make sure it doesn't then.'

They followed Vee up the stairs and onto the rampart, a stiff evening breeze snapped flags overhead and buffered their chests. Vee stood at the door to the cell tower, and at a nod from Lidan, knocked three times.

The door swung open and a young ranger stepped into the twilight, leading Thanie by a leather collar and rope. The woman blinked, lifting bound hands in a futile attempt to shield her face. Even with the sun setting and night creeping in, it had been several days since the witch had been outside her gloomy cell.

'I'd like it noted that this is a fucking stupid idea,' Lidan muttered over her shoulder.

'She needs to know who's in control, that we can give and take at whim.' Ran recalled his short stint in his father's dungeons as readily as the sweet relief of freedom when fresh air had touched his face again. He'd never have gone back to that cell if he'd an opportunity to negotiate a way out. Would Thanie be disposed toward their demands if it meant even the slightest reprieve from the oppressive claustrophobia of her prison? Her cloud-grey eyes darted across the vista, then closed as she took a deep breath, savouring the fresh air. They might just be in with a shot.

'Thank you, Wiley.' Ran nodded to the ranger as he tied the rope off on a rail. At a gesture from Vee, the two of them retreated, leaving Lidan and Ran to face Thanie together.

'Interesting choice,' the witch croaked without looking at them.

'I'm sorry?' Ran asked, resting his hand casually on the pommel of his sword and leaning against the rampart wall as if he hadn't a care in the world. In truth, his magic boiled, a swirling torrent under his skin, rushing to his fingertips in anticipation of a fight.

Thanie gave him a long look. Could she feel it roaring through his veins? 'At a guess I'd say no one else knows about this. Where *is* your father these days, girlie?'

'Planning a war, as far as I know.' Lidan put an elbow on the parapet and rested her chin in her hand. Whether their collective nonchalance made any impression on Thanie, Ran couldn't tell. 'You're literally the last thing on his mind. He'd probably forget you were here at all if I didn't remind him.'

'Oh, a *war*? That does sound fun. Who's he going after now?' A smirk danced on Thanie's lips. Her thaumalux was faint, barely more than a dim glow, but Ran put little stock in that. She'd demonstrated quite a talent for concealing power should the need arise. Was she shielding it now, hiding its return, or was she still so weak?

'Yorrell Namjin.'

'That self-important turd. Yes, your mother told me all about his little attempt to match you to his son. He's got a pair—snatching his own niece's children.'

Lidan glanced at Ran and shrugged. 'She's not wrong. He is a turd.'

'I doubt you brought me out here to discuss such things,' Thanie pressed, turning back to the flood plain. Far below, the swollen river churned, an angry rush of brown water and debris from upriver, another bank of storm clouds flashing in the distance. He'd never seen anything like the relentless afternoon storms that grew fat on the day's humidity.

'You said you could help us.' Ran dropped all pretence.

'Did I?'

Lidan closed her eyes and shook her head, frustration birthing a grimace. 'Yes, you did.'

It wasn't an unexpected move by the witch. Perhaps she'd changed her mind since she'd spoken to the daari's daughter. Perhaps she'd realised she had nothing to trade, or no longer thought it worth her while.

Ran cleared his throat and called her bluff. None of them had time for this. 'If you can't, that's not a problem. Wiley, please take—'

'I never said I *wouldn't*.' Thanie snapped around to glare at Ran. 'I merely forgot, boy.' She rolled her eyes so hard he thought she might lose her balance. 'Orthians always were shit at negotiation.'

'Excuse me?'

'The war would have been over decades ago with a bit of careful manoeuvring, but no. Accept it and let it go.' She dismissed him with a wave of her bound hands.

'What war?' Lidan cut in, frowning as the conversation moved to a part of the world she had likely never heard of.

'I'll tell you all about it one day,' Thanie assured her. 'But for now, let's keep to the issue at hand. What do I have that the both of you so desperately need?'

Lidan took a deep breath and drew out the pause. 'More like what can you offer us that might alter your fate.'

'Ah,' the witch said finally. For a long moment she said nothing, perhaps collecting her thoughts, perhaps rifling through her plans. Eventually she laced her fingers together and cleared her throat. 'I'm not sure either of you know what you want. You both reek of uncertainty and indecision. Frankly, you want someone to tell you what to do.'

'I do *not*—' Ran hardly got the words out before she levelled him with a look that stole the breath from his chest.

'You do. Nothing you planned will come to pass, Ranoth. None of it.' Thanie came toward him, moving as far as the rope would allow. 'Did you really come all the way down here to capture the Lackmah witches and take them back to the dear old duke? Sellan was right when she said they hunted you from your home. Yet you want to go back, risking everything, just for the chance they'll pin a medal on your chest. You're not that stupid, surely? You set foot in Usmein and they *will* kill you. So now what? How can you possibly show the world just how wrong they are, if not by crawling back to your father?'

Clenching his jaw, Ran averted his eyes and strangled the sword pommel. It was as scathing a review as Sasha had given of his intentions before he left the Keep. What was it with these women and their painful ability to see straight through to the truth of him? Thanie might as well have stripped him naked right there, exposing every boyhood desire he held close. Lidan glanced at him, wide-eyed, then looked awkwardly away.

'And you,' Thanie continued, scrutinising Lidan with an expression that could have been a sneer if it held any less pity. 'You're like a kicked pup without a master now your mother is gone. You want purpose. Perhaps a little revenge. She wronged you, then abandoned you, and now you're left in the aftermath of her destruction. You know what she'll do. I told you as much, but you know it in your gut. She can't stop herself, so who will? Who has the strength and desire to stop that woman from breaking the world?'

'I don't see what my plans for you have to do with *any* of that,' Ran growled.

'Because I can help *both* of you get what you want. All of it.'

Silence breathed between them, broken only by the crack of pennants in the wind. The sun had left the sky now, the remains of its warmth lingering in the stained clouds, shadows cooling in the breeze. Darkness crept in from the east like ink spilled across the land.

Thanie leaned toward the edge of the parapet, peering over the side. 'Of course, if you aren't interested, I might just throw myself—'

'No!' Lidan cried.

Ran darted forward and Thanie lurched away from the edge, snapping the rope taut as Ran caught hold of her shoulders. She strained against the leather collar, and he realised she wasn't trying to escape, but to get further back from the edge. Her eyes trained on the lip of the wall, all colour drained from her face, and he released her, holding his hands up. 'What?' he demanded. 'What's wrong?'

'Cut me loose,' Thanie croaked, her voice harsh against the collar.

'Like fuck,' he sneered as Wiley and Vee came to their feet in the little awning.

Thanie turned a manic glare on him and Ran froze beneath it. 'Cut me loose, you idiot boy, or condemn this settlement to death at the hands of the marhain.'

'What's a marhain?' Lidan reached for her knives but Ran couldn't move.

He couldn't breathe.

He knew that word.

It was Woaden, sharing the same ancient roots as his own language. His mother spoke it, as had his tutor. Almost all high-born or military trained Orthians did, if only so they could sling insults across enemy lines and interrogate prisoners of war. What he didn't understand was why Thanie uttered *that* word so far above the flood plain, at the top of a sheer cliff. He moved to the edge of the wall and threw a glance over the side.

Barely visible against the rocky face of the cliff, figures slithered upward. Spinning back, he caught Lidan's eye. 'Oh fuck. You call them ngaru. Marhain are ngaru.'

CHAPTER ELEVEN

Tingalla, Tolak Range, the South Lands

Ran yanked his sword from its scabbard while Lidan looked over the side then lurched away, spitting a mouthful of curses. Grabbing at Thanie's collar, she pulled her in close. 'Did you bring them here?'

The same question throbbed through Ran's mind with his racing pulse. 'What?! Are you mad? Why the—'

'Did you *bring them here*?' Lidan demanded, bordering on a scream. 'Did you call them to you?'

Thanie jerked back on the collar, her pale hands like claws, raking at Lidan's leather bound wrist. 'No! Why would I do—'

Something in how the woman moved, the genuine terror in her eyes, told Ran the witch spoke the truth. Her face a picture of rage, Lidan let the woman go and turned to Vee and Wiley. 'Sound the alarm! We're under attack!'

Wiley darted past at a sprint, racing along the top of the wall toward the gatehouse while Vee glanced nervously at her mistress. Shuddering out from under his terror, Ran hefted the sword as Lidan drew a knife and handed it to the slave.

'Go and tell my father the ngaru are coming over the wall,' Lidan ordered. 'Make sure the children are inside the hall and lock it down. No one in or out until a ranger tells you otherwise.'

The young woman took off, the knife held awkwardly in her hand, leaving the three of them alone on the top of the wall. With a swing of his blade Ran cut Thanie's rope and took her collar in one hand, pulling her back to the edge, forcing her to stand closer than she liked to the approaching threat. She fought him all the way, as a dog might when dragged toward a bath it didn't wish to take. The dark figures of the dradur continued upward and he started to count.

One, two, three...

'There's more around here!' Lidan called from a distance. She began to jog, knife in hand, glancing over the parapet as she went. Abruptly she whirled to face him. 'I think we're surrounded.'

'You have to let me—' Thanie wheezed.

'Shut up,' Ran and Lidan snapped in unison.

The witch was at least fifteen years his senior, but he was more than equal to her in height and well and truly stronger. Dragging Thanie to Lidan, he leaned over the side again, heart hammering.

His throat contracted.

More dark figures wormed their way up the cliff. 'There has to be two dozen at least!'

Lidan groaned. 'More, I'd wager.'

A bright horn blasted over Tingalla, the sound echoing against the walls and disappearing off into the evening, silence falling across the settlement in its wake. Clan folk emerged from buildings, doors opening to the dusk, rangers hurrying to open spaces and pausing to watch the gatehouse. The horn sounded again; a long low call repeating three times before the village burst into action.

Someone started screaming and Ran turned to the sound.

At the far northern edge of the village, a hundred feet away where the cliff stood at its highest, something menacing crawled over the lip of the wall. The few rangers on patrol, distracted by the horn blast, turned to meet the dradur in a flash of steel and whir of stone axes.

Thanie thrashed and Ran pulled her in as close as he dared. 'Fucking stop this *shit*.'

Lidan forced herself between them, snarling at the witch. 'How are they here? They've never attacked a village—'

'Yes they have, you stupid girl! They just haven't attacked a village *you've* been in!'

Lidan started. 'What?'

The sound of fighting dulled in Ran's ears. 'The crissan web...' he muttered.

'The fucking *what*?' Lidan snapped, glaring at them both in turn. She shifted her weight, agitated and eager to move. They had mere moments before the dradur crested the wall beside them and the rangers defending the settlement nearby could well be overrun by then. 'What the fuck language are you two talking?'

'You saw the web?' Thanie asked and he nodded. The lines of power flared in his mind, laid out like glowing flower petals around the village of Hummel, a magical barrier to ward off the evil lurking in the bushland.

It was to keep them safe... Iridia whispered quickly, Ran's fear mirrored in her voice. *A wall no one but the dradur could see.*

His grip slipped down what remained of Thanie's rope, giving her more slack. 'You laid that spell to keep them away from Hummel, but there isn't one here, is there?'

'No!' The woman's gaze darted to the edge of the wall, her bound hands coming up as she tried to pull her wrists apart. 'I kept them away from here with an active frequency. I didn't have the time or opportunity to lay out a proper web and—'

'And *what*!' Lidan demanded, shoving her knife up at the soft flesh under Thanie's chin.

'Unless I have magic, the defences fail! Sellan took what I had and the walls fell. I hoped they wouldn't sense me as easily once she was gone, but—'

A snarling dradur pitched up over the rampart and Ran lunged, his sword spearing it through the eye and knocking it back into another, tipping them both off the wall. They screamed all the way down. He turned back to Thanie.

'Untie me! I can help!' she begged.

'Not likely,' he snarled.

The village was awash with screams and the sound of battle, rangers racing to the walls with weapons drawn, two clans fighting as one while those too young or unable to help hurried to shelter in the hall.

Lidan shoved him aside, slashing at a dradur behind him, cutting its throat to ribbons until it slumped on the ground, its head hanging from a thread of flesh. Thanie pulled away from Ran and he found himself drawn along the wall to the stairs by the cell tower. A fourth dradur clambered up and Lidan staggered under the flailing assault of an axe-bladed arm. It was huge, taller than Ran and broader in the shoulders, vile pus-streaked spit drooling from its grisly maw. Thanie's pull on the rope was relentless, frantic, the fibres cutting his hand as he fought to anchor his feet and stop her dragging him from the fight.

'Lidan!' he cried as she ducked and darted away from the attacker.

'Coming!' She was fast and she was strong, but that collar bone, while healed, was still weak. It was a disadvantage she could ill-afford, and it showed in the way she guarded the shoulder, pushed onto the back foot while Ran struggled to control Thanie. He was useless while he held her restraints, his sword arm hampered and his magic blocked.

'Fuck it,' he cursed, switching to drag Thanie toward the stairs. He couldn't defend himself or anyone else up here. With a glance over his shoulder, he saw Lidan hurrying after him. It had to gall her to run from this fight, but they were better on open ground. 'Come on!'

She caught them as they made the top of the stairs, two more dradur slithering over the rampart and across the walkway, clattering toward the stairs as Lidan and Ran hurried down, Thanie staggering to keep up. All around the village the creatures tumbled over the defences. Some met with the business end of a well-aimed weapon, others overcoming the defenders and boiling down into the settlement.

Rangers waited for them, but the numbers weren't in their favour. Ran cast around desperately. 'Where the fuck is everyone?'

'Out on patrol, looking for Namjin raiders,' Lidan shouted. Together they formed a wall before Thanie, protecting her more by instinct than anything else.

Dradur scrambled down the stairs, others leaping from the wall. Some landed heavily, snapping bones they didn't seem to realise they needed. Others hit the ground running, launching at the defenders with wild, glaring eyes and snapping teeth. Weapons whirled and monsters screamed alongside rangers and villagers, tine-slaves fighting with their masters to slay the invaders.

Somewhere nearby, the distinct sound of magic cracked the air and Ran turned to look for his friends amongst the fray. Blue flashes illuminated the deepening darkness. Not too far off, a building flared bright with orange flame. Dradur tore toward them and he swung his sword single handed, catching one in the gut and deflecting it toward Lidan. She cut it down, staggering and slipping, falling hard to her knee and taking too long to find her feet again.

Thanie took her chance and snapped back on the rope, ripping it from Ran's hand and whipping him around to face her. The front of his shirt caught in her bound hands, and she dragged him in, inches from her face; her voice a hard, vicious growl, her grey eyes darkening to near black, ominous with threatened intent. 'Cut me loose or everyone in this compound will be dead by dawn.'

His mouth ran dry. Her fear was gone; as if it had never been there at all. 'Cut. Me. Loose.'

He pulled at her hands and brought up his sword, the blade slicing through the bonds. The rope tore as she wrenched her wrists apart and spun away, hands out, fingers flexed. The air shifted, the pressure changing, rising and folding in as Thanie moved. She trembled, the screams of the defenders fading to a roar, a sharp squeal bursting in Ran's ears as they equalised.

Lidan called out, and Ran turned his full attention to the fight. He sheathed his sword and let his magic go, dropping his walls, bringing it to the surface and feeling the weight of the power, the rush of the release. Hands burning with icy heat, blue lightning snapped between his fingers, forming an orb, then a snake-like rope. The crackling magic then straightened into something that looked like a two-foot-long shard of razor-sharp glass.

With a lunge and a flick of his wrist, the shard cut straight through the torso of a dradur bearing down on Lidan. In the murk of the early night, the blue blade flashed and the ichor of the creature's spinal fluid sprayed across the dusty ground. It glowed bright in his Sight, a sparkling constellation across the soil. The magical discharge of his companions, somewhere off in a corner of the compound, burned brighter as he let his power radiate, drawing on his reserves.

Dradur thaumalux oscillated in the air, catching his attention. Each trail that made it over the wall and down into the compound snaked toward him and Lidan. Most were cut short on their journey, but many—too many—drew closer, the rangers unable to hold them all off.

There was little doubt the monsters were coming for him.

No.

Not him.

Thanie. They came for the witch.

He turned and found he'd left her behind, following Lidan instead, as if his mere presence could dissuade her from doing something she shouldn't. He cut another dradur down and his blade of magic sputtered, dying in his hand as his power snuffed out.

Thanie stood alone in the common, somewhere near where Sellan had disappeared into thin air. The witch turned to face him. Her voice reached over the screams and the bellowed orders, though she didn't seem to move her lips more than to whisper.

'I can't do this alone.'

He drew his sword. Surely that's what she meant? Thanie shook her head and lifted her hand, a single blue spark snapping between her fingers. She didn't need to speak—her eyes said it all. They would die unless he gave her what she needed. There wouldn't be single living soul left in Tingalla by sunrise unless he gave in.

Brit roared something, Lidan calling back then screaming orders in her own language as fire and death consumed the village, dradur swarming over the walls. Had they been waiting in the hills and ravines, biding their time for the summons that would surely come when their prey was defenceless?

Thanie screamed at Ran, no longer asking. Demanding, without room for dissent. A desperate hand reached for him and he sprinted across the common. A dradur darted in close and he whirled to cut it down, spinning with his sword and slicing it from shoulder to hip, the momentum enough to carry him straight into Thanie's grasp.

Her outstretched hand caught his throat, her fingers hard as dragon's claws, nails biting his flesh. She squeezed and for a moment he thought she'd choke the life from him where he stood.

'Let go, Ranoth,' she ordered, her voice deep and distorted, eyes dark pools.

He did as commanded, unable to find a reason not to, defenceless against her will, crushed beneath the mountainous weight of her power. Magic tore from between the bones of his spine and through the pores of his skin, his scream a faint cry in the distance as his legs collapsed.

A torrent of blue flame erupted from the palm of Thanie's other hand, held forth as if to ward off the creatures tearing across the common. Light

83

bloomed in the dark, flooding the compound and revealing the location of the creatures. They hissed and shrunk away from its brilliance. The blue fire caught the dradur unawares, those nearby scrambling to escape as Thanie aimed the magic their way.

She trembled like a leaf in a storm and all Ran's veils fell; veils he'd not realised still held firm across his Sight, barriers he hadn't known confined his magic cracked and peeled away. His Sight stripped clean of all protection, he looked up and saw Thanie for what she really was.

She blazed before him, swathed in a brilliant aura of oscillating light. Her gaze narrowed to a single point, a darkening glare of fathomless depths brimming with a power of its own, a force to be reckoned with. Her lips pulled back, she unleashed upon the dead, scorching them as they leapt and scattered. Ran had never seen anything so terrible and magnificent in his life.

Heart pounding, blood raced through his veins, his spine warming, then burning as Thanie drew more of him away than he thought he could possibly stand, more than he knew he had to give. One hand managed to reach, leaden and numb, to clutch at the waist of her tattered dress, the slightest tug on the fabric his weak signal to her to stop.

With the excruciating slowness of time caught in amber, Thanie's fingers lifted from the skin of his neck and he fell sideways. At her feet, tingling in every inch of his being, every fibre aflame, he stared up, unable to move. Vaguely he registered Lidan fighting her way through a whirling storm wind to crouch at his side.

Thanie's hands met in front of her chest then she threw her arms wide, a concussive boom shaking the village to its foundation. A wave of blue magic swept away in a fiery circle, coursing through the common. It consumed the dradur and knocked the living from their feet, throwing them backward, sending them skidding across the ground. Animated corpses were engulfed, disintegrating into ribbons of flesh, devoured by blue flame until nothing but flurries of ash remained.

The fighting ended abruptly, and the storm wind fell away.

Above him, Thanie glowed from within, her blue aura visible to everyone in the common. Her power stood naked before them, shining through her skin like sunlight breaking through cloud. Her hair lifted and fell as if carried on a breeze none could feel. She turned to look at him. The restraint collar had vanished, probably burned away, and Ran gaped as people emerged from the shadows between buildings, torches held high. Lidan's hand tightened around his arm, neither of them moving as the witch looked them over. She glanced at her hand, her once grey eyes an eerie, luminescent azure.

'Thank you,' Thanie whispered. He read nothing in her gaze, none of the malevolence he expected from a magic-weaver of her strength, no intent or purpose. She was completely closed to him, as blank as a sheet of parchment or a fine polished stone, unmarked and unaffected by the loss of power or exertion. She hadn't been weakened by the spell cast to defeat the dradur, not even in the slightest. If anything, she seemed renewed and stronger for it.

Slowly, her power subsided, and the blue glow faded from her skin, from her eyes, from the very air around them. Her internal sun set, and she stood before them once more, an unremarkable woman in tattered clothes. With a slight tilt of her head, the witch turned to look at Lidan and the girl flinched.

'Now will you let me help you?'

CHAPTER TWELVE

The edge of nowhere...

Time wheeled overhead. Untracked and unmeasured.

Voices came and went. Something wet placed against his lips and forced down his throat. Hands manipulated his body, binding and unwrapping, then binding again. He shivered. Moaned. Then the tremors eased. Sweat beaded his brow from the warmth of the air, no longer from the heat of his own skin. Calm washed through him, relaxing muscles that had been consumed with rage and terror and hate.

He lay quiet. Still. Watched shadows dance across the covering above his head.

Light shifted slowly from one side to the other, then faded to darkness. He began to count.

Three times the light came, followed by darkness. Small bright spots would appear as the light faded, dancing and darting, eventually extinguished, giving over to the hunger of greedy shadows.

Darkness came now, shadows bleeding into one another, forming one enveloping abyss above him. Sounds from beyond the covering changed. Tittering songs became rhythmic chirrups and high-pitched calls. Sounds of creatures akin to the dark.

Once, the darkness had been torn apart by blood curdling shrieks that set his heart thumping and raised the hairs on the back of his neck. Others cried out and soon the shrieks and screams were silenced. A foul stench of burning flesh filled the air, brought forth by a bright orange glow he had not seen before. It remained strong in the darkness long after the smaller points of light had gone out. He knew it was different but could not remember why.

Could not remember much at all.

He heard voices and knew they were like him. From their tone he felt they were not to be trusted. Rage flared in his chest at the recollection of the voice he knew. It was still there. Outside the covering. It shouted orders and swore and barked a cruel laugh that set his teeth on edge. He had thought to leave the covering and find the voice, if only to silence it. He did not care why, it only mattered that he made it stop. But his body would not heed his commands. He lay impotent under the covering, staring as darkness ate the light once more.

The covering split apart, a small man stepping through from beyond. The man paused, a bowl in his hands and several lengths of cloth draped over one arm. Sharp, dark eyes surveyed him. Neither of them spoke. Slowly, the man retreated.

'Go get the daari,' someone said in a low tone.

'What? Why?' replied another.

'He's awake,' the first growled. 'He wanted to be told as soon as the prisoner opened his eyes. You want to be the one to explain why we didn't tell him straight away?'

'Not fucking likely,' snapped the other. 'But I've got orders. You do it.'

'Fucking rangers,' the first voice snarled and spat. 'Dumb as fucking rocks.'

The sound of stomping boots faded, returning a short time later, multiplied and surrounded by hurried voices. The covering parted and someone at least twice the size of the first man stepped through.

No…

A malevolent smile broke across the large man's face. 'Well, well, well. The dead man wakes.'

The dead man… I was dead. I am the dead man…

'I hardly believed them when they said you lived. I thought they were joking when they said you'd woken.' He tilted his head to one side. 'You're simple, surely. Those rocks must have knocked you senseless.' Thickset with a mop of brown curls, the man sneered. 'That is, of course, assuming you weren't already dumb as horse shit. Wouldn't be at all surprising for a Tolak.'

Tolak.

The word hit the dead man like a punch to the gut. Shock sucked the breath from his lungs, his stomach clenching. He gasped and fought to remain still.

That word meant something. He had no idea what, but his body responded as if heeding a call.

The large man crossed the space under the covering, slow deliberate steps intended as casual and nonchalant. He crouched a few feet distant and put something on the ground by his boots. It was long and wrapped in pale cloth. Those hard, cool eyes never left the face of the dead man.

'You're the only one we didn't kill, you know. The only one not left for carrion. More than you deserve, but you might be useful. We shall see.' Dark eyes continued to rove up and down. The dead man shivered under their scrutiny. 'We don't know who you are, of course, but we know by your tattana that you were high up.'

The sneering man pointed, and the dead man glanced down. His arms were bare above the rough cloth of a blanket, burnished brown skin etched with black markings drawn to look like the shadows dancing above his head when the light came.

'Erlon was always so proud of his rangers parading their years of service with those branches. Too bad they were nothing more than targets for our bows.'

Erlon. He knew that word too.

And the marks were branches. Branches of what?

A whooshing whisper swept overhead and the dead man glanced up, as if he might see through the covering if he tried hard enough.

Trees. That was the sound of wind through trees. Tree branches.

His marks were tree branches, winding up his arm toward his shoulder, black bands at his wrists empty of the meaning given to them somewhere in another lifetime. A lifetime where this all made sense and he didn't have to unravel the meaning from every single word.

The big man moved, unwinding the cloth from the long item at his feet. Pale light shone along its length, and he flipped it, driving the point into the soft earth. It wavered, shivering with energy, reflecting the dead man's face in the highly polished surface.

His throat tightened, a cold shiver breaking across his skin.

At the top, something like a handle wobbled back and forth, the very extremity crowned by the stylised head of a creature he felt he should know. The length of it shone, sharp despite notches and marks along the edges. It was worn but had been cleaned—that much he could tell.

The large man watched him carefully. 'You've seen this before.'

He did not answer, though he knew he had.

'You know who it belongs to, don't you?'

He did not move, though his mind screamed at him to do so.

He *did* know, yet he did not. He knew it in his soul, and even if he'd had a voice to use, he could not have said the words. It was a weapon and it belonged to a presence within him that he could not name, could not place, could not feel. It had filled him once, consumed him in the places where now torrid anger seared. The presence was gone. The significance of what he had lost betrayed only by the scale of the emptiness left behind. A loss obscured by blinding desolation, yawning up as if to consume him.

The big man leaned forward, his meaty hand on the object's handle, fingers squeezing until the skin paled at the knuckles. He licked his fleshy lips and smiled. 'It's all right. You don't have to tell me. There's only one person I know who carries weapons like this, and I plan to return this to them very soon.' The smile broadened and the shadow in the depths of his eyes darkened. 'Would you like to watch?'

CHAPTER THIRTEEN

Baleanon, the Woaden Empire

The handful of days it took Sellan's ribs to stop spearing her side were enough to cure her of the will to live, filled as they were with unending boredom and the utter inability to complete the smallest tasks without assistance. The calm, attentive hands of Eddark, undeterred by her cursing, made the experience even more frustrating as the days wore on, sunlit afternoons reclining in her quarters broken only by his arrival to check on her.

She barely left her room to begin with, sleeping the days away until her back ached and forced her to swing her legs from under the covers and struggle into a fresh change of clothes. At least the pain in her chest had eased enough for her to pull on a linen underdress and belt a finely-woven woollen tunic over the top. The hem brushed the floor, obscuring her soft leather sandals. Eddark and the slaves she'd seen all wore shorter summer attire, but Sellan found herself searching through a trunk by the wall and then the standing wardrobe, hunting out a fur lined hooded cloak to throw over her shoulders.

Pulling back a heavy curtain she found a window fitted with a pane of translucent glass. Her fingers traced its cool, smooth surface. Oh, how she'd missed proper windows. By the door, she paused, her eye caught by the glint of fine metal. Nestled amongst the detritus of a long-abandoned dresser was the tulla charm her parents had gifted her on the one hundredth day after her birth. The circular swirl of her tribe's symbol gleamed, a stylistic representation of a snake poised to strike. It was a wonder the Burikanii still represented themselves as such, given their centuries-long failure to take back what had once been theirs. After so many years in political exile, they were about as threatening as wet lettuce.

Sellan sighed and dropped the necklace back on the dresser, her fingers brushing the statuettes of household gods, shifting aside dried, brittle flowers and half-burned candles. A single statue stood out amongst the collection—three figures carved from a single block of timber, all in similar attire to hers; each with their hair covered, their faces angled downward as if in conspiratorial discussion. One had a slight hunch to her back, another a little shorter with finer facial features, while the figure in the centre had strong shoulders and a defined hourglass shape.

The Dead Sisters, her mother had called them until Sellan became a woman, old enough to learn their true name, the name unspoken before men or the uninitiated. To those brought through the veil, they were the Morritae—winged death, callers of fate, spirits of childbirth and a warrior's death.

Some northern cultures saw them as one woman, a single entity encompassing all that power and ferocious grace, but Sellan knew the truth of their form. She'd seen the faces of the queens of the unseen realms, seen their darkness and eternal patience. Her throat contracted and she shuddered, gently placing the figurine back on the dresser and clearing a space around it. She needed new candles and a proper silver bowl, offerings and the like, before she even attempted to re-enter their good graces. She was nowhere near ready. Not yet. They would have to forgo their due deference a little longer. Better to ask forgiveness for her absence than to make a half-hearted offering in the meantime.

Beyond her door a stiff northerly breeze cut through the attempted warmth of the sun beaming down from the azure sky. Thin clouds scudded overhead, nothing thick enough to promise rain, but she knew well enough the fickle heart of the northern summer. This south-eastern corner of the Empire would waver indecisively between the chill of a South Land spring and the sweltering heat of a raging summer on the flip of a coin.

She pulled her cloak a little closer about her shoulders and limped along the verandah overlooking a large private courtyard below. Her quarters had always been on the second floor of the house, offering uninterrupted views of the atrium garden and an obscured entrance to the kitchen. If she ignored the stable yard and storage warehouse beyond that, she could make out the high walls of other well-to-do homes. Most of the town's high-born inhabitants had some link to the Burikanii tribe of old. Why else would they live in such a backwater shithole when they might have chosen any-where in the known world.

In the nebulous days of childhood, Sellan had been elated to break away to the capital at the end of each summer, sick to death of the lack of culture and fashion. It wasn't until her first few months on the run that she'd yearned for the simplicity of this small regional city and its behind-the-times garment stores and months-old plays performed in the plazas and squares. What had once seemed so quaint had quickly become the calling card of home, something she missed so dearly after so many years. Had she not held some nostalgic longing to return, she might not have thought of Baleanon when making her escape from Tingalla.

No matter.

She was here now, stuck with the consequences of that mistake. She would have to work with what she had.

'I wouldn't go down there if were you.'

Sellan spun from the balustrade to find Eddark leaning against the wall near her door. 'Go where?'

'The kitchen, or the stables, or the streets, or anywhere you might be seen. Not yet, anyway.'

'Despite what you may have heard, I'm not completely insane, nor am I an idiot.'

He shrugged. 'Just saying.'

'Well don't.' She scowled, her words so salty they could have seasoned a stew. Freed man he might be, but he was still low-born and well beneath her. Being made a citizen didn't change that. Her mother was getting soft in her old age if this sort of behaviour was acceptable in the house of a lady and a rook.

'Can't blame me for being careful. You get found out, this house will burn along with everyone in it. Maybe you are what they say you are. I wouldn't know—I've hardly seen you in twenty years.'

'You haven't seen me *at all* in twenty years.' She met his gaze and saw he was deadly serious. The breeze hissed through the trees and shrubs of the garden below. Overly bold, but he was right. Again. She fucking hated that.

'Your mother wants to see you,' Eddark told her, then turned to leave.

'Why?' Sellan ground her teeth and followed him, pushing through the pain and walking as normally as possible.

Eddark shouldered his bag and shrugged again. 'No idea—I'm not her errand boy.'

'Aren't you?' She cocked her head to one side and pursed her lips to suppress a smirk as he glowered, dark eyes narrowing under a frown. He had the lightly bronzed skin of someone from the coastal colonies, vaguely reminding her of Lidan; a thought Sellan snatched away before it could hurt her again.

'I've got patients to see. Do you remember where the Primrose Patio is?'

Sellan scoffed. 'Of course I—'

'Good.' Eddark walked away, bounded down the stairs to the ground floor and disappeared through to the front of the house.

She blinked hard at the place he'd been, stunned by his insolence. He was perhaps a year or two older at most, but at their age it was hard to tell. She'd seen younger men with less hair and more grey than he had at his temples. His arrival at her parents' home had occurred before her earliest memories had formed, and growing up he'd been a ubiquitous presence, always lurking somewhere nearby when she came home for visits. She'd always wondered if her mother hadn't favoured him, and his ascension to freedom confirmed her suspicions.

Throwing a look over the balustrade to make sure he had in fact gone, Sellan made her way gingerly down the stairs in his wake.

She kept to the shadows of the colonnade, limping around the garden, surprised at how she enjoyed the scent of the blossoms on the breeze. It wasn't that she'd been without such things in the south, or that her return had kindled some sentimental memory. She simply hadn't cared enough to notice. Securing one's own survival tended to substantially occupy much of one's mental faculties.

The slaves and attendants kept their distance, but their eyes lingered longer than she thought appropriate. Sellan pulled her cloak a little closer around her shoulders; she hadn't seen either of her parents since the night she arrived—neither of them had been to check on her or enquire after her health. Eddark had surely given her mother daily reports, and she'd heard

Mediia's voice beyond her door more than once. Her father seemed to have all but vanished.

Stepping past the small chamber that had always been his study, she found the door open but the room empty, the desk a riot of parchment and scrolls, broken quills and dried up ink pots abandoned on the surface for some unnamed soul to clean up. Evidently, that person had never arrived.

On the far side of the garden, near the entrance to her mother's sitting room, a long, paved patio overlooked the flowers, fruit trees and herb beds. The whole place had a clipped nature to it, no weeds or unwanted plants poking up from the dark soil lest they risk decapitation. Lady Mediia sat reclining on a day bed against a mound of cushions, her ledgers piled nearby, a low table set with platters of breakfast foods. Blown glass goblets stood alongside a tall jug of something that could be a fruit juice. How long had it been since she'd had a glass of juice? She honestly couldn't recall, and that fact bothered her more than she liked to admit.

'Daughter,' Mediia said without looking up. She licked the tip of a finger and turned a page in the ledger.

'Mother,' Sellan replied. 'Where is Father?'

Mediia sighed, more with exacerbation than actual concern. 'At this time of day, I'd wager he's sleeping off a headache after vigorously fucking something young and payable. Should I send someone to find out?'

'Gods, no.' Sellan suppressed a shudder, took a few dried apricots from a bowl and leaned back into the cushions of the opposing day bed, her mother's candour difficult to stomach so early in the morning. 'He's clearly not changed then.'

'No, dear,' Mediia said with an air of resignation, 'and he never will.' She snapped the ledger shut and looked down her nose at her daughter. 'What are you doing here?'

Sellan frowned. 'I'm sorry?'

'After all these years. You know how dangerous it is, how great the risk, so what are you doing here? You've not come to see me or your father, this isn't some leisure jaunt.'

'I...' There was no subtlety to this woman, no massaging the edges of the conversation to ease into the central point. Was she trying to peer through Sellan's walls at the truth she thought must lie beneath? Sellan drew up her defences and relaxed the muscles of her face, looking down at the handful of dried fruit as she focused her mind on the story she chose to tell. 'The less you know, the better. For you and everyone here.'

Mediia grunted, tossing the ledger on the pile. 'Keep your secrets if you like, but you're under my roof now, and I have expectations. At the very least, we need to decide what your story is.'

'Story?'

'Who you are and why you're here. I trust the household of course, but your arrival may just be too much for some of them to resist mentioning, even if they have no earthly idea who you are. We need to get in front of it, so to speak—control the narrative and project a sense of control and calm. For instance, it should be known that your arrival was expected—'

'Ever the politician.'

'Someone has to be, dear.' Lady Mediia scowled and put her glass back on the table a little harder than necessary, as if to punctuate her point. 'The Sisters know your father never has been, and you haven't exactly been able to fill that void. So, the story. You're a distant relation visiting from the south-western colonies. No one knows much about that pirate-riddled coast, given its fairly lawless nature. You'll need a name, a backstory—'

'Mother, I really wouldn't bother. I won't be here that long.' Sellan rubbed at the bridge of her nose. Such a complex ruse would be difficult to establish and tedious to maintain—both things she had neither the time nor the energy for.

'Oh?' Her mother's brows rose in surprise.

'I'm going north,' Sellan told her, regret pooling in her belly. *Keep it simple. Tell her only what she needs to know.*

'North?'

'Yes.'

'To the capital? To Wodurin?'

Sellan rolled her eyes. There wasn't anywhere else up there worth visiting. 'Yes.'

'No.' Mediia sat back on the cushions and looked out at the garden as if that was the end of it.

'What?' Heat tingled in Sellan's fingers and she tightened them into a fist, pushing down on the magic.

'No, you are not. Well, not as yourself. Whatever it is you have planned—which is obviously some sort of suicide mission if you're going anywhere near that place—won't be achieved under your old name.' Mediia stabbed a finger toward the front door and the town beyond. 'If you so much as *mention* your name out there, you're dead by sunrise. If they find out we harboured you, we'll be joining you on the blocks, and unless it escaped your notice, I quite like my head where it is. You need an alias and a story to tell.'

Frustration simmered in Sellan. She shouldn't have come here. She'd complicated things too much, involved people who shouldn't have been anywhere near her plans. Now, everything stood to fail, and the element of surprise she'd hoped to wield slipped through her fingers like an icy mist. 'I don't need anything of the sort—'

'Sellan Parben, where the fuck have you been all these years?'

Her mother's tone slapped her in the face, and she gaped at the ferocity of the words. They dripped with pain and sorrow, humiliation and years of worry snapping out to cut at the child who had almost brought her family to their knees. Perhaps she had, and they'd spent the last two decades clawing themselves back from the hole she'd dug for them.

Sellan lifted her chin and looked away into the garden. 'Away.'

'Have you been to Wodurin lately, or at *all* in the past twenty years? If you had, you'd know things are desperate. Expansion into the colonies has stalled, the emperor's hold on himself and his government is slipping, and our Empire stands on the brink of a future we cannot see. Desperate people are scared people, and scared people are stupid. They are violent and dangerous and cannot be trusted. The capital is the centre of that stupidity, a vortex of idiocy that has sucked all that is good and proper and reasoned into its ugly maw. You go anywhere near that place without proper preparation and it *will* consume you.'

Her chest tightened. 'I had no idea...'

Adjusting the skirt of her long tunic dress, Mediia composed herself. 'I shouldn't have thought you would, but if you think things are as they were, then you are more a fool than I thought. The Empire is...' She waved her hand, as if trying to pull the correct phrase from the air. 'I don't know what it is, but it has changed, and continues to change. We must protect ourselves, and as much as I would like to admit that an alias is simply for your own protection, it is for *all* of us. If you wish to remain under this roof, you will do as you are told, Sellan. I will not be moved on this.'

There was no jest in her mother's gaze, no hint of innuendo. Mediia meant every word.

Sellan worked her jaw and released an unsteady breath. What impact this news might have on her plans, and what she'd intended to inflict in the capital, she had yet to understand. It could change everything, or it may be just the opportunity she needed. First, there were things she'd neglected for too long, things she needed to see to, or all further efforts toward that end would be for naught. Without this next step, nothing else mattered.

'Very well,' she said reluctantly, collecting herself and standing. 'But this "story" will take time to formulate, and I'm afraid I can't wait that long. I need some things from town.'

'I'll send one of the girls for you then.' Mediia reached for a small bronze bell on the table, but Sellan waved her off.

'No, I… This I have to do myself.'

Her mother leaned back slowly, studying her face for meaning. There were only a few things a Woaden noblewoman would insist on leaving the safety and comfort of her home to buy herself, rather than sending a slave in her stead. This was non-negotiable for such women, something that signified the importance of the items and the ritual itself.

Realisation dawned and Mediia gave a small nod. 'Have you maintained your observance?'

'I wasn't able to; at least not properly. So I didn't, just in case.' It had been Thanie who warned her off trying to worship the Morritae once the two of them arrived in the south—another rule meant to keep them safe. Sellan had argued that the deities could have helped them, perhaps looking kindly on their fate and steering it from the path of harm, but Thanie had been adamant—do it properly, or not at all.

An uncomfortable silence fell between mother and daughter as Mediia's lips pressed into a line. 'It is perhaps for the best that you didn't try. A poorly made offering can draw their ire just as easily as none at all. Still, you have few excuses now. You'll need to disguise yourself before you set foot out that door. As a slave most likely. I'll have Eddark escort you, and you'll use your middle name for the time being—am I clear?'

Suppressing an exacerbated groan, Sellan nodded.

Mediia slipped one of her ledgers from the pile and flicked open the cover. 'He'll be back in short order, then you may go.'

'He spends a lot of time here, doesn't he,' Sellan remarked.

'He should. He lives here.'

This time she did groan. She should have known there was no way her mother would let him live anywhere *but* here. 'I suppose you gave him the Parben name when you freed him, too?'

'Of course,' Lady Mediia said casually, glancing over the top edge of the leather-bound volume. 'I had to give it to someone. You weren't here to carry it.'

Sellan caged the retort behind gritted teeth. Her fingernails pierced the palms of her hands, channelling the rage surging from within. As much as that final little cutting statement hurt, an outburst did not serve her needs.

'I'll wait in my room,' she ground out, and turned to go. How could her mother give him their name, like it was a throw away item, something to dole out? How could she—

She barely heard Lady Mediia clear her throat over the thump of her pulse in her ears.

'Where is your cousin?' the woman's question reached through Sellan's wake to slice her heart.

She faltered to a stop, covering the slight stumble with a wince, as if pained by her ribs, then drew a deep, shuddering breath. That word should not have hurt this much. Barely glancing over her shoulder, Sellan kept the tears at bay. 'I don't know.'

'Don't lie to me.'

'She remained where we found succour. She was perfectly safe when I left.' Sellan had no idea if that remained true, but she had nothing else to offer. The reality of what she'd done was something she would never admit here.

Mediia gave an unimpressed grunt. 'You'd do well to think of a better explanation than that. An alias might fool the masses, but your uncle will see right through it. Lord Orel lost his heir thanks to what happened at the Academy, and no amount of lies and trickery will keep him from the truth.'

Their eyes met.

'Consider the web you weave, daughter. He will know the truth of what happened to Thanie, and I will not be able to stop him if he chooses to force it from your lips.'

Chapter Fourteen

Baleanon, the Woaden Empire

Stepping through the doorway and into the warmth of the sun, Sellan drew the veil up over her hair and adjusted the wrap around her neck and shoulders. It had been quite a while since she'd worn a head-covering in public, or felt the need to, but in a built-up area like Baleanon it was expected a woman of her age did such a thing. Posing as a slave of a great house made it crucial she drew as little attention as possible. Running around town with her distinctive auburn hair showing, a well-known mark of House Corvent, would certainly attract notice she did not want.

She moved ahead of Eddark, then lurched to a stop as he caught her elbow.

'At my shoulder or behind me, Abrial,' he muttered, using her middle name as she'd promised her mother she would. 'Slaves don't walk in front of freed men.'

'You're going to enjoy this, aren't you?' she hissed, falling in half a step behind and hurrying to keep up.

'I'm sure I have no idea what you mean.'

'Horse shit,' she spat.

'At least you swear like one of us. Now, where's this shopping list of yours?'

Sellan scoffed. 'I know where I'm going.'

He threw a dubious glance over his shoulder as they passed the fountain in the centre of the city's great plaza, positioned in the space between her parents' home and that of her uncle, Lord Orel. 'It's been a while since you were here last. Things might have changed.'

Pulling her gaze from the front door of the Lord of Baleanon's house and the thought of what he might do if he found out she was here, she focused on Eddark and their path into the merchant quarter of the city. 'There was a woman on Mere Road who sold what I need. If she doesn't have it, she'll know where to get it.'

The plaza itself wasn't busy, but the crowds grew as they moved down the main road, milling around, talking amongst themselves, or hurrying off to some important appointment or another. Slaves carried curtained litters down the centre of the street, shirtless and sweating as the high sun beat down on their backs. Had Sellan been allowed to move through the city as herself, she would have been in such a litter. On reflection, she was glad she hadn't insisted on such a conspicuous mode of transport. On foot she was mobile and unencumbered, easily disguised in the hordes of folk seething along the ever-busier roadways.

'Mere Road is down by the docks,' Eddark said in a low voice, shuffling around a group of townsfolk exchanging loud midday greetings and promises to meet soon for a drink. Their overly exaggerated mentions of preferred establishments left her in no doubt they were more interested in the perception that they were wealthy enough to frequent such places, rather than an actual arrangement to meet there. She shook her head and stepped through the gap in the crowd after Eddark.

'I know where it is—I told you that.'

'The docks aren't exactly your kind of place though, are they?' He kept his gaze on the people around them, speaking as if she weren't actually there.

'How would you know?' Sellan snarled. How dare he presume to judge? 'You know nothing about me.'

'True, but I'm the one stuck babysitting you as a favour to your ma. I'd rather not be the one who has to explain how you managed to get yourself shanked by some thug who mistook you for a whore he could rob.'

They rounded a corner and headed west, the street sloping down as it came off the ridge where the plaza and her family home stood, and into the river valley. The Bale River ran through town from the southwest to the north, providing an important trading artery connecting the city to the farms outside its walls. It allowed for the transport of goods up to the great Skree River, just south of the capital. As important as it was for commerce and trade, the Bale stank to the heavens, fetid water sloshing around the quayside in summer, largely stagnant until the autumn rains came to flush it clear again. Sellan recalled the news reports that made it to her parents' house of a morning. She'd rather not end her days as one of the many bloated bodies found floating in the murky waters.

'We won't be down there long enough to run into any thugs,' she assured him, catching the scent of a bakery nearby and putting a hand on her stomach as it grumbled. That handful of dried fruit a few hours earlier really hadn't touched the sides, and she was suddenly ravenous.

Eddark sighed heavily. 'Whatever you say.'

The sweet scent of the bakery vanished beneath the weedy stench wafting up from the docks, and instead of grumbling, her stomach flipped. She blocked her nose and pushed on, eager to have her business done and return to the safety of the house before the sun even thought about setting.

Brenna's shop had always been in a dark little alley off the dockside, carefully positioned to shield the comings and goings of her patrons from the watchful eyes of those with loose tongues and too much time on their hands. Seeking out the remedies and items she sold wasn't illegal, but it could spark a scandal, especially if someone suitably noble was seen frequenting such a place more than once every few months. Sellan wondered if Eddark had ever been here in search of herbs or utensils for his work, but he showed no sign of recognition as he followed Sellan into the narrow, shadowy space between a warehouse and a grimy stone building.

The door stood behind a stack of pallets draped with a torn sheet of canvas, and Sellan had to shove it with her shoulder to release it from where it jammed on the step inside. The room beyond wasn't any more spacious than the alley, packed to the rafters with shelving units groaning under the weight of Brenna's wares. Weaving between the stacks, Sellan shuffled across the dusty floor, a single small window at the front of the shop providing the only natural light, the rest of the place illuminated by sparse candles. It was no high-end store, but it was exactly what she needed.

Glancing back, she saw Eddark cast around, then reach a tentative finger toward a stuffed animal paw on a nearby shelf.

'No touching,' Sellan warned. 'She'll have that finger for her tea if she catches you.'

His hand fell quickly to his side, and he kept close as she approached the counter at the back of the room. He might be the man in charge outside, but this was Sellan's domain, and it showed. Hopefully Brenna still ran the store, if she was even still alive. She'd been in her middle years when Sellan last saw her, and in reasonable health, so the chances were good.

Oddly, despite the noise they made coming through the jammed door, no one appeared to greet them or tell them get out. Sellan frowned as she came to a stop near the counter, glancing at a small bronze bell on the bench top.

'This place is fucking creepy,' Eddark muttered. 'Is that... What *is* that?'

Sellan followed his gaze to what looked like a man's head in a jar, perched on a shelf behind the counter. She chuckled under her breath. 'You surprise me, Eddark. I'd have thought a medical practitioner would know his anatomy better than that.'

'Why the fuck has she got a head in a *jar*?'

'How else is she meant to pickle it? In a bucket?'

He stared at her in shock for a moment, then looked back at the jar. 'She's a healer, isn't she?'

'Of course she fucking is, you idiot. She studies the body, as I imagine, do you. Or at least I hope you do, or I'm telling my mother to find herself another live-in medic.'

'Is that what you think I am—a resident medic?'

Sellan turned to glare at him. 'At this point, you're a pain in my arse. Shut up and let me get this done!'

She rang the bell, the bright jangle of the bronze harsh in the silence.

Nothing.

A sideways glance at Eddark earned her a shrug and a pair of raised brows. *Useless.*

She reached back to the bell and rang it hard, the loud clang echoing and setting a ring in her ears.

'What!?' a voice snapped from behind a curtain.

Sellan and Eddark started, but Eddark recovered first. 'You the owner?'

'Depends who's asking?' An older woman shoved the curtain aside and hobbled into view, her distinctive gait one Sellan recognised immediately. Brenna—older and a little worse for wear—still as prickly as a cactus and about as friendly as a viper. 'You from the Congress? I told those ball-bags last month that I paid my licence fees, and if they can't find the receipts, then maybe they should employ some bookkeepers with actual brains instead of just a nice pair of tits.'

Age hadn't softened the fierce old bitch, and Sellan loved her shrivelled black heart for it. 'I come seeking observance wares,' she told Brenna, ignoring Eddark's affronted expression.

Brenna's eyes narrowed. 'You brought a *man* with you to fetch such things? Are you looking to get smote, or what?'

'He's an escort, nothing more. The docks are hardly safe, even in the day. I'll have him leave if it matters—'

Brenna waved Sellan's concern away. 'Just making sure you know what you're doing. Not my business if you want to break the covenant.'

Break the covenant? She was doing no such thing, and opened her mouth to say so, but Brenna was already moving away, unbothered and apparently uninterested.

'What do you need?'

Sellan sighed. 'Everything.'

The old shop keeper stopped and levelled her with a look that would have made Lady Mediia proud. There was only one reason a woman of Sellan's age needed *everything* for an observance ritual—her complete failure to maintain her altar and keep up with her offerings.

'Right then,' Brenna grunted when Sellan offered no explanation. She reached under the counter and pulled out a black satchel, dumping it on the bench with a clank and a thud. 'You'll need a starter kit, I imagine. Still have your effigy, or did you lose that too?'

'Of course I—I didn't *lose* anything, I just...' Sellan's protest died as a wicked smile spread across the woman's face. Brenna was toying with her, teasing and prodding for a reaction, and she'd given her one.

With a loud plonk, another smaller bag landed on the counter. This one held candles that rolled around in the confines of the linen sack. The shop keeper pointed at Eddark. 'Time for you to step away, sonny.'

Eddark lifted his hands in surrender. 'By all means.'

Brenna didn't move again until he stood near the door, not completely out of earshot but far enough away that the two women could talk without being understood word for word. The old woman leaned forward. 'Have you a sacrifice?'

'I'd intended to use my blood,' Sellan whispered. 'Or is that not enough these days?'

'It *has* been a long time for you, hasn't it?' Brenna's brows drew together as she studied Sellan, and she fought the urge to pull away. 'The Maiden and the Mother are more amiable to a sacrifice of seed, though they will accept lesser offerings. The Mourner insists on it.'

'Seed? As in *male* seed?' Sellan scowled. Since when had the Morritae desired such a crude sacrifice? Blood had always been their currency of choice. Something had changed while she'd been gone, the goddesses of the unseen realms shifting as if they were sand beneath Sellan's feet. Would the deities recognise her at all? When Brenna nodded, Sellan couldn't help but pull a face. 'Where in the Underworld am I going to find *that*?'

Brenna threw a glance at the front of the shop where Eddark stood peering at things he knew he shouldn't touch. 'He'd do.'

'You cannot be serious!' Sellan hissed, her veil slipping off her head as she took a sharp step toward the counter.

The flash of recognition was so brief she would have missed it had she been more than a few inches from Brenna's face, and as quickly as it came, it was gone. A long, pregnant silence settled between the women, until Brenna leaned back and shrugged. 'Up to you. You can try blood and see what happens, but if you've been out of contact for as long as I think you have, you may find you need something stronger.'

Without another word, Sellan pulled a purse from the hidden pocket of her gown and drew out a few coins. It was more than enough to cover the cost, while the rest was for the woman's discretion. She handed over the coins, dropping them into the shop keeper's creased palm.

Brenna's aged hand seized Sellan's wrist before she could pull away, yanking her in close—close enough to feel breath on her face, close enough to sense the power surging beneath parchment thin skin.

'I couldn't be sure it was you when I came through that curtain, but there's no mistaking those eyes, is there?' The old woman studied her slowly and Sellan clenched her jaw, fighting down the magic rising in response to a perceived threat. 'They all said you were dead...'

Sellan met Brenna's gaze, defiant. 'They were wrong.'

A shrewd smile broke along Brenna's dry lips. 'Best you keep your head down, or else it might get chopped off.'

Sellan snatched her arm from the shop keeper's grasp, red marks glowing where her hard fingers had been. With one swift move, she collected her bags from the counter and corrected her veil, adjusting the end of the wrap that hung over the back of her shoulder.

'Best of luck, sister. May the whispers of fate be in your favour.' Brenna's eyes gleamed as she offered the traditional farewell between the initiated.

There was little risk in speaking it near Eddark, but still Brenna's mouth twisted into a smirk. Eddark would ask questions now, wondering what she'd said and what they'd discussed. He may not ask aloud, but he would want to know things Sellan could not tell him. This alone would place an obstacle in her path. His curiosity could sabotage the entire endeavour if he were stupid enough not to steer clear.

Sellan turned for the door as Eddark lifted a small, hard ball of sweet-smelling resin from a bowl on a low table. He held it up toward Brenna. 'What's this?'

'A pain killer, dear. Take some,' Brenna called back. 'The first one's free.'

Now it was Sellan's turn to catch Eddark by the elbow and march him out of the shop. They bustled through the door and into the darkened alley, the afternoon sun sliding lazily across the sky to the west, the wind off the river cold in the shadows. Eddark hurried to keep pace with Sellan as she rushed into the light, stuffing the smaller sack inside the larger black bag, then slinging the strap of the satchel across her body.

Clutching at the veil, she pulled it a little too close under her chin, walking a little too quickly toward the edge of the quay and the water lapping at the pylons and the hulls of river boats. Several deep, shaking breaths calmed her nerves, and she stood staring across the water, blinded by the reflection of the sun on the wavelets.

Brenna's words echoed with warning and threat. She'd risked so much to get the things she needed, an essential gamble if her plan was to work at all. The Morritae would accept nothing less than the best, and a half-arsed observance would not do. But was it worth it if she was caught? Worth it if she was executed before she could finish what she'd started? If Brenna had recognised her after so many years, who else might?

Glancing around, she reasoned there were few people in this small city who knew her face as well as Brenna. She'd spent many hours in that shop as a young girl, following her mother from the litter to the doorway and scurrying amongst the shelves, marvelling at what seemed like trinkets to a child's eyes.

'What was that all about?' Eddark asked, appearing at her side and looking out over the water.

'Nothing you need worry after,' she replied, hard and final. There would be no discussion of this.

'She recognised you, didn't she? If she's a threat, we need to tell your mother. She needs to be silenced—'

Sellan rounded on him, hissing, 'You will do *no such thing*! Mention this to my mother and I will personally see that you are disgraced. You will *never* work in this city again, understand?'

Eddark didn't flinch at her tirade, he just stared at her and blinked slowly. 'Very well,' he finally said before turning to look at the water. 'But you should know that if I get the slightest hint she has revealed your presence here, I *will* act. I may or may not tell Lady Mediia, but I will act. This you should understand.'

Slowing the pace of her racing heart, Sellan glared at the healer. 'Why the fuck would you do that for me?'

'I won't be doing it for you. I'm a Parben as much as you are. I have been for many years, and a threat to that family and House Corvent is a threat to me. I will not let it stand.' His expression was one of calm contemplation, as if the thought of taking such action didn't in any way conflict with the ethos of his profession. It struck her then that he was truly loyal, truly committed to her family, perhaps in a way she never had been. Her chin quivered, and she bit the back of her lip to stop it.

Eddark lifted the small ball of resin to his nose and sniffed. 'What is this anyway?'

'You don't want to know.' Sellan snatched it from his hand and tossed it into the river. The medics of the Empire had yet to realise the dulling effect of the substance, though it had circulated amongst the womenfolk for years. 'There's a reason the first one is free.'

A sickly-sweet smell clung to her fingers, wafting up as she wiped them on her clothes. Stuttering, faded memories of swirling smoke and a blurred face tried to claw their way to the surface as she started back along the dock. The smoke had muffled her senses and muted the pain inflicted by the blurry face, the years since scrubbing it from her mind like she'd scrubbed the blood from her clothes. But neither time nor any substance could completely cleanse her of the truth. It was a stain she would always carry.

'Why?' Eddark called, hurrying to catch up.

'Because you'll always come back for more.'

CHAPTER FIFTEEN

Baleanon, the Woaden Empire

Along the dockside, warehouses loomed two, sometimes three storeys into the sky, dockers and sailors working to swing loads to and from the hulls and holds of the river boats. The raucous sound was punctuated by the screech and chatter of river hawks circling above on the promise of a mouse or rat amongst the cargo stacks. Ratting dogs patrolling the quay barked, and other birds honked from the reeds on the far bank. By the time Eddark jogged to catch up and walk silently at her shoulder, Sellan had almost grown used to the smell, but the noise could not be shut out.

At least Eddark knew when to be quiet.

They wove around cargo wrapped in canvas, and sacks of grain piled up on timber pallets, until a herd of sheep bleated into Sellan's path and pulled her up short. The pause forced her to stop and breathe, glancing around to get her bearings. 'Where are we?'

Eddark pointed down river. 'That's Saddler's Bridge. We might have gone too far...'

The stone bridge reached out toward the centre of the river, where it morphed to a timber construction that could be raised and lowered to allow masted boats and small ships to pass through.

Yet, as interesting as the engineering might have been to someone who cared about bridges, her attention drifted back along the wharf until a familiar figure caught her eye. Squinting against the glare, she vaguely registered Eddark thinking aloud as he tried to locate the junction of the road.

She hadn't expected to find her father in this part of town. He stood talking to another man, close, as workers moved around them like water around a stone. The other man gestured at the river boat moored by the dock, her cargo swinging on ropes as it was hoisted from the hold and onto the quay.

'I've never understood why they don't use magic to move that cargo,' Eddark muttered.

'Because mages have better things to do than lift bales of wool on a stinking dock,' she replied, studying her father as he watched the unloading.

No, he wasn't simply watching. He was *supervising*.

Sellan slipped behind a cargo stack—ostensibly to make use of the shade—without taking her eyes from the men along the quay. The man with her father wore clothes similar to the boat crew, albeit of a finer cut—three quarter length trousers under a thigh-length tunic, belted at the hips beneath the slight paunch of his belly. Her father was dressed down, not in the usual fine white robe with a thin blue trim she expected a rook to wear about town. He might be a minor noble, a brother to a lord in another province and the husband of a lady, but he was a noble nonetheless. Presenting himself like this was intentional.

'What are you looking at?' Eddark asked from behind her, his low voice raising the hairs on the back of her neck.

'Someone I thought I recognised...'

'Ah, shit.' He must have followed her gaze.

'What?' She spun to glare as he shook his head.

'We need to go.'

'What is he doing down here, Eddark? My mother said he was holed up somewhere with a hangover and a whore, not supervising a delivery of goods.'

'I'm surprised he's out in the open like that. We should go back to the house.' He made to take her by the arm, but Sellan snatched it away, turning back to her view of the dock.

Rook Warrin Parben was gone.

Stepping from the shelter of the cargo, Sellan scanned the quay. The man from the boat was also missing, but the unloading continued. 'Shit!'

As quickly as she dared, she took off toward the boat, darting behind the cover of pallets and crates. Eddark swore and hurried after her through the crush of slaves and merchants and dockers. It was one thing to be down at the docks, but it was quite another for a noble to be dressed down and apparently supervising the unloading of goods. What possible interest did her father have in such a thing?

The ruling classes of the Empire were above menial tasks like running businesses or more laborious work. The magically-blessed among them might take up lucrative positions assigned by the Congress, but otherwise slaves conducted their affairs and tended their homes, coin spent on supplies and investments as and when needed. Their estates made their fortunes, bolstered by the plunder of conquered lands when such men were called to campaign with the emperor. Never would they stoop so low as to earn money directly. Should they find themselves in such dire need as to require a single hour of honest labour, they did so in absolute secrecy. They did not *ever* do it in the open streets, or on riverside quays where they might be seen.

Rage bubbled in Sellan as she stopped near the boat, watching the crowds. Her father and the other man had disappeared inside a building on the city side of the dock, leaving her to glare at the entryway. What was going on with her family? What was her father doing down here? The potential disgrace was almost too much to fathom. Surely he had a good reason for this, but first she needed to know what *this* was.

The building Warrin and his companion had entered stood two storeys above the dock, glass-paned windows set into the stone walls at regular intervals. At the end closest to her, an alley not unlike the one where she found Brenna's shop stretched off, awash with shadows. Perhaps down there was a door or window she might peer through. Crossing the quay, she slipped into the cool gloom.

Fuck.

No windows. The wall was solid stone blocks from the ground to the roof.

Eddark barrelled in after her. 'Are you *insane*? What are you doing down here?'

'Are you going to tell me what he's doing in there?' she snapped back.

A loud voice boomed down the alley and they both darted behind a stack of old sacks and broken timber pallets. Another voice laughed and two men walked past the dockside end of the alley, joking about something crass but entirely uninterested in what was going on in the shadows.

'I don't know what he's doing, but I'm extremely fucking sure I don't want to,' Eddark hissed in her ear.

Sellan watched the mouth of the alley, her back pressed against the cold stone. It was chilly down here, her coarse slave tunic warm enough while she'd been in the sun, but now her skin prickled and she shivered. 'How long has this been going on? Does my mother know?'

'I've no idea. I stay out of their business.'

'Horse shit,' she spat. 'Tell me the truth.'

When he said nothing, she leaned out past him, spotting a door a few feet away. She moved before he could stop her, easing it open and creeping inside. Not a moment later he was beside her again, scowling and hunching low as he scanned the room.

'You're fucking nuts, you know that?'

'Maybe the rumours were true,' Sellan whispered. Sliding her satchel around to rest in the small of her back, she crept forward. The room looked to be for the storage of supplies, holding nothing more interesting than some small barrels and crates. A stack of wine urns stood to one side, and a chair or two, but not much else. At the far wall, a set of timber stairs led up to a landing and another door. Silent as a cat stalking prey, she made for those stairs. Eddark's heavier footsteps followed, but paused at the bottom as she began to ascend.

Turning back, she looked down into his dark glare, reading the thoughts written across his face. 'Tell me what you know, and I won't have to go up there.'

Eddark shook his head. 'I can't, because I don't know. But it won't be good, Sellan, that I can promise you.'

Infuriated, she kept moving. She'd never been inside a goods warehouse, but she expected there to be guards, or at least some form of security. How did people stop things being stolen, especially if rear doors were left open to all and sundry? At the landing, she pressed down the iron latch, slowly lifted the bar and released the door. Holding her breath, she eased the door inward and peered through the gap.

Beyond stood a walkway, perhaps four or five feet across, with a timber railing the other side. At the railing, the floor dropped away, voices echoing around the space within. Sellan frowned and pushed the door further, prompting a hiss of warning from Eddark. Glancing in either direction and seeing no one, she risked it, and stepped through.

The warehouse was cavernous, stretching to cover at least the same footprint as her parents' residence, and perhaps half again. The timber walkway encircled the entire level, reaching around to the far side and a collection of rooms that overlooked the floor below. As she peered down, Sellan's fingers tingled with the heat of magic, fuelled by anticipation and, to her shame, fear.

Her mouth ran dry.

There were a few men on the warehouse floor, all congregating at the far end and occupied by the stock moving in and out of the double doors to the dock. Goods packed in crates had been brought in on flatbed sleds and left to one side, while others stood nearer to her and the far wall of the warehouse. Some were open. Others remained shut tight. She scanned the floor, noting each face until she found her father. Taking a quick step back out of Warrin's line of sight, she bumped into Eddark and his hands steadied her against his chest. She shrugged him loose, hating herself a little more as she found that fleeting touch reassuring.

'Fuck,' he breathed. Expecting him to pull her back through the door, she stepped forward again and peered down at the open crates.

Swords? She tilted her head to get a better look. The shine of the steel was unmistakeable against the dull, coarse packing cloth at the bottom of the long crate. A stack of neatly wrapped parcels stood nearby. There weren't many open crates, but those she could see appeared to use false bases to conceal hardware like crossbows, blades and spears, the cloth-bound parcels waiting to be placed on top. Someone laughed, the barking noise echoing off the rafters and stone and making Sellan start backward again.

By the door, other crates stood waiting—closed and sealed—apparently ready to be shipped, the timbers branded by a stamp she could not read. What was her father doing packing swords into the bottom of shipping crates?

'Sellan,' Eddark hissed.

She waved him off and leaned over the rail. In a crate almost directly below her feet was a collection of urns packed tightly with wool, their lids marked with a symbol she *could* read. Fear tightened her throat, and this time she would not have been ashamed to admit it. Her magic rose to roll across her skin as she straightened, her gaze sweeping the warehouse floor to find her father again. He hadn't noticed her standing at the rail. He hadn't realised she was watching him make a deal with someone he never should have been seen dead with.

A sharp tug on her tunic pulled her attention from the warehouse floor. She rounded on Eddark, ready to unleash a withering rebuke. He pointed before she could open her mouth and she turned. A man moved toward them along the walkway, through shafts of light from the windows, his eyes trained on the floor below.

'We need to leave,' Eddark whispered, taking a step back.

'Yes, we do.' She moved to follow and scuffed her shoe on the rough timber boards.

Oh no.

The guard looked up, registering them immediately. It took a second for his hand to reach for his blade and his arm to come up, pointing as his mouth opened to shout.

Fuck!

His alarmed cry bounced off the walls, following Eddark and Sellan through the doorway and down the stairs. They scrambled down into the storeroom as the man slammed into the door and thumped after them.

Eddark hit the ground floor first, racing for the alleyway and the promise of freedom as the guard's hand snatched at the back of Sellan's tunic and the veil over her hair. That small purchase was enough to yank her backward, but she leaned into the motion, spinning and jabbing with her elbow as she did. Her other hand came around as the man clutched his face, her palm shoving at the plane of his forehead.

Her magic boomed, a hot flare of blue light exploding in the dark little storage area, almost blinding her. The back of the man's skull erupted in a grisly blast of blood, brains and bone, the force of her magic shattering his skull and showering the wall and the stairs behind him. Ears ringing, she staggered and collided with something, sending a pile of urns or pots crashing to the floor.

Vaguely she registered Eddark's hands on her arm, forcing her to move, forcing her to run. He shoved her through the door and into the alley, urging her out into the dockside cacophony and dragging her through the crowd.

She couldn't hear a thing beside the sound of her own breath and the thud of her pulse, drawing curious glances of the dockers as she and Eddark streaked past.

She didn't turn to see if they were followed.

They didn't stop until Eddark pulled her into a winding side street some distance down the dock, not far from the brothels where their presence as a pair, sweating and breathless, would raise little notice or interest. With a rough flick, he pushed her into a doorway and stood watching, his eyes trained on the end of the street, his chest heaving.

As they waited, life went on along the dock as if they hadn't been there at all. Folk passed by, some arm in arm, some staggering drunk while others laughed and called out to friends. After what seemed like a lifetime, Eddark turned and looked her up and down.

'That was far too close. Have you got any idea what would have happened if we'd been caught?'

Sellan glared but couldn't find the words to fire off a retort. Pain flared in her hand, tendrils of invisible fire licking up her arm as her stomach tied itself in knots. She was either going to collapse, or shit herself, or both, and she didn't want to do it here. Leaving her in the doorway, Eddark took a few steps down the lane and dipped his hands into an open rain barrel, returning and reaching for her face.

Lurching away, Sellan banged against the door at her back. His hands found her face and began wiping, cold water smearing over hot skin. 'What are you doing?' she demanded, flinching uselessly, unable to escape.

'You're covered in blood,' he growled, ignoring her protests and attempts to shift away.

One of his hands tightened around the underside of her jaw and Sellan froze. Eyes wide, she stared, realising that with her back to a locked door, in an underused laneway off the city docks, near the worst brothels in town with her hands up near her ears, she was completely at his mercy. Even if she screamed, no one was coming to help her.

Memories laced with barely forgotten horror surged through her mind.

Magic crackled between her fingers and Eddark slid back, a single finger pointed at her face. 'Don't.'

Curling her fingers into a fist, she lowered her arms and lifted the end of her veil to wipe the drops of bloody water away. Evidently the guard's brain had not just sprayed the wall and the stairs, but all over her as well.

Glancing down, she traced the blood splatter from her veil to the hem of her tunic. There were even specks on her shoes. Made of soft, embroidered linen, they were the most expensive thing on her person, and the only thing she wore that she actually owned.

'Well. That's not going to wash out,' she muttered.

Eddark grunted, shifted some of the abandoned rubbish at the side of the lane and looked like he was about to settle down on a pallet by the opposite wall.

'Don't get comfortable. We need to get back to the house,' she warned

He waved at her clothes and snorted a derisive laugh. 'Not looking like that you're not, and there's nowhere down here to buy you a change of clothes. The tailor's stalls are at least three or four streets away.'

'Excuse me? We can't stay down—' She took a step forward and her leg collapsed under her. Eddark caught her with one hand and she froze again, waiting for her head to stop spinning and her muscles to cease trembling.

'You're in no fit state to make it back up the hill, and covered in blood, people will stare. Unless you want some more unwanted attention, we wait here until nightfall, then make for the house.'

Straightening, she shook her head. 'I need to speak to my mother. I need to find out if she knows what's going on, and if Father has some sort of contract with the Assembly or the emperor.'

Eddark's brow creased in a brief frown. 'Why would he have a contract?'

'For the weapons?' Sellan replied, whisking her hand through the air, somewhat bewildered and wondering if she was making any sense.

The ringing in her ears faded, and she shook all over, the release of her magic shocking her system into almost complete shutdown. Other than travelling to the city from the South Lands, she hadn't had access to the power for a very long time, nor had she been required to manage or control it herself. Turning her hand over, she was surprised there wasn't a glaring red burn on her palm where the energy had discharged into the guard.

'If my father is dealing in weapons, then it must be for the war effort,' she added. Eddark's expression didn't change. Exhaustion overcame her, and Sellan slid down to sit on the step at the foot of the door. 'A noble wouldn't work as a trader unless it was required for the good of the Empire.'

Eddark crouched and studied her face. 'That's not how it works, Sellan.'

'What?' Her voice was hoarse and her mouth cotton-dry. The sickened sensation in her gut hadn't shifted and she began to wonder if it ever would.

'It's illegal to profit from providing supplies or services to the government, especially for the war or the expansion of the colonies.'

That makes no sense... Her thoughts must have been written all over her face, because Eddark checked the end of the lane and leaned closer.

'The emperor got sick of paying top coin while merchants got rich off the war, so he passed a law making it illegal to sell weapons or anything else to the government for more than cost. The Assembly even went so far as to set up their own production lines. They pay the workers bare minimum, and anyone caught skimming or gaming the system faces exile. A few years back a trader was caught selling extra ration packs to soldiers. He wasn't *technically* selling them to the government, but they cut off his hands to make an example.' Eddark shook his head. 'If your father is dealing in weapons, he's not making a profit, and if he's not making a profit, then why get involved in something that could bring shame and scandal on his family?'

A cold shudder coursed through Sellan as she sat curled up on the step, shivering uncontrollably. She narrowed her eyes, still unwilling to believe what she was hearing. 'Then w-who are the weapons for? W-why go to all the trouble of hiding them in the bottom of the...'

Her question trailed off to a silence she didn't dare fill.

'If they aren't for the Imperial Army, then there's really only one other option.' The look on Eddark's face, the knowing and the disappointment, the fear and the uncertainty were mirrored in his eyes. 'He's selling them to our enemies.'

CHAPTER SIXTEEN

Baleanon, the Woaden Empire

Night fell across Baleanon, and Eddark and Sellan remained in the laneway, huddled against the walls as much for warmth as to disguise their presence. A city guard loitered at one point, but moved farther down the dock, more interested in the sailors' taverns than what might be lurking in a dark alley. No one from the warehouse came looking, though that didn't mean Warrin or his business partners didn't have people watching, waiting for someone to come by who looked like they'd just committed a murder.

The shock of the magical discharge eventually eased, and Sellan finally sat still, free of tremors and able to breathe normally. She'd forgotten how brutal and unwieldy her magic was. Had lost touch with it and its ferocity, the damage it left behind becoming a thing of distant memory, faded by years of trauma and denial. Thanie had kept it contained, and Sellan would likely never know the toll that had taken on her cousin. Yet had she not made that sacrifice, it would have killed them both.

Most youngsters whose power grew faster than they could control became derramentis, entirely at its mercy. Sellan hadn't ever breached that barrier, allowed to mature while her magic lay dormant in Thanie's control. She'd never *actually* become derramentis, despite her enemy's liberal use of the term. It was only thanks to Thanie that Sellan had managed to survive to adulthood at all. She picked at the skin around her nails, wondering if her cousin regretted that choice now.

'When your mother asked me to escort you today,' Eddark said from nowhere, 'I wondered if you'd do something like this.'

Sellan glanced across the lane, his face only barely visible in the deepening darkness. 'Like what?'

'Go off on some tangent or mad quest or whatever and get us killed.'

She didn't dignify his statement with a response. He'd made his assumptions and there was little she could do to change them. Not that it mattered. She wasn't here to make friends—she was here to do a job.

'Was it worth it?' he asked in a low whisper. His hand indicated at the bag by her feet. 'Was that worth the risk?'

She looked out at the dock. 'It will be. Once I'm done...'

The first crescent of the moon glistened on the river, and if it weren't for the hoots and caterwauls of tavern patrons, it might have been a beautiful night. It was a dangerous, deceptive beauty though, like the false sense of security the city begged her to fall in to. Threat lingered below the surface and there was not a single building in this town, or any other in the Empire, where she was safe. At least not until she'd done what she'd come back to do. But time slipped from her grasp, running away toward an end point she could not yet see. She had to get moving. Staying in Baleanon any longer was a mistake.

Eddark leaned out from the shadows and into a shaft of new moonlight. 'You didn't come back here to reclaim your place in the family, did you?'

Their eyes met and Sellan slowly shook her head. 'A merchant I am not, but I am owed, and I will collect.'

'Ah, I know something of that feeling.' His sad little chuckle tugged at a small part of her heart. 'I thought being freed would heal that wound. Turns out the scars run deeper than I ever imagined.'

That slapped her mind clear. Was he talking about her family and their ownership of him, or something else? Was this an older hurt he carried from before he'd arrived in the Parben household? Did she even dare ask?

Then he looked her dead in the eye. 'I'm not sure I want to know what you're up to, but have a care for the destruction you'll leave in your wake.'

'Don't worry,' she sneered. 'You'll have your idyllic existence back in short order. I don't intend to stay.'

A black silence spread through the laneway, unspoken pain filling the void until he stood and brushed himself off. 'We should head back.'

She dismissed his proffered hand with a sharp flick of her own. Leaning against the wall, she staggered to her feet. Sellan didn't need his help or anyone else's. She'd manage just fine on her own, even if it killed her.

They burst through the doors to the kitchen and the dish girl scrambled backward, squeaking with fright.

'Where is she?' Sellan snarled as she stormed into the room.

'W-who?' the girl stammered.

'Abrial—' Eddark began.

'Drop the act, Eddark. They all know who I am,' Sellan snapped then whirled back to the girl. 'Lady Mediia. Where is she?'

'In the—her sitting room. She's in her sitting room!'

Leaving the girl cowering by the trough of steaming water and Eddark's hurried apologies echoing behind her, Sellan hurried through the internal kitchen doors and along the colonnade beside the garden. It was well after dark now, having taken quite some time to wind up through the city to the great plaza before cutting around to the back entrance of the house. Sellan hadn't noticed anyone that might be looking for them, either for good or ill, but then she didn't expect her mother could justify sending men out lest it rouse suspicion.

Sellan shoved the door aside and her mother started from where she reclined by the hearth, surrounded by scrolls and cradling a glass of wine. 'What is—Sellan, where have you *been*?'

'Did you know?'

'Did I know what? Where is Eddark?' Mediia glanced behind her daughter and the man's footsteps slowed from a jog as he entered the room. 'Oh, there you are! I've been worried out of my mind!'

'I can see that,' Sellan said brusquely, smiling sourly at the wine urn on the table beside the lounge.

Mediia baulked and looked Sellan up and down. 'What in the name of the Sisters has gotten into you? You're filthy.'

'Did you know what he was doing at the docks?' Sellan's question exploded into the room. For a moment, time stilled, trapped in a quagmire of unspoken truth. Sellan's gaze locked with her mother's, challenge written all over her face. As if punched, Mediia's shoulders hunched as she let out a sigh. Her mother's cheeks bloomed red, and she looked away, her eyes darting across the scrolls and books scattered around the lounge.

'You went to the docks...' Her whisper was barely audible over the crackle of the fire. Sellan would usually have been glad of its warmth, but tonight she was ablaze with indignant rage. 'Why?'

'Brenna's shop, Mother. I went to Brenna's shop.'

Suddenly, the woman seemed old; aged and shrinking before Sellan's eyes, as if the news was a weight she could not carry. She sank back on the lounge, her wine glass clinking gently as it came to rest on the table. 'Of course you did…'

What was going on? Why hadn't Mediia dismissed her with a wave and a simple explanation?

'Ma?' Sellan ventured, concern softening her voice only slightly. Her father, once again, was nowhere to be seen. It was possible he lurked somewhere in the house, but by now he would have heard the commotion and come to investigate. That he had not, told Sellan everything she needed to know. He was probably still at the warehouse.

Mediia shook her head. 'You weren't supposed to see that. No one is supposed to know, not even me.'

A pulse of heat shuddered through Sellan and she staggered, gasping as the truth hit home. Her eyes narrowed. 'It's illegal? He's trading weapons *illegally*?'

'What else was he supposed to do?' Mediia snapped, glowering up at Sellan, tears shimmering in the firelight. 'What were *any* of us supposed to do?'

'Excuse—'

'You *left*!' Mediia shot to her feet as her words cut at Sellan. 'What do you think all these ledgers are for? The household accounts? Tell me, daughter, do you *ever* recall me poring over our household accounts with such attention and care in all the years you were here?'

Sellan gaped. She *had* thought the books were the records of the house, assuming her mother was simply a studious manager of their affairs. Others left it to a trusted senior slave like Paud, but Sellan had assumed… She had assumed… 'What are they for?'

'Brothels, you foolish girl. With so many years behind you, how can you still have no idea how the real world works?'

Brothels? No. That was a lie. She scoffed, 'You don't own any brothels.'

'Don't I? How do you think I know where you father spends all his time when he's not at home? I own every single one of his favourite establishments, and I have done so since I realised he was fucking our money into the purses of the city's pimps and madams, fattening them up on

121

our misfortune while our reputation disintegrated in the wake of our daughter's disgrace.'

Sellan flinched. Surely her mother knew why she'd acted as she had done. Surely, she understood. Mediia had known about what was going on at the Academy, and while she'd supported Lord Orel's insistence that Sellan not protest, she'd surely only done so to make her brother happy. Lady Mediia had to have known…

Unless…

'My girls and boys watched your father for months before they discovered the weapons business, and yes, it is entirely illegal. But what he makes from his trade he funnels into my houses and that, my dear, is what pays the fucking bills around here.' Seething, Mediia picked up a ledger and dropped it on the table, the wine glass jumping with the impact. 'All of *this* is because of what you did.'

'You *know* why I did that,' Sellan growled, her voice thick with emotion, her heart pounding. She would not wear the blame for this. She would not carry the entire weight of her family's fall from grace. That faded, blurry memory of a face, seen through swirled smoke, lanced her mind and she shoved it away. 'You knew all along, so don't you tell me it came as some big surprise when I finally snapped.'

'Don't give me your excuses. All you had to do was keep your mouth shut and your legs open, and none of this would have ever happened!' Mediia's accusation echoed against the walls and Sellan reeled as if someone had kicked her in the chest.

There it was.

The truth. The thing she'd done that was so horrific it had almost ruined her entire family, her entire tribe.

She'd fought back.

Her top lip curled. 'I will not apologise. Not now. Not ever.'

Lady Mediia lifted her chin and glared; her hands clenched tightly into fists. 'Then you will find no succour here.'

A frighteningly huge body-slave all but threw Sellan into the darkness of her room and slammed the door. The tumbling pins of the lock thunked as they dropped into place, leaving her alone in the silence. Despite herself, a small sob escaped her throat as she peeled her soiled veil from her head and unwound it from her neck.

That was that, then.

Mediia had been willing to help her and she'd burned that bridge to the waterline, all because she couldn't keep her mouth shut. Again. It had always been her way. She'd seen it in Lidan, creeping in as the child grew ever more wilful and determined. As much as she'd quietly admired her daughter's strength, it was as likely to get her killed as keep her alive. Beating it out of Lidan had been about as effective as Mediia's efforts to beat Sellan into line. It was a wonder she'd even bothered.

Still, none of that mattered now. She was destined to be reported to the Congress office by morning. The mages would take her away, posturing and preening at their cleverness when they'd done absolutely nothing to assist in her capture but show up with the shackles. If she was lucky, they might execute her quickly, but something told her they would take her to Wodurin, unable to resist the opportunity to parade her before the emperor. Tamyr would reward anyone who brought her low and allowed him to watch, even after all these years.

She wished she could have seen his face when he heard of her escape from the Academy, instead of facing the death sentence he'd engineered for her in the Disputed Territory. But she'd slipped through his grasping fingers one last time. This wasn't the return she'd hoped for, but it afforded her one last chance to spit at his smirking face before a crowd of baying citizens. Going to her death in the capital would be well worth it.

Lifting the strap of her bag over her head, she let it drop to the ground. Eddark's question repeated in her mind. Had that bag and its contents been worth it? Glancing at the dresser, faintly visible in the gloom, she thought perhaps it had. The Morritae had spoken—albeit indirectly—weaving her fate to this point. What became of her now was their will. Her fingers found the statuette amongst the scatter of items, her hand aching as she held it to her chest and sank down beside her bag.

Should she try and speak with them before it was too late?

No, there was little point. If they wished to see her, they knew exactly where she was.

Right here, on the floor of her room, in the dark.

The first tap on her door was so light she thought she'd dreamt it. When the second came, a little louder and more insistent, she sat up from where she'd fallen asleep. Had they come for her already?

A quick glance at the window told her night still held dominion over the sky. It was doubtful the mages from the Congress office would be called in the middle of the night. Perhaps it was her mother, come to seek an apology, or to insist on one in exchange for her life. The old bitch was barking up the wrong tree if she thought—

'Sellan,' Eddark whispered from beyond the door.

What in the name of...? She scrambled to her hands and knees and crawled to the door. 'Eddark? What are you doing up here? She'll flog you—'

'It's illegal to flog a citizen.'

'Well she'll have you thrown in a cell if she catches you defying her.'

'Shut up and listen to me,' he hissed. 'I haven't got long.'

'Where is everyone?'

He paused, and she shuffled closer. 'They're asleep, I think. I don't believe anyone is too worried about you breaking out.'

She frowned. 'Is there a guard?'

'Not that I've seen.'

Didn't her mother expect her to use magic and attempt an escape? Why not at least post a guard? She blinked hard as the realisation dawned in the darkness. Her mother had no idea if the magic had returned or not. The last Mediia knew, she was as weak as a day-old babe and unsure when or if her power would return. The truth wasn't too far off. Sellan hadn't tried to escape because her sole weapon was unreliable and extremely weak. Bone tired and hardly able to lift her arms above her head, she might have killed the guard in the warehouse, but it had exhausted her for a good few hours afterward. There was zero chance of sustaining the power long enough to fight her way out of town, and even if she did, they'd find her collapsed in a ditch by the road before sunrise.

There was another reason her mother hadn't posted a guard, of course. If Sellan couldn't get out on her own, there was no one within these four walls who was going to help her.

'When we were in the alley, after dark, you mentioned a debt owed to you...'

When Eddark didn't elaborate, she nodded to herself. 'Yes, for something that was done to me.'

'Does that have anything to do with what happened in Wodurin before you disappeared?' His voice drew closer, as if he leaned as near the door as he could manage. 'Is that what you and Mediia were fighting about?'

Her stomach clenched and she licked at dry lips. He was circling the truth, but how close could he get without being burned by those flames? Turning her back on the door, Sellan stretched her legs out into the room and looked up at the ceiling. What did it matter now if he knew? She was dead at dawn. Secrecy had only been required to earn the trust of the Morritae, and through that, their help. That possibly was long gone. She was alone now, her truth about to be scoured from the world. Someone might as well know.

'Yes,' she whispered, all caution falling into the wind.

He had almost certainly heard the official accounts, detailing in vivid fiction how she wantonly attacked the young Prince Tamyr and his closest friend, accusing them of heinous crimes before murdering the friend and injuring the prince. It would be another year before Tamyr became emperor, but he still wielded immense power in the capital. It took him less than a day to have her declared derramentis, then sentenced to serve out the remainder of her life on the eastern front as a battle mage. There hadn't even been a trial.

What Eddark could not have known until tonight, and perhaps only barely suspected now, was why Sellan had attacked Tamyr in the first place.

She opened her mouth to lay out the truth and the lock clicked.

What?

The door swung outward to reveal a moonlit sky smeared with clouds dark enough to promise rain.

'What are you doing?' she whispered, glancing along the balcony outside. Surely someone would have heard the creak of the hinges.

'I've my own debt to settle in the capital,' Eddark muttered. 'And I wager neither will be easy tolls to extract.'

'No, they won't.' Sellan stared at him in disbelief. So his wounds were the acts of another, not her family's doing. His reasons would have to wait though. They didn't have time for them now.

'I assume you have a plan?'

She hardly dared believe this was happening. Mediia would drop dead from shock if she knew. Sellan nodded.

'Thought so. Get your things.'

Her body reacted while her mind whirled, trying to catch up, trying to understand. He was actually doing this. He was actually *helping* her. She scrambled to collect the black bag and her veil, stuffing an assortment of random clothes into the bag then scooping the cloak and the statuette from the floor. 'Have you lost your mind?'

Eddark shrugged and allowed himself a wry smile. 'Probably, but then I'll be in excellent company, won't I?'

CHAPTER SEVENTEEN

Somewhere in the Western Tablelands

The darkness came and the sounds of life beyond the covering faded again. The dead man waited, listening to those beyond as they prepared for something. They'd spent the time of light running back and forth, shouting and ordering each other around, the big man's voice booming and setting the dead man's teeth on edge.

He'd begun to test his hands and arms, working his feet and legs beneath the blanket. As darkness fell, he thought he had just enough strength, but no idea where it came from. Deep inside, a fire burned, stoked by rage and something unknowable that told him to move, to rise and to act. Laying here was defeat and he'd already lived through that. He'd fallen, and now it was time to get up.

A clean set of clothing and a pair of well-worn boots lay beside his pallet, a signal that his keepers would take him with them when they put their plan in motion. He had no intention of waiting that long. With trembling hands, he set about dressing. Clothing went where blurry recollections indicated they fit best, muscle memory overriding any reservations about what he was doing. Instinct was his only beacon in the dark.

At the opening of the covering, he paused, hand hovering at the threshold. A tent. It was a tent, he reminded himself.

Move, a voice commanded. He recognised it. It had greeted him in the realm of the dead.

Where?

Trust yourself. You know more of this place than you remember.

Have I been here before?

The voice said nothing more and he sighed, giving himself over to the pull of his own mind.

Turning from the opening, he crouched at the far edge of the tent and slithered under, his belly in the dirt. Faint light washed through the trees from nearby fires, the wind whispering through the branches high above. With a deep breath, he greeted the bush once more, memories of childhood creeping back. He *did* know this place and these smells. The air stuck to his skin, warm, clinging, his vision clearing as he huddled at the back of the tent.

There were many more tents just like his, the sounds of sleep drifting from within their walls to mingle with the chitter of night creatures. The largest would belong to the big man. A man like that showed off at any opportunity and his sleeping place would be no exception. Most likely it stood at the centre of things, where the bodies of others shielded him from the hands of those who wished him ill. Faded memories and a deep sense of wrong simmered, a repeating tale of death and misery in the big man's wake. There was no doubt many wished this man ill.

Sneaking through the camp, stealing through shadows and the protection of the soaring trees, a tent larger than the others came into view. The dead man stopped and waited.

Footsteps crunched through the undergrowth, and he sank into a crouch. Instinct had him reach for something at his waist yet his grasp found nothing. Heart lurching, he glanced down. A weapon had been here once. Now only an empty belt loop remained.

Someone had taken it.

That would not fucking do.

His jaw clenched. *Find the big man. Find the weapon.*

He took two quick steps between the tents and left the sound of footfalls behind. The biggest tent loomed across a circular firepit, and he skirted around to the back, senses straining for any hint that he'd been discovered. The camp slept on, snuffles and snores, coughs and grumbles all as natural as the snort of beasts tethered nearby. There was just enough noise, just enough shadow to hide his movements from the few sentries at the perimeter. He took his chance.

Breath held, he slipped inside the tent and stood still as stone.

No one stirred.

A bird squawked in the distance, but he remained as he was, eyes adjusting to the gloom.

On the far side of the space, a large chest stood open, its contents strewn across the floor. A small table stood beside that, cluttered with tankards. There was no sign of the weapon he knew, nor the weapon the big man had shown him the night before.

There was, however, a dividing curtain hanging across the space, obscuring the sleeping quarters. It parted easily and beyond he found a plush pallet heaped with furs, a figure slumped across it. The man hadn't even taken his clothes off before falling into a deep sleep.

The big man was alone.

Turning from the bed, the dead man scoured the darkness, scanning for the faintest glint of light. The long weapon was incredibly shiny and the big man had coveted it with a hungry gleam in his eye. It would not be far.

Perseverance proved fruitful as his gaze fell on a low bench to the far side of the bed. A cluster of weapons lay in a pile, the long one amongst them with another he recognised. His hand ached for the haft of the one he knew best, but as he skirted the end of the cot with silent steps, his fingers reached for the long weapon. It was cold and unfamiliar, a presence nestled at its core—the ghost of someone he knew, someone who'd held it and spilt blood for love.

He slid the weapon free and hefted the blade. What little light filtered through the tent shone along its length and the big man groaned, rolling over. His arm flopped across the furs and smacked into the dead man.

Eyes flew open. 'The fuck—'

The dead man spun the blade and dropped his shoulder, the point angled at the big man's throat, his free hand hovering above the head of the pommel. Together they froze, one in fear of his life, the other at a precipice.

This must be done? the dead man asked the night.

It must, replied the voice.

Why?

It is the first step back to who you were.

A wicked smile broke across the dead man's lips as he reconciled what he was about to do, revelling in the satisfaction of the moment, connections forming between who he had been and who he was now. Though his purpose here remained uncertain, the murk of the past cleared just enough to see the path ahead. Just enough to remember exactly who the big man was and what he'd done.

'None survived?' he asked the big man.

'Some,' he croaked. The whites of his eyes shone; nervous sweat beaded on his skin. 'They fled.'

'The one who carried this blade?'

The big man twitched a nod.

Heat flared in the dead man's chest, a flash from deep within the chasm. The piece he sought was still out there. It was not gone, merely misplaced, just like the blade.

'I lost a lot under those stones, but not everything,' he whispered, leaning down as the big man flinched. 'I may not remember much, but I remember *you*. I remember what you tried to do and how you made her feel. She wasn't the only one you tried to take, was she? She was the one who got away.'

Their eyes met, terrible comprehension clashing with cool, unwavering purpose. The big man saw his fate and realised it was vengeance. His vile acts and the horrors he had inflicted, were all to see his desires met and his thirst slaked.

'She survived you, Yorrell.'

The blade point speared down, parting skin and bone and muscle and sinew. A wet crunch echoed through the tent and Yorrell jolted. Blood vomited from his mouth, spurting out over the bed. The blade wobbled as Loge stood back and took his axe from the table. Its edge made short work of Yorrell Namjin's neck, cleaving head from torso with more care than the brute deserved.

The horse shied as he drew it to a halt at the gates.

Mounted folk had watched him since dawn, shadowing his approach to the river, eyeing him from a distance. None approached, seemingly unsure of what they saw. One woman stared, her eyes brimming with tears, mouth agape. He thought he knew her face. She turned and rode off without a word, leaving him to plod across a timber bridge on his stolen horse as a hot, red sunrise bled across the western sky.

It took two days and nights to reach the edge of the tablelands, overlooking the flood plain and the village atop a promontory. The Namjin camp had been farther north than the rockfall, his vague and cloudy memory sending him off on the wrong trail at least twice. At the edge of the trees, he'd made camp and waited for daylight, unwilling to risk an arrow to the head if he surprised a sentry on the wall.

The extermination of those in the camp had taken longer than anticipated. A largely silent affair, watched from a stump by Yorrell's severed head. Some of the sentries tried to run, but Loge threw stone axes and flint knives, drew arrows and trained them on their fleeing backs. Everyone else had been sent to Dennawal in their sleep. It was the least he could do for the Shadow Rider—a sacrifice, a bloody toll taken—for the power that had brought him back.

With that grisly task complete, Loge's purpose had fixed on returning the long blade. Why Dennawal wanted this, he did not know, but the Rider's need was as present in him as his own heartbeat. In fact, it was the only reason his heart beat at all. The blade's importance was lost on him, and he found he didn't much care.

The gates were open through the earthworks toward the top of the hill, left so by the woman he saw riding off. He'd pushed his stolen horse across country but did not hurry the animal in her wake. Instead, he carried on calmly until he found the final gate closed in his path. The horse protested the delay with a pawing hoof and indignant snorts, perhaps eager to rid itself of the bloodied head hanging in a makeshift sack from the back of the saddle. More likely, the creature could smell the stable on the far side of the wall and knew too well that a decent feed and a drink awaited.

Someone spoke in hushed tones from the lintel above, hidden in the shelter of the gatehouse, and the gates began to open with a creak and a groan. The horse needed little prompting and Loge Baker rode back into Tingalla.

The place was silent save for the warbles of birds and the odd snort or stamp of a horse. No one ran forward to take his reins, but he didn't mind. They watched him instead. Someone would see to the animal's needs once he was clear of it. For now, *he* was far more interesting.

The open space at the centre of the settlement stood empty for the most part. The remains of a huge fire smouldered near the middle, folk milling at the edges, watching and whispering. A large hall dominated the far end of the open space, a crowd gathered at the steps, faces he should recognise but could not place. One of them was the woman he'd seen on the horse, huddling beside a shorter, pale woman with bright hair. Both looked on him as if they knew him yet could not reconcile what they were seeing. They had thought him dead.

They weren't wrong.

Loge swung from the saddle and untied the sack, the weight of its contents straining the stitches of the linen shirt he used to fashion it. Silence lay heavy as he approached on foot, wind whistling across the common, dust kicked up into whirls as the head bounced against the outside of his thigh.

A sudden movement caught his attention and a young woman broke from the crowd, jogging toward him, slowing to a stop as her wide green eyes registered his face. Her thick, dark curls were pulled back into a braid, stray ringlets dancing in the wind at her temples.

Loge's heart gave a hard thud of recognition.

He knew that face.

Yet, he did not.

It's wrong. It isn't her.

He frowned, and his hand began to shake as his throat contracted. Deafening buzzing filled his ears, his chest tightened as he breathed out, struggling to expand again as his vision narrowed.

It's not her...

'Loge?' the young woman asked. 'Is that you?'

'What?' He blinked. It was difficult to look at her, knowing she wasn't the one he sought. The resemblance was so strong, it was like staring at the sun.

She took another step forward, tentative yet courageous. 'How is that you?'

'I came back.' His voice cracked, his strength waning as if the power that carried him wore thin.

'But you're *dead*,' she insisted. 'They told us you died...' She glanced at the remains of the fire and he realised what it was. A memorial pyre; not for a body, but for someone lost. It gave his people something to bury, something to scoop into an urn and inter in the tumals. Had someone collected ashes for his parents?

'I did die,' he agreed. The buzzing became a roar he barely heard her over. 'I was dead.'

'Then how…' Their eyes met and a flash of realisation crossed her features.

'I came back.' He held up the sack, then let it go. It hit the ground with a wet thud louder than any sound in the common.

The young woman didn't take her eyes from his face. 'Who is that?'

'Yorrell Namjin.'

A wave of astonished gasps and muttered curses split the crowd and the young woman held up her hand. He remembered her now. This was Marrit. This was her sister. With another step forward, ignoring the head in the bloodied makeshift bag, she studied him, the voices of the gathered folk fading away. 'Loge?'

The pounding of his heart stopped, the shaking of his hands eased and the screaming in his ears faded. 'Where's Lidan?'

Marrit's chin quivered, and his heart plummeted. 'She's gone.'

Chapter Eighteen

Tingalla, Tolak Range, the South Lands

They interrogated him for the rest of the day, leaving him alone in an ante-room of the hall for long stretches while they discussed something beyond the edges of his hearing. A man stood guard; dark, narrowed eyes watching with unbroken scrutiny. Arms crossed, his muscles bulged under pale scars and black tattana that matched Loge's. This man was like him, but older.

'Do you remember me?' the man asked after someone brought a platter of food and a cup of bitter brown water.

A flush of heat rushed through Loge's chest. Should he? 'I think so,' he said instead, hedging his bets. He wasn't sure if he liked the strange brown water, but not drinking it might be an insult.

'Must have knocked your head pretty hard then.'

'Must have,' Loge agreed without conviction, picking at the food. With a quick, furtive glance at the man, he put some in his mouth. It tasted of ash and dust but he ate it anyway, if only to banish the look of curious bewilderment and raised brows from the man's face.

'I'm Siman,' he said eventually.

'Loge,' he replied.

Siman frowned. 'I know.'

'Just making sure.'

'What happened—' Siman's question fell away as someone came through a door, striding around from behind Loge's shoulder to fill the room to the brim. This man was bigger than Yorrell, at least in the shoulders. He looked as if he could have held up the sky with one hand.

'Where did you get this?' he asked, stabbing a finger at the long blade on the table.

'Yorrell had it,' Loge said around a mouthful of food.

'And you killed him with it?'

He shrugged half-heartedly. 'He wasn't a very nice man.'

The mountain of a man turned and looked at Siman, who mirrored Loge's shrug. 'He's not wrong.'

'He *cannot* seem right to you?'

Siman snorted a sour laugh. 'Of course not! Have you heard him? He's half senseless, but he's got Yorrell Namjin's head in a bag and Lidan's sword, so he's not entirely without his wits.'

'Can I go now?' Loge wiped greasy fingers on his trousers, stifling a bored yawn.

The tall man rounded on him with an indignant glare, nostrils flaring as he drew himself to his full height. 'Oh, I'm sorry. Are we delaying you?'

Loge sucked at his teeth and thought for a moment. 'A bit.'

Another exasperated look shot between the tall man and Siman. 'How am I going to explain this to his father?'

'Where have you got to be?' Siman stepped forward, his head tilted, his question cutting across the tall man's frustration.

'Somewhere else.' Loge didn't honestly know where, but it wasn't here. *She* wasn't here, so he couldn't be. Beyond that was only light and silence. Dennawal gave him nothing else.

The tall man shook his head. 'Ancestors only know what kind of mess he's made across the border—'

'Hold on, Erlon.' Siman slowly crossed the room, waving his hands in a placating gesture. Loge let him come, curious but unafraid. This man meant him no harm. That was evident in the dancing lights at his back.

That's interesting... Loge blinked, his brow furrowing briefly. If he squinted just a little, the lights brightened, then faded as he lost interest.

'His eye... Does it look black to you?' Siman asked Erlon. They both edged closer. 'Where are you supposed to be, Loge?'

That question had weight and it dropped between them like the heavy, severed head he'd carried to their door. Loge's left eye twitched and he shuddered. 'Not here.'

As one, Siman and Erlon leaned away.

'I've heard stories,' Siman whispered.

'We all have, but they're *stories*.' A dark cloud of confusion settled over Erlon.

'I think she was right...'

Erlon sighed and rested his hands on his hips. 'Marri usually is.'

Siman turned his back on Loge, as if to conceal his words. 'If it's true, then it's best we don't stand in his way.'

Distress crept across Erlon's face and sent a chill through Loge; tiny, icy lances of pain prickling across his skin and shooting into his bones. The tall man was afraid, and it showed in the creases of his brow and the hard, taut line of his mouth. He hurt, too; genuine anguish for something he'd lost, or was about to. 'Can't be true. He's just had a knock—'

'What if you're wrong?' Siman hissed, jabbing a finger at the settlement beyond the walls. 'After what I've seen these past days, I will *not* be convinced there isn't something far fucking bigger at play here. Hands so large we can't even begin to see them at work. I for one won't tempt their wrath. Jessah said she saw the rockfall. There's no way he survived with just a knock to the head.'

Loge thought it all fairly obvious but felt no need to enlighten either man. What he needed was to leave. Telling the whole tale would likely land him in a cell somewhere. Mad men rarely walked free for long. Erlon's dark blue gaze came to rest on his face and remained fixed, studying his features. After a while Loge wondered what he saw.

'Where are you going, Loge Baker?' Erlon asked softly, his voice thick and his eyes glistening. His fingers curled into tight fists until his knuckles grew pale against his brown skin, his tattana faded by time and exposure to the harsh southern sun. Shadows of confusion darkened the man's features. Things were beyond his comprehension now.

In truth, they always had been. Loge understood them only because he'd been to a place that existed in fireside fables and tale-keeper's warnings. He hadn't thought to ever play a part in such games, yet here he was, a piece on the board, moving as instructed for reasons he could not fathom. Perhaps this had always been his fate, he just hadn't the eye to see until now.

'I need to find Lidan,' he said.

Erlon's eyes slid closed, fists relaxing. He nodded. 'Of course you do.'

'I need to go *now*,' Loge pressed. Would he be denied? Thoughts and plans rushed his mind, spinning through him as his heart began to pound and the buzzing roar shivered at the edge of his hearing. She was moving away from him, each moment farther than the one before, each heartbeat a step into the distance. He stood and they didn't move to stop him, his long finger unfurling to point. 'I need that, too.'

Erlon followed the gesture to the table and the sword gleaming in the ruddy light of oil lamps and tallow candles. Despite the heat of the day outside, a bitter draught washed through the room.

No one moved.

'Why?' Erlon didn't look back at Loge, his fingers twitching as if they itched to hold the blade. Did the man have the skill to end him with it? Loge knew he had the power in his bare hands. Should the need arise, Erlon would do anything necessary to protect his people. But his pained grimace told Loge he would not.

'She needs it,' Loge replied.

The blade passed between them in silence only broken by a sharp intake of breath and the sound of Siman's boots scuffing the floor as he stepped back.

'You'll need a scabbard and supplies. These will be ready in the morning. I'll have the tines arrange lodging. Private lodging, I think.' Erlon glanced at Siman, who nodded and left.

They didn't want him near other folk. That was fair. He didn't much like the idea of being around them either. Their noise hurt his head and the bones around his eye ached when he looked at some of them. Something to do with those funny lights he'd seen around Siman.

'You're not to leave the compound until these arrangements have been made, understand?' Erlon's warning echoed against the quiet, filling the space beneath exposed beams and thatch. Certainty hardened his eyes. Should Loge defy him, his purpose would be thwarted, and with force.

'I'll stay until dawn.' The loop on his belt opposite his axe was just wide enough to carefully carry the sword, and though the blade hung exposed, the cross guard prevented it from falling to the ground. It would do for now. 'Should you have need of me, I won't be far.'

He reached the door before Erlon cleared his throat.

'Loge?'

He turned back, a steady hand on the latch.

'I once told her you can only row with the oar you're given, but I didn't tell her that there's no map for this life, no course charted. We're all bound to get lost along the way.' Sorrow and regret deepened the lines of Erlon's face. 'It's how we find our way home that matters.'

A heartbeat passed in silence.

'You keep her alive, whatever it takes.' Words as sharp as thorns scored their way out from the daari's throat.

Loge did nothing but nod. 'Always.'

The bed seemed familiar, as if he could reach through time to a place where the memory of it stood fresh and clear. Instead, the recollection blurred before his eyes, darting away as he fell asleep. He hadn't opened the trunk across the room of the small hut, though it beckoned as he pulled on a clean shirt and laced his trousers. Belongings he knew to be his own were delivered along with a meal after the sun set, but none of the items ignited any great sentiment in his heart. Each one shone with vague familiarity and that was all. Had someone asked where or when he'd acquired the bronze knife or the little tokens tucked inside a leather pouch, he couldn't have said.

Shouldering the saddlebags left by the door, Loge stepped beyond the threshold and into the cool pre-dawn. None of the rangers patrolling the settlement challenged him, nor did they bar his entry to the stable block. They observed from afar, silent in their assessment of what he must be alongside what they had no doubt heard. He'd be gone before the sun broke the horizon and in time their memory of his face would fade. In time he would be naught but a story recited to spellbound children as the cold of the dry season dug its claws into the land. They wouldn't see him again.

The torches by the stables had long ago burned out their oily fuel, and he ducked through the door into the musty darkness. A new scabbard and leathers had arrived with his things and the sword now rested snug between his shoulders. It wouldn't get in the way should he need to fight or hunt. It wasn't his to use, so it would remain there until he found where it belonged.

Horses snorted and he glanced into each stall as he passed. In the gloom they all looked much the same, until they didn't.

'Striker,' he murmured. The horse stamped his hoof and Loge smiled. 'I wouldn't forget you.'

'What are you doing?' Her voice cut the quiet and his axe was halfway from his belt before he turned to see her face. It was the face he thought he'd recognised, younger by a few years but no less fierce. She had her arms folded and her hip cocked, scowling as she watched him through the semi-dark.

He dropped the axe back into its loop and opened the stall. 'Leaving.'

'With my horse.'

Loge hands grew still, and he turned slowly. '*My* horse.'

She shook her head. 'No, she gave him to me. You up and got yourself killed, and I got left with this big bastard to look after. He's mine.'

He went back to bridling and saddling Striker. She understood that he'd died and seemed unbothered by it, not questioning why or how he'd come back, not revolted or frightened by the possibility he may not be entirely as he appeared. Maybe if he ignored the girl in the corridor of the stable, she might go away. Striker's saddle sat on a shelf at the back of his stall, all his tack hanging on a peg beside it. At least he didn't have to go rummaging through a storage room to find what he needed. With a glance from the corner of his eye, Loge realised she hadn't moved.

Fuck.

'Where are you going?' Her scowl deepened, if that was at all possible for someone with a face that young.

'Why does everyone keep asking me that?' Loge muttered to the horse. Striker didn't reply.

'You can't save her.'

He stopped, heart stuttering then thumping back into time. Buzzing crackled at the back of his mind. Somehow, he knew that to be true. He was not here to save anyone. Turning, he met her gaze.

Marrit. Her name is Marrit. Marrit is her sister. He remembered now.

'I'm not going to save her. She doesn't need that.'

Marrit's eyes narrowed briefly and the taut muscles holding her posture so rigid, primed for a fight, softened. 'Then why are you going? That *is* where you're going, right?'

Loge nodded, fastening the last of the girth straps and hefting the weight of the saddlebags across Striker's rump. 'Because I'll always put myself between her and the darkness. I'll die a thousand times if that's what it takes.'

'You're fucking insane.'

'Probably. Love does that to people.' Pain lanced his chest and his fingers clutched at the coarse hair of Striker's mane. He hadn't meant to say that. He hadn't wanted that truth freed. He hadn't even known it *was* the truth until now, and it hurt.

'You're not going alone.'

He fumbled a stirrup on its strap. 'You're *not* coming.'

Ignoring him, Marrit swung open a stall door and led a horse from the shadows. It was saddled and provisioned, ready to leave at a moment's notice. Her clothing should have been the first give away, yet he'd missed that too. Trousers and a loose shirt, a leather jerkin laced at the front, a knee-length oiled leather coat, sturdy boots and an expression that warned him she would not be dissuaded. She'd been waiting; hiding in the stable, knowing he'd come before the sun cut the night.

'You're not the boss of me, Loge Baker.'

A moment of shining clarity dawned, and a smile tugged at the corners of his mouth. 'You're a lot like her.'

'Yeah, well…'

'Why?' He wasn't sure he cared, but curiosity tickled at the edge of his awareness. Was it even *his* curiosity, or did something else, some*one* else, watch the world through his eye? How many of these feelings belonged to him alone?

'Why am I coming? Have you got any idea where she's gone? Any idea where to even start looking or which way to go?' Marrit snorted. 'I'm coming so you don't get fucking lost or end up dead again.'

'And how do you know where to go?' Scepticism laced his voice, his smirk hidden. She looked all of about fourteen summers but used to a certain authority that others bowed before. A belt rested on her hips, heavy with leather pouches and a massive hunting knife in a sturdy sheath. A healer's belt. That settled it then. *No one* was the boss of her, least of all him. Marrit would go exactly where she wanted, whether he liked it or not.

'I've got a map, you fool. Have you got a map?'

'Ah...' He didn't. He'd thought to follow his gut as he had after leaving the Namjin camp, but on reflection, that seemed idiotic. The maze of canyons and ravines between here and the camp had confounded him plenty. What chance did he have beyond the borders of his childhood home? He didn't even know where Lidan had gone, just that she had.

'Thought so,' Marrit mused as he led Striker from his stall and she climbed into her saddle.

Loge put himself between her and the door. 'Give me the map.'

'No.' Marrit lifted her chin in defiance.

Something shifted under all her bravado and self-confidence, and he narrowed his eyes at it. An aching throb bloomed in the orbit of his left eye. He winced hard, bit down on the inside of his cheek. A corona of colour burst to life around Marrit's body, oscillating green and yellow with a scintillating blue that washed over Loge in a crushing wave of fear and anxiety. Marrit's fear, Marrit's anxiety, carefully concealed beneath audacity and strength. All her reasons seemed good enough until he peeled back the mask to see the truth hidden beneath. Good enough wasn't *actually* good enough. Stance wide, he blinked the lights away and folded his arms across his chest. 'Why, Marri?'

Avoiding his gaze, Marrit shrugged with the feigned nonchalance all young people try at least once. It didn't suit her. 'I was born seven nights after the longest day. Today is my fifteenth birthday.'

There it was. He recalled enough of clan law to know what that meant. First daughters and sons were kept from matching until they were eighteen, largely to improve the likelihood of any daughters surviving childbirth. As a minor daughter, Marrit was considered old enough to match at fifteen.

'I can't stay here any more than Lidan could.' When that wasn't enough to shift him from her path, Marrit sighed, deflating as his question pierced through to the truth. 'While I may not understand all of what's happening out in the world, I know my sister hasn't simply gone with the northerners to be a witness like she told our father. They're going after our mother, and that's as much my fight as it is Lidan's. I need to help, even if it's as small a thing as making sure you get to where you need to be. You came back for a reason. Fuck me if I know what it is, but there is a reason.'

'You're insane,' Loge murmured.

She gave him a sympathetic smile. 'Love does that to people, I guess.'

CHAPTER NINETEEN

South of the Malapa, Tolak Range, the South Lands

It took five days from her departure from Tingalla for Lidan to accept the choice she'd made. Five days to understand and measure its weight. Five days to know she couldn't turn back from what she'd started. Still, she replayed the day over in her mind as she rode north, wondering if there had been another way, wondering what she might miss now she was gone.

Had she been able to orchestrate their departure in the dead of night, without the notice of a single person in the village, she'd have done it in a heartbeat. Had she been able to avoid the look of disappointment and concern on her father's face, she'd have gladly traded everything she'd ever owned. The hardening of her heart against the tears of her sisters had begun with the healing scars of Loge's loss. It was a burden she hadn't ever wished to carry. Still, she bore it anyway.

Their journey had required preparation, the best part of the day following the ngaru attack spent defending Thanie against Erlon Tolak and the leadership of the two clans gathered in the settlement—a thing she'd never thought to do. No one needed convincing that Thanie should leave, the only question was whether her head would remain attached to her neck. Her terrifying display of power had shaken the Tolak and Daylin to their core. Another day more than necessary in the village was another day closer to breaking point, and whispers hissed between folk of a plan to execute *all* the northerners, just to rid themselves of the threat of magic in their midst.

Vee brought Lidan news of the murder plot the night after the attack, then hurried the revelation to Ran. By morning they had a skeleton of a plan. It was missing half its bones and barely looked like it would hold together, but it was a plan. Lidan couldn't be sure why she'd agreed to it at all, but deep within she knew Thanie was key to stopping whatever Sellan planned to do next. And whatever it took, Lidan knew she had to be there to see it done. Sellan was *her* mother, and like it or not, she simply couldn't go about her days knowing she'd done nothing to stop what was surely coming. Besides, nothing remained for her in Hummel or Tingalla but a life as the wife of someone she didn't know or care for.

The first step was getting out.

As morning broke over Tingalla and the funeral pyres for the dead were erected beyond the walls, Ran had announced that Thanie must face northern justice and that Lidan was required as a witness to her misdemeanours in the south. It was a bare-faced lie. Ran had no intention of returning Thanie to his father's lands. Instead, they'd head for Aelish's home of Kotja in Isord; a truth they couldn't afford to reveal to the daari. Marrit alone knew their plan, she alone was the only one Lidan had ever been able to trust.

Erlon's dubious expression had dropped Lidan's heart into her boots, a sure sign he considered refusing altogether, but in the end the man had little choice. The northern prince offered him a tidy solution to a very messy problem, taking the witch who'd saved Tingalla off his hands. Erlon also knew well enough that he'd have to imprison Lidan to stop her leaving, something that would fall flat in the eyes of his people given all she'd done to protect them.

The more onerous separation had been from Vee and Marrit, both young women insisting on coming as well. That idea had been quickly shot from the sky, and Lidan charged them both with the care and protection of Ehran. Vee had taken the task to heart and immediately set about attending Farah and the two youngest Tolak children. Even so, Lidan kept watch over her shoulder for days, expecting to see Marrit picking her way along the trail behind them.

It was only when she'd gone a full five days without sight of her sister that the reality truly hit—she was never going to see Marrit again.

She turned from the sorrow, spinning in a dusty clearing, feigning blows at Aelish as Eian scrutinised their form. Driving her anger and pain into her training had been the only way to expel it as the days stretched on, weaving her grief into the muscles and sinews, laying it down to add strength to the fabric of her being. How much more pain could she endure? How many more losses? How many more goodbyes?

Had she truly, *really* said it for the last time? Had she meant it? Had Marrit known? Something in the girl's eyes told her she did. Somehow, she knew there was no coming back from what Lidan intended to do.

Perhaps it was for the best.

The villages of the Tolak range had become too small. Too full of ghosts, echoing with memories that pulled at the thin skin over old wounds. As a girl she'd dreamed of the day she might break away and forge her own path, but when that day had finally come, the moment Theus carried her out of Tingalla's gate and across the river, a part of her died. All she had lay ahead, shrouded in a mist she couldn't penetrate.

Without her sword, she focused on knife skills and honing hand-to-hand combat techniques under Eian's watchful eye. According to Ran, he was somewhat of an authority on the under-appreciated art of brawling, and while she had some skill, she'd lost conditioning thanks to her injuries.

Aelish threw a flurry of jabs, forcing Lidan into a defensive crouch as she shuffled backward. Her arm came up to block and she snuck a quick blow in under Aelish's guard, connecting with the soft side of the trader's torso.

Eian let out a high whistle. 'You're dead.'

'Fuck it!' Aelish arched away from the blow, lifting her hands up to yield. 'You said you were slow?'

'*Slower,*' Lidan replied with a sly grin. The time spent grieving and healing had cost her dearly, but her strength had returned at a pace.

'She's luring you into an attack then turning it back on you,' Eian explained. He tossed Aelish a water skin and leaned back against a tree. 'Hold your guard. Be sure you can defend before you go on the offensive.'

Lidan pulled her hair from its braid and set about re-tying it, scraping dark, fly-away curls from her face. 'If I had my knives, you'd be full of holes by now.'

With a roll of her eyes, Aelish stoppered the water skin. 'You won't always have them.' The trader furled and unfurled her fingers, flexing the joints. 'Though I'm not sure these particular skills are worth the bruises.'

'Smooth talking and manners aren't enough sometimes,' Lidan reasoned. She knew little of the Woaden, but what she'd heard left her in no doubt.

They were war-like and quick to anger. If they were caught, even a skilled negotiator like Aelish couldn't save them.

Aelish nodded. 'That much is true. The Woaden practice diplomacy by the sword more than anything else.'

'That's enough for today,' Eian told them. 'The food shouldn't be long. Although, with those two in charge, I have my doubts.'

The three of them turned to watch Brit and Zarad, crouched by the fire, exchanging heated whispers about what should or shouldn't be going into the pot. Brit hissed something about the best way to cook a hopper, to which Zarad growled, levelling the point of a paring knife at the big northerner. Groaning inwardly, Eian left Lidan and Aelish alone, seemingly intent on preventing a dispute. Lidan didn't like his chances.

'Are they always like this?' she asked.

'When it comes to the cooking, yes. Brit spent too many years on his own, doing things his own way,' Aelish said with a weary smile, unwrapping the bindings from her knuckles. 'And he's still not convinced any of us are healed after that fight.' She sighed and the mirth faded from her eyes. 'I'm not sure how he's going to handle the city. It's been a long time for him. So many people in such a small space. It can be too much, even for me.'

A little thud of anxiety pulsed through Lidan and she cleared her throat. 'Is it very crowded?'

Blinking under a confused frown, Aelish's mouth opened to speak then snapped shut again in embarrassment. 'Oh no…'

Shrugging a shoulder, Lidan balled up her hand wrappings, squeezing them between her aching fingers. 'I've never been to a city. I'm not even sure what one is. Rick used to talk about them but I couldn't ever picture it in my mind.'

'Lidan, I'm so sorry!' Aelish stared, mortified. 'I should have realised—'

'No!' Lidan insisted, her hands coming up as she stepped forward to quell the trader's worry. 'It's all right! You couldn't know!'

'I should have guessed. I should have said something…'

'How could you have guessed that?' She looked flatly at Aelish until she relented with a nod.

'Well, Kotja isn't a big city, not compared to somewhere like Wodurin.

That's the centre of a whole empire, while Kotja is just the tiny capital of a kingdom hemmed in by mountains. *They* are the reason we haven't been overrun by the Empire. That and our allies.' A shadow passed over Aelish as she spoke of the Empire, perhaps the ghost of a memory long ignored. Lidan didn't want to follow where that shade led, lacking any desire to dig up the sun-bleached bones of someone else's past. She had quite enough of those to carry herself without taking on the burdens of others. Still, it intrigued her.

There was an ancient hate between these nations, running deeper than she could fathom. It was in Ran and Brit, less so in Eian and Zarad, and she wondered what they'd seen. She shuddered. Was her mother at the heart of any of it? Had she or her ancestors—*Lidan's* ancestors—been party to the pain she sensed here?

For now, she didn't want to know, turning her mind back to the city of Kotja, and Aelish's wistful recollections.

'It's beautiful, though. Small, but very pretty—especially in winter. Towers and spires nestled in the head of a valley, some buildings even carved into the stone of the mountains. Bridges span the river through the middle of town, and at midwinter every window in the city is lit with a candle or lamp.' A faraway look overtook her face, light dancing in her eyes as if she could see it twinkling in the distance. It was alluring in its mystery, and despite the dangers of travelling so far from home, Lidan desperately wanted to go there.

For a moment, longer than a held breath, Lidan let herself fall into the notion that she might live in such a place one day. She wouldn't. She knew this. Doubted she'd ever walk the road back from where she intended to go, but for just a little while, it was nice to pretend.

'Have you seen snow?'

Lidan nodded. 'Not up close, though.'

'It glistens. It's the only thing in the world that sparkles like the stars. It's as though diamonds fall from the clouds themselves. In summer you can see it on the peaks, but in winter it blankets everything. It's the most beautiful city in the world.'

Shame slid down Lidan's back like a cold drop of rain. 'Is it wrong that I'm excited? I should be—'

A hand caught her wrist, pale as ice, marked by a spider web of fine scars but warm as the sun. Lidan looked up into Aelish's eyes. They were green, like her mother's had been, shining with unshed tears.

'No. After everything that's happened, everything you lost...' She glanced at Brit, his dispute with Zarad diffused by Eian and a joke told at Ran's expense, the three of them laughing as he smirked from the edge of the camp and made a rude gesture. Loge's memory still tormented Lidan, a dark abyss at her back wherever she went. The others seemed to have put aside their hurt, living each moment as it came without always holding the weight of the past. 'We have to take what little joys we're given. That's not wrong. You can't live under the yoke of hate and sorrow forever. You might as well drink poison.'

Lidan ate her supper in silence, held in the murmuring embrace of her companions' rambling conversations. They passed the time joking and making fun of each other, reminding her of a ranging party. It was a comfort, though she didn't understand half the jokes or the words. They spoke only in common, though that may have come from necessity rather than any specific kindness to her.

The only one amongst them who didn't speak at all was Thanie. She remained close to the fire, hands bound, carefully sipping broth from the side of a wooden bowl. As the others drifted away, either to sleep or to find more firewood, Lidan watched the flames until eventually, she felt she was alone at edge of the fire's warmth.

A scatter of stones clattered beside her and she started sideways, her hand grasping for a knife only to find empty air, the weapon laying in its holster on her bedroll a few feet away. A blue-black bird, made entirely of smoke and shadow, hopped toward her and she sighed.

It was the craw—the mysterious spirit of a dead bird that had followed Lidan since she'd freed it from the bonds of a cursed toy. Though only a few weeks had passed, the moment stood at such a distance it seemed like a lifetime had come and gone. The bird bounced closer and tilted its head, the shine of its black eyes catching the orange of the flames. The last time she'd touched it, it had snatched her away to a place between worlds. It hadn't been a pleasant experience. She'd sworn off voluntarily making such a shift again, but as the bird approached, one tentative hop at a time, she wondered. Would it be so bad if she just let go of this place and left it all behind?

Would anyone notice?

The tip of her finger twitched toward the silky feathers.

'Don't.'

'Fucking shit!' Lidan jumped, her heart leaping into her throat. Her hand snapped back against her chest and the bird squawked, flapping and scrabbling backward before settling on a fallen log to preen. Lidan swung around to glare at Thanie, sitting completely still across the fire. 'What is *wrong* with you?'

'I know what you're doing,' she said smoothly, her unnerving grey eyes passive in the firelight.

'You don't know anything about me.' Lidan scrambled to her feet. She didn't know where to go or what to do, but she wasn't staying here to have this conversation. Several days had passed without a word exchanged between her and the fugitive magic-user. There was no reason to break that run of good fortune now.

'Oh, stop being so dramatic. I know more about you than you could possibly guess.'

'Dramatic?' Rounding on her, Lidan towered over Thanie. For the first time in a long time, perhaps even ever, she held the upper hand. Powerful in the face of Thanie's captivity, she loomed over the woman as she seethed.

Thanie flicked her fingers out from the pads of her thumbs and the binding on her wrists unravelled. 'You're my second cousin. I know your roots like the back of my hand. They are more a part of you than you realise.'

The fuck... Lidan leaned away, eyes growing wide. 'Wait, how did you—'

The witch moved her hands in a sweeping motion like scooping water from a basin and the fibres of the bonds rewound, twisting in reverse and confining Thanie's wrists once more. 'Ignore that.'

'Ignore it?' Lidan hissed, leaning down so she couldn't be overheard. 'What were you *thinking*?'

'Just getting your attention. It worked, didn't it?' The witch lifted a finger and pointed across the fire. Following the gesture to the craw, Lidan slipped into a crouch, then to her knees. None of this made any sense. 'That little stunt you almost pulled will lead to nowhere but the darkness you seek to escape.'

She turned her scowl on Thanie. 'I wish I didn't need a translator every time you speak. Do you know how to have a conversation that isn't in riddles?'

'Ha!' the woman laughed, throwing her head back. 'All right, I'll give it to you straight. You touch that creature, it will drag you to the unseen realms. The unseen realms are the places where the living dare not tread without the proper preparation or sacrifice. You get caught there, you aren't coming out *ever*.'

Lidan's stomach twisted with dread. The original purpose of the bird's spirit, trapped inside a small wooden horse her brother had played with, had been a malevolent curse. 'Why would you make a curse like that and bind it inside a children's toy?'

Her indignation was met with nothing more than a shrug. 'It was the only option at the time. You mother wanted a curse and a priggin doll was a convenient way to kill two birds with one stone. Or solve two problems with one dead bird...'

For a moment, Lidan didn't reply, watching the witch's face for a lie that never materialised. Thanie wasn't making this up. She believed all of it.

'Say I believe you,' Lidan ventured. 'I understand the curse. My mother wanted to make Ehran ill, possibly even to kill him.' She glanced over her shoulder to check the clearing for the others. Ran was nowhere to be seen, while Brit and Aelish had taken a torch down to the creek to wash the bowls. Eian and Zarad were several feet away, talking amongst themselves as they tended the horses and secured them for the night. None were within earshot. She turned back to Thanie, closing the space between them. 'What was the second problem?'

A sly smile twisted Thanie's lips. 'For your mother to do what she did, to create the marhain, she needed more than just her own magic. She needed help. It took time and enormous sacrifice, but eventually she got that help. In the end, she fell at the final hurdle. She made promises she didn't keep, and beings of incredible power were betrayed.'

If the story were a trap to snare Lidan in the shadowy mysteries of the past, it worked. She fell hard into the tale.

'The raven is the messenger of those beings. The bearer of tidings good and ill, their eyes in our world, allowing them to weave the fates of mere mortals between them. Almost all the people of the north tell it the same, no matter the distance between them.' Thanie shook her head, her voice dropping lower, drawing Lidan deeper. 'I made that priggin doll to send them a message, to tell them that Sellan, their servant in this world, had failed. She had betrayed their trust and squandered their power, unleashing a vile pestilence on the realm of the living without care for the consequences. That *thing* was never meant for you, Lidan.'

Her throat tightened and Lidan pulled away as the wind cut across the clearing, guttering the fire. It sputtered against the logs, darkness curling around them.

'The craw's spirit powered the curse and the message. It was designed to be triggered by one of your blood, one of *my* blood. Every time you touch it, it attempts to enact its purpose.'

'To send the message,' Lidan whispered. A shiver prickled across her skin, down her arms and across the back of her neck. She'd thought the priggin doll a malicious thing when its intent had been to poison Ehran. Now it reeked of a whole new darkness, a deeper magic than she could have imagined. She hadn't thought Thanie willing to commit such treachery behind Sellan's back. What they had all seen as an inseparable pair had been no more than a pretence, a facade rotting from within.

Thanie nodded. 'To *take* the message to the unseen realms and deliver it to the power behind all this horror.'

Her hands splayed to encompass the clearing and the bush beyond, and though the binding remained in place, Lidan knew what she meant. The ngaru—the monsters that had haunted their steps for four years, hunting her people into a bloody battle for survival. A chill caught on Lidan's skin as Thanie went on, trembling down to her bones.

'The only reason you've escaped the unseen realms before now is that this was not meant for you. They're waiting for *her*, Lidan. They know she failed, and that failure will have cost them dearly. Promises were made and betrayed, and if you fall through the veil again, I'm not sure your father's blood will save you.'

CHAPTER TWENTY

North of Baleanon, the Woaden Empire

Sellan hated horses.

She hated how they smelled and how they looked. She hated how they juddered along, flicking their heads, and swishing their tails. She especially hated how they managed to make every mile of road jar through the bones of her backside. But on balance, if her arse was sore, then at least she was alive.

The same couldn't be said for the inn keeper who caught them stealing one of the mounts and some supplies from his stable as they escaped Baleanon. He'd met a rather grisly fate at the business end of a pitchfork. The other horse had been taken from a farrier's yard across town. Eddark insisted it was a bad idea to take horses from the same place. Sharing the misfortune made the thefts difficult to connect and therefore harder for the authorities to track them with a description. Something told her he'd done this before. So confident they'd made a clean break from Baleanon, she hadn't the heart to tell him a thaumalux tracker with half a brain could find her in a few days given sufficient time and power.

The magic coiling in her soul, growing and recharging as each day passed, darted erratically between aching weakness and roaring strength. Its return had doubled in pace in the five days since their escape, leaving her light-headed and nauseous, breaking out in night sweats despite the chill, huddling with them in hollows well off the road. Her hands shook and her skin tingled from her nape to the small of her back, the conduit of power throbbing up her spine as it once again grew accustomed to the force of nature that had been the cause of so much anguish and consternation for her family.

Her parents had been thrilled when the same test of Thanie's magic had sparked their only child's talent. At age five she'd been shipped off to join her cousin at the Academy with all the fanfare and fuss one might expect. It hadn't taken long for elation to turn to worry. Had her only challenge been a disruptive inability to relate to her inferior classmates in any meaningful way, Sellan's transition to Academy life might have been smoother. But the rampant growth of her magic quickly outstripped her capacity to control it. By age ten, Thanie actively quelled Sellan's power. The memory of the cool rushing sensation as her cousin doused the magic still brought a shiver to her skin. It had been for the best, Sellan supposed. It bought them five more years of peace.

Her rebellious nature, in full flight at fifteen, brought the whole house of cards crashing down around them. That, and the attentions of a boy used to getting exactly what he wanted.

Try as she might, dark and dusty memories haunted her steps and stained her waking hours in the week it took her and Eddark to reach the Skree River. She barely spoke to her would-be rescuer, preferring silence rather than attempting to explain her past or how she'd come back to her parents' doorstep. They travelled at night and rested by day, taking ever more arduous routes through hills and thick forests. Eddark reasoned it would make them harder to find, and she didn't once give voice to her doubt. She just watched their backs and waited.

Nothing came, though. The dust in their wake settled on an empty road, their only pursuers lurking in the murky crevasses of Sellan's imagination. The greater threat loomed ahead—their food had run out, forcing them into a town to resupply.

Enough coin had been pilfered from the coffers of the Parben household to last months if they were careful. A spending spree would draw attention, and theft was just as likely to attract the wrong kind of notice. Eddark had many hidden talents, but she doubted he could carry off anything more complex than swiping a few loaves of bread. Neither of them was adept in the burglary field. Sellan still couldn't believe they'd managed to steal the horses. Their only option was to creep into the river town of Myrtford and find a tavern dingy enough to not ask questions of two bedraggled travellers.

The evening darkened and they turned to the east, approaching the town along the river road. Eddark reckoned anyone asking after them would be looking to the south of the town, not the east.

Sellan scowled at him from the saddle. 'How much of this kind of sneaking around have you done?'

'Me? Not a lot.' He was lying.

'Bullshit. No one just *knows* how to evade capture or throw pursuers off their trail. You learned this from somewhere.'

He kept his gaze trained on the road. 'I've got some nefarious friends.'

'Oh really?' Suddenly the ache in her legs seemed less important. This was the most interesting thing he'd said in days. 'Anyone I know?'

'Folk who help people like me get away from people like you.'

Their eyes met and Sellan's heart skipped. The horse's hooves continued to thud against the road, the leathers of the saddles continued to creak, the buckles and clips clinking gently over the sounds of dusk birds calling through the scent of evening blossoms. Clouds continued to build, the world moving on, ignorant of her indignation.

'Rebels. You're friends with rebels?'

Eddark shrugged. 'One man's terrorist is another man's freedom fighter.'

'Did you *help* them?' she hissed, urging her horse closer and leaning forward as if to prevent the roadside trees from hearing. 'You could have been executed for that, Eddark! Think of the fallout—your career as a medic, your family name—'

His frown had her shut her mouth with a snap. 'What does it matter if I did or I didn't? I'm out here with you. All of that is dust.'

Didn't he understand? He'd involved himself with the lowest and most hated of the Empire and he just shrugged? What about her family—*his* family—the name he'd taken and used to advance himself? 'Had you been caught, though...'

'I wasn't, and none of it matters now. What matters is that the things I learned might just keep us away from the Congress and their mages for a little longer.'

Down the road, the dim lights of Myrtford blinked through the soft rain leaking from the clouds. She couldn't put her finger on why Eddark's dirty little rebel secret galled her so deeply. Was it *that* surprising for a freedman of a prominent household to be involved in smuggling escaped slaves and fostering rebel activity? Was it really so shocking that he'd played her mother with one hand while holding the Empire's enemies firmly in the other? Would Sellan have done any different?

Of course not. She'd done much fucking worse.

What shocked her was not *what* he'd done, but that it was perfect Eddark—apple of her mother's eye—who'd done it. The blessed glow around him suddenly cracked and yellowed, wearing thin as she understood he was not all he appeared to be. There was more to him than obedience and a kind heart. Darkness simmered behind his deep brown eyes, a sharp edge lingering behind his easy smile.

Still, she couldn't help wondering what other little tricks he'd acquired, what stories he might reveal. That sort of a villainous tendency was bound to come in handy.

The town emerged from the drizzly gloom, the persistent fall soaking everything. Somewhere off to the right, the river hushed along, a dock of some kind lending a familiar stink to the air, banishing the scent of summer blossoms that had, for a short time, perfumed the early night. Sellan snorted to herself. Northern summers really were some malevolent god's idea of a joke.

Probably Aeris. She was into that sort of tricky shit.

The main street of Myrtford stood largely empty, the last of the town's stall keepers hurrying to close and protect their wares from the rain. Folk already indoors stayed there, those with a home to go to quickly disappeared. Anyone out in the damp by the time Sellan rode past had nowhere else to go.

Still, a single figure lingered in a darkened doorway, huddled away from the coming rain. Ordinarily such a woeful sight would have turned Sellan's attention but this time her gaze caught on the edges of the shape. There was something eerily familiar about what crouched by that door.

Its stillness, the way it held fast in the drizzle—unbothered by the mud caking the hem of its cloak—was unsettling. Unnatural. But who could know a person's mind in such a state? No face was visible amongst the shadows, the intensity of its unseen gaze following her along the road nonetheless. It couldn't be anything more sinister than a beggar, glaring at someone with enough to eat who was unwilling to share such good fortune. Sellan sniffed. She might be down on her luck, but she'd not be caught dead passing her coin to the unwashed poor.

Eddark's horse plodded ahead through a slick crossroad until they came to the river, a muddy bank built up with rough stones and timbers that served for a quay. The Skree River made a direct journey west from here, and though it was a crucial trade route for the capital, Myrtford was not an important town. A stop-off at best, a blink-and-you-miss-it speck on the map at worst. Not far to the west, the bigger and more influential settlement of Naemii stood where the Skree joined with the southern Bale River, hoarding the trade and the subsequent profits to itself. Of the two, Myrtford was just the kind of place they wanted to be.

An inn materialised through the grey drizzle, right beside where the north-south road thought about crossing the river with the aid of a barge. Sellan peered through the misting rain at the sign above the door. 'The Dripping what? Bucket? Does that say *The Dripping Bucket*?'

'Seems so,' Eddark replied with barely a hint of interest.

'What kind of name is that?

He shrugged, pulling his horse to a stop and swinging from the saddle. Cobbles hid somewhere under the mud, the townsfolk unconcerned with maintaining any semblance of civilisation so far from anyone who might care. 'I heard the owner is a retired fletch-singer.'

'An archery mage?' Now that *was* interesting. A rare and unique kind of frequency mage, Sellan had heard of only a few capable of controlling the flight of arrows or an airborne projectile with devastating accuracy. If the Woaden could find and train more of them, they might have won their litany of never-ending wars long ago, but there were fewer than a dozen in each generation, and to a man they all ended up a single degree off full derramentis madness. More often than not, they didn't survive much past their twenties, let alone into retirement.

Leading their horses through an untended gate, Eddark and Sellan offloaded their mounts to a weary, disinterested stable-hand. If the lad thought them suspicious, he was an exceptional deceiver. Sellan wasn't entirely sure he even looked at their faces. They paused for a moment in the shelter of the stable door, looking across the sloppy yard to the entrance of the tap room, their meagre possessions in the handful of bags they clutched in icy fingers.

'He must have been good to live this long,' she mused. Neither of them seemed in a hurry to step into the rain again. Eddark's thick hair was plastered to his head, his clothes soaked. Sellan suspected she looked even worse.

'They reckon he came back from the Battle of Obsidian Pass a bit... screwy.' He made a circling motion with one finger beside his temple. 'Changed the name of the inn and never looked back. Mad drunk, but not a bad sort.'

'Any of your dodgy friends ever teach you how to pick a lock?' Sellan asked without preamble. The server clattered their empty plates into a pile and moved off.

'Excuse me?' Eddark coughed, choking on dark ale thick enough to stand a spoon in.

'Lock picking? And not one of those provincial, basic things. A proper inner-city lock.'

He eyed her, chewing slowly at the remains of his mouthful. The beer was so dark it might as well have been beef broth. It looked vile but had an odd earthy scent that was mildly appealing. 'Maybe. Depends on the where and the why.'

The tap room of *The Dripping Bucket* was almost as dark as his beer, lit only with a few dull oil lamps, struggling candles and smoky hearth fires instead of underfloor heating. Figures hunched at tables, their attention on their drinks and the food, puddles of rainwater in various sizes pooled at their feet. A place like this was a crossroad, but a backwoods one. The kind of folk seeking shelter here were unlikely to be the sort one might consider as a new and trustworthy friend. Best to keep to oneself, and the patrons seemed intent on doing just that.

Sellan glanced suspiciously at the tables nearby. Several feet stood between her and Eddark and the next cluster of guests, who seemed uninterested in the newcomers picking at a heel of bread left over from their meal. She leaned toward Eddark and lowered her voice. 'My family have a house in Wodurin; a big flashy thing in the north hills. You know it?'

'I've been there almost as many times as you have,' he replied, sucking stewed meat from between his back teeth.

As dank as this place was, the food was good and warm. A contented sensation slid along Sellan's limbs to coil in her chest. It was a deceitful feeling, a taunting lie that told her she could relax, that she could rest.

She could do neither.

'Are they still maintaining a staff there?' she asked, trying not to seem too interested.

Eddark shook his head, speaking around another piece of bread dipped in oil. 'Just a housekeeper. Everyone else is down at the main house for the summer.'

'Good. We need to get in there.'

His expression became dubious, and his incessant chewing slowed to a stop. 'You're kidding, right?'

Gods, the questions! 'No, I'm serious.'

'That's the first place anyone will look for us. They might not recognise you, but they know me—all of them do.'

Sellan swirled her cider. It wasn't as good as the wine she was used to, but it was cheaper than the coastal vintages gathering dust on the barkeep's back shelf. They didn't have enough money to waste on expensive drink. The cloudy liquid spun in her tankard and she sighed.

There was a limit to how much she could safely tell Eddark, an upward point at which he would start to question their alliance. He was a healer, and with that came all sorts of complications about the value of a human life, not murdering innocent people and so on. These were concerns she was aware of, even wary of, but they couldn't stand in her way. There were things that needed to be done, no matter how gruesome and amoral they might be. The less Eddark knew, the better. Still, if he were to be of help, he needed to know the basics.

'I don't want to live there. That would be too obvious. And as you say, people know you. It's too easy make the connection. I need the money hidden in a the cellar.'

'And then what?'

'What's wrong with you?' she growled over her drink. 'I'm not going into detail *here*.'

Didn't he care if someone heard? The walls had ears in places like this, and sometimes weapons. If Congress mages were on their tail, the tavern would only be safe for so long. They might already be here, imitating travellers. Sellan had little affinity with thaumalux, so sensing another magic-weaver in a room was outside her remit. 'We need the money to get somewhere to live and set up our cover. They aren't going to let us just walk into the Assembly or the palace, are they?'

'Are you—' Eddark paused, stifling a laugh and a grin. '—going to wear a disguise?'

Staring at him deadpan, Sellan cocked an eyebrow. 'Not just me.'

Eddark blanched and pulled back, looking around the tap room with feigned nonchalance and a slow, bleary blink. 'Oh. Well. That could be fun.'

'*Fun*? Are you mad?' She felt like spitting knives. What was wrong with...

Their gazes met and she registered the glassy sheen and the deep rose flush to his bronzed cheeks. What she had thought was the heat of the fire was in fact the drink. She licked her lips, realising they were numbing, along with her face. This backwater barkeep was turning out cider strong enough to melt steel and a glance at the line of tankards at the end of the table filled her with dread. Eddark was well ahead of her, with at least double the drinks under his belt. From the looks of things, he didn't hold his liquor at all well for someone of his build. 'You're drunk. Brilliant.'

Throwing a glance across the room, she found the barman busy serving a new pair of customers. It was time to get Eddark away from the beer or they'd be stuck here past midday sleeping off a hangover and losing time they couldn't afford.

Sellan sighed. 'I'm going to sort the rooms.'

Before she could stand, a key clacked onto the table, staring at her from between Eddark's fingers. 'Paid for it when I got the last round.'

'Just one key?' Her eyes narrowed. 'Two beds?'

Eddark snorted. 'Of course!'

CHAPTER TWENTY-ONE

The Dripping Bucket, Myrtford, the Woaden Empire

The door swung open and Sellan groaned.

A bed just wide enough for two stared at them from across a pokey room. Cosy would have been a generous description.

'No, I'm not falling for that old trick.' Turning, she tried to push her way back through the door to the corridor and the taproom. 'I'm going to get—'

Eddark tossed his bag past her into the cupboard of a room. 'Wouldn't bother. Was the last one.' He hiccuped and she glowered, barely enough space to breathe standing between them. Had he been sober, he might have felt the rage radiating off her skin. As it was, he was flushed, her anger barely seeming to register as she glared hard into his eyes.

'You did this on purpose,' Sellan growled.

'The fuck I did.' Leaning back against the door frame, he poked a finger toward her face. 'Last woman who shared my bed was a blanket-stealing harpy. The bloke before her was like a starfish. You ever seen a six-foot man starfish across a bed? Ever seen a starfish? They go like *this*.'

Eddark's impression of the pool-dwelling sea creatures filled half the hallway with a display of outstretched legs and arms. If only to save herself the embarrassment of being seen with such a fool, she groaned and conceded, retreating into the room. 'I have, in fact.'

'The fish or the man?'

Her saddlebags thumped onto the floor and her slightly damp cloak found a home on a hook by the unlit fire. 'Both. My husband was a giant and I was at the same sea-side holidays as you.'

The shift in Eddark's expression was nearly lost in the corner of her eye as she glanced at the hearth stacked with firewood. A crack in his drunkenness allowed a glimpse of his usual, pensive self. Was it her mention of a husband or the summers spent at her parents' villa in Port Dava? He'd been a peripheral presence in her childhood, and when she had noticed him, it was to resent the attention lavished on him by her mother. A slave boy not more than two years senior and yet somehow treated with more kindness than the woman's own daughter.

Without thinking, Sellan rubbed two fingers together, urging a spark to ignite the timbers in the hearth. It struck and caught, a gentle wave of her hand fanning the flames, stoking it with her magic.

'Haven't seen that in a while,' Eddark murmured, entranced by the dancing glow. She glanced over and he read the question in her eyes. 'You were the only one in the family who ever had magic. When you left, it went with you.'

'Wait, you don't…' Her words trailed off into confusion, reminded again of how little she knew of him. 'I thought you used magic in your healing, like the medius mages?'

He laughed and stumbled to the bed, slumping down to pull off his boots. 'No, not me. Just herbs and potions and good old-fashioned study of bones and muscles and bodies.'

'And how do you manage that?' The smallest glimmer of an idea sparked in Sellan's mind. 'I don't imagine there's a surplus of those just laying around?'

Eddark squinted at her through his drunkenness. 'What, bodies? No, they aren't easy to come by. Most folk burn their dead down our way. Sometimes you can pick up a stray, someone who hasn't been claimed and the city has to cremate them. They charge through the nose for a fresh corpse, but it's worth it.'

Sellan's heart rate slowed; a chill crawled over her skin. She hadn't expected that. 'Unclaimed bodies?'

'Folk who've no family, or who've been missing a long while, lost in the churn.'

It hadn't ever occurred to her that such people—those who were the leavings of society, scratching at the margins, abandoned by a system not built to care for them, but to intentionally pass them by—were forsaken in death as well as in life. Life in the Empire was harsh, from the top to the bottom, for a myriad of reasons. Yet somehow it escaped her notice that there might be an entire population in a place like Wodurin who, on the event of their deaths, would not be missed.

Eddark tossed his boots toward the door, having at least the presence of mind to turn his back while she dug through a bag for something clean and dry to sleep in. A lone, unworn underdress was the best she could manage, leaving nothing to the imagination. It was only marginally better than the bare skin she was born in. By the time she wriggled under the covers, Eddark had stretched out on top of the blankets, dressed in what she suspected might be his last clean pair of pants and a shirt. This was all they had until they found somewhere in the capital to make their lair.

The bed, while seemingly big enough for them both, suddenly shrank until the sides of their arms and legs pressed together. It took Sellan a moment to realise the mattress ropes had sagged, rolling them toward each other. An awkward, silent tension seeped into the room, the pair of them staring at the ceiling.

'You never mentioned a husband before,' Eddark muttered into the semi-darkness.

Her heart gave a single hard thud and her stomach roiled. 'He didn't warrant mentioning.'

'Is he back where you came from?'

Please don't... The conversation edged toward a path she did not want to tread. 'I assume so.'

'Parted on bad terms, then?' he whispered. Sellan didn't reply, hoping he'd leave it alone if ignored. That hope died as Eddark took a deep breath. 'Does he know what you're planning?'

'If he did, I doubt he'd care.' Rolling away, she tucked her hands under her chin and crushed a shiver in her fist. 'None of them would.'

'You had a whole family, didn't you?'

Don't take that step...

'Children?'

Fuck you, Eddark Parben. 'No.'

'Liar.' His softly slurring voice cut her like a shard of glass. 'Gods, if they could see you now.'

Anger trembled through her body, her nails biting the soft flesh of her palm. 'Like I said—they wouldn't care.'

'Oh, but they would, Sellan. Family always does.'

She spun back to face him, his features obscured in undulating shadows. 'Family? The fuck do you know about family? They didn't lift a finger to protect me—not any of them, not once, not ever. They threw me to the wolves, then shoved me into the pit when I dared to claw my way back out.'

'Just like mine,' came his reply.

She grew still. 'They what? How do you... How could you know that? You can't have been more than a toddler when you were sold to my mother. Younger even...'

'Research. Years of it. Following stories that seemed too mad to be true, comments heard about the house when no one thought I was listening. It's a tale for another night and a lot more beer. Actually, I'll need something stronger than beer.' Eddark leaned toward her, his breath on her skin, the earthy scent of drink not nearly as repulsive as she'd hoped. 'You get me some of that Harbern mash your father keeps hidden in the cellar of the big house. Then we'll talk about all *this*.' His hand circled in the tiny margin of air between them.

'This? I've no idea what you're—'

'What we're doing. What you're planning. You think I don't know you're keeping things back?'

'So what if I am?' Sellan replied sourly, not knowing if her feigned dismissal of his concerns even made a dent.

Eddark's voice dropped, low and rumbling. He didn't move any closer, but his presence seemed to encircle her, filling the room like heavy fog. 'We want the same thing, Sel. We just don't know it yet.'

Not more than a few weeks ago she couldn't have cared less if someone disapproved of her methods. In fact, she would have actively encouraged them. It made for a more entertaining journey to her destination; watching them struggle against her, trying to thwart her every move without knowing she was ten steps ahead. Yet Eddark calling her out, challenging her, demanding answers, sent a lance of shame and fear through her chest.

She hated him for it, but it didn't change the reality. What she'd thought to do alone was no longer possible without help. She fucking needed the bastard, and if he turned away now, she'd be dead within a week.

Had she not heard the exhaled breath from the far side of the door, Sellan wouldn't have known someone waited beyond the threshold of their tiny room. She'd escaped the covers, in need of a dripping bucket of her own, padding across the cool timbers and threadbare rugs as quietly as their creaking moan would allow.

Eddark didn't wake, stirring and snuffling before settling again to sleep. At first, she thought the sound a trick of her ears, reflected noise made by Eddark, not someone lurking in the hallway. A pause longer than a heartbeat was all it took, the scuff of a boot and the protest of a floorboard giving it all away.

She stood from relieving herself, regretting the last three tankards of cider and her lack of foresight in collecting a jug of water from the server before retiring. Her mouth as parched as a dry season plain, she slid her bare hand along the guestroom wall. A gentle shunt of frequency magic, no more than a spark, rippled away from her fingers. Eyes closed, she let the vibration tell the story; a pale blue image reflected through the frequency, a vivid if obscure picture of what stood beyond the confines of the room.

The attention of the lurker piqued, their gaze coming up to scan the corridor as Sellan watched in her mind's eye. They'd felt it but didn't know exactly what she'd done. They didn't seem to know she was there.

A shining star crest gleamed on the breast of their robe as her magic rippled over it and moved on. The Congress of Mages. Not a tracker, or they would have felt her pulse like a stab to the eye. Likely an elemental, either a local or an unfortunate soul too weak to warrant a better posting. Had she been sent to a shithole like Myrtford after graduation, she might have welcomed the opportunity to serve on the eastern front. Might have even volunteered for the navy, just for a change of scenery. That this dull edge had ended up here didn't speak highly of their skill or intelligence, but they'd found her and they were right outside her door. Underestimating them would be a grievous error.

A glance over her shoulder found Eddark sound asleep, his frame illuminated in the glow of the half-moon beyond the window. What he didn't know couldn't hurt him. What he didn't see couldn't colour his mind against her.

It was an easy decision in the end.

The door swung open and she was in the hallway before the robed figure had a chance to blink. At the flick of her fingers a light gust of wind brought the door to a gentle close behind her, her body weight cannoning into the mage and throwing them into a cluttered storeroom. That door shut with the same assisted silence and Sellan's hand hovered over the mage's throat.

A winded grunt was all they managed before they realised what had happened, freezing the instant they registered the position of her hand and the glow of her fingertips. No time to retaliate, no time to defend themselves, frightened eyes darted around the storeroom. The enlarged closet, barely smaller than the space Eddark had rented for them, was stuffed with all manner of cleaning equipment and linens. There was no exit besides the door they had come through. Nowhere to run and nowhere to hide. Eventually, the mage settled their wide-eyed stare on her face.

'You're up late,' Sellan whispered.

'So are you.'

Snappy, given their unenviable position. Did they have backup in town? Were they the nightshift, while other more powerful mages lay in wait for a proper arrest tomorrow?

'I had business to attend to. What's your excuse?'

The mage licked their lips, a slight tremor to their movements that no degree of bravado could disguise. 'Much the same.'

'Ugh,' Sellan muttered, rolling her eyes. This was going to take forever, which was probably the point. Her fingers twitched, contacting the mage's neck. If they hadn't been still before, they practically turned to stone at her touch. Her expression flattened, eyes dead to the fear. 'This is the single chance you will be given. Your mission, your crew, your timeline. Who sent you and what were their orders?'

'You can't run from us.'

'That is *not* what I asked.' Her fingers pressed harder against flesh and the mage winced. 'Who sent you and what are your orders?'

'You were reported to the Baleanon office.'

Sellan's heart pounded like a battle drum in the heat of a fray. 'By who?'

'As if it matters!'

Her nails bit hard and she ground her teeth. 'It fucking matters!'

Their laugh tore shreds from her confidence. Whoever they were, they were unafraid to die. Such conviction *had* to mean they had back up somewhere, but how close and how many, she was never going to find out. It could all be a bluff, of course; an elaborate ruse to shake her resolve and send her running. Getting the most basic information was like squeezing blood from a stone. 'It was an anonymous tip. I figured you'd reveal yourself. Messages came up the road days ago.'

'I? So, there's only one of you… Did they promise reinforcements? Someone to help you bring me in?'

They snorted. 'What would I need that for?'

'Oh dear,' Sellan purred, leaning in until her breath washed across the side of their face. 'That wasn't very smart.'

Their face twitched, tiny lines of betrayal signalling their truth. Confident they might be, but they didn't have all the information. They knew to look for her, but the why was unknown. She was an enigma, and their facade began to thin.

'You have no idea who I am, do you? They didn't tell you and you thought you could bring me in on your own. A nice clean arrest? Something to crow about on rotation back to the Congress?' With a click of her tongue and a shake of her head, Sellan feigned pity and sympathy she would never feel. 'I wonder, what did they tell you?'

Her grip tightened on the mage's neck until they jerked against her hold, gasping as the glow from her fingers sliced through their skin. 'You're wanted for questioning. Something about a break in. That's all I know!'

'If only that's all there was.' Their eyes met and a cold smile tugged at the corners of her mouth, a mirthless thing that did nothing to warm the black stone crusting over her heart. 'I wonder if the Academy still tell stories of the girl who got away, the one who left ash and scars in her wake? I wonder if anyone still walks those blackened Academy halls, or did they pull it all down and start again? Did they ever get the stench of burnt flesh out of those ugly purple drapes?'

Her memories flashed fresh and bright; the Academy in flames, the lock on the door that no one would ever break. The screams had been enough to turn her stomach, but it was all for a reason. No death at her hand was ever a waste. She *always* had a reason.

The mage's eyes grew bulged as their airway collapsed, flailing arms and legs in a panicked, vain effort to throw her off. Knowledge blazed in those eyes, denial and disbelief feeding the frantic thrashing against the storeroom wall. They *had* heard the stories. Spoken in hushed tones she imagined, but the memory endured. The girl who turned the Empire on its head and escaped, never to be seen again, had come home.

Did they know she was coming? Did *he* know?

This poor being didn't have the answers. Someone had severely misinformed them of the nature of this arrest and the nature of the mage they would come up against. If the Baleanon office knew Sellan was here, they wouldn't have sent a junior lackey, they would have sent an army. They would have turned every blade and magic-weaver they could muster on her, if only to stop her taking a single step toward the capital. Whoever had reported her didn't know who she was, and their mistake would end the life of this backwater mage in the broom cupboard of a grotty inn.

Their death would not be in vain. It would not be a waste. Magic poured from the bones of their spine, the thrashing becoming a seizure, Sellan's fingers burning white-hot. Absorbing what little magic they had took mere moments, light fading from their eyes despite the blazing glow around her hand.

In the end, there was more blood than power, a slick pool gleaming at her feet in the faint light. Tingling coursed through her body, singing along her limbs, her skin sparking as the power soaked into her soul. Trembling from the release, Sellan gasped as the last of the power settled, warming that cold, empty place once more.

No death was a waste.

She left the body to cool on the floor of the storeroom, closing the door without touching the timbers. There would be a laundry here somewhere, a quiet place to wash away the blood and discard the stained underdress. She might even find that jug of water. By the Dead Sisters she was parched.

CHAPTER TWENTY-TWO

South of the Ice Towers, Tolak Range, the South Lands

By the time they reached the foothills of the Ice Towers, Ran had tried every trick he could think of to pull Iridia into the realm of the living, including insane ideas he didn't realise he had the capacity for. An exercise in frustration and wild trial and error, he'd done everything from attempting a split in the fabric of reality to physically hauling on her soul with his magic. Contact with her manifestation of skin didn't make a scrap of difference and neither did manipulating her presence with power.

Each night they'd sneak off after the evening meal under the pretence of collecting firewood, searching instead for a nice, secluded hollow in which to practise. Desperation had wormed its way in. Try as he might to deny it, time was running out to keep things just as they were. The gods knew once they reached the northern side of the Towers, there wouldn't be a hidden hollow to retreat to. The expanse of open grassland stretching northward to the woodlands of Arinnia wouldn't disguise his efforts, nor was he ready to admit what he was trying, and failing, to do. Once they crossed under the mountains, he had to stop.

By day Thanie watched him from the corner of her eye, keeping her distance and her peace. Something in her narrowed gaze told him she knew more than she let on. Could the witch sense the discharge of magic? He sometimes thought it left a scent on the air, a kind of burnt fume that clung to his clothes. Perhaps she felt his magic surging back to life, so much faster than it ever had before. Had Eian or Zarad sensed it?

He often stared at his hands as he walked into the trees, wondering if his contact with Thanie hadn't triggered the release of some terrifying potential, hidden for years, banked up behind indelible walls, unable to be turned to use. *Something* had changed. Something deep within. A breaking of a final seal between the young man he'd been and who he was becoming.

His Sight cleared and his registry of frequency heightened, naturally occurring plumes of shimmering magic became visible in the bush. He hadn't known such things existed before. The fire under the cooking pot and the water rushing through the creek called to him, but not with a voice he could hear. He *felt* them; their structure, their particles moving in unison, now obvious when he narrowed his eyes and peered through the veneer of reality. Iridia noticed the change. Any time they were alone she drew down on the magic more than in times past. Less gently and with more confidence, until she became almost completely solid.

She walked beside Ran now, following a game trail to a creek-side beach warmed by the failing light of the summer night. Her bare feet crunched across the coarse sand, the sound filling the easy silence. Her physical presence soothed him more so than when she existed as just a voice in his head or a gleaming presence at the edge of the light. Whatever the changes in his power, he didn't truly care. As long as it opened a door to saving Iridia from a fate in the place beyond.

'Have you noticed how many dradur we *haven't* seen since we left the village?' Iridia murmured as they reached the edge of the bank and sat on the sand.

Ran nodded, glancing into the dappled evening shade. 'I wouldn't mind betting there aren't many left. There can't have been more than a few thousand to begin with. Lackmah wasn't a huge town.'

She laid back, closing her eyes, and folding her hands behind her head. 'Before the massacre it was the biggest it had ever been. War was good business. It almost doubled in size in the time I was alive.'

'Even so, the dradur are finite—there were only so many of them made,' Ran reasoned. 'Any of them south of the Towers would have been drawn to Thanie once her wards fell.'

Their eyes met. 'Then it's likely she's warding them now. Why wouldn't she? She wouldn't go stomping through the wilds without protection, would she?'

A reluctant nod was all he would concede, stripping a thin twig of its leaves with fidgeting fingers. 'Suppose not.'

When Iridia didn't reply, he glanced over and found her watching him, solemn blue eyes piercing right through his walls. 'We don't have to keep doing this,' she said. Her low voice rumbled with sincerity that cut to his core. 'At some point we need to stop.'

'Is that what you want?' Ran asked. The barbs of truth caught in his throat. It was only a matter of time before they had to admit defeat. He'd happily follow Iridia's lead. He didn't want to push something on her that she didn't want.

But...

But what if they tried one more time, another way, with a bit more effort? What if the next time was the time it worked?

Iridia sat up, crossing her legs, and tucking her shift into her lap. Sometimes Ran could ignore the state of her by focusing on her face. Sometimes he could glance past the blood stains and the wounds and hold her gaze, listening to her voice. Half the reason he didn't want the others to know what he was doing was because he didn't want to admit just how far gone he was. The sensation building in his chest gained weight with each passing day, fuelled by magic and sheer fucking desperation.

How long did they have? How long before Iridia's time ran out? How long before he had to accept that no matter how powerful he became, she was going to vanish? How long until he had to pull himself together and get on without her?

'No, Ran. It's not what I want and you know that. But you're exhausting yourself.' For a moment she looked like she wanted to touch him, fingers twitching outward. Instead, she curled them back into a loose fist. 'You're pouring everything into these futile attempts to pull me through. I'm not sure it's worth it.'

'I'm not exhausting myself,' he lied, clearing the truth from his throat before it betrayed him. She must have seen it though. Her head tilted in that way it did when she knew he was lying, and he turned away before the flush of his cheeks completely undermined his argument. He'd pushed the limit of what his new reserves could take and still it wasn't enough. Iridia only ever got as corporeal as she was now—translucent enough to see the shadows of trees and rocks through her frame. 'Just once more,' Ran urged, on the verge of pleading but not yet falling into that pit of despair.

Iridia raised a brow, pushing the curtain of her silver-blonde hair back from her face.

'Just once more. That's it. I promise.' The last word barely made it out.

The pause dragged until he felt sure she'd refuse, cruel, hot prickles of certainty crawling up his back.

Iridia stood and brushed herself off. 'Do your worst.'

The sun had all but disappeared from the western horizon. Darkness had begun to wrap its long, fathomless arms around them. Biting insects zoomed past Ran's ears, undeterred by the magic radiating from his skin, many falling victim to the hot flashes of light snapping from his hands. A graveyard of charred, shrivelled bug corpses littered the sand.

He didn't have long. Someone would come looking soon and he hadn't even started on the armful of firewood he was expected to bring back. Eyes closed, hands held toward Iridia, his magic formed a cocoon around her. In his mind he imagined power pulling her through from wherever she was tethered.

The force shook the coarse sand of the beach, sending it in fizzing, vertical sprays as the frequency of the spell vibrated the rocky ground beneath. The air crackled with hot, humid lightning, dry enough to spark a wildfire. Sweat dripped into Ran's eyes, his mouth tacky and his muscles aching with the burn of magic. If he kept this up, he'd blister his hands so badly they'd peel sheets of skin by morning.

Yet despite the extraordinary power rippling through the fabric of space by that chattering creek, the bond between Iridia and the place between hadn't weakened in the slightest.

'Ran,' Iridia gasped. 'It's time.'

'I can do it,' he grunted, 'if I give it a little longer.'

'Ranoth, please…'

'I can do it!'

'You can do what?'

The demand pierced the twilight and Ran's eyes snapped open. Several paces away, Thanie watched them with an expression of curious bemusement. Ran's magic held despite his surprise, cast in ropes from his hands to Iridia's waist, pulled taut, oscillating light coursing between. His attention narrowed on the witch.

Her bonds hung loose from her wrists, dangling in the breeze. One hand came up and made a downward motion, forcing gentle pressure against Ran's arms until they dropped to his sides. The sizzling magic winked out with a loud cracking sound, releasing Iridia from its embrace. 'I suggest you stop this before you give yourself a brain tumour.'

He screwed up his face. 'A what?'

'Nothing. Never mind. Stop pushing so hard. You'll only end up hurting yourself.' The witch wandered over and stood directly between him and his ghost, folded her hands, then eyed them both. 'Did you think I wouldn't notice?'

'I have no idea—' Ran started. At least she had the grace to pretend she was surprised, even if it was entirely for show. Feigned consternation fell to cold assessment, Thanie's cloud-grey eyes somehow luminous in the deepening dark.

'I don't know what you think you're doing, but you're lucky it didn't work.' Her gaze settled on Iridia, and the younger woman lifted her chin in defiance. Thanie chuckled. 'You always were a spark, even to the end. I don't remember many of them, but I do remember you. One of the last, if I recall. There were *too* many, all told. A ridiculous endeavour I should've stopped before it began. But, here we are.'

Surprise tingled up the back of Ran's neck and Iridia's mouth fell open. 'You can see me?'

'Of course I can see you! You're drawing magic off him like a snake absorbs warmth from the sun. You always have. Only now there's more to take than before.'

Ran glanced at his hand and flexed his fingers. Thanie was right. He'd expelled untold energy in his fruitless attempts to bring Iridia through the veil, yet his magic seemed to refill at a pace. 'Why should I be glad it didn't work? You told us she had to make a choice. That's what we're doing.'

'Had your exercise worked and brought her back to a fully corporeal form, your little power ropes would have ripped her in half.' Thanie's words echoed across the creek, cutting through Ran's stunned silence. A glance at Iridia showed his horror reflected in her eyes. He could have killed her in the act of saving her? The witch looped her long, dark hair back into a knot tied off by a leather strip, then cracked the knuckles in her left hand. 'I believe *this* is the spell you're looking for...'

Her fingers splayed wide and she pushed her hand toward Iridia. With the aching slowness of poured honey, Thanie twisted her hand as if turning a wheel, curling her fingers around into a fist. The air thrummed; deep, soundless pulses thudded through Ran. Iridia lurched, falling through the surface of something invisible, the membrane of reality peeling back from her skin until her cheeks flushed pink.

Gasping, Iridia toppled, slamming hard onto her hands and knees, sand spraying out from the impact. Ran darted to her side and caught her by the shoulders. Warmth bloomed beneath his hands, the weave of her shift smooth against his trembling fingers. The wound at her throat oozed dark blood and she wheezed, her desperate blue eyes locked with his as she choked for breath.

'Wait—she can't breathe! Thanie, she can't *breathe*!' Ran rounded on the witch and Thanie flicked her fingers outward from the fist. The air pressure shifted and the temperature plummeted, a concussive force shoving Iridia out of his grasp and back through the veils between worlds.

She crashed to the ground, sprawling across the sand and clutching at her neck, sucking in deep, heavy breaths. Except they weren't true breaths; Ran knew that now. Dread clenched his stomach, the truth laid bare in such vivid colour he couldn't dismiss it as speculation. Iridia could survive where she was, wounded and mostly dead. In between, she could exist. Out here, in the realm of the living, she was a fish out of water, too broken to survive. His hands ached for the warmth of her skin as the flush in her cheeks faded and the ooze at her throat evaporated.

The pressure in the air returned to normal as the seconds ticked by, the heat of the evening creeping in, close and tight.

Despite the humidity, Ran trembled, impotent rage welling up from the deep place he liked to keep such feelings of self-pity. He turned on Thanie and snarled, 'What did you *do*? How did you do that? Is that the spell you used to heal Lidan's arm?'

Thanie shrugged as if it were a small thing, a trifle. 'I pulled Iridia through the veil from the unseen realms. And no, Lidan's shoulder was a simple medius incantation.'

'A what? Why didn't you tell me you could do that?' Shaking with fury and unrecognised exhaustion, Ran swung a hand in Iridia's direction. 'Why couldn't she breathe?'

'Because the full spell requires more than the exertion of a lot of power in the right place, Ranoth.' Thanie's tone wasn't unkind, so much as it was apathetic. She could well have been scolding a schoolboy error on a history exam. 'All I did was pick a lock. Unfortunately, without the rest of the things you need, it isn't, and can't ever be a complete resurrection. You can't just wave your hands and mutter a few words. If returning someone to life were even remotely easy, people would do it all the time. Sellan had to beg the power of the gods to make the marhain, and even then they are barely more than slavering insects in need of a queen.'

Words? Ran frowned. He'd never said words when doing magic before. He'd only lifted his hands and let it out, hoping it might do what he wanted.

Thanie stabbed a warning finger at his face, all apathy dissolving into a snarl. 'You keep pushing yourself like that, expelling *that* much energy every day, and you'll end up bursting something vital in your brain, or breaking your own spine.'

That got his attention. 'Magic can do that?'

Thanie rolled her eyes. Sighing heavily, she slumped onto a boulder and dug her boots into the sand as Iridia climbed back up to sit. 'Your magic exists in a reservoir, an organ deep in the pit of your gut. Everyone has one, but not everyone's develops enough to use. The spine is the conduit, the very reason beheading is the only proper way to make sure something magic stays dead. I've seen power like yours do much, much worse than break someone's back. It corrupts. It rots. It turns the mind into something dangerous. It does things to people that cannot be undone. Not by anything.'

'So, what, you came down here to save me from myself? Is that it?' Ran sneered. Fatigue bored down into his bones and an icy shiver wracked his body. 'Forgive me if I wear a mask of shock when a prisoner wants to kick start her journey back to redemption. Sorry, not having it.'

Thanie snorted a laugh and turned to Iridia. 'Is he always like this? So whiny. Are you sure you want to come back to this world?'

Iridia's expression darkened, her lips pressing into a hard, unforgiving line of judgement. Thanie would find no allies there.

'Fine,' the witch conceded with another long-suffering sigh. 'What you seem to misunderstand, young Ranoth, is that I don't want to help you out of the goodness of my heart. That organ is as black as the night is dark. I'm a Woaden mage—we don't *do* altruism. We do self-interest, so if you really want to know why I came all the way out here to get eaten alive by fucking bugs, then fine. You aren't allowed to die from some ridiculous misadventure, blowing your brain into a thousand pieces trying to save your sweetheart from the Underworld. That's not how this story is supposed to end.'

'I'm sorry, *sweetheart*?' Iridia broke in, affronted by the mere suggestion. Ran, on the other hand, trained his scowl on Thanie. It was all he could do to stop the shameful heat of being so blatantly exposed boiling his face red.

Thanie ignored the ghost's fury and locked eyes with Ran. 'You have a job to do, Ranoth. Killing yourself in a foolish attempt to save Iridia isn't going to help anyone.'

'I know when to stop.' Even as he said it, he knew it was a lie.

Thanie slowly shook her head. 'No, you don't. No one ever does. Iridia begged you to stop and you insisted. I can't even start to unpack how problematic that is. How do you think magic-weavers like Sellan become who they are?'

No... Iridia whispered to him.

'Derramentis...' Ran gave voice to what they were both thinking. 'This is the path of the derramentis?'

'Not yet, but mark me—the potential is there. What you're becoming is what you were always meant to be, what you would have if you'd been born in the Empire and trained properly. Whoever taught you to do this—' Thanie whisked her hands in the air, indicating the magic he'd shaped. '—failed in the most important of ways. They didn't teach you anything more than how to control your power as it breaks out. They taught you some fancy tricks and some flashy moves, but they barely scratched the surface of what you truly are. Sadly, the more powerful you become, the more dangerous you are.'

A chill prickled across his skin. Her sincerity terrified him more than her rage and magic combined. Malice and trickery, he expected. Deceit and outright lies, he'd prepared for. But honesty? That was the last thing Ran thought to hear from Thanie, and it rocked him to his very foundations.

'I'm not dancing to the tune of a prophecy,' he murmured.

She smiled sadly. 'It's not a prophecy. It's fact. You're one of the most powerful magic-weavers I've ever seen, or at least you will be. You have no idea what sleeps within you. On any other day, I'd be thrilled at the prospect, truly. But now...' The witch shook her head, and he swore he saw her shudder.

A ripple of fear rolled away from Iridia as she moved closer and a frown briefly creased Ran's brow. 'What?'

'Your feet are on the path to who you were born to be. That can't be stopped, nor should it. To dampen or contain you would be folly. But you're at a precarious point. You aren't strong enough, nor are you without power.' Thanie leaned forward, hands folded in her lap, her voice low and coarse with the weight of her words. 'What I'm about to offer isn't a favour. It's self-preservation. I don't want to die in the fallout when you finally crack. Usually, you'd walk this path with a mentor for years. That's the usual way. But you don't have years to master this. You can't walk, Ranoth. You need to run.'

Iridia shifted, Ran's heart rate rising as her anxiety pressed up against his. 'That sounds a lot like hard and dangerous work,' Iridia ventured, 'but nothing to fear.'

A sour laugh and a shake of her head told Ran that Thanie knew better. She bit her bottom lip and glanced away, a vain attempt to disguise the gleam of tears. 'No one in their right mind would take this course. Every-one I know who tried to rush the process ended up dead.' She met his gaze, and it was his turn to shudder. 'This is a sprint you may not survive but we have no choice, not if we want to stop what's coming.'

So, it all came down to this.

Sellan.

Sellan in the north, planning and plotting, doing unspeakable things to only the gods knew who. The creator of the dradur, the ngaru, the marhain, bending her will to make more abominations to stalk the land.

'I need to be stronger than I am, or it isn't even worth attempting to stop her, is it?' Dread pooled; a heavy, solid mass of fear settling at the centre of his being. What would it take to dislodge? 'If I do as you ask, will it end this mess and the monsters Sellan is trying to create?'

'Yes, if we get it right. She won't go down without a fight and she'll likely be beyond powerful by the time we get there. We may already be too late.' With another shrug Thanie looked northward, staring at where the mountains hunched in the darkness. 'I can only guess at where she ended up. I can't know for sure. But if I'm right, we're swiftly running out of time.'

He released a long, shaking breath and threw a glance at Iridia. Neither of them liked this. It wasn't what they'd planned, and it certainly wasn't how he'd seen this day ending. Regardless, Ran had a choice—trust Thanie and her claims, or not. The enormity of the task lurked behind its simplicity. It cut to the very core of him and demanded to know what he was willing to do to end the nightmare. Would he risk himself, his friends, his life, Iridia and her chance at a future this side of the veil? Could he put that all aside in the hope of stopping Sellan? 'The danger to me could save millions?'

'It risks us all. None of us stand much chance at walking away from this.' With a tilt of her head, Thanie indicated back in the direction of camp. 'The rest of them have a role to play, but you're the card up my sleeve, the force Sellan won't be expecting.'

'Because?' His brow furrowed. Maybe it was the weariness clouding his mind, but Thanie seemed to be talking gibberish. He wasn't special. This couldn't all hinge on him.

'She handed you your arse last time!' Thanie's arms stretched out in exasperation, and she fought back a hysterical, frustrated laugh. 'You're the last person Sellan will expect an attack from. She certainly won't think you can actually defeat her. It's my job to make sure you can. Without the right training, she'll flay you in seconds and go right back to doing as she wishes.'

'Can't *you* stop her?'

Thanie scowled. 'I only held back her power because she consented. She let me cage her because she knew it was that or death. An easy choice in the end, but not one she'll make again. She's never had access to her full-grown power and now there's nothing standing in her way. She's far more than I can handle on my own.'

'And Lidan?' Did he really want the answer to that? Did he really want the certain knowledge that he was it? The last line of defence, the shield standing between the world and the wrath of the Woaden witch?

'Lidan is resigned to this fate. It's in her eyes. Singular purpose toward a singular goal. This is the final thing she has to do, the last task. She knows what needs to be done, how it might end—in some ways she always has. She doesn't expect to survive it. She may not even want to...' Thanie slapped a biting insect from her arm. 'What hope she had for a life beyond her parents' whims died with that ranger in the tablelands, and nothing any of us say will change that.'

Silence swept the clearing, broken only by the rush of the creek and the sway of branches on the stifling wind. Thanie turned away from the shine of the moon, keeping her feelings between her and the darkness.

Ask her, Iridia whispered. Meaning passed between them like the breeze, intent and curiosity, a need to know if the dream they held might ever come true or if it was nothing but a waste of time to try.

Ran cleared a lump of anxiety from his throat, bracing himself for a scathing rebuke, aware he might sound like a needy child. 'Will I be able to bring Iridia back if I learn all this?'

'Unwinding the bonds that hold her requires one important ingredient. Without that, she remains trapped, drawn ever more toward the realm of the dead and the dominion of Ortus.' Thanie pointed at the shimmering luminescence that was Iridia and Ran stepped closer, intent on catching every word. He'd commit this to memory despite the chill it sent down his spine. 'It will take enormous power and a great deal of sacrifice, but without this one thing, no mage—no matter how powerful—can bring her back.'

Then there *was* a way, an answer to the knotted riddles. Ran crossed the space between them, boots crunching through the rough sand. The world seemed to shrink and contort as he stepped over a line he never thought he would. 'I'd go to the Underworld myself if I had to. If you swear on your life to help me, then I'll do as you ask.'

The witch's gaze narrowed, studying his features. 'You're certain? There's no going back from a bargain like this. You make it and you see it through, no matter the price.'

Ran nodded. He didn't care. He'd asked Iridia what she would pay for her freedom, and she'd wondered if the cost were too steep. Reckless it may be, but he was too far gone, too undone to be put back together. Even if Iridia walked out of his life the very next day, it would be enough to know he'd made good some small amount of the hurt and damage wrought that winter in Lackmah. 'Show me how. What's the key? Where do we find it?'

'It can't be found. It has to be *done*. A life must replace a life. The one who killed Iridia must die and take her place. The years the killer would have lived then belong to the returned soul, the victim of the crime. A clean swap, the scales balanced—a soul for a soul, so to speak. Ortus will accept no less, and even then he'll resist. There will be further sacrifice, but that's only worth discussing if we survive all this.'

Ran's heart began to pound. 'Wasn't that you? Didn't you kill her?'

'No, dear boy. Not me. Sellan killed Iridia—cut her throat while she held her paralysed in a magical trap.' Thanie's sad, knowing smile held the ghost of a wound that would likely never heal. 'To free Iridia, Lidan's mother has to die.'

Chapter Twenty-three

Fracture Pass, the Malapa, Tolak Range

Thanie's words tumbled through Lidan's mind for days after their fireside confrontation, shunting aside repeating images of Loge and disrupting her efforts to etch his face in her memory. He slipped from her grasp despite her frantic clutching, her thoughts caught in the snare of the looming fight and the revelations of the witch.

Sellan had enemies. Not just in this world, in this *reality*, but in the places between that Lidan couldn't or perhaps shouldn't have ever seen. Like Dennawal, the Shadow Rider, the shepherd of souls to the domain of the ancestors. Exactly the kind of entity one would expect in the margins of reality. It made sense for him to be involved, but the being Thanie spoke of sounded altogether different; a wicked, power-hungry malevolence. The Rider Lidan had seen didn't seem to fit that description.

Lidan kept these disturbing details to herself as they trekked the foothills and valleys, approaching the Pass and climbing steadily out of the humidity and into the chilly slopes of the Malapa. The information was of little use to her companions. Surely it didn't matter how or why Sellan had obtained the power to do what she'd done. What mattered was stopping her from doing it again, finding her before her plans gained traction. Achieving that end weighed heavy on Lidan, sickening anxiety drawing her thoughts in an inevitable spiral toward a truth she was not yet willing to accept.

Balanced precariously on top of that burden, her cycle had come and gone with its usual headaches and cramps, destroying the last slim chance of keeping a small part of Loge in this world. In many ways, she was grateful. Carrying another life into the battle ahead was not a thought she relished, hardened though she was to violence and blood. Another part of her mourned that loss as heavily as she did the rest. It was not the passing of something that had been, but something that never would—an idea, a hope, a dream—the final spark of her time with Loge.

More than just a companion or a lover, he'd been a doorway, a chance at something else. He'd offered her an impossible possibility—there was more to be had from this life than a position and title as a daari's daughter and then a daari's wife. Lidan had clung to these things since his death, only to watch them flit away on the wind, more pressing concerns taking their place. Abandoning that hope left an open wound to fester; an injury she wasn't sure, when all this was done, she would survive. All she had left was the path ahead, one foot in front of the other, until the end of this final task. A brave face and silent, hidden tears her only solace as the days dragged on.

A day out from the Pass they decided to walk the horses, picking between the twisted trunks of snowy gums and tough, scrubby groundcover, over blue-grey boulders peeking from beneath the soil, and along trails worn by wild high-country horses like Theus. After the rugged beauty of the ridges and valleys, the tunnel under the mountains sounded anything but inviting, Eian's assessment of the place not exactly filling Lidan with excitement.

'What if it's still blocked?' he called up the line to Ran. The northern prince walked beside Lidan and Theus in the baking heat of midday, the whir of insects belying the chill in the shadows that cut through their clothes the moment they stepped from the glare of the sun.

'We'll find another way,' Ran replied over his shoulder.

'*Is* there another way?' Lidan muttered.

Ran shrugged. 'I have no idea, but I'm not telling him that.'

'If we get attacked again, I'm done,' Eian went on. 'I'm going home.'

'Doesn't he have to go *through* the Pass to get home?' Heights troubled Lidan more than the dark depths of a cave or tunnel, yet trepidation circled the prospect of what they might find down there.

Since childhood, tales of ice serpents had travelled with rangers and traders, exaggeration and embellishment impossible to unwind from the truth. In the four years Lidan had patrolled the northern range, she hadn't come across one. She'd almost begun to wonder if they existed at all beyond the recollections of old men and tale-keepers. At least until these northern-ers had come to her door.

With a shake of his head, Ran glanced at the sky, as if calling down help from whatever power his people prayed to. 'Not reminding him of that either.'

'We'll just use frequency magic like last time,' Zarad said in a noble attempt to soothe his partner's frayed nerves. For a man with the brawn of a wrestler, Eian seemed mightily unnerved. Lidan couldn't tell what worried him more—the Pass or the dragons.

The big blond man gave a bitter laugh of dissent. 'Forgive me, I'd forgot-ten. That worked *so* well last time. Almost brought the entire mountain down on us. *Excellent* plan.'

Several paces ahead, wandering between Lidan and Ran, Brit and Aelish, Thanie led her mount and turned to glance over her shoulder. 'Frequency works on serpents?'

After a considerable pause, Ran replied, 'In a manner of speaking.'

'Huh,' the witch grunted. 'Interesting.'

'I love how she talks as if she's never been near the place,' he muttered. He'd become more irritable than a teething baby as the days passed, snap-ping at anything that didn't go right, from the buckles on his saddle to the cooking of a meal. 'It's *her* magic that allows the serpents to be in the Pass at this time of year.'

That didn't surprise Lidan. She didn't imagine there was much her mother and Thanie wouldn't have done to throw off their pursuers. She *was* surprised to learn the curses were still working after so long.

'Why don't you ask her,' Lidan suggested dryly. Ran's only reply was a sour scowl and she shrugged, squinting into the sun to gauge the hour. 'You two spend a lot of time together.'

A fleeting eye twitch, blinked away as quickly as it appeared, exposed the raw nerve she'd so roughly stomped on. If he thought no one had noticed or remarked on his nightly disappearances with the witch, he was fabulously naive. 'After the dra—sorry, ngaru—attacked Tingalla, something happened to my magic. Thanie can't tell exactly what, but *something* changed.'

Lidan eyed him. 'Can't or won't?'

He shrugged. 'Does it matter? She's not telling either way. This isn't the first time something like this has happened to me. Whatever it is can't be stopped either.' He paused, hesitating at the edge of an admission as his fingers squeezed the reins. 'She's been teaching me to control it, how to channel it better, so I don't hurt anyone.'

'That's it?' Such generosity on Thanie's part struck Lidan as odd, if not out of character. The older woman wasn't a stranger to helping others, offering advice or guidance in her own twisted way, but there was always a price.

'Eian's been teaching you to fight, hasn't he?' Ran countered brusquely, his infamous temper rearing up.

Lidan rolled her eyes and lifted the collar on her sweat-soaked shirt, encouraging a breath of fresh air to cool her skin. 'Yes, he has. Not sure the two are comparable, though.'

Just as the prospect of the Pass unnerved Eian, the idea of Ran taking instruction from a woman supposed to be his prisoner made Lidan's skin crawl. She hadn't snuck in close enough to watch without being noticed, nor could she understand the small glimpses she caught through the tress. He spent a lot of time with his eyes closed, maintaining an oscillating ball of light a foot or so in front of his chest. To what end, Lidan couldn't tell, and frustratingly, he wasn't about to let her in on the secret.

'How is it *not* the same? You're preparing for what's coming. So am I.' Anger flashed in his fever-bright eyes, bordered by dark smudges of fatigue.

'What the fuck, Ran? It's not even *close!*' Lidan hissed, all too aware they were at the centre of the group spread out along the trail with Thanie barely a half dozen paces ahead. 'I'm training with an ally, someone I hope to call a friend. I'm learning in the open, right beside the camp. You're off in the fucking bush doing fuck knows what with a woman you personally declared your *enemy!*'

'Enemy is a matter of perspective, isn't it?'

A growl rose in her throat and she rammed it back down, if only to preserve their fledgling friendship. 'Ah, no. It's not.'

What was wrong with him? For the past seven days he'd spiralled. Now it seemed he'd cracked. Thanie's influence mouldered at the root of it; a fact Lidan failed to miss as she watched her companion eat himself alive. With a swift strike of her hand, she caught the reins of his horse and led them both off the trail and up a thin game track, nodding at Eian and Zarad's raised brows as they passed.

'We'll catch up,' she told them with a stiff smile, ignoring their sidelong looks and the suggestive elbow Eian dug into Zarad's side. Let them think what they liked. Nothing but furious words and curses were about to be shared here. Ran seethed, stalking up the track to loop his horse's reins around a low branch, then he paced away, hands on his hips.

'Right,' Lidan snarled, rounding on him. It was time to deploy a weapon so deftly wielded by Loge that she couldn't help thinking he'd be proud. 'You tell me what the fuck is going on *right now*, or I'll kick your fucking teeth in.'

'Oh, really?' Ran spat with a sneer.

'Yes, really! We don't have time for this! We don't have time for your moods to swing with the wind, or for you to fall apart at the seams. I need you together, in one functional piece, not scattered and fractured and snarling at every word someone says. If I didn't know any better, I'd say you were on your cycle!'

Ran whipped around, incredulous. A little spark of blue crackled between his fingers and Lidan fought the instinct to recoil. 'My *what*!?'

'You heard me.' Drawing herself to her full height, Lidan stared him down. 'I can't help you if I don't know what's going on. I can't keep you and the others safe if I'm blinded by lies. I'm hauling my own baggage up this mountain, Ran. I can't carry yours as well. We have no idea what's waiting in the Pass. By the sound of it, we might not even be able to get though. We may actually be fucked. *Really* fucked. I can't have you throwing your toys out of the cot as well. I need you in your own head and ready to fight, or we're dead.'

For a while he didn't answer, preferring to glare at her for daring to challenge him and this vile mood he'd fallen into. She'd weathered worse storms than this. Numb as Lidan was, dull to anything that hurt less than the pain she already felt, Ran could glower at her all day and not reach the inner bastion of the walls she'd built. Eventually, he relented, running his fingers back through the lengthening dark waves of his hair and turning his face to the sky, eyes closed this time.

'I'm sorry,' he said, voice coarse and thick. 'Not long after we left Tingalla, she... Thanie told me I had to make a choice.' A pause drew out as he considered how best to put his thoughts into words. 'The interaction with her powers triggered something in me—a reaction that must be harnessed. She's teaching me to control it so I can stop the things your mother is planning.'

A shiver of revulsion rolled through Lidan. 'Her ngaru army.'

They'd done little more than guess at Sellan's plans. There was no way to know what she was doing or even where she was. All they had was Thanie's sense of the woman's whereabouts and her assumptions about her plans. It seemed obvious Sellan would try and recreate the creatures, turning them to the same ends she'd sought to achieve before Lidan was born. Thanie assured them the original monsters—those Sellan had made in Ran's homeland—could not be bent to her will, no matter what spells or curses she called down.

What Sellan needed was a fresh batch—new, properly finished creatures—that would operate entirely within her control. *That's* why the spirits in the unseen realms wanted her. *That's* why Thanie had tried to send the message with the craw. Sellan was disturbing the laws of nature and drawing on the strength of even more powerful beings to do it.

'Yes...' Ran seemed to want to say more but held back. Did he understand it himself? In truth, Lidan didn't want to know. She didn't care for more detail. Whatever Thanie was teaching him suddenly seemed to fade into insignificance. What mattered was that their pursuits were changing Ran in ways Lidan didn't like.

His dry, whip-fast humour had all but disappeared. His banter with Brit and the others hadn't been heard in over a week. He'd hardly spoken to anyone but Thanie unless it was urgent. Lidan hadn't even sensed his conversations with Iridia, finding herself wondering if the ghost woman had survived the trials Ran had embarked on.

She sighed and offered her open hands in desperation. 'At what cost? It's consuming you, Ran.'

He nodded. 'She warned me it would. I didn't expect it to effect me so quickly. There's no choice, Liddy. If I don't do this, then I won't be ready to face what comes next.'

He wasn't telling her everything, the sense of deceit deepening, unable to hold eye contact for more than a few seconds. Perhaps he was just tired, but she knew in her bones something else was going on. What could she do? Begging him to stop was a waste of breath. He wouldn't have given over to Thanie's teaching if there was another way. If this was how they rid the world of her mother's monsters, then what choice did they have?

'You know you can talk to me? If it gets too much... I'd rather you fight at half strength than not at all,' Lidan pressed, and again he nodded. Unspoken truth hung between them. Preparing for what faced them was one thing. Surviving the changes was something else. She released a breath, pushing down on the fatigue and the worry, glancing away into the trees as if the answer to her problems lay amongst the fallen leaves and branches. 'We should make camp early. Get some rest before the Pass tomorrow.'

'A wise idea.' The shadow of a memory darkened the faint light in his eyes and Lidan shivered. 'We'll need all the strength we can get.'

Stones crunching under foot broke Lidan's reverie, scattering the whirl of Ran's revelations across her mind. Aelish approached with a steaming bowl of watery broth. The trader folded her legs beneath her and settled back against the same fallen tree as Lidan, handing her the bowl and a battered metal spoon.

'He might look like a thug but Brit makes a mean soup.' Her smile was genuine but weary, and Lidan nodded her thanks. Basic yet edible, the group were entirely reliant on Lidan to gather wild greens and root vegetables to throw in with whatever game they'd shot that day. 'How far north have you been?'

Lidan sputtered her soup a little; she hadn't prepared for a conversation, fatigue muddling her mind. Taking a moment, she narrowed her eyes at the winking stars, blowing on the broth to cool it and stealing a few minutes to sift through the memories of the last four years. 'Just south of the Pass. We checked it for ngaru, but never went too far into the mountains. Never as far as the snow line. The serpents got too bold.'

Aelish pointed her spoon at Lidan. 'Those things are a curse.'

'They're just doing what they do.' Lidan shrugged a shoulder. 'It's in their nature.'

'No, not these. They should stay high up in the peaks in the summer. These days...' Aelish scanned the trees as if a dragon might burst from the shadows at any moment. 'The Pass isn't as it used to be.'

Lidan followed the trader's gaze until it fell on Thanie, sitting several feet away, hands bound if only for show. Ran had begged off training after his confrontation with Lidan, blaming the need to rest before entering the Pass in the morning. The witch had caught Lidan hovering within earshot and kept hold of her tongue, unspoken meaning in her glare muttering loudly enough. 'Good thing she's coming with us then.'

It was Aelish's turn to stumble, coughing down a mouthful of soup. 'Good?'

'If she did put a curse on the Pass, then surely it's in her interest to change it back or stop it. Serpents will eat her as eagerly as the rest of us.'

Aelish scowled. 'Perhaps. I still don't trust her.'

She looked much like the hundreds of traders who came south to Hummel in Lidan's childhood—pale, light-eyed and fair-haired—and Lidan couldn't help wondering if everyone north of the mountains looked the same. Where Lidan had thick, dark curls more like Ran's, Aelish had flaxen waves she bound in braids and a wiry figure that seemed petite against Lidan's taller, more athletic frame.

Lidan snorted a sour laugh. 'I've known Thanie all my life and still I don't trust her. It's a good way to be.'

'Not even now Ran's in her pocket?' The question was formed with such care and precision, it was almost casual. The edge to Aelish's tone gave it away. Had the others been talking?

'You noticed that too?'

The little spoon clacked against the bowl as Aelish scraped the dregs of the soup into her mouth and wiped her chin with the cuff of her sleeve. 'It's hard not to. He's been a surly shit for days. Brit says he mutters in his sleep, but I haven't heard.'

Lidan had dismissed it as bad dreams, not unlike the horrors that stalked her own sleep. It would have surprised her if Ran's dreams *weren't* haunted, given all they'd seen. But could she tell Aelish what she knew without breaking Ran's confidence? He'd been honest with her for the most part.

'He didn't tell me much. It's got something to do with my mother and what she's planning.' Lidan finished her soup and put the bowl on the ground with a sigh. 'This whole insane venture relies too much on Thanie; on trusting what she knows about the north and my mother.'

'And if she's lying?' Aelish closed the space between them and lowered her voice. 'What if she's just using us to get home?'

Lidan's heart thudded harder, the thundering beat of her barely-reined fears threatening to gallop away, her sanity dragging in the dust behind their flashing hooves. Aelish had given voice to the niggling thought tugging at Lidan's consciousness. She'd examined Thanie's motivations, such as she knew them, at every angle she could manage. No matter how hard she looked, that particular end did not seem to justify Thanie's means. Something else lingered behind Thanie's actions thus far. Something she couldn't yet see. Slowly, Lidan shook her head. 'I'm not sure that's what she wants.'

The woman titled her head and blinked in confused. 'Why not?'

Lidan looked back at the fire. 'She showed me something long ago. I thought it a confused nightmare. Dismissed it as the muddled thoughts of a frightened little girl.' Their eyes met. 'I was wrong.'

Ran knew this tale. He'd been there when Thanie revealed the truth about Sellan. Lidan hadn't the time to tell anyone else, nor had it seemed important until now.

'Thanie was manipulating my dreams—'

Aelish's eyes grew wide. 'She can do that?'

'—and she showed me a vision of something that happened when she and my mother were barely more than children. Young women at best, certainly no older than I am now. There was an accident, or something, where they lived. A fire. They ran farther than most people travel in their whole lives. If they were welcome in their homeland, why didn't they go back? Why flee into Orthia then travel all this way south? Why leave your home for a place so far away if you have any other choice?'

The pop and crackle of the fire and the murmur of men's voices filled the clearing. As one, they glanced at Thanie. She hadn't moved an inch.

Lidan went on in a hissed whisper. 'Something happened in Wodurin that meant my mother and Thanie could never, *ever* go back. She said something about derramentis, but I don't—'

'No...' Aelish cut her off, leaning back as if absorbing a blow. 'No, please tell me you misheard that.'

'Derramentis? That's what she said. My mother was declared derramentis and—'

In a whirl of movement Aelish came to her feet and rounded on Ran. 'You never told me they were *derramentis*! Are you insane!?'

Her voice echoed off into the trees, silencing Ran and Brit, frightening a flock of unsuspecting birds and drawing the attention of Zarad and Eian from their food. Thanie's eyes closed, and a bitter grimace twitched at her lips, sending a shiver down Lidan's spine.

Glaring at Ran, Aelish stabbed a finger at Thanie. 'You never told me she was derramentis!'

'I'm not,' Thanie murmured. Her eyes opened and her gaze locked on Lidan.

'Shut it, witch,' Aelish snapped. 'I'm not interested in your lies.'

A look of feigned offence creased Thanie's features. 'Lies? I speak only the truth, you waspish little ice wench. I was never declared derramentis. In fact, I was well on my way to a comfortable career as a Congress mage before I left Wodurin.' The woman lifted a finger and pointed at Lidan. '*Her* mother was the derramentis.'

Lidan didn't know the significance of the insult, but it was enough to stun the trader into silence as she turned to gape at Lidan. Suddenly she felt very small, the instinct to shrink away as strong as the urge to run, the eyes of each northerner turning to scrutinise her as if she were the mad witch and not her mother.

'I should have known.' Aelish slumped onto a boulder, rubbing the bridge of her nose.

'Did you really think she'd be anything else?' Ran asked, as if the answer were obvious, his tone heavy with weariness and frustration. 'You saw what she did in Tingalla and the creatures she created. How could a properly trained mage do those things?'

Thanie scoffed. 'A properly trained mage could do it easily. They just have no reason or need to. That's the problem with derramentis mages— they don't *think* like the rest of us. They don't *reason* like the rest of us. Everyone and everything is a threat; the very shadows conspire against them. You'd best get that into your heads now.' Her warning cut across the clearing, her storm-cloud glare settling on them each in turn.

'If you can't do this, you had best abandon this endeavour here and now. If you can't face the danger, if you can't stomach the truth of what you may be required to do, then I suggest you turn for the coast and take the fastest ship to Pandea, because that far-flung frontier will be a damn sight safer than this continent should Sellan have her way. Make no mistake—this is the fight you win, or you die.'

For a moment, no one spoke or moved. Lidan wasn't sure any of them even breathed.

'I don't trust you,' Aelish murmured.

'I don't give three flying fucks if you trust me. Should Sellan succeed, she will create something worse than any dradur or ngaru you've ever faced. It will be worse than every nightmare that has ever stalked your dreams.' Thanie shook as she spoke and Lidan knew it was the truth. Trust was a formality they could no longer afford. They *had* to believe her, truly believe, or they would fail. 'Trust me, or not—I don't care. But know that you will not defeat her without me. She will redraw the maps of the world if you fail, and everything you know will be left in ashes.'

CHAPTER TWENTY-FOUR

Fracture Pass, the Malapa, Tolak Range

'Well, fuck me,' Brit breathed as they broke from the trees.

Drawing the horses to a stop in the early dawn, silence washed through the clearing. The destruction at the mouth of Fracture Pass stole Lidan's breath before she had a chance to utter her own curse. Where an open space had been for caravans of wagons to assemble, a jumble of jagged boulders collected in a slump, blocking the dark throat of the tunnel.

A shiver prickled over Lidan's skin, the unnatural cold of the valley not the only reason her skin rushed with goosebumps. The eerie similarity of the rockfall—the sharp stones, the scar in the face of the hill above, the heavy silence pressing into the space left behind—made her stomach churn. Though it stood miles and miles away, she saw nothing but the catastrophic collapse that killed Loge.

The hot sting of tears met with a furious rebuke, quickly blinked away. Now was not the time.

Shrugging her thick pelt-lined coat closer, the fur tickled her chin in the bluster of the wind as she squeezed the cold from her gloved fingers. It shouldn't be this bitter so close to midsummer, even at this altitude. The temperature had plummeted as they crossed the last few miles, the call of bird song fading away, the rustle of small creatures in the trees falling silent. Something abnormal had a grip on the Pass. Nothing was as it should be.

Aside from the near freezing temperatures, the terrain was clear and unencumbered by cloud or mist, giving them an excellent vantage to assess the absolute clusterfuck that was the mouth of the Pass.

Thanie leaned out from the line of travellers and raised her brows at Ran. 'Did you do that?'

'*That* was me,' Zarad corrected, red ringlets falling in front of his eyes as he sketched a mockery of a salute. Was he fighting back a grin? He had a history of breaking mountains, then. At least this time he hadn't killed anyone. Nausea rolled through Lidan and she tore her gaze away.

'You'd best hope you can undo it,' came Thanie's retort.

'You're joking? I can't—'

Ran stepped forward and lifted his hand, a hush falling over the clearing. Fingers curled as if to grip the boulders from afar, the horses' hooves thumped against the soft soil at the change in air pressure. Theus snorted hard, flicking his head high. Rubbing at the horse's nose and cooing gently, Lidan glanced back at a burst of blue light pulsing from Ran's hands.

The boulders trembled, tiny stones flicking free and skittering across the clearing. A deep, resonant groan pressed against her ears; a sound felt as much as heard. The first boulder began to shift, grinding at the earth and sliding awkwardly away. Ran reached through the fabric of the world and bent it to his will, his fingers trembling, his face a mask of calm.

Curiosity overcame any instinct to fear, her need to know just how much Ran had changed drawing her forward. Lidan's mouth fell open with a sharp gasp, a cold sweat breaking across her skin. Instead of clear, bright blue eyes, luminescent, blistering-white orbs glared as Ran turned his power on the stones. The air thrummed, a metallic taste not unlike blood settled on Lidan's tongue.

She backed away.

Who was he now? This was not the Ranoth she had come to know. This was someone—some*thing*—else.

None of the other northerners looked like they knew what was happening. Zarad reached to stop Eian marching forward to grab at his friend, while Brit angled between Aelish and any threat the prince might pose. For once, the trader didn't object to the overprotective reflex, and Lidan didn't blame her. The only one among them seemingly unbothered, if not a little pleased, was Thanie.

The older woman watched with a smug smirk, her gaze trained on the violent blue light oscillating from Ran's hands and the uncanny movement of boulders that weighed more than ten men could lift. Was this what he'd been training for? Was this what encountering her power had done to him?

Tense minutes dragged by; a collective breath held while boulders scraped away from the tunnel mouth. Soon a space wide enough for the horses gaped in the jumble of rocks, like a tooth knocked out in a fight. With aching slowness, Ran lowered his arms. By the time he turned back to the group, the incandescent white had faded from his eyes, leaving them bloodshot and bordered with deep shadows.

'What the ever-loving fuck was that?' Eian demanded. He'd let his beard grow; his jawline now about as curvaceous as a brick. The terrifying effect it had on his scowl made Lidan's heart skip.

Ran glanced at his hands with a somewhat bewildered expression and Thanie stepped forward, leading her horse toward the opening. 'A proper deployment of frequency and elemental magic, dear. Maybe one day you'll let yourself learn something more than party tricks too?' She glanced over her shoulder and winked at Eian, who growled in his throat.

Zarad put a hand on his chest again. 'Leave it, my love. She's not worth it and she knows she can beat you.'

'She's still allergic to pointy steel like the rest of us,' Eian snarled. He practically vibrated with impotent rage. They all knew Thanie was an uncomfortable necessity to the achievement of their ends, but the means were beginning to wear. How long before some of their party stepped away from that grindstone in favour of a little peace? The ancestors knew some days Lidan wished she could. Her face and neck ached from clenching her jaw while she slept, exhausted by maintaining their fragile alliance while Thanie shoved at the boundaries.

Zarad watched the witch disappear into the tunnel. 'That she might be, but for now we need her.' How he maintained the voice of reason, Lidan didn't know.

'Problem is,' she ground out as she collected Theus's reins, 'the bitch knows it.'

Her comment drew a few choice words and grunts of agreement from the others, and the three of them turned to Ran. The man went about his business as if he hadn't heard them at all, checking the buckles of his saddle and bags as Eian and Zarad moved into the tunnel, muttering between themselves and leaving her alone with the northern prince.

Lidan took a step forward and cleared her throat to say something she would probably live to regret when a glimmer of light moved through the trees behind Ran.

She started, her heart thumping, mouth running dry. One knife was halfway drawn when the gleam of light became a figure, translucent and luminescent through the boles of hunched snowy gums. A fine-featured face and long hair the colour of moonlight emerged, framed by shadow and shafts of sunlight, dressed in nothing but a plain white underdress, barely thick enough to hide the nakedness beneath. The figure turned with the languid grace of a sleepy cat, their bright eyes just like Ran's.

Iridia?

The figure blinked from view and Lidan gaped, heart thundering as the minutes slipped by. Ran went about his tasks unperturbed, turning as he collected his reins and lurching to a stop at the sight of Lidan's face. 'What?'

'Nothing,' was all Lidan could croak out, shivering from a wave of cold rushing her core.

'Are you sure?' Ran turned and scanned the clearing for a threat he might have missed.

Nodding and swallowing the tightness in her throat, Lidan glanced to where Iridia had been. A trick of the light, surely? 'Of course. Tired. That's all.'

'Was it the magic?' His gaze darted to the boulders, cheeks blushing crimson. 'I forget sometimes how that isn't normal for you.'

Her mute nod became a stiff shake of her head, a forced smile her best attempt at reassurance. 'It's fine.'

It was not fine. The changes in him and their very direct link to Thanie were impossible to ignore. She'd tried—she really had—to trust and to believe, but his eyes just now... He hadn't seemed present as he moved the rocks from the tunnel. Something else had been in control, a presence as cold and unknowable as the mountaintops.

'You can trust me,' he murmured, as if reading her thoughts.

Lidan tried not to stumble as she tugged at Theus' reins. 'If you say so.'

A hand reached for her arm, gentle this time, careful not to pinch and she refrained from flinching. Instead, she turned back. Lifting her chin, she met his gaze, holding it steady as the sun swung into the blue haze of the morning. When he didn't elaborate, Lidan filled the void with the only words she could think of, brutal and hard as they were. 'How can I *possibly* know that?'

Ran shrugged. 'Do you have any other choice?'

A dismissive scoff broke her facade of control. 'You're changing so fast I don't know who you are anymore.' Lidan stabbed a finger at the Pass. '*They* don't know who you are anymore. I won't ally myself with a puppet, Ran. I'll kill you before I let you become Thanie's weapon.'

She meant it too. Her entire life had been lived at the mercy of her parents, dependant on the magnanimity of people who cared for little more than themselves. She would not allow that to happen again, nor would she allow Ran to blindly wander such a path.

Dropping his reins, he took her shoulders in his hands. Their eyes locked and the air vibrated. A sense of him washed over her, a scent enveloping her completely. The tension in her shoulders fell away into the tight grip of his hands.

'Feel that?' Ran asked, his voice as thick as the air around them. It shifted, swirling without bothering the trees. 'That's who I am at my core. That's the centre of me. What drives me, what keeps me going.'

Try as she might to deny it, Lidan did feel it. So much pain and yet... hope. Ran had hope.

Hope that he could win, hope that he could save Iridia and the people he loved. Hope that one day he might go home. That people like him would one day live without fear. That he could rid the world of a growing evil that ruined every good thing it touched.

He meant this knowledge to ease her mind, to calm her worry, but Lidan hardened against it, muscles rigid under his grip. Hope was a frivolous extravagance she could no longer indulge. She admired him for holding onto something in the darkness, but her scars ran too deep.

'We *will* survive this,' Ran pressed, ignorant or perhaps oblivious to the wall she hastily built against his reckless pursuit of an unattainable future. 'We have to. But I need your help. I need you at my side to fight these things, to destroy them. Can you do that? Can you trust me long enough to do that?'

'I will,' she agreed flatly. There wasn't another answer that would release her arms or end the conversation. He probably expected her to tear up, to thank him for his sincerity. Instead, she found her edge and cradled it close.

There would be hard choices to make if Ran took a turn toward darkness. Such an end wasn't beyond possible. Her mother had walked that road. What made him so different? Lidan would finish him before he got the chance to become her mother. Cool certainty steadied her voice. 'I'll kill you with my bare hands if you betray that trust.'

Ran's expression hardened; he knew she meant every word. 'I would expect nothing less.'

Darkness overtook them not more than fifty feet into the tunnel, the world collapsing to a black abyss. With a flick of his hand, light bloomed at the ends of Ran's fingers, a sphere of illumination forming as they moved underground.

Time passed unmeasured in silence, the events of the past few days stewing in Lidan's mind. The others continued ahead without them, her stomach's growling silenced by a handful of dried meat and a few sips of water. Alternating between riding and walking the horses, Theus only baulked at the shadows once or twice. When the fatigue became too much, Lidan climbed into the saddle, hunching away from smacking her head into the roof. By the time she thought it must be sundown, her back ached something cruel and her hunger refused to be sated.

Sound didn't work as it should down here. It echoed and it didn't, the hard surface of the walls keeping voices close while the ground reflected the loud clop of hooves off into the distance. The people of the South Lands told stories of the spirits who slept under the Malapa. The Cooderi, builders of the peaks that held up the sky, who fell asleep beneath them, exhausted by their efforts. She didn't imagine they would appreciate her companions stomping all over their resting place. Perhaps that was why they kept the ice serpents near—a deterrent for anyone too stupid to be put off by a place as dank and oppressive as this.

'Can you sense them?' Lidan wondered, keeping her voice low, her mistrust ebbing away beneath waves of trepidation.

'The serpents?' Ran asked and she nodded when he glanced over his shoulder. 'A little. They'll hear us well before we hear them. They sense vibrations in the rock. The sooner we cross to the other side, the better.'

'How long?' She narrowed her eyes at the faint glow in the tunnel ahead, ignoring the rapid thud of her heart.

'Takes a day to make the halfway post, then another to reach the exit.' He shifted in his saddle. 'If there was anything I could do to cross that distance faster, I'd do it in a second.'

'No tricks like my mother used?' Her heart fluttered, wondering if he hadn't considered the possibility even once.

Ran chuckled dryly. 'That's a kind of magic I'm not sure I even want to learn, let alone use. Imagine if you dropped in wrong? Appeared inside a wall or underground? No thanks.'

'So, we go the old-fashioned way,' she said, reaching tentative fingers to trace the cool, wet stone of the wall.

It had been many years since a caravan of traders had come south to Hummel and her instincts screamed over the sound of plodding hooves. This place was wrong, twisted somehow into a false version of itself. What should be, was not at all. Her heart told her to flee, to make a break for the other side before hungry jaws came hunting. Her mind stood firm against the onslaught of fear. There was little point in running from the inevitable. Better to save her energy for the coming fight. And there would be a fight. Of that she was certain. Predators learned fast where to find a meal. They would come.

'If we're quiet, we might slip by them.' Ran lifted his hand to illuminate the tunnel and Lidan wondered if he really believed that. 'If we're very lucky, we'll all make it out alive.'

'Such confidence...' Their eyes met and she saw the shadow of the truth. They'd only barely escaped with their lives last time. Did they stand a better chance now with two more added to their number? Or would the noise simply bring the serpents sooner?

A glow against the rock ahead shivered and vanished.

Lidan blinked hard. Had she imagined that?

A scream cut the close press of air and Theus shied violently, dancing sideways and missing the wall by a hair's breadth. A roar followed, tearing up the tunnel and chilling Lidan to the bone. Her thighs gripped the saddle tight, hands fighting for control of Theus' bit. Ran dug his heels into his mount's side and the mare launched into a canter, clattering toward the shattering sound of fighting.

Lidan wheeled Theus around and gave him his head. She wasn't about to be left behind in the dark.

A few hundred feet away, the left side of the tunnel opened into a cavernous space, the entry lit by a torch dropped in panic. It might have been an awe-inspiring sight if it weren't for the terror. A serpent filled the entryway, pinning down her companions and blasting them with super-heated jets of water.

A long tail slithered across the floor, coiling under its body as it prepared to strike. Scales of ice rattled violently together as it pressed up against the ceiling, crystalline armour made possible only by the frigid temperatures of the tunnel. Thanie stood with hands outstretched, a barrier of blue webbing throbbing with magic between her and the dragon.

The beast wound up, swelling its throat until it seemed fit to burst then unleashed another torrent on the cluster of people cowering before it. The barrier flexed and Thanie cried out in a wordless, grunting protest, shoving back against the blast of water and steam.

Aelish's crossbow fired in rapid succession through the shimmering wall while Eian flung spheres of magic, striking the dragon's muzzle and neck. Despite the onslaught, the barrage did little more than irritate the creature, pinging off scales made of rock-hard ice. Crumpled beside Eian, Zarad lay useless at the foot of the tunnel wall, eyes closed, blood leaking from a gash on his forehead. Had it been his scream splitting the silence as the creature took a swipe with its scythe-like talons?

A hurried glance at Ran revealed the reflection of her own horror. 'No,' was all he could whisper as his horse baulked and danced backward. He seemed frozen, unable to comprehend. 'Too soon.'

Not waiting for him to move, Lidan abandoned Theus and her knives. Rolling from the saddle, she drew a weapon she had all but forgotten. Her bow came free of its sleeve, and she snatched a handful of arrows before racing to a lump of rock jutting from beside the cavern entrance. Within seconds the bow was strung, an arrowhead trained on the back of the dragon's skull.

'Wait!' Ran's command pierced the chaos and he slid into the blind beside her. Breathless, crouching in the sparse safety of the lip of rock, he held up a hand. 'Wait.'

'For what!?' she hissed. Heart hammering, she held her aim as the dragon recoiled and shrieked, keening in a voice that surely reached a pitch beyond her hearing. The tendons along the back of her hand burned, the weight of the bow rammed back into her achingly weak shoulder. Were there more dragons out there, racing to answer that call?

'You won't get through the scales. Wait for it to strike. Wait for the scales to expand.'

Eian staggered and collapsed, exhausted, reaching to drag Zarad back into the cavern. The rapid fire of the crossbow faltered and Aelish relinquished the weapon to Brit, who returned fire with renewed energy as the trader moved to replenish his stock of bolts.

That couldn't last long. They only had so many to shoot.

'We need to move now!' Lidan shouted. Her arm began to shake. Loge had warned her against holding for too long. Heavily strung from when she'd shot with it often, the string shivered, the arrowhead wobbling despite her best efforts. The bones in her fingers ached, her shoulders screamed with the strain.

Thanie took a step forward and their eyes locked, intent written plain as day. She was about to goad the creature into attacking.

The shield crackled and bulged toward the dragon, shoving a ripple of energy up to catch the end of its snout. It jerked back, writhing away with an incredulous hiss. Surprised but not defeated, like a great pale snake it drew itself up to full height and loomed over Thanie.

A sizzling sound rose beside Lidan and she risked a glance at Ran. His eyes blanched to white, lightning snapping between his fingers with furious frequency. Burnt air coiled up her noise and she gagged.

'Ready?' he asked, his voice distorted, deeper and harsher.

Across the tunnel, Thanie roared and lunged, again thrusting her shield toward the dragon. It swung its claws, the hard points of talons screeching across the translucent surface. The witch ducked and Ran took his chance.

He stepped from the shelter and launched a volley of magic at the dragon. It swivelled and screamed, the pitched cry cutting through Lidan, stealing her breath and eroding her resolve. In one fluid movement it lost interest in Thanie, she and the others darting into the darkness of the cavern. Falling to its forelegs and flexing its scales, the creature arched its back like a threatened cat, instantly filling the tunnel.

Lidan blinked away a hot wave of realisation. Did it recognise Ran?

Magic tore from his hands, shaking the tunnel with consecutive booming explosions. If he brought the place down around their ears, that dragon would be the least of their problems. Fury built in the serpent, roaring and shrieking in a language only it understood. It reared onto its hind legs and swung its tail in a wide, scything arc.

The tip caught Ran, tossing him across the tunnel. He smacked hard into the ground, skidding over loose stones until he came to a halt mere feet from where the dragon slammed back onto its fore claws, opening its massive jaws to scream at his groaning form.

Lidan didn't think.

She un-nocked the arrow and ran.

Darting from the rock shelter, she sprinted the final few feet and slid to a stop between the dragon and the fallen northerner. Crouched between them, she stared up at the serpent, arms outstretched; bow in one hand, the arrow dangling precariously between the fingers of the other.

The dragon baulked and snapped its mouth shut with a loud crack.

If this thing had recognised Ran, if it had recognised and targeted Zarad, then it was smart. This wasn't some instinct-driven predator with its reptilian mind locked on the hunt. It was intelligent.

But would it understand what she was about to say?

Heart pounding so hard she thought she might vomit, Lidan crouched further, lowering the bow and arrow without taking her eyes from the dragon. It huffed and bunched its muscles, recoiling but not retreating. Preparing.

'Lidan...' Ran groaned.

'Shut up,' she snarled through clenched teeth. The beast's head, just barely out of reach, was scarred. Skin had been torn back, scales dislodged, leaving patches of soft, pallid flesh exposed. The tips of its wings were scorched black. One front paw continually lifted, never completely bearing full weight and a scar had formed at the creature's throat, visible as its scales flexed in and out.

Her lip trembled along with her hands as she placed the bow and arrow on the ground.

If this doesn't work, we're all dead. Please. Let it work...

'You hurt it, Ran.' Lidan didn't look at him as she straightened. 'It's in pain.'

'It tried to fucking *eat us!*'

She rounded on him. 'It's a dragon! That's what they do! Defend territory and eat things! We need to make this—'

An ominous groan rolled into the tunnel and the dragon's head swung to stare at the gloomy abyss of the cavern. The groan came again, resonating deep in Lidan's chest. She followed the dragon's unwavering gaze. Nothing moved in the darkness beyond the torch light burning at the margins of the fight.

Searching the gloom, Lidan found Thanie at the edge of that light. The older woman's face drained of all colour, leaving her gaunt and stricken, squatting at the lip of the entry beside Eian and Zarad.

The witch didn't move. She didn't even blink.

A strange, truncated squeak echoed from the cavern, followed by another threatening crack.

The dragon fled.

Chapter Twenty-five

Fracture Pass, the Malapa, Tolak Range

For a creature so large, the ice dragon vanished with shocking speed, racing away into the darkness in complete silence, its prey and their quarrel forgotten. Lidan stared at where the massive reptile had been, not quite believing it was gone.

Another crack and a groan echoed from the cavern and Ran rolled over, heaving himself to his feet. With a grunt Lidan scooped an arm under his shoulder and hauled him back to standing, watching Thanie and the gloom beyond.

'What was that?' Lidan asked. Did she really want to know? It had been enough to frighten a full-grown ice serpent. It couldn't be good.

'I have absolutely no idea.' Brushing himself off, Ran straightened and nodded at the cavern entry. 'But she does.'

In a heartbeat Thanie was gone, disappearing beyond the reach of the light, her thick overcoat flapping like a wind-torn flag in the lull left by the fleeing dragon. Aelish gaped after the witch, the same stunned expression on Brit's face. Eian ignored them all, his attention squarely on Zarad. He crouched over his partner, gently trying to rouse him from unconsciousness.

'Is he all right?' Lidan asked as she and Ran drew near.

Eian barely registered her approach. She wasn't even sure he recognised her voice. 'He's alive…'

Alive would have to do for now. With a deep breath she stepped past them, hefting an abandoned torch and leaving Ran to help bring Zarad further inside the cavern.

'Is that wise?' Aelish asked.

'We can't stay out here…' Ran told her. Their conversation faded behind Lidan, a series of suggestions and counters about what to do next.

Ahead Thanie darted through the ruins of what looked to be old buildings. Huts mostly, built of stone and timber and all in a state of collapse. The remains of a half dozen wagons lay scattered along a thoroughfare dividing the outpost, but there was little sign of the people who had brought them here. Nothing worth salvaging had survived; no weapons or food stuffs, no clothing or tools. Most notable was the conspicuous absence of human remains. Thanie jogged past as if it didn't exist, coming to an abrupt halt at the edge of a lake.

Lidan narrowed her eyes and followed. The lake didn't lap at the shore, nor did it shimmer or ripple in the faint torchlight. It was a flat, opaque expanse that disappeared into the shadows, reaching off into an unknown distance. Was it frozen? It was surely cold enough down here.

'Thanie?' she murmured. Suspicion gave way to apprehension, her breath clouding. 'What's wrong?'

The older woman shook her head, lengths of dark hair tied back in a riot of braids, her coat hunched up under her chin. She didn't speak.

Lidan took another step forward. 'What was that noise?'

'We need to get out of here,' came the hoarse response. Still, Thanie didn't turn.

'That's fairly obvious,' Ran scolded and Lidan started, sliding back from his sudden appearance at her side. 'It won't be long before the dragon comes—'

'That lizard is the least of your worries, boy.' Their daily training hadn't quite thawed all the frost from their relationship, then. Thanie glanced over her shoulder, her lips set in a hard line of resignation. Lidan could have sworn she saw the woman's chin tremble.

'What are you not telling us?' A growl crept into Lidan's demand. All her life she'd been sheltered from the truth, and she was more than done with accepting that from anyone anymore. She snatched at Thanie's elbow, yanking her around to face them and their questions. Let her lie to their faces. 'Fucking *tell* me!'

'She laid a curse in this cavern to draw down the dragons,' Ran said into the silence. 'She's the reason Zarad is half dead by the door and all these trading caravans never made it home. It's her fault. That's what she's not telling you.'

Thanie's features didn't even twitch. That wasn't it. There was something else—a deeper secret.

The groan came again, followed by the odd, high-pitched squeak. A terrifying cracking noise tore through the cavern and Thanie lurched away from the lake, shoving past Ran and dragging Lidan with her. 'We need to leave. *Now!*'

Lidan dug in her heels and pulled away. 'Not until you tell us what that is!' She stabbed a finger at the lake. The echoing sound of a thousand tiny cracks splintered the air. The ice was about to break.

'The curse wasn't to bring the dragons.' A new voice spoke and the three of them whirled around.

Glowing at the edge of the ice, Iridia watched the three of them, her expression flat but her gaze sharp. She found Thanie and pinned her, the force of the stare washing over Lidan. To her credit Thanie didn't so much as flinch as the others behind them swore in a myriad of languages. Lidan's thoughts cascaded into confusion, her mouth opening then snapping shut. The ghost held her form so firmly that she could barely see through her at all. A sharp pain lanced through Lidan's skull as magic rippled from the dead woman.

'Was it, witch?' Iridia continued, her accusation bitterly merciless as she fought to hold herself in the realm of the living. 'The curse you put here was for something else.'

A shudder rolled through Thanie, and Lidan glared at her. For a moment the woman struggled for words, her lips moving without sound until finally, Thanie sighed. 'The dragons were an unintended consequence. The curse wasn't for them, though it turned out to be—'

'Tell us what that is!' Ran roared. 'That lake was frozen solid the last time we came through here. What's changed? What's going on?'

'The wards are failing,' Thanie snapped. 'They can't take the pressure. It's been too long. They would have held as long as it didn't stir, but now I've returned, it's all failing.'

Their bickering faded to a muted rumble and Lidan stared across the lake, eyes widening as cracks opened in the ice, dark rents in the pale surface.

Two fluid steps brought Ran within inches of Thanie's face. 'Wards against *what*?'

Their eyes met and a chill rolled over Lidan.

'Marhain…'

Ran's guts turned to slurry as the lake continued to splinter. 'Marhain? The wards were against the dradur?'

Thanie gave him a sharp, stilted nod and her throat contracted as she swallowed. 'We need to leave.'

'We've fought ngaru before. We can fight them again.' Lidan's confidence lay as a thin veneer, barely disguising her hesitation and uncertainty. There was more to this, and Ran knew it. Thanie's panic had been tangible when the dradur attacked Tingalla, but this went beyond fear. This was a visceral, bone-deep urge to run and never stop, her entire body trembling as she stared at the lake.

'Not this dradur,' Iridia whispered, drifting to hiss in Thanie's ear. 'Tell them what you did. Tell them how you made him.'

Now it was Ran's turn to shudder. They didn't have time for this shit!

The witch licked her lips and Iridia moved toward Aelish and the others, who stared in equal parts horror and awe. Lidan should have been just as shocked, but she watched Iridia retreat as if she'd seen it all before. They would have of questions he had no time to answer. He needed to focus.

'*Him*?' Ran repeated, fingers curling into tight fists of rage. All he seemed to do these days was ask questions of this woman and spend the rest of the time wondering if she was actively trying to fuck him over. Already Lidan's hard-won trust was faltering under the strain. If he lost her, what was the point? He couldn't end this on his own—that much he knew.

Frustration boiled in Ran and Thanie lifted a hand to where Lidan gripped her sleeve, as if seeking comfort from the younger woman's touch. He crushed his magic down, held it close lest it unleash a furious deluge he could not control.

'We—*she* needed a leader, one strong enough to keep the others in line if she wasn't nearby to control them.' The witch's voice shook, and Ran's heart raced. 'It pursued us. Almost caught us as we trailed a caravan through the Pass. I set a trap and hoped…'

Thanie's eyes met Ran's and he shivered. Wherever this was going, he didn't like it.

'I left a lure in the lake. An imitation that reflected my thaumalux. It was a weak copy, but it worked. The ice trapped—'

The lake exploded with an earth-shaking boom, water and ice showering the shore. They staggered back as a massive sheet of ice lifted at the farthest edge of the weak light. The lake groaned again as the sheet teetered and shifted, then slipped below the surface, leaving a gaping black chasm in its wake. The violent motion of ice on water eased; the groaning and cracking faded away.

For a moment, stillness.

'My power is stronger than the lure, Ran,' Thanie whispered. 'It knows I'm here.'

'Iridia.' Ran didn't know if she could hear him. Eyes trained on the opening in the centre of the lake, he didn't dare turn to find out. 'Who did they choose?'

'He was the last one left. Once they killed the rest of us, they swept the town one final time. Found him in the lockup under the Watch.'

He spun to stare at his ghost. 'A prisoner?'

Utter disgust rippled across Iridia's features, her top lip curling. 'Tried and convicted of the most heinous crimes. An army deserter who returned to Lackmah after he'd passed through on the way to the front. He'd seen the girls. Wanted to find out how they tasted, he said. The magistrate had him down there while they thought up a suitably brutal death sentence.' Her gaze pinned Thanie again. 'Until *she* showed up and did for all of us what he'd wanted to.'

A low growl rumbled across the ice and a cold hand of fear dragged a ragged nail up Ran's spine. Slowly, he turned to the black water. Far across the shattered surface, a dark shape separated from the inky abyss. A wet slap cut the air as something heaved up onto the remaining ice sheet.

'Oh fuck,' Eian muttered.

'Aelish,' Brit managed to croak. 'Get the horses. Be ready to leave.'

'What about—'

'Get back to Zarad and the horses *now*!'

Ran didn't need to see their faces to register their terror. Two pairs of boots sprinted away across the stones, but Brit stayed. With a rustle, Lidan shrugged Thanie off, shedding her coat and drawing her knives. Steel shone in the torchlight, no doubt deadly but he wondered how they would stand against the thing crawling out of the lake.

A drip, drip, drip echoed against the cavern walls, a slosh of displaced water falling against the surface of the ice.

Ran put a hand on Brit's chest, pushing him toward Aelish. 'Get them out of here.'

The move met a solid wall of resistance, the big man standing his ground. 'Not leaving.'

'Get them away from here!'

The watcher took Ran's coat in his fist and drew him in sharp and close. 'I'm not running this time, mate.' Determination blazed in his eyes. Brit wasn't leaving unless he or the creature lay dead. A nod of reluctant agreement released Ran's coat from the watcher's furious grip.

Magic pooled in Ran's hand as he lifted it, casting light across the lake. It had only broken in the centre, leaving the rest—while cracked and groaning—intact. Sturdy enough at least to support the grisly monstrosity writhing toward them.

Two feet taller than either Brit or Eian and twice as broad, the creature moved on all fours like a mountain cat; molten ease in its careful, intelligent motion, considering exactly where to place its weight on the ice. Claws of steel scraped the surface with a screech, flicking sharp chips away into the dark.

'Fuck,' Lidan breathed. Spinning the knives in her hands, she began to pace, slipping off into the dark then shifting back again.

'What is *that*?!' Brit drew his sword and dropped into a crouch, glancing between Ran and Thanie in the hope of an answer before the thing decided to launch itself across the ice.

'That is *not* a dradur.' The statement was pointless, but it dropped from Ran's mouth anyway. It clearly was a dradur—a creature that had once been a man, with all the obscene hallmarks of Sellan's gruesome handiwork—but unlike any he had ever seen. Thick slabs of muscle shifted over the hulking frame, free of any rot or pus. Where the others had decayed before his eyes, this dradur looked as fresh as the day it had been unleashed on the world.

For a breath it paused, lifting its chin, drawing in a long, deep breath. Ran froze, his gaze roving over the parts of the monster the light managed to catch. Something about its face made no sense. The way it swung its head, nose up, chin out. Long, hungry breaths drawn in, sniffing. Then a deeply satisfied sigh.

Ran stared, straining to make out the lines of a face that didn't match; planes and features mangled like melting wax down the side of a thick candle. 'It's eyes…'

Where eyes should have been, where the glisten of light should have reflected, there was nothing. No shimmer, no gleam. Only a scarred, muted darkness. Skin pulled down to cover the holes left behind, not even a chasm in the mutilated face.

'The magistrate took them,' Iridia murmured.

'How does it know—'

'It can smell my thaumalux,' Thanie whispered. The dradur sniffed again and Ran swore he saw it lick at the air. A wet clicking noise echoed over the protesting ice and disgust crept across Ran's skin. There was no fear in its stance, only calculation. The same repulsive drive that had brought the man to the attention of the Lackmah Watch lingered on beneath the surface of what he'd become, only now it hungered for the flesh of its creator. It wanted this prey, craved it so desperately that twenty years under that ice hadn't dispelled its need. It could smell Thanie, tasting her power from across the cavern. It wanted her, and it would take her.

Ran's hand went to his sword, but Thanie gripped his arm. 'You'll need more than that, boy.'

'Tell them why. Tell them what you did,' Iridia snarled, returning to taunt Thanie, her anger perfuming the air.

'It was changed. Made bigger…' Thanie muttered. Resignation and anguish creased her face and Ran suddenly understood. She'd never meant it to come to this. It had all gone far beyond her control, beyond what she could recover. What had begun as simple revenge had become something horrific and unwieldy in its fury, unstoppable no matter how Thanie tried to slow it. 'This is only the beginning of what Sellan will do if she's not stopped.' Magic ignited at the tips of her fingers and her eyes flared white, brilliant light flashing across the darkness of the cavern.

The dradur's shriek shredded the darkness. It charged, drawing a bead on Thanie's power and launching itself forward.

Brit darted onto the ice, pitched his momentum into a barely controlled skid and swung his blade low at the creature's feet and hands. The sword connected with its foreclaws but served only to flip it into a forward roll, the creature coming up to a loping run and tearing toward the shoreline as Brit slid past.

Ran staggered back, stunned by its speed, the lightning-fast reaction of senses honed by the absence of its sight.

Thanie's magic boomed and the dradur leapt sideways, dodging a stream of power that should have torn its head off. It corrected. Came in hard, claws swinging. A shield flashed between the witch and the beast and Ran called his own magic. A sizzling shot skimmed past the dradur and he followed it with another, narrowly missing the monster's thickly-armoured back and shoulders.

Horses screamed, hooves clattering on the stone floor in a deafening cacophony. Faint voices tried to calm them. The gods knew if they bolted, the rest wouldn't matter. Win or lose, they were dead without the horses.

The pressure in the cavern changed and Iridia vanished. Ran's magic surged and he fired a furious hail of magic at the roaring beast clawing Thanie's shield. From the darkness, Brit came back swinging, his sword carving through a leg, scouring muscle from bone. The monster yowled and whirled, claws and teeth bearing down as the watcher scrambled away, blocking and parrying the attack. He hardly had time to breathe between blows.

Running footsteps echoed over the chaos and Lidan sprinted from the black. Knives in hand, she leapt from the ruins of a wagon and onto the back of the flailing dradur. The twin blades carved through flesh to bite into muscle. Yanking them free one at a time, she used them as picks to hold and climb.

The beast arched, arms whipping and thrashing with renewed rage. It spun, desperate to unseat its attacker, wildly swiping at the source of the pain.

'Now, Ran!' Lidan screamed.

What?

The creature arched again, tilting its head back, exposing the softer flesh of its throat. There was no armour there, no thick bands of meat to protect the delicate spine. He could almost see the cord—blue veins of liquid energy pulsing up the column of bone and shining through the skin.

The dradur wheeled, roaring, snatching at Lidan as she cut and stabbed at the base of its skull. The blades dug savagely into the creature and blood spurted in inky gouts.

Thanie's hand caught Ran's and he took a single quick glance at her face. 'You need more than you have.'

His magic surged again, and his entire body jolted as if struck by lightning. Her power burned through bone and his free hand kicked up. Every fibre begged, demanded, screamed at him to unleash the torrent of magic banking along his arm. He fought, wrestling for control. Just a few more seconds, just a breath longer to make sure he wouldn't kill Lidan as well as the dradur.

A final wrench from the monster and Lidan slipped, losing her grip on a knife and dropping below the line of the creature's shoulders. All Ran could do was aim and fire.

Blue flame poured from his palm, blasting through the exposed neck of the monstrous dradur. A deafening roar shook the cavern and the creature's head exploded, severed completely from the neck and obliterated by the force of the combined magic.

Globs of dark, wet flesh slapped onto the ground, the fight over as soon as it had begun. Headless and extremely dead, the corpse dropped to its knees and slumped forward, Lidan rolling away and staggering to her feet. Covered in muck, she gasped, her upper torso painted with the black, sticky ichor of the dradur's brains. She was filthy, but she was alive.

Somewhere near the shore, Brit groaned.

'You two all right?' Ran called into the echoing silence. His ears rang as if his head were stuck inside a temple bell and he drew a sliver of power to illuminate the cavern, banishing the gloom. The tiny spark sputtered but held, and he glanced down. Apparently, he'd found his limit. Thanie sank to the ground behind him with a thud and curled into a ball. 'What about you?' he asked, surprised he actually cared for the answer.

'That was not fucking fun.' She groaned and rolled away, holding her belly as if someone had kicked her.

'Lidan?'

She staggered backward and he reached to steady her before she fell. Her brow furrowed, and she squinted at him. 'What?'

'Can you hear me?' he asked. 'Are you all right?' He searched her face, then looked her up and down. She didn't seem grievously injured.

'Ringing in my ears,' she said too loudly. 'Can't hear you!'

Hurt or not, she was unlikely to die in the next few moments, so he guided her to sit beside the witch. The older woman lay shivering, eyes squeezed shut, knees pulled up to her chest. Hopefully, that wouldn't last long. They needed to get moving.

'Are there any more of those things in there?' Brit demanded, limping from the lake's edge and pointing his sword across the ice. Thanie managed a shake of her head and another groan. It would have to do. Ran hoped for her sake she was right.

He turned as Aelish approached at a run, leaving Eian with the terrified horses and a semi-conscious Zarad. 'We need to get moving in case the dragon comes back for another round.'

'Are you—' Brit began, cut off when Aelish threw herself at him and banished his words with a desperate kiss.

Thanie lifted a single trembling finger and pointed at Ran from the ground. 'You put me anywhere near a horse right now and I'll cut your fucking balls off.'

Lidan snorted and eased onto her back, then closed her eyes.

'We really do need to go,' he reasoned. Somewhere nearby a sword clattered to the ground. He spun to the sound, realising Brit and Aelish had disappeared into the dark. Panic gripped his heart and he searched the depths of the shadows, willing his magic to brighten the cavern.

'Leave them alone,' Lidan muttered, not opening her eyes. 'They don't need an audience.'

'Or a chaperone,' Thanie put in.

For fuck's sake... Really? At a time like this? Didn't they see what he saw? Didn't they have the same sense of urgency? Ran finally registered their exhaustion, and it triggered his own. He stumbled, weariness shoving him backward and setting his head to spinning as he sat down hard.

'And there he goes,' Thanie muttered.

With a moan, Lidan rolled over and climbed to her feet, staggering sideways as she aimed for the cavern opening. 'I need to check my horse…'

A hand reached to pat at Ran's arm. For once he didn't feel the need to recoil from Thanie's touch and a thin smile broke across her lips. 'You'll be right as rain after a sleep and some food. But none of us are fit to ride or walk.'

'But…' The watery protest was all he could manage. Gods, he was exhausted. The training had been worth it, but it hadn't prepared him for the strain of sharing Thanie's magic. Giving in to her demand at Tingalla had been easy, submission requiring nothing more than a single moment's thought. The opposite exchange left him trembling, nauseous and dead tired, every fibre tingling, singing at a frequency he hadn't before heard.

'That dragon won't come back for weeks. It knew what was under the ice.' The witch peeled an eye open and met his gaze. 'Thank you, Ran.'

Thank you? Iridia shimmered at the edge of his awareness, confusion etched on her face. Weak and drained, there was precious little magic to draw from, Ran's reserves so shockingly depleted it felt like someone had ripped out his bowels.

'For what?' Ran asked on behalf of them both.

'For giving me a chance to right that wrong.' Thanie squeezed his arm again and grimaced. 'I wish I could say it will be the last.'

CHAPTER TWENTY-SIX

Wodurin, the Woaden Empire

The north gate emerged from the haze, obscured by road dust and the lingering miasma coughed out when a city as large as Wodurin exhaled. They called it the Morgen Gate, opening toward the northern mountains and drawing every important trade route from Marlow to the High Tund and across to Redona City into its yawing jaws. The road teemed with activity: wagons and riders, travellers on foot and long snaking goods caravans choking the width of the gate in both directions. The entire scene had a sense of organised chaos, one Sellan was counting on to get them into the city unnoticed. So far, it seemed to be working.

Guards posted at the entryway watched the newcomers, but she and Eddark hardly stood out. Neither of them was clean after ten days on the road, nor did they look out of place amongst the dusty stream of people jostling to get through the walls. They'd attached themselves to the tail of a caravan from somewhere up north, keeping their heads down and dropping back when someone glanced in their direction for too long. No one seemed to care about the weary riders near the last wagon in the line—they were just two amongst hundreds, and no one was out here to make friends.

Again, they used Eddark's tactic of approaching town from the wrong direction, taking an extra day or two to travel straight past Wodurin and continue north before circling around, hoping that anyone alerted to their arrival would have their eyes trained southward. Had her mother a mind to send one, a messenger could have reached Wodurin and the Congress days, if not weeks ago. But would Mediia turn her daughter in? She hadn't reported her to the Baleanon office. Someone from her father's warehouse had done that, without knowing her identity or why she'd been in the storeroom that day.

Sellan doubted the disgraced sister of a lord would dare draw such attention to herself by alerting the Congress directly. Plausible deniability was her mother's shield. How could Lady Mediia inform the Congress mages of something she knew nothing about? How could she know her errant, fugitive daughter had returned? She hadn't seen the little traitor in years!

That was the line Sellan would have taken in such a situation; she could only hope her mother had the same instinct for self-preservation.

Her breath grew shallow as she rode toward the guards, daring them to recognise her, willing them to look just to prove that she hadn't spent the past week searching every shadow and sound for pursuers. It took days to scrub the blood of the Myrtford mage from under her nails and she didn't fancy repeating the experience.

Their caravan came upon the Morgen Gate and shuffled through, a sliver of shade passing overhead where the lintel managed to block a little of the bright midday sun. It wasn't the baking, humid heat of the south, yet it beamed down on her veiled head as paranoia tightened its embrace around her chest.

None of the guards wore the shining star crest of a Congress mage and she released a sigh of relief, then melted into the crowded streets. Perhaps she simply didn't look as much like herself as she thought. Twenty years had passed since she escaped the city at her cousin's desperate insistence. More than that, the skin of her face and arms had turned from pale to a stinging shade of red before morphing into a sad attempt at a tan. She couldn't recall ever having a tan before. Parading around half-dressed in the sun hadn't been a common pastime. That, combined with the road dust in her hair and clothes, suitably disguised her as anything but the daughter of a noble family.

Eddark glanced at her from the corner of his eye. 'See, no fuss.'

'That could have been a disaster,' Sellan growled. 'There will be trackers in the city, mark my words.'

'There may be, but how many magic-weavers? Did you ever hear of any trackers good enough to simply pick a thaumalux thread from thin air and know exactly who it belongs to?' He gave her a dubious smirk. 'The crime rate would plummet if such a thing were possible.'

Sellan rolled her eyes and followed him through the guild plaza and business district crammed against the north wall. She'd kept the secret of the corpse in the tavern cupboard to herself—no point mentioning deeds that could not be undone—until Eddark's insufferable optimism became so irritating that a day out from Myrtford she spat out a warning. Trackers could be in their wake. They weren't home-free by any means. To her indignant shock he'd laughed so hard he'd almost choked on his dinner. He knew what thaumalux tracking was. Always had.

His villainous rebel friends used it to disguise themselves and the escaped slaves they spirited across the country, weaving back and forth along main roads until anyone with a hint of magic was lost in the tangle. Eddark had done the same, a move she had obliviously followed. By now even the best tracker in Baleanon didn't stand a chance at picking her from the mess left by the thousands of magic-users traversing the Empire's roads. There was some solace in this and the hope that her mother hadn't sold her down the river, but nothing strong enough to unwind the anxiety crushing her chest.

In truth, she wouldn't feel safe until they had the extra coin from her family's coffers and a place to settle and build the shield of their cover story. Even then, her peace of mind hinged on whether she could complete her work, ridding herself of the dark spectre that had loomed over her entire adult life.

Each wide, cobbled thoroughfare paved across the Empire led to Wodurin and the busiest of these roads ran like an artery toward the centre of town, past the games arenas and on to the market quarter by the river. The press of folk pulled them with the crowd, and Sellan thanked the Sisters they didn't have to fight the flow of humanity to change direction.

The place reeked.

So many bodies, so much life creating so much waste, all tangled together in a space that had expanded very little since she was a child. The defensive walls were largely unchanged along the lengths she'd seen, the city extending upward rather than out. Where the tallest buildings on the north side of the river had once been the games arena, the Congress and the Academy, the guildhalls and the newest structures in the business district had overtaken them, growing by at least two storeys. The freshly hewn sparkle of marble and limestone was a stark contrast to the baked brick and rough stone of the poorer buildings, the market quarter almost entirely made of timber and daub. In places, folk attempted to disguise the rude construction of their homes or shops, whitewashing the outside or sometimes only the facade.

The scent of humanity was doused by a wave of strong spices as they broke onto the Surian Way, following it to the high arched bridge that would take them over the Ullis River and into the more civilised side of the city. Mastless river ships bobbed in the sluggish waters, the breeze meekly blowing the stench of the docks downstream to the slums and tenements. It drifted in from the north, cooling the city and ensuring the best of Wodurin didn't wake to the odour of those less fortunate. That was the side of town where Sellan and Eddark needed to be, both to uncover the fortune lurking in the basement of her parents' home, and to find somewhere ostentatious enough to support their ruse.

Gaudy colours adorned statues of ancient emperors and generals, war lords and fabled tribal queens remembered in squares and plazas too numerous to tally. Off to her left, looming above the extravagant homes of the Empire's elite, the city's tallest and most imposing building stared as Sellan guided her horse along somewhat quieter streets. Perched on the jutting ridge of a hill, the imperial palace commanded the northern skyline, glaring, dark voids watching her and Eddark weave through a maze of plazas and avenues, coming around the base of the ridge-line and ascending it from the south.

For the first time in her life, she pitied the slaves hauling litters up the slope in the heat, their skin shining with sweat as the over-fed men and painted ladies of the noble classes lounged inside, hidden by sheer curtains worth more than most people earned in a year.

Here, now, Sellan finally registered the excess of it all.

Years spent in the south, subsisting on what could be caught, grown or gathered, relying on the more visible hard work of others to survive, her eyes had been opened to silent and unrewarded toil. Sellan hadn't escaped the last twenty years without doing some measure of work herself—as little as she could manage, truth be told—but still far more than if she'd stayed within the iron embrace of the Empire's nobility. Without realising, she'd come to know exactly how the other half lived; how the structure of a society rested its foundation upon the labour of those she had not and did not want to see. A tiny tingle of shame shivered through her, and she glanced away from the truth.

Perhaps things would change once she'd achieved her goal, but she doubted it. Her objective was not to change the world. She couldn't. She had come to avenge a wrong. Whatever grew in the wake of that act was neither her problem nor care.

There was always another rat ready to climb to the top of the heap and take the place of the one slain. None of the so-called nobles were about to sacrifice themselves for the betterment of anyone else. It had ever been thus since the six tribes of the Woaden had come to heel under the rule of the Ultimii; families tearing each other apart through successive generations, all to reach the summit of some imagined pile.

The physical manifestation of that pile continued to glare as she rode, as if it knew her intentions. That palace would outlive them all. When they were nothing but dust and half-remembered stories, it would endure.

***

Waiting in the shadows of an alley beside her parents' city house, Sellan's legs shook with fatigue and her hands throbbed from gripping the reins for days on end. Time and necessity had proven cruel teachers. Eventually, she'd become a little more comfortable in the saddle. Still, she couldn't see what appealed so much to Lidan that she would willingly put her life in the trust of such a beast on a daily basis. Sellan's whole body ached, right down to her toes, and she willed Eddark to hurry the fuck up breaking through the locks on the inside of the gate.

Beyond the high timber panels set into the painted limestone walls, a stable and courtyard waited to greet slaves and deliveries to the kitchen, with housing nearby for guards. It all stood empty for a good part of the year. According to Eddark, such travel had been rare in the past two decades—Mediia and Warrin keeping to themselves in Baleanon, no doubt too ashamed to show their faces at court since their daughter had disgraced herself.

The place was as close to deserted as they could hope to find it. Watching the gates and doors as the sun slipped into the west, shadows lengthened across the roads, revealing no signs of movement within. At the end of the alley stood a bustling avenue faced with dozens of similar homes, all serviced by lanes at their back or side walls. Across that avenue, in the deepening shade of one such alley, a dark figure huddled at the base of the wall. Perfectly motionless, at first Sellan thought it a pile of discarded rubbish or one of those unclaimed dead Eddark had mentioned. But as the hours ticked by, the bells in the temple district marking the time, what looked to be its head turned slowly toward her.

Her breath caught and her mouth ran dry.

She'd seen that figure before.

Or at least, one just like it, crouched in the alleys and dark crevices of every town she'd passed through since arriving in the north. It wasn't simply a series of homeless or transient beggars. It had watched her with unseen eyes and unmeasurable purpose each time. Revulsion crawled across her skin and she squeezed the reins tighter. Was it the thaumalux mage she'd feared all along, or something more sinister?

'Where's the housekeeper?' she'd asked Eddark before he'd climbed the wall, tearing her gaze away from the figure and tracing the baked tiles of the roof as folk bustled past about their business.

He'd narrowed his eyes at the structure and dragged his fingers back through his dirty, dark blond hair. 'They don't live here if that's what you mean. He's only around every few days, maybe less, just to check in and make sure the state doesn't reclaim the land as abandoned.'

The likely time for the housekeeper to arrive came and went without an appearance and the north wind grew teeth, pressing Eddark to get them inside before the warmth of the day dropped away entirely. As dusk chased people from the streets, his nimble ascent to the top of the wall and disappearance into the courtyard went unnoticed.

A click echoed in the alley and the gate swung outward just enough for Eddark to peer through. He waved, opening it a little wider and she urged the horses into the yard before he pulled the gate shut with a whisper on the paving stones.

Memories flickered to life of winters spent in the rooms and hallways beyond, sounds and smells seeping back from a time she'd forced herself to forget. Roasting lamb to celebrate the turning of the season and her parents' farewell before they departed for Baleanon, fresh bread dusted with salt and herbs baked in large, thick discs. Stola and veils of the finest fabrics from beyond the Empire, jewels mined in provinces annexed or outright conquered by magic and the sword. Sellan glanced down at her grotty clothes and sweat-streaked skin. How far she had fallen since those bright years of childhood, darker memories blinded by nostalgia that did not belong. Swallowing self-pity like bitter tea, she worked in silence beside Eddark to tend the horses, then followed him and his lock-picking hands into the gloom of the house.

'We can probably afford a small fire, but candles are less risky,' he whispered. 'We don't want people wondering at smoke belching from a chimney when no one is supposed to be home.'

Her stomach growled. 'What are the chances of some food?' It was a selfish request, but surely he was as eager for more than the plain fare they'd purchased or stolen along the way.

'Go check the cold stores beside the cellar.' Eddark reached to take her bags. 'I'll get one of the internal rooms lit. Keep away from the windows.'

Coaxing a small glow of magical light from the palm of her hand, Sellan descended into the bowels of the building. The chill air burned her nose, her fingers tracing the wall of the stairwell. It was dry at least, free from the scent of mildew, mould and the sensation of moss or slime on stone. If something was stored down here, be it preserves or cured meats, it should have survived abandonment better than anywhere else in the house.

The cold room door gave in with a shove, reluctant even when forced by magic, groaning open to reveal a long room lined with shelves. It wasn't packed; nor was it bare. Stoppered urns waited patiently on the shelves while large, bulbous jars with sharply pointed bases stood in a sloping timber rack at the far end of the room. Cured meats of various shapes and sizes hung from the ceiling, tightly wrapped in thin cloth to protect their salted skins. A few rounds of hard cheese hid at the very back and Sellan gathered what looked like a cured pork joint, a lump of something cheesy and an urn of savoury brined berries her people liked to serve at the beginning of a meal. They came from some far-off place on the coast, arid in the summer but famous for its—

'That's a lot of food for two people.'

Sellan screamed, spinning wildly. The urn toppled from her hands and smashed on the flagstones, slicing the silence with shards of kiln-baked clay. Staggering back and slipping on a puddle of brine, she dropped the rest of her bounty and brought her arms up, one hand drawing a defensive ward in the air while the other flung a ball of energy at the doorway.

A dark figure swatted the magic away, tearing through the ward with unnatural speed and slamming the butt of a pale hardwood staff into Sellan's stomach. With a gasp and a flare of blinding light, Sellan folded in half, crumpling to the floor. She drew the ward again, muttering an incantation she only half remembered and flicking her fingers. The figure swung the bulbous end of the staff down on her forearm with a crack.

'You are sloppy, unrefined, and out of practise. I should strip whatever pathetic power you have left and save those mewling fools at the Congress the trouble of worrying about you.'

Not a Congress mage, then.

Blinking up at the dark shape, Sellan kept her bruised arm—useless as it was—in front of her face for good measure. 'Who the *fuck* are you?'

The butt of the staff settled on the floor with a hollow tap and pair of gnarled hands grasped the shaft. The figure scoffed. 'You have forgotten too much, little wasp.'

There was only ever one person who called her that and she wasn't sure they could truly be called a *person*. They were something else, of myth and smoke and time-warped tales spoken only in whispers by those who knew the truth.

'Urda?' Sellan croaked, blinking orbs of light from her vision and gulping breath into her lungs. Her skin tingled as an arthritic hand reached to pull back a black veil, her throat tightening as the face of an old woman peered down.

The Mourner and the Liar, the eldest and wisest of the Morritae, Urda studied Sellan, casting her brilliant violet gaze from the top of her head down to her dusty boots. She was ancient and beautiful, fierce intent in her eyes unlike any Sellan had seen in a mortal. Hair falling in curtains of silver-grey, her proud chin and nose were not those of the malformed hag many thought she was.

Urda had seen things Sellan could only dream of, witnessed the passing of eons as seconds, watched as the threads she wove of mortal lives played out to their inevitable ends. While lesser beings enquired at the length of a piece of string, Urda knew. She *always* knew, those knowing eyes watching Sellan with a creeping air of disgust and disappointment she wasn't sure she could endure.

'Was that you? Outside in the alley?'

Urda shrugged in a way that would have made Brenna proud. 'Does it matter? You ignored that poor wretch, though they clearly needed aid. Would you have done differently if you thought it was me?'

Panic surged through Sellan. Had it been a test? Or was Urda here for a reckoning? Had she come to watch the final moments of her once-favoured protege play out?

'Don't be so naive, girl.' The goddess of fate waved her hand and clicked her tongue. Sellan was hardly a girl anymore, but she supposed by comparison she was no more than an infant to this ancient. 'You're not ready to go to Ortus just yet. You've got a plan, haven't you?'

'I...' Sellan paused, glancing at the door beyond Urda's shoulder. Had Eddark heard the smashing urn? 'I do have a plan, but I need—'

'I know, little wasp. I heard everything you did and did not say.'

'So, you'll give me what I need?' She sat up, cursing the desperation in her voice. When had she become so pathetic as to beg?

Urda grunted, dragging a finger casually through a layer of dust on a nearby shelf. 'No.'

'What?' The retort echoed through the cellar before she could bite it back and Sellan cringed, anticipating a savage strike from the staff.

'You vanished.' Urda leaned forward, her voice whispering like the last fallen leaves of autumn. 'You made promises and then you vanished from our sight like you had never existed at all.'

Sellan rolled that admission across her tongue, tasting its implications. 'My cousin... she disguised my thaumalux when we fled the village. I didn't know it hid me from you as well.'

'What she did and why are not important. The fact remains that you reneged on your end of the deal. We both know how my sisters look upon those who go against their oaths.'

Her sisters...

'They want you dead many times over. They want to see you suffer.'

Had Urda come without the blessing of her younger siblings? Macha and Neuna had always been less trusting, less willing to place their faith in such insignificant creatures as mortals, while their eldest sister hardly seemed bothered. Was it that she knew their fates and therefore didn't fear the outcome? Or was it that she enjoyed the sport, watching the living twist themselves in knots trying to avoid the inevitable?

Sellan shuffled up to sit against the rack of urns, not daring to take her eyes from the goddess. 'If you won't help me, why come here at all?'

A smile tugged at the corner of Urda's mouth. 'I didn't say I didn't *want* to help, little wasp with the stinging tongue. I said I won't give you what you want *for free*. Disappearing from my sight was not part of the plan. It changed the course of everything. *You* did that. I have no idea what your fate is now. What happens in the future is entirely up to you.'

An opening like that couldn't be ignored. The Mourner had all but laid an offer on the table and Sellan lurched forward, snatching a handful of the woman's black robes and holding them to her breast. 'I will do anything, Mistress of Fate. Name the price and it will be paid.'

Rampant desperation echoed against the walls. If she were to succeed, she needed the power the Morritae had once seen fit to gift her. Without it, there was no hope of the revenge she sought against the man who had shamed and wounded her so grievously.

'Anything?' Urda asked with a smirk, her head tilting coyly.

Fuck it. 'Yes, anything,' Sellan repeated, tugging at the robes for emphasis. She'd kill and maim whoever and whatever they wanted. She'd walk across fields of broken glass if they asked. She'd spill the blood of thousands.

The smirk deepened to a sneer. 'Sister Brenna already told you the price.'

Sellan's blood ran cold and every muscle in her body seized. Unable to look away, she stared up at the goddess, gobsmacked. 'What?'

'She told you the sacrifice my sisters ask, and that's only the beginning.'

A shudder of revulsion coursed through Sellan. There were a hundred things she would rather do than that. Urda didn't flinch and Sellan sensed no lie or jest. She was as serious as a sucking chest wound. 'What about a blood sacrifice? It was enough last time.'

Memories of the fire in the Academy flared in her mind's eye, her hands locking the dormitory doors, her whispered incantations sending licking flame up the heavy drapes. She never did find out how many perished that day, but it had been enough to slake the Morritae's thirst and satisfy their need. It had been enough that they'd agreed to give her everything she'd asked for.

'That may have been a worthy sacrifice last time but that was before you failed us.' The ancient shrugged, the staff creaking as she leaned onto it. 'We were weakened by that failure.'

'How?' Icy dread slipped a hand around Sellan's throat. What had she done? Had she known, she might have done something, anything, differently...

'The souls you promised would have rejuvenated and replenished the power we gave you. They would have fed us for decades, if not centuries. Even longer had you continued your work and created more of those repulsive creatures.' Urda eased into a crouch, her aged appearance belying the strength and flexibility of her immortal form. She didn't even wince as she came level with Sellan's eyes. 'Those souls you abandoned and left wandering fed neither us nor the cursed rider, Ortus. They were lost to the wind, and we paid dearly for our trust in you.'

There was no point pleading her case, no point professing her sorrow at her failure. The ears of the mighty would not hear her.

'A worthy sacrifice or none at all,' Urda said finally.

Sellan choked on a mouthful of bile, glancing away for the slightest second. She'd sworn never again, sworn to never stoop so low. 'You wish me to defile myself?'

'How badly do you want this? How desperately do you need this revenge?' Urda swiped a hand through the air in a sharp, dismissive gesture. 'You were willing to give yourself to a man to secure your safety once before. You whored yourself to him so many times it gave you two daughters who you have yet to bring to us.'

Rage evaporated Sellan's fear. 'What has this got to do with them?'

'Nothing beyond illustrating my point. You did it once, little wasp. You did what was required. If you want this, you will do it again.'

'I had no choice!' Sellan cried, yanking furiously at the folds of the robes. Tears stung her eyes. Fuck, this could not be the only way.

Giving herself to a man and pledging his seed to the Morritae could *not* be the only path. But the Dead Sisters had a thirst not only for life but for the power held in its mere potential. She couldn't bear to look at the malicious gleam in the goddess' eyes.

'That, my dear, is why they call it a sacrifice.'

CHAPTER TWENTY-SEVEN

Wodurin, the Woaden Empire

Staggering from the cellar and hauling the food and a bottle of Warrin Parben's favourite liquor with her, Sellan bit back tears and the heaving urge to vomit. The gods had spoken. What had once only been the suggestion of a mad old shop keeper was now a decree from on high, one she could ignore if she so wished, but at her peril.

It surprised her that Urda alone had appeared in the cellar, unaccompanied by her sisters. But the goddess was willing to give her another chance. In every old story, it was Urda at the fore of any scheme to knock Ortus off his pedestal. As the shepherd of the dead, he maintained the flow of souls from this world to the next, and with that came power, fuelled in equal measure by the adoration of the dead and the fear from the living. He didn't decide the time and place of a mortal's death, but the nature of their afterlife. *He* balanced the scales between the seen and unseen realms.

Long had the Morritae ravenously coveted his place at the head of the vast Coraidic pantheon, other gods and spirits going about their business, unbothered by the petty politics played at the top. Long had the Sisters fought Ortus in his many forms, lashing out in their myriad of manifestations, across all the nations of the northern continent. Sellan couldn't know how far beyond Coraidin their feud stretched, but it raged here like an unattended forest fire.

She imagined there had been a short lull while the Morritae regained their strength, twenty years no more than a blip in time to them. Had those years of peace ended with her return, old wounds opening anew? If the Morritae gave her the gift she sought, it would not be for her benefit. Sellan would become a tool, a means to an end in the victory they sought over the Dark Rider, a way to starve him of the souls sustaining his very being.

Yet without the blessing of the Morritae, her plans were no more than smoke and glowing embers. To make matters worse, there were rules. Sacrifices required sincerity; a genuine desire to serve and to give something precious, something that mattered. Anything less was a waste of time. Pouring a libation at a feast without the right words and spirit in your heart did nothing but feed perfectly good wine to the dirt. For her plan to work, Sellan had to *mean* it. She had to want it. It had to matter to her, and that required feelings she did not have.

Along a corridor branching from a smaller atrium garden, a glimmer of candlelight flickered under a door. Pausing and gasping a steadying breath, Sellan leaned against the wall, licking at dry lips and glancing at the bottle in her hand. Would this be enough?

What if Eddark needed more? What if he rejected her?

She shuddered and looked back at the atrium, stars blinking in the blue-black summer night. The moon had turned toward last crescent again and she was close enough to the end of her cycle that foul moods had begun to plague her days, her chin breaking out in at least one angry spot. If she were to commit her act of self-sacrifice tonight, the risk of anything taking root was extremely low. Waiting any longer would put her out of action for at least a week. After that, the risks rose again—risks she was in no mood or mind to entertain. She was not of such an age that another child was an impossibility. In fact, Macha the goddess of mothers and a warrior's death, might just conspire with her younger sister to ensure such a quickening, if only for a laugh. Waiting until it was again safe to lay with a man meant delaying an entire turn of the moon. Time she did not have.

Sellan squeezed the neck of the bottle until she thought the fine glass might shatter. She sighed and resigned herself to the fate she had apparently written for herself.

Tonight would have to do.

Eddark looked up at her entry, dark eyes tracing her steps under a deepening frown. 'You all right?'

'I'm fine,' she replied, holding back a frustrated snarl. Dumping the armload of food and the bottle on a table, she stood back, hands on hips and sighed again. 'Just tired.'

It wasn't a lie, and it was an easier sell than explaining the unannounced appearance of the goddess of fate in the cellar. She ached to her very bones and needed sleep like she needed air. If she managed to stay awake long enough to seduce the man, she would be genuinely shocked. Still, needs must, and she turned to survey their accommodation.

It was one of the smaller receiving rooms—a place her parents had entertained individual guests or close friends who didn't require the employment of extravagant excesses. Those were saved for new or influential guests, rolled out to impress as and when required. This was the sort of room where her mother slumped onto a day lounge with a glass of wine and an old friend to gossip about the latest court scandal, their bare feet on the upholstery, their airs and graces left at the door. The only windows faced the atrium, both shuttered against the night.

Eddark set about inspecting the food and carving slices of cured meat off the joint. On a nearby table a basin of clean water gleamed beside a pile of soft towels and little bottles of scented oils.

'Thought you might want to wash up,' he said, nodding at the basin.

Looking him up and down, she realised he'd already scrubbed the road dirt from his tanned face and shaken most of it from his hair. His clothes were clean and fit too well to be pilfered from someone else's wardrobe. Sellan scowled suspiciously at the garments. 'Where did you get those?'

'I keep clothes here,' he replied, stuffing meat into his mouth and lifting the bottle of liquor to inspect the text inscribed on the glass. 'Harbern mash? He might be a sucker for a whore, but Rook Warrin has good taste in liquor.' Eddark glanced at her apologetically. 'No offence.'

'None taken,' she replied, genuinely nonplussed. Eddark's assessment of her father couldn't be closer to the truth. She slipped the bottle from Eddark's hands and tucked it under her arm.

'Oi—'

A single raised finger stalled his protest, and she sank gratefully onto a day lounge across the room. 'You promised me something in exchange for this, or were you too drunk to remember?'

Recollection drew him to a pause and Eddark's fingers played idly across the rim of his empty glass. He remembered, but was he still willing to pay the price? Were either of them ready to admit why they were here? Sellan waited, tapping her nails on the bottle and arching a brow at him.

'That's a two-way conversation, Sel.'

One of her eyes twitched and she glanced away. He seemed committed to resurrecting that diminutive from their childhood, not that he'd ever used it in the presence of others.

He wanted a list of her intentions, but how likely was he to fall for her seduction once he knew her plans? Eddark wasn't going to give ground, standing there stubbornly scrutinising her face. Some of Thanie's tonics or the supplies to mix a tincture would have solved the problem of desire. She could have lured him in as easily as a hungry fish. But this needed to be genuine. He had to want it, as did she, otherwise there was no point in doing it at all.

'Fine.' Sellan held the bottle out for him to take. 'Pour two. Each. We're going to need it.'

For the length of a breath he hesitated, eyeing her as if to see the motivation hidden beneath her skin. Then he set to work. She took the time to wipe her face and arms, and when she turned around, four glasses of amber liquor waited on a little table alongside a selection of meat and cheese. Suddenly, Sellan found she wasn't hungry.

'It doesn't take a genius to guess you're here to take that rage out on Tamyr,' Eddark began. His chair creaked as he leaned back, took a long sip and licked his lips, waiting on her response like a cat watching prey.

Sellan snorted a laugh to cover her anxiety, her nails picking at a dried spray of mud on her clothes. 'Am I so easily read?'

'After what your mother said and what you told me at the inn, there's really little doubt.' The intensity of his stare sent a shiver down her spine. 'I'm a medic, Sellan. I'm trained to watch for the things my patients can't or won't tell me. Things happened at the Academy that folk don't know about, or perhaps won't admit.'

He wasn't wrong. If all this failed, she was dead anyway. Telling Eddark the truth meant at least someone knew before she stepped off the mortal plane.

Draining her drink in three quick gulps, she slammed the heavy base of the glass onto the table. Shock flashed across Eddark's face, barely there before it vanished, his features settling as he waited.

Sellan pressed her lips together and sucked at her teeth. Where to begin the dredging of a lifetime of pain? 'At first I was flattered. Who wouldn't be? The son of an emperor even looking in my direction was a coup. We were of an age, perhaps no more than a year between us. His skill put him a few classes above me and almost ready to graduate from his studies. I was the niece of a minor noble, albeit of a tribe defeated and humiliated by the Ultimii in the Unity Wars. He shouldn't have even shared the same air as me. Yet there he was, smiling and laughing at my jokes.'

She drew a deep steadying breath. This should not be this hard. Why were her hands shaking? What was this churn in her stomach?

'I'm not sure Tamyr ever knew what love was, or how to show it. He knew how to pretend well enough, how to wear a mask and the appearance of caring. In the light, he was charm and humour and wit, but in the dark he was brutal. He hurt people. Not just me. There were so many more than just me. He was chaos in human form, destruction writ large in the body of a young man with strength and power far in excess of my own.'

Bile rose, burning her throat and she blinked away the heat prickling her eyes.

'The wounds he left in me festered until I couldn't take another beating. I couldn't face being used by his friends while he watched.' She sniffed and met Eddark's eyes, recoiling from his horror. His top lip curled, and his hand shook where it strangled the glass. This was a mistake. She shouldn't have stepped onto this road, but her feet were already running. She had no choice but to go on. 'I broke.'

'How old were you?' Eddark whispered, his words torn as though his throat were made of shards of glass.

'No more than fifteen.'

Silence coiled through the room like a chill mist and Sellan shivered. Wasn't this supposed to make her feel better? Wasn't letting it out supposed to release her from the hate she carried? Instead, rage simmered in her gut, not unlike the dark emotion creasing Eddark's brow.

'One of his friends liked to hold my throat. The marks held on for weeks, then just as I healed, he'd ask his master for another turn. Tamyr wasn't the jealous sort but he guarded me like a wolf. They needed permission, and only then if it suited him.'

'You didn't run?'

'Where the fuck would I have gone, Ed?' Sellan's retort snapped against the walls, echoing hard and startling Eddark. 'Home? Where my letters begging for rescue were ignored? Eventually my mother wrote and told me to be grateful for the attention. She said there were more important things than what *I* wanted. Girls all over the Empire would give their right hand for a place in the prince's bed. Just because I didn't like it rough wasn't reason to rock the boat.'

His eyes narrowed. 'She actually fucking said that?'

'If the letter hadn't gone up in flames with the Academy, I'd show you.' Sellan held back the part where her own magic had caused that fire. Eddark didn't need to know that little detail. This was bad enough. Shame flared hot in her cheeks, mingling with anger and impotence.

'What happened?' Hesitation cracked his voice. He didn't really want to know, but he was caught in the thrall of her disaster—too terrified and fascinated to turn away.

The second drink went down smoother and faster than the first, and the glass almost dropped from her grip. She didn't have to ask for a refill, his reaction automatic as he stared across the table.

'They sent for me one evening, after all the doors were supposed to be locked. Tamyr never came himself, always sent some servant or slave. This time it was a guard, so there was no ignoring that summons.' Candlelight blurred and a tear trickled free. Fuck him for making her cry. Fuck this shit right into the sea. Once this was over, she would never speak of it again. Flay the skin from her bones and she would still take it to her grave. 'I went. Tamyr always went first, then his mate. He put his arm across my throat this time.'

Eddark's hand went to his mouth, fingers flexing as if to throttle something that wasn't there. His body twitched, fit to burst from his seat, his anger barely contained. Sellan's revulsion receded into numb distance, gaping emptiness opening in her chest as the scabs fell from old wounds. There was no pain where she had expected the find agony. The edges of the void blackened. She couldn't feel it because she was already dead inside.

'It was so much worse than before. I snapped.' Her throat tightened as the words forced their way out. Even now the weight pressed down on her neck, the lancing agony, the blood. She couldn't remember his name, nor did she want to; his face and Tamyr's burned into her memory. The little balls of resin Brenna sold chased back the nightmares and eased the pain. The smoke had been her only solace. 'I ripped his head off.'

Eddark baulked. 'You did *what*?' He hadn't expected that.

'Like pulling the head from a rose.' She put her forefinger and thumb together and made a tugging motion, as if plucking a bud from a branch. 'One hand at the back of his neck and it popped right off. Made a fucking riot of a mess though. I was scrubbing his blood off me for days.'

'Wait,' Eddark waved his hands and sat forward. Reconciling these facts from the fiction he and the rest of the Empire had been fed would take effort, but at least he was trying. 'That was how Prince Orrin *actually* died?'

Orrin... That's what they'd called him.

'He was hardly a prince,' Sellan scoffed, gulping another drink to wash away the salty taste of her tears.

'He was the emperor's *cousin*!' Eddark hissed.

Sellan leaned forward and pointed a finger. 'He was a cunt.'

'And Tamyr?'

'Pissed himself,' she said flatly. After copping a spray of his cousin's brains, Tamyr had scrambled over the back of his luxuriously upholstered lounge, screaming bloody murder and calling for the same guards deaf to her cries for help. The future emperor had literally pissed his pants as Sellan stalked across the room, magic blazing in her hands, her fury and pain finally unleashed from the cage Thanie had built to hold it. 'I got a few hits in before they took me down.'

Eddark's eyes grew wide. 'The burns?'

With a nod, Sellan sat back. 'I think you know the rest. Tamyr had me declared derramentis without trial and sentenced to life service in the Disputed Territory. I escaped when the Academy went up in flames.'

'You were a child,' he murmured.

'They didn't care. You don't get to decapitate a prince and disfigure another and get away with it. What would the masses think if such a thing were left to lie?'

Swirling his drink, his gaze fell to the amber liquid and silence swept in after it. For an age he did nothing but stare, not a word passing his lips as he absorbed the ugly, painful truth she'd placed at his feet. Some small part of her did feel better. Someone else now lived with the knowledge of what she'd endured. Regret lingered at the margins, that of all the people she knew, it had become Eddark's burden to bear, but no one else had volunteered. At least her fury had direction now, a place to settle in her breast, accepted and acknowledged. Justified.

She stoked that flame of hatred, promising it nourishment. Never again would she leave that fire unattended. Ignoring her wounds had almost killed her, poisoning her rational mind, injuring any chance of forming a meaningful and healthy relationship with another man or her daughters. Her fears for their safety had turned violent, the scars of Tamyr's wrongs almost consuming her entirely. Now she stood upon a path to justice. She would be the one to pass judgement and inflict the sentence because no one else would.

'Seems my own trauma pales in comparison...' Eddark muttered.

'Another's sorrow doesn't negate your own.' Her response surprised her; a rare moment of wisdom she hadn't thought she was capable of. Yet, she meant every word. His suffering might be different, but likely no better than the pain she'd endured. He'd spent most of his life a slave. Who could know the kinds of deprivations he'd survived?

'Not sure you'll ever look at me the same once I tell you.' Eddark's fear permeated the air, mingling with hers in a heady mix of trepidation and anticipation. He shifted nervously in the chair, unable to meet her gaze. Leaning down, elbows on his knees, he nursed his drink and held his tongue.

Minutes ticked by. He wasn't going to speak. That was it. She'd scared him into silence, she was sure of it. Then he sighed. 'People think I'm an archipelago slave, descended from the islands, but that's wrong. My mother's family were islander, many generations removed. They lived in Bata for at least a century before I was born. My father is of entirely different stock.'

'She was a coastal slave?' Sellan asked with all the tact of an axe. Even as she said it, she cringed.

'Not even close.' His gaze drifted to the shuttered windows and a past Sellan couldn't see. 'She was a noblewoman of Bata's ruling family, of similar rank to Lady Mediia. The sister of a lord, destined to marry a man of sufficient stature to maintain some semblance of decency.'

Shock tingled through Sellan. *A noblewoman?* Eddark was the son of a noble house? That couldn't be right. Biting her tongue until it bled was all she could do to hold back from firing a hundred questions at him.

'My mother was once Mediia's closest friend.' He met her eyes then, unspoken truth passing in the pause. 'That's why she took me in, albeit disguised as a slave.'

'Wait... Your father... Were your parents married to other people?' There weren't many social mores the Woaden tribal families held, but above all else was that children were only useful if born into a legitimate marriage. Even a betrothal would do. Anything to ensure the lines of succession and inheritance were clear. Wars had been fought over less.

Eddark shook his head and drained another glass, leaving the empty for Sellan to fill as he stood and paced across the room. Agitation bunched in his muscles, tension forcing his shoulders into a hard ridge, his face a grim picture of a man unsure if he was ready to reveal this deeply held truth. 'My father was untouchable, a man beyond reproach. And yes, already wed.'

The liquor stopped pouring, the smooth bottle frosting in her hand as her fear manifested as icy magic.

Sellan looked up and her heart gave a hard thud. 'Oh, fuck.'

'Holidaying at the coast, he took a liking to my mother. The records are sparse, some letters and diary entries. Rumours. What little my associates found was hard won, but there's no doubt. There was only one man allowed near her that summer.' Eddark paused again, his throat contracting as he swallowed. 'Guarded her like a wolf, you could say.'

Sellan's blood ran cold and for the briefest, fleeting moment, their eyes met. What the fuck was he trying to tell her? 'Eddark, I don't understand.'

'My father was from one of the oldest and most powerful families of the Empire—*the* most powerful. First among men, the highest in the land.' He shuddered, hands perched on his hips, his face paling. 'My father was Emperor Senivus.'

CHAPTER TWENTY-EIGHT

Wodurin, the Woaden Empire

'Don't fucking lie to me.'

'I wish I *was* lying. I wish any other truth were mine, but this is all I have.'

'You're Tamyr's *brother*!?' Sellan launched from her seat, hands extended in exasperated claws of confusion. 'You don't even fucking look like him!'

'Half-brother, thank you very much,' Eddark sneered. 'Islanders have stronger blood than Woaden, especially the Ultimii. They're so pale you can almost see through them.'

'Inbreeding will do that to a family,' she snarled, stalking away. 'If this is true, and that is a very big if—'

Turning back, her brow furrowed briefly. They were so different. Where Tamyr had skin the colour of milk, Eddark wore a sheen of bronze. Where Tamyr had a head of straight blond hair, Eddark's fell in slightly darker waves when he let it grow. Tamyr had been lean, almost wiry, but strong. He may have grown some bulk by now, but Sellan doubted it. The Ultimii were ever a weedy lot. Eddark stood as tall as any of the Imperial family, but broader in the shoulders, muscled where they were svelte. She just couldn't see it. Perhaps she didn't want to.

Her chin quivered and she savagely rammed her teeth together to stop it. 'What happened to your mother when they found out?'

'Tamyr wasn't born yet, but his mother fell pregnant soon after mine. There's no more than a year between us. But I'm the eldest. I had to be disposed of.'

That Sellan understood. When faced with the same choice, she'd prevented pregnancies that threatened Lidan's title rather than waiting. It was just many of the silent battles she'd waged to protect not just herself but her daughters. Without positions of authority in their father's clan, they faced uncertainty and death. As Erlon's heirs, Sellan could heavily influence her daughters' futures. Her daughters had position and rank; the only shield afforded to them in a world dominated by the will of men.

But could she have actually *killed* Farah's little runt once he was born? Could she have ordered someone else to do it? In the end she'd left it to fate to decide, her word given to Lidan that she wouldn't act, the choice taken from her hands and no longer her concern.

Understanding prickled across her skin. 'You're Senivus' true heir, aren't you?'

'That I know of, yes.' Eddark shrugged. 'There's probably more just like me lurking in the coastal towns and cities of the Empire, but I don't know of any others born before me or Tamyr.'

'Most likely never lived long enough…'

'Probably not. He wasn't going to come and marry their mothers, was he? Their families would have dealt with things much the same as mine—turning me out like rubbish on a midden.'

Deep breaths brought her some sense of calm. Tamyr's brother Eddark may be, but he was not the monster his father or half-sibling had become. Eddark was different, and not just in appearance. Perhaps the years in the Parben household had fashioned him into something else. Favoured or not, he still endured the same deprivations as any Woaden slave.

'So Mediia took in her friend's son rather than letting him die,' Sellan wondered, thinking aloud as the numb warmth of drink settled in her bones.

'I suspect so. I never had the chance to ask.'

He took the glass she offered him, their fingers brushing for no more than the briefest second. A jolt of energy snapped through Sellan. Flinching away, she ignored a flare of heat deep in her belly. It was the liquor talking, nothing more.

Eddark went on without noticing. 'My mother's family weren't easy to find. They retreated to their ancestral lands in the archipelago. From what I've heard, Senivus destroyed them.'

Slumping back onto the lounge, Sellan cradled a drink twice as strong as the previous two. Stunned to the edge of dumb disbelief, she shook her head. 'Why flee? Surely they wanted you dealt with as much as Senivus?

Your existence threatened your mother's prospects as much as it did his succession plan.'

'Senivus paid them to kill me, and they didn't. There are documents proving undisclosed payments from the Crown to her family. But proof of death was never given. He couldn't know where I was, but he knew I was alive.' Eddark stared at the flickering candles, lost in thought as the weight of the truth settled on Sellan. Now she understood his hate. Now she understood his need for a reckoning. 'Senivus ruined my mother and her family to discredit any claim they might make on the throne. Without proper standing, no one would take them seriously. No one would listen.'

'Is she still alive?' Sellan asked in a whisper. If she were, there might still be a way. They could bring down the whole house of cards, poisoning the entire Ultimii dynasty and its creeping, insidious branches at its very root. They could besmirch the ascension and turn the Assembly of Lords against—

Eddark's face fell, his features crumpling. 'She killed herself after I went to your mother. At least, that's the official story.'

'Official story, my arse.'

There were any number of ways the leviathan of the imperial court could silence a threat before it did damage. Staged suicide was a long-held favourite. That, and liberally seasoning a rival's supper with poison. Rare occasions of less subtle action could be found in the annals of history—emperors sending guards after their meddling mothers, brothers mysteriously dropping dead of fever on a distant battlefield, their wives and children inexplicably perishing on the journey back to the capital. Ruling was a brutal business and the Woaden did it well. Eddark's mother may well have taken her own life for grief and despair, but the stink of the court lingered all over this like a putrid cloud.

Their eyes met. Did she dare hope that Eddark hated the Ultimii family as much as she did? Did she dare hope he wanted to watch them burn?

'I can't truly avenge her, but I can bring the apparatus of her humiliation and murder to its knees.' Finally unleashed, his truth spoken, his anger boiled to the surface. Tears glistened in Eddark's eyes, his teeth bared, his body poised to fight. He stabbed a finger at his chest then pointed at the city beyond the walls. 'I can't free every child who grew up like me; dressed in rags and believing they were no better than the dirt on a high-born boot, but I can free the world of the likes of him. Tamyr may not carry the sins of his father—he has enough of his own and he'll answer for those—but he is the keystone. If he falls, the rest may well topple with him.'

'He has heirs by now, surely?'

'One. A daughter. Mad as a cut snake by all accounts.'

Sellan leafed through her dusty recollection of Woaden history. Had the Empire ever been ruled by a woman in her own right? Had it ever stood strong against its enemies with a woman at the helm? The girl couldn't be much older than Lidan. Would she survive the Purge if her father were to perish?

Perhaps... Sellan raked her teeth across her lip, narrowing her eyes as she considered the spiralling possibilities through the fog of drunkenness. With only one heir, and a girl at that, Tamyr and his legacy were as vulnerable now as they would ever be. She'd come seeking vengeance on him alone, reasoning that whatever followed was not of her concern.

This changed everything.

This could be her chance to not only ruin him, but to return her own family to its rightful place. The Burikanii had long ago chosen the poised snake as their sigil. Was now the time to strike, not just for herself, but for her ancient and noble tribe? Could she carve a way back to the top for House Corvent?

'How were you going to bring him down?' she asked.

Eddark started and blinked. 'I'd hoped *you* had a plan.'

Of course she did, but admitting how she would take Tamyr's empire out from under him would surely turn Eddark against her. Still, she might not have a choice. 'You came all this way without a plan?'

He looked at her deadpan. 'It was a spur of the moment decision, Sellan. I wasn't exactly expecting you to show up on our doorstep and profess your undying hatred for the emperor. You said you'd tried to ruin him before.'

'You don't want to know the details.' Sellan dismissed him with a flick of her fingers and took another few mouthfuls, letting the warmth spread. All her aches began to fade, old wounds slowly closing. Thanie had only stayed with her through sheer desperation. She'd hated Tamyr enough for vengeance to burn bright in her too, but time and distance had worn that need away. In the end, the gruesome reality and the price to be paid for their weapon had become too heavy for Thanie to hold.

Sellan was alone in this. Eddark wouldn't knowingly follow her into that darkness. He was simply too good. Too good for the father who rejected him, too good for the family who sent him away. Too good for the family he'd spent his life serving.

Too good for her.

'You think you can't trust me,' Eddark said, his voice thickening and wavering under the influence of the liquor. It was strong stuff and neither of them had much practise at holding their alcohol. 'I can't help you if you don't trust me.'

'I don't trust anyone!' she snapped, her drink slopping over the rim of the glass. 'Everyone I ever put my faith in returned it with betrayal. What makes you any different?'

'We want the same thing. We want him to fall and never get back up.'

'And what would you do to achieve that? How far would you go against your morals and your precious ethics? What darkness would you condone to meet that end?'

He watched her for a moment from beside the cold brazier. His dark gaze watched as she raked her fingernails back through the filthy lengths of her auburn hair. Gods only knew what a state she must be in. She hadn't seen a mirror in weeks. But still he watched, studying her carefully despite the drunken gleam in his eyes. He was as tense as a mountain lion, bunched and poised. Yet he held it, maintaining restraint she'd never mastered.

She'd give anything to know what he was thinking, almost anything to peek inside and turn his needs to her ends. Slowly, her anger and anxiety wound down, his steady gaze calming Sellan against her better judgement.

'At this point, there's very little I wouldn't do to see him rot, Sellan. Very, *very* little.'

'Good,' she nodded, drawing a shaking breath. 'Because to kill a man like Tamyr, with as much influence and magic as he has, you need something stronger than steel or power alone. You need a weapon unlike *anything* the world has ever seen.' She leaned closer, as if proximity would drive her point home. 'I almost did it once, long ago, but I failed. This time, I'll finish what I started or die trying.'

Eddark's brow furrowed, his expression darkened. 'What do you mean by "weapon"? What are you going to do?'

'Make something he won't be able to outrun or negotiate with. A weapon so powerful it takes the strength of the gods and a sacrifice so bloody you'll question the very essence of your humanity.' Her hand opened toward the door, her mouth running dry. 'You can still walk away, Eddark. There's still time. But if I tell you what I mean to do and you abandon me, I will come for you and I will kill you. Understand that nothing can stand in my way this time. I may come to trust you, but for now, you have to trust *me*. I will bring you the revenge you seek, I promise you that. But first you must swear that you're with me, no matter how dark or gruesome things get. You have to trust that there is no other way. Can you do that?'

He could turn and leave right now. She'd opened the door and shown him a sliver of what waited on the other side of this choice.

What if he walked away? Could she do this on her own? She could try, but she would most likely fail. Without Eddark, she'd never receive the power she needed from the Morritae, nor could she subdue the sheer number of subjects required to build her army.

And she would build an army—a legion of undead to scour Tamyr and his progeny from the surface of Coraidin. He would rue the day he wounded her, humiliated her, cast her out and sentenced her to die for defending herself. She was a repugnant excuse for a human being—an awful wife and a more loathsome mother—but nothing she'd ever done came close to the agony Tamyr had inflicted. One day she would atone for her mistakes and the damage she'd done, but not before Tamyr had paid his debt to her.

She needed Eddark for that and she prayed harder than she ever had that he wouldn't leave. Not now.

Slowly, he opened a hand, his palm up, his gaze holding hers. 'Swear to me that it's worth it. Swear that this is the only way.'

Her hand clasped his wrist, the oldest form of a binding oath without mingling blood. 'I promise you, on my life and the honour of my ancestors, on the ash of their bones and the spirits of this house, that this is the price we have to pay. I can't defeat him on my own. He was always more power-ful, always the strongest. But I promise if you help me, he will fall and *never* rise again. They all will. Whatever punishment I face after that is mine to carry, but I will go to my death knowing I did everything to take him with me.'

'I believe you.' Eddark lifted his chin and set his jaw, defiant. 'And I'll follow you. I'll see him suffer as my mother did, if it's the last thing I do.'

They ignored the sleeping chambers of the house, limiting themselves to one room. Evidence of their presence had to appear innocuous, as if left by any transient or hopeful burglar. When they found their permanent base, the story would be different. As night closed in, Sellan coaxed a tiny glimmering fire to life in the brazier, just enough to chase the midnight chill from the room without pumping out great clouds of smoke. They drained the bottle of her father's favourite liquor and she confessed the first steps in her plan, drowning in dread as she did.

Eddark would use his contacts to find a house for rent, somewhere suitable for a visiting noble, for that was exactly who he'd imitate. Sellan would stand as his household mage and their business in Wodurin would concern an offer to the emperor. A weapon of war had been discovered by this nobleman's mage in their tiny port city, just across the border in Arinnia. A weapon that would smite his enemies and raze their armies to the ground; a gift to the Empire in the war against the Free Nations.

Posing as defectors, unknown to the court of Wodurin and untraceable since official diplomatic communication with Arinnia had disintegrated years ago, they would offer a demonstration. At this point, Sellan left the conversation unfinished. She knew the steps beyond that point of no return, but there was little point in telling Eddark unless everything else fell into place. The rest would wait until he was too committed to withdraw, too invested to abandon her.

For the slightest sliver of time Sellan wondered if the sacrifice Urda demanded had a dual purpose—to feed the goddess' need for power and to bind Eddark to Sellan in their pursuit of vengeance. It hardly mattered. She was fucked either way. In the meantime, the less Eddark knew, the better.

She lay on lounge mats tossed onto the sitting room floor, staring at the ceiling through the gloom, restless and unable to find peace. Her own daughter had looked upon her with disgust when she'd discovered the truth. Lidan didn't want to know the reasons for creating the marhain because the reasons didn't matter. Sellan had fashioned an abomination. That simple truth was the end of the discussion.

Had she been able to explain herself—given a chance to speak rather than fending off an attack from some puffed-up Orthian princeling—then she might have convinced Lidan that there wasn't another way to kill Tamyr of the Ultimii.

And Sellan *had* to kill him.

At first, she'd make fifteen or sixteen, little more than a section in military terms, but enough to begin with. The creatures her husband's people called ngaru, the things she called marhain—the wandering dead—would this time be under her complete control.

She couldn't wait until she had a hundred, or even two dozen. *That* had been her mistake in Lackmah. She'd been greedy, wanting more bodies to throw into her ranks, more steel to turn on Tamyr when the summer season came. But time was not on her side now. The longer she waited, the greater the risk of discovery and arrest.

If Tamyr so much as caught a whiff of who she really was, she was dead. If he thought her an imposter of any kind, she was dead. She had one chance to dazzle him with her undead soldiers, to bend him to her ruse and convince him that she only served his needs. If she fucked that up, she was dead.

Her disguise had to be more physical than magical. Tamyr and his court mages would see straight through a glamour such as Thanie had used. There were chemics to change her hair, even one that would drain the green from her irises, though it stung like a motherfucker when dropped in the eye. When all was said and done, Sellan wouldn't look anything like the wounded, angry girl Tamyr had violated in his Academy bedchamber. She'd be just another court mage offering her services to the lord of the north.

Beside her, Eddark groaned and Sellan froze.

Slowly, with all the elegance of a great, shaggy hound, he rolled over. His long, muscled arm flopped across her chest, and he absently buried his face into her hair. Heart pounding so hard it was a wonder he couldn't hear it over the gentle crackle of the fire, Sellan turned her head. Was he awake? Did he know what he was doing?

Eyes closed, breathing steady, he settled again, seemingly unaware. She could use this…

No. Not yet.

But it had to be now…

She rolled away, putting her back to his chest.

Not today.

Groaning again, his arm tightened and she slid backward across the matting. Now every inch of him pressed against her, along the back of her thighs, his heart beating through the thin fabric of the sleeping shirt she'd found upstairs. Parts of him were certainly more awake than others, willing to give her what she wanted.

It couldn't be this easy. It *shouldn't* be this easy.

What if he woke up fully and realised what he was doing?

Shifting again, Sellan gave in, twisting in the circle of Eddark's embrace until she faced him. Fingers tracing his jawline, she wondered if she'd ever trust someone the way a lover should. Was she even capable of it, or would she forever hold back?

'Sel?' he murmured, eyes closed, his embrace relaxing.

'Hmm?'

'You awake?' The whisper smelt of amber liquor and sweet wine.

'Yes.' Curse her heart for racing. Was she actually nervous?

One eye peeled open and he pulled back. 'Sorry, I didn't mean—'

'Shut up.'

She kissed him and her body fired; tingling rushing her limbs, heat bursting in her chest. She didn't care anymore. It had been so long since anyone held her without demanding something in return, so long since anyone had looked at her without fear or revulsion. So long since anyone had seen her for who she was.

Eddark knew.

He saw what she was. He knew what had turned her down that path to darkness and he knew she planned violence. Yet he remained.

He hadn't hurt her either. It was a sad indictment on her life that the bar had been set so low. Her affection, thin and mealy as it was, should have cost more than basic kindness, but that was all it took.

What began as a business-like exchange immediately and urgently became something else—a release of tension, a destruction of walls, a final blow to the barriers standing between them and the partnership they needed to survive what was coming. Neither spoke with words, only hands and limbs and lips. Neither waited on the other and she realised he wanted this. Perhaps he always had.

Perhaps she had too.

The words to the Morritae came without prompting, floating through her mind as she gave herself to risk for the sake of reward, as she gave herself to fate once more. Sellan acknowledged the awful, destructive person she had become, accepted it and let it go. She would see this end, her justice and Eddark's.

She would give her life for it, if that's what it took. And she would not stop until her truth was heard, no matter the cost.

Chapter Twenty-nine

Fracture Pass, the Malapa

A fortnight of oppressive humidity began to peel away as they cut higher into the foothills of the Malapa. Insects whirred as the afternoon dragged on, undeterred by the cooling air, invisible amongst the trees yet so loud Loge almost had to shout to be heard. 'Do you have any idea where we are?'

'Yes,' Marrit snapped from her saddle, her horse wandering along behind Striker.

He turned and scowled. 'Can I see the map?'

'No.' She artfully avoided his glare, gazing up at the sky splintering through the trees.

'Why not?'

Marrit released a sharp sigh of frustration. 'Because you'll gallop off and leave me here. Your horse will be dead in a day, and you'll end up walking all the way to the North Lands.'

'I won't.'

An eyebrow lifted into a cynical arch. 'Yes, you will.'

Their pace was sluggish at best, Marrit insisting on sparing the horses if they had any hope of reaching a place she called Isord. A city stood there—whatever a *city* was—the place Lidan and the northerners were taking the witch. Loge had missed some crucial events while dead, namely the revelation of Lidan's mother as the creator of the ngaru, and that she and her elderly companion were both magic-weavers in hiding from some far away authority. He vaguely recalled a man who had come south looking for something, or someone, but the memory snaked away into the mists of his mind before he could catch it.

Marrit passed the evenings of their journey regaling him with tales of what he'd missed: the battle between Sellan and the northerner called Ranoth; the ngaru attack on the settlement of Tingalla. He wondered at the size of the balls Ranoth must boast to take on a woman such as Sellan. Was he brave or stupid or both? A sense of vague animosity remained toward the man's name but Loge couldn't clearly remember why. When he made mention of it one night by the fire, Marrit placated his apprehension, assuring him that Lidan left with Ran of her own free will.

Loge asked her to speak of Lidan often, pursuing any reminder of the life they'd once shared. None of the stories stuck. Scrabbling against the shifting scree of his broken memory, they failed to gain purchase. By morning they'd vanished like ghosts fading with the night.

'We need to move faster than this,' Loge insisted in a low growl. Drowning in frustration, he turned his anger on Marrit.

'No, we don't. They're only three days ahead. We're on their trail, we have the marks of their passage through the hills, and we'll follow them through the Pass to the other side. If they slow or stop, then we might catch them. We aren't flogging the horses dead to get there.'

She's arsey.

Didn't she know how important this was? Loge did, though he wished daily to truly understand why. Dennawal hadn't given him further instruction since driving him to kill Yorrell and slaughter the Namjin raiders. The Drover of the Dead remained silent yet present, lingering, never truly gone, ignorant to Loge's silent pleas for some sign, anything he could cling to beyond this mute, relentless purpose.

A yawning emptiness gaped at his centre, a void he longed to fill. A honeycomb of punctures stretched through his mind, steering his moods in wild directions, propelling the constant yearning to find the woman who had once held the sword. That was his only goal.

He railed against rest or sleep, chafing at any delay. Food tasted of ash, though it did silence the meek voice of hunger mewling at the end of each day. He cared not for things that would allow him to complete his task, only that the task was done. Even as night fell beyond the canopy of the trees and the rumble of a distant rainstorm drew near, he itched to ride into the night.

Instead, they turned up a trail and angled toward the base of a rocky outcrop. Loge's thoughts screamed in protest, begging him to continue. Need clawed at the flesh of his mind, dragging him back to the main path, away from shelter and the promise of succour from the coming rain.

Marrit was right. If she let him anywhere near that map, he'd be gone before she could blink. He'd ride Striker into the ground, and he wasn't sure he'd care enough to move the poor creature off the track.

That thought drew him to a pause as he unsaddled the horse under the overhang of rock. Could he truly do that? He wouldn't enjoy it, but he'd do *anything* to close the gap between him and Lidan. With a shudder, Loge pushed the thought away. Best to follow Marrit's lead. At least she still had a grip on her morals.

'The Pass isn't far now,' Loge said, breaking the heavy silence as he served out the meat roasting over the fire. Darkness found them as the edge of the storm moved west, washing the bush clean and leaving the foliage to drip to its own beat.

The temperature plummeted with the setting sun and a fire crackled in the shelter of the rude cave; barely more than a naturally formed awning, eaten into the side of the steep valley by the bitter wind and rain of the high-country winter. Despite his general apathy, cold still bit at him as sharply as any living folk. Loge just didn't care quite as much as Marrit seemed to. Coats of tightly sewn pelt, abandoned during the day, were gratefully shrugged around their shoulders as night crept in, icy fingers seeking any loose stitch to sink their talons through.

He handed Marrit her portion of the dark meat and she stared out beyond the cave mouth, her gaze following the lazy smoke into the sky. Did she know he was testing her? Her eyes traced the stars, seeking the markers he'd shown her each night out from Tingalla, the chill northern wind lifting the tendrils of her hair, begging them to dance. If something were to happen to him or the map, she'd have only the sky to find her way. Tracking her sister would take more than just surveying the ground and the bush.

Finding a cluster of stars in the south would be her first step, then the bow of the sky serpent would give her north. Judging the distance to the mountains wasn't easy in the dark, but if she'd been paying attention, the young healer would gauge such a thing by the way their looming height blotted out the stars along the horizon.

'Maybe tomorrow?' Marrit guessed.

'Before noon,' Loge corrected.

Marrit flinched, her gaze falling to her lap, and he paused. She hadn't been wrong, only less specific than he would have liked. He should say something to reassure her that she'd done well, he just didn't know what.

Instead, he said nothing.

His next mouthful didn't touch his lips before the hairs on the back of his neck prickled to standing. A shiver rushed across his skin, a whisper of a warning in his mind. Loge lowered the greasy joint of meat into the rough timber bowl and put it to one side.

The sound of Marrit's chewing stopped. 'Loge… What can you see?'

It was her favourite question. She'd asked about his blackened eye, and he'd told her what he knew, which was precisely nothing. He left out the part about the auras and the sense they gave him of a person's intent or mood. It was enough that he was a walking and talking dead man, kept alive on the whim of a meddling death spirit. Marrit didn't need to know just how changed he was, just how unnatural and inhuman.

'Nothing.' Silence fell again and he came to his feet. It wasn't what he saw in the fire-lit wall of trees, but what he felt.

Something had changed.

A shift in the air, a pressure he hadn't realised was there until it dissipated. His black eye twitched and he tilted his head. They hadn't seen or heard a ngaru for two weeks. Marrit reasoned the creatures were wiped out when the witch incinerated them in the village. Many of the Tolak believed they were the last of the monsters remaining in the south, seeking out their creator only to be destroyed.

Loge had accepted this and left it alone. It wasn't his problem. He had no quarrel with the creatures so long as they kept out of his way. For a time, he'd allowed himself to believe as his people did. For a time, he'd been a fool.

What he *had* seen was an invisible presence along the trail—a pale shimmer he'd paid little heed to until now—one he hadn't truly understood until he and Marrit broke away to camp several hundred feet from the path.

That shimmer didn't continue up to the outcrop, and neither did its meagre protection against things that meant them ill. The Tolak were wrong. The ngaru were not vanquished. And they were about to become his problem all over again.

'Can you fight?' he asked Marrit without taking his eyes from the trees.

'Ah, what?'

Spinning, he glared at her, hefting his axe and hatchet. 'Can you hold a knife at least?'

Marrit scowled and discarded her bowl, climbing to her feet and drawing a long hunting blade from a sheath at the back of her belt. 'With more precision than those meat mallets.'

Loge baulked and she upended a pot of water onto the flames, reducing the fire to glowing coals. 'Don't fall on that. I don't have time to nurse your burns as well as stop you doing something stupid.'

'Excuse—'

A scream tore the night to ribbons and the death of the fire plunged the camp into darkness. Three fast blinks and his sight adjusted, his weird left eye fracturing the dark, absorbing even the faintest light from the stars shining on the rain-soaked bush. The moon was on its way out, the visible half glowing brightly enough to make out the shapes of trees and Marrit, sinking into a crouch.

'Who taught you that?'

'Who do you think?' A glance over her shoulder revealed a pearlescent gleam to her eyes in his night vision. 'She wouldn't leave me defenceless.'

Spinning his hatchet, he took a careful step away from the cave, scanning the trees for a shiver of movement that should not be there. 'Have you fought them before?'

A growl rolled from the bush not ten feet distant and Loge's fingers squeezed the haft of his axe, reassured by its weight, his heart thudding merrily and muscles tingling at the prospect of danger. Perhaps he *was* still capable of feeling something more than the cold.

'Nah,' she replied, an unseen maniacal grin echoing in her voice. 'But I like to learn on the job.'

A pair of monsters burst from the trees and flew at Loge and Marrit. Steel caught the light, flashing in the darkness. Screams of hunger and desperation shredded the air and Loge's axe clashed along the edge of something hard. He drove against the onslaught, his hatchet coming around to hack at the flank of the ngaru flailing an embedded steel limb at his face.

Ducking under the arm, he snapped around, hooking the beard of his axe around the creature's arm. With a hard yank and twist, the limb dislocated, crunching out of its socket, dangling by threads of disintegrating tendons and rotting muscle. His sight penetrated the puckered dead skin of its back as he buried the hatchet in the soft flesh at its nape. This one was starved, its throbbing blue spine barely glowing, its torso an emaciated rake.

Time slowed by a heartbeat. Loge's blood sang through his veins. The creature whirled to face him, swinging its useless dangling arm in a vain attempt to wound. Violence surged in him, and for the first time since Dennawal sent him back, Loge felt alive.

With his hatchet still wedged in the back of the ngaru's neck, Loge swung the axe in both hands, scything upward at the beast's jaw. Steel met flesh, bone and gristle, a nauseating crack echoing against the trees as the weight of the axe ploughed into the ngaru's skull. Something let go and the head tore from the neck, skin parting like bread fresh from the oven. A long cord whipped out behind it, snaking through the air, still throbbing pale blue as the decapitated head sailed off into the night.

Abandoned, the trunk of the corpse shuddered and staggered, momentum holding it upright for the length of a breath before it flopped to the wet ground like a dropped doll. Dripping with sweat and sticky ngaru ichor, Loge looked the corpse over with his blackened eye.

Nothing.

Not even a spark of life remained.

Nearby someone grunted and Loge snapped up to glare across the clearing. A small, lithe figure staggered back, skidding to a stop in the mud and wet leaves. Staring down its opponent, a defiant ngaru opened its unnaturally wide mouth with a throaty hiss, unfazed by the great gouts of thick, dark blood pouring from a constellation of holes in its trunk.

Marrit flashed Loge a look and stabbed her knife in his direction. 'You stay the fuck over there!'

She threw herself at the ngaru, unleashing a battle cry that would have woken the dead, launching from the ground and taking it down in a brutal tackle. The creature crumbled and she pinned it, her knife tearing across its neck as it screamed fury in her face.

The scream became a wet, gushing gurgle but Marrit kept sawing, her knife an unstoppable, deadly whir. Loge slipped his axe into its belt loop and levered the hatchet from the remains of the beast at his feet. Urgency vanished into the wind, his heart rate calmed, the tingle across his skin eased. He headed slowly to where Marrit crouched over the mangled ngaru.

If she heard him, she didn't turn. He put a hand on her shoulder and she sprang up, knife drawn back, her face painted with the gleaming muck that had once kept the ngaru moving.

'What?!' she snarled, teeth bare, eyes wild.

'It's dead.'

'And?'

Perhaps she didn't have as good a handle on her morals as he thought.

'There isn't much left to cut,' Loge told her. 'But if you have unresolved issues you want to work through, I can leave you—'

'Oh, fuck off.' Marrit spat ichor and shoved past him. This time he caught her elbow and squeezed until he was quite sure a flick of his wrist would snap the bone. Marrit didn't flinch.

'Do you?'

'Do I what?'

Loge rolled his eyes. She was smarter than this. 'Have unresolved issues? I can't have you going to pieces out here.'

'You're worried about me?' Marrit's bitter laugh cut the night. 'That's fair, coming from the dead man who has no idea why he's here. *Obviously*, I have issues. With a family like mine, how the fuck could I *not* have issues? I've spent every day since I was eleven years old, stitching up the damage done by these things. Don't you fucking judge me for wanting to give some back.'

Her accusation echoed loudly. Too loudly for him to ignore, too furious to let him sleep.

...the dead man, with no idea why he's even here...

The truth of it stung, piercing through the numb shell around his mind until it was the only thing left to feel, the only thing worth thinking about. His companion washed her face with a grimy cloth and climbed into her bed roll, falling asleep as her head hit the crude pillow of a rolled-up coat. Loge remained by the fire, his gaze caught in its depths.

Questions edged along his thoughts, scratched to be heard above the cycling, persistent need for one single answer.

Why?

Muscles relaxed, time slowed into a heavy stream, flames shuddered to a stop. Loge's sense of the world lurched hard, and his vision stuttered, stomach clenching. Blinking rapidly, he recoiled, heat bursting from the campfire and blasting his face.

Loge lowered the shield of his arm from his eyes.

He was not alone.

In truth, he never had been, but now something else sat in the cave, hidden only because he had not the heart to admit it to himself.

'You're loud, you know that?' The voice of death rolled through the cave, as heavy and timeless as the mountains. The figure seemed male for all intents and purposes, though Loge wondered if it was anything but an affect, a ruse to put him at ease. If the face he saw fit the stories from his childhood, then perhaps he wouldn't run screaming.

Violet eyes studied him across the fire, a hulking man with skin the colour of onyx hunched by Marrit's feet, poking a stick into the fire. White specks decorated the man's cheek bones and brow, reminding Loge of the stars. For all he knew, they were. A pelt hung around the man's shoulders, loose trousers of hide about his legs, his feet bare against the sharp stones of the cave floor. Those violet eyes followed Loge's gaze to Marrit's sleeping form, and the man waved a hand in casual dismissal. 'She won't wake.'

'How do you know? She's more cunning than you think.' If anyone could break a spell through sheer force of will, it was Marrit.

'We're outside of time. If she were to open her eyes, she'd see nothing out of the ordinary. I'm not sitting at her feet because it's not her time to see me. My task here doesn't concern her.' Dennawal's slight smile didn't ease Loge's apprehension. The spirit lifted the end of the fire-stick and pointed. 'I came to shut you up.'

Loge scowled. 'Excuse me?'

'You think I can't hear all those questions?' Dennawal swirled the stick as if trying to swat the thoughts from the air. 'So many times; why,

why, why. I know not all of you came back, but this? This is too much.'

'Whatever you did to me, whatever is *wrong* with me, is your fault!' Loge hissed across the fire. His finger jabbed toward his black eye, a sneer curling his lip. 'You gave me this *thing* and no explanation of what it's for. Took parts of me I can't get back—memories, places, feelings without purchase or—'

'That's all that was left, Loge Baker.'

The words smothered the tirade and Loge stared in confusion. 'I don't...'

'I know. You were dead when I found you. Making the journey to my side before your passage could begin to the realm of your ancestors. What you lost was gone before I found you.' The spirit's brows drew together, sympathy in the lines of his face. 'I did not do this to you.'

'What about...' Loge gestured at his eye, the anger melting away. 'This. I don't remember this from before.'

'That is an artefact of death, an unavoidable necessity for sight in the afterlife, I'm afraid. Your people know of it. The tale-keepers see it when they travel through my realm to seek the counsel of their forebears. Marrit knew it when she saw it. She paid attention when her father spoke of the old ways.' Dennawal tapped his temple. 'You, I fear, did not.'

Uncertainty coiled in Loge and he fought the urge to pull his knees up under his chin. This wasn't a special power or gift. It was evidence of his death, proof of just how close he'd come to joining his ancestors. It was all nice to know, but it did nothing to answer the real question. 'Why?'

Death looked up from the fire, his expression blank. 'Why are you here? I told you why.'

'Ah, no, you did not.' Of all the things he'd experienced since his return, the certainty that he knew nothing of his purpose was the clearest, strongest sense Loge had.

Dennawal scoffed. 'You're not done here, that's why. It really couldn't be much simpler.'

Fury built like a swelling storm, thunderous rage rolling to a crescendo. Loge leaned dangerously over the fire and glowered into the spirit's purple gaze. 'You dragged me back here, gasping like a landed fish, half-dead, untethered and deformed and *that's* all you've got? That's not a fucking reason. Why am I here? I need to find Lidan—you made that abundantly clear—but you never told me why. Why does she need me so badly?'

'She doesn't need you,' Dennawal replied simply, dropping the truth between them and sitting back against the cave wall. Casually folding his arms, he shrugged. 'Her life didn't revolve around you when you were alive, and it doesn't now. But Lidan is one part of a task so crucial that should it fail, the balance of the very universe is at stake. What she needs to succeed is what you *represent*, and that doesn't work if you're dead. Your death took away the thing she needs to win this fight.'

Loge let the pause settle, let the words sink in. Memories twitched to life, of riding, of fighting, of love. They lanced through his chest with enough force to make him gasp and he pulled back from the intensity. 'What could I possibly give her that she doesn't already have in spades?'

'Hope. Your death destroyed her hope.'

It was the single thing he had not considered. How had Lidan fared when he'd fallen under that cascade of rock and soil? How had she borne that loss? Had it torn at her heart, crushed her spirit even further than her abysmal parents had with their unrealistic expectations and horrific judgement? Had she flayed herself in misdirected guilt, thinking that somehow she was at fault?

She'd do it too, blaming herself for his stupid refusal to treat his injured knee. The same refusal that damaged the joint and slowed him down, made him vulnerable to a stray kick or a well-placed strike of a club. It left him in the creek bed of that gorge, unable to run, unable to do anything but stand between Yorrell and Lidan's retreat. Hazy as the memories were, he'd done that knowing he'd die and leave her to face whatever horror her parents managed to cook up.

I left her...

'You represent a future she never thought she could have. Something beyond her existence as the daughter of a daari. You embody the hope for what she could have had if none of that mattered. That she was worth something more than her title and her birth right. That she was worth more than her womb and what's between her legs.' The spirit shook his head and aimed a finger at Loge. 'You reminded her that she mattered.'

'Is,' Loge corrected.

'Pardon?'

'She *is* worth more than that. Always was, always will be.'

The Drover of the Dead opened his hands. 'I rest my case. I didn't bring you back to save her. She doesn't need anyone to do that. I brought you back to remind her that she has a reason to save *herself*. You always were stronger together. She needs to be the strongest she has ever been to face what's coming.'

Marrit's stories slotted into place—the disappearance of her mother, Sellan's creation of the ngaru and the need to stop her before she birthed something even worse into the world. The Lidan that Loge remembered didn't need a protector, yet her father and Siman had trusted him to keep her safe for years. Had it been their choice or had Dennawal forced their hands? Had this spirit planned all along to wield Lidan as his weapon and placed Loge between her and danger? 'There's more at play here, isn't there?'

'There always is,' Dennawal said quietly.

'This is more than just stopping a woman from creating a monster. This is a war.'

Dennawal nodded. 'A war for the balance of all things. There are beings that your people call the ancestors or spirits—others call them gods—who'd happily tip the scales into chaos just to feed their greed. The Morritae are such a force. They stand at the other side of this, and if they succeed, if they get their hands on the power Sellan has promised them, there will be nothing to correct the balance but destruction. This is a war I have fought for eons, a war you cannot see. That you should *never* have seen. Yet here you are, right at the centre, on a path you were never and always meant to walk.'

Loge sighed, resignation heavy across his shoulders. 'Will we survive it?' Already emotions tore at him in ways they had not in weeks. It was a sensation he despised. Purpose bit deep once more, fortifying and crystallising his resolve, insisting that he move, that he act, that he fight beside Lidan until the danger had abated or there was nothing left of him but dust.

'You might. You might not.' Dennawal shrugged and time shifted as he began to fade. The reply did little to quell Loge's uncertainty. 'Other beings decide such things, not I. All *you* must do is stand between Lidan and the fate that comes for her. She will do the rest.'

CHAPTER THIRTY

Eastern grasslands, Arinnia

Night poured over the plains, seeping from unnamed mountains in the east. Stars blinked bright in the moonless sky, the eaves of a woodland to the west plunged into murky darkness as the hazy warmth of the day nestled beneath the blanket of night.

Lidan waited for her companions to settle, for the soft sounds of rest and the gentle murmurs of relaxation after a long day in the saddle. Summer heat radiated through her bedroll and despite its sultry call, she couldn't sleep. Instead, she lifted her head and glanced around the camp.

Coals glowed in a crude hearth, the remains of their spare dinner crisping at the edges of the ash and dusty rocks. By that dim light she crawled quietly to her feet and picked her way amongst sleeping forms. Five nights after they stumbled exhausted from the Pass, they were within reach of the great forests of Arinnia, angling north-west to cross the River Arris and hike once more into mountainous terrain.

Tonight was the first where, in near absolute darkness, she could slip away, the risk of discovery at its lowest. Brit stood watch somewhere, wandering in the dark. If she was smart, or perhaps lucky, she'd get past him and a few paces away before she vanished. It wouldn't take much. She just had to get clear of Ran and Thanie.

She allowed herself a bittersweet smile as she stepped past Eian and Zarad, orange firelight gleaming on their features. A tangle of limbs, they rested in each other's embrace. She remembered what it was to feel that, to slumber beside the person she most trusted in the world. The chasm left by Loge still beckoned, as raw as the void left by a freshly pulled tooth. A weak numbness remained and she forged a path past the ache.

Lidan couldn't bring back her love. She didn't know how to dull the pain, either. But she did know how to hunt monsters. There was simplicity and beauty in that, a perfect unison between action and reaction, predictable and knowable in the chaos. She could stop her mother too, but to do that, she needed information.

Ran, Thanie and Aelish had become her tutors of the ancient and not-so-distant past—stories of the world beyond the borders of the South Lands, the war between the Woaden Empire and the Free Nations of Arinnia, Isord and Orthia, and the chain of islands the Empire had yet the will nor the strength to conquer. They told her of the gods her mother's people worshiped, their creation tales not so distant or different from her own people's stories.

Almost all of what these northerners attributed to their gods, Lidan's people gave to their ancestors; the good seasons and the bad, the rains and the fertile soils. They were the ones who blessed babies at their first breath or fortified a warrior in the heat of battle. Besides Dennawal, there were no other named entities in the south, but she knew this was not the way across the world. Others saw life as the workings of many, or sometimes one being. All of this sat right with Lidan. It all made sense, in one way or another. It was the female deities of the Woaden she didn't understand.

Thanie had told her the barest bones of the Woaden legends, holding back at least some truth of the Dead Sisters. She'd skirted at the edges of what they controlled, the facets of life in their dominion. Her features had warped as if she had a mouthful of sour milk at Ran's mention of the Dark Rider, a deep mistrust rearing no matter how she tried to brush it away.

Had Lidan not seen the reactions, not noticed the gaps in the stories, nor wondered at the glaring inconsistencies, Thanie's secrets may have remained just that. Lidan might have left them well enough alone. But she prodded and probed, peeling away layers until the words the witch left unspoken said more than the woman intended to reveal.

The Dead Sisters were connected to Sellan and the ngaru.

They'd helped her mother, but why or at what cost, Lidan couldn't say. Without the power gifted by the Sisters, Sellan couldn't make the first army of tormented dead. Following that down a logical path, Sellan would need their help again to resurrect her plans for conquering the north. Thanie's assertions that the deities were furious with Sellan left Lidan with the bitter taste of suspicion on her tongue. They may not be willing to lend such aid again, but there remained a small kernel of horrifying possibility.

What if they did?

All Thanie gave her were warnings, murmured caution that she should never again touch the blue ghost of the craw, for it would take her to the unseen realms where no magic could save her if she fell too far.

It burned at Lidan until she couldn't sleep, scratched at her until she couldn't train properly or sit still. She paced the camp night after night, a plan forming, and she'd waited. Tonight, in the darkness of the absent moon, she made her move, all hope resting on the thin edge of a knife. Could she prevent the needless yet utterly inevitable bloodshed that loomed in their future?

She'd go where her craw beckoned and hang the consequences. What she'd do when she got there was another matter entirely. Need drew her into the evening until the soft flutter of feathers announced the arrival of her guide.

Its pale radiance split the night as it banked through the air, alighting amongst long blades of sun-parched grass. A deep breath, released slowly, did nothing to calm Lidan's nerves. She glanced over her shoulder at the glow of the camp beyond the gentle rise of a hillock.

'I hope you know what you're doing,' she muttered, as much to herself as to the bird. The grass rustled and the craw hopped closer. She dropped into a crouch. 'If we get stranded, no one's coming to save us.'

A shiny eye studied her, winking at her hand as if asking for an invitation. Tentative fingers unfurled from a fist, a slight twitch beckoning the messenger-spirit. Heart in her throat, she crushed her fear and squeezed her eyes shut.

A pair of taloned feet scratched her skin, and reality tore.

Beyond her closed eyes, the brightness of the white place bloomed, stinging at the edges of her sight as the close warmth of the night evaporated into a chilling void.

With great care, Lidan opened her eyes.

The expanse of white hadn't changed. The same featureless ground lay at her feet, the dirt on her boots leaving no marks as she stood. There was no discernible sky, nor edges or margins to the place, no way to measure how far she'd gone or if she moved at all.

Behind her right shoulder, emerging as she turned, a black smudge stretched out along what might be a horizon. She'd seen it last time she'd fallen through the crack in the world, but today it seemed a little closer. Was that where she'd find answers? Or was it the doorway to the place Thanie warned her about—the realm she stood no chance of escaping once she threw herself in?

The craw made the decision for her, launching from her hand and lifting until it became a speck of iridescent blue against blinding white. Wings beating hard in the silence, it streaked toward the black smudge, trailing blue smoke from sleek feathers.

'No, wait!' Lidan's shout echoed, fracturing into a thousand shards of sound. She darted after the bird, desperate not to lose it in the glare.

Her boots pounded the ground, splintering cracks squealing as they raced away from each footfall. Like an endless sheet of opaque ice, the pure white beneath her feet buckled, an agonised groan wafting from deep below the surface. Lidan threw a frantic glance over her shoulder and stumbled, tripping over her own feet.

Oh, fuck.

Her boots had carved into the white, leaving dark, ragged pock marks in the otherwise perfect surface. Spiderweb cracks screeched away from them, growing as she watched, the edges crumbling and tipping into darkness beneath. The cracks pursued her. She ran harder, no longer chasing the craw but racing to outpace the ravenous cracks.

Ahead, the black smudge vanished along with the craw. The blue smoke was gone, the trail lost. Without a sound, the ground beneath Lidan's feet opened, lips retreating as it yawed.

She fell.

Time doesn't flow in darkness.

It has no measure, no way to mark it against the movement of anything else. All her life Lidan measured time against trees and plants, stars and seasons, the moon and the very people at her side. Now, Lidan fell through darkness so complete it had no end or beginning. It was entirely without time, without limit, without comprehension. It was at once vast and minute. At once empty yet stuffed with everything that had ever or would ever exist. She was so insignificant beside its magnificence that she barely warranted attention, and yet it knew she had arrived.

It knew and it did not want her here.

Something cold placed its fingers around her throat and her scream came out as a weak puff of air. The hand didn't squeeze, it only held. The rest of her body came to a point of quiet stillness; no longer falling nor on solid ground. She simply existed; held firmly but gently by an entity she couldn't see.

A presence leaned in beside her cheek and a shiver rolled down Lidan's back. A careful, deliberate intake of breath drew chill air past her face, her skin crawling as the entity exhaled. A dusting of ice prickled along her cheekbones, and Lidan went rigid.

'You are not what I expected, nor what I was promised.' It wasn't a question or an accusation, simply a statement of fact. What might have been a woman's voice, deep and husky, slid into Lidan's ear and began to search. A physical presence, the voice slithered inside and perched on the edge of her consciousness, a cool hand caressing the scars of her life. The largest—a ropey, puckered thing, standing proud, fresh and tender—drew the being's attention. 'That must have hurt.'

Courage surged in Lidan. That was not for anyone but herself to see. 'How would you know?' she snarled.

'I know scars. I know the tales they tell. I know the creases on an old man's brow speak of worry while the lines at the corners of his eyes recall his laughter. The lines on a woman's thighs and stomach might tell of life created, or of years of hardship and struggle. I know this ragged thing here is the death throes of your sister, the sound of her final breath as you gave her true mercy. These are the many stinging losses of too many friends. This one,' it murmured, tracing a cold finger of awareness along the largest puckered wound, 'is a pain so terrible you dare not even look at it. All of them battle wounds, all of them won in a life too short to have warranted such strife. You are far too young to have suffered such torment.'

'You don't know anything about me.' Lidan's denial rang so hollow it echoed.

The being made a sound that might have been a chuckle. 'I know your blood, small one. I know the line from which you come. I can smell it on you.'

Light flared in the dark. Clear violet eyes glowed inches from Lidan's face. Her sharp intake of breath cut like knives as the being began to squeeze, fingers tightening around the soft flesh of Lidan's throat. A long straight nose materialised above full, pale lips in a snow-white face. The being's hair blazed with the fury of wildfire, the light of her eyes pulsed, illuminating her monstrously tall form.

'*She* is the one I want, small one. *She* who shamed and weakened me. Are you helping her?' the being demanded in a voice as vast as the world itself. 'Or are you here to challenge me, an irritating distraction while she thinks to court my sister in secret?'

Terror danced on Lidan's tongue, and she laughed. 'Aren't you all knowing? Don't those eyes see everything?'

The fuck is wrong with me?! Had she just sneered in the face of a god, the embodiment of her ancestor's power? She was so utterly fucked.

The being's lips pulled back into a dreadful grin and this time, she laughed, the sound shaking the fabric of reality.

'Oh dear. I'd know that defiance anywhere.' Her head cocked to one side. 'You are her daughter but...' A long, deep inhalation tore the air and the being blinked her enormous violet eyes slowly, as if savouring the knowledge she garnered in that single act. 'You do not travel with her. You are not *with* her at all, are you, small one?'

This time Lidan knew better than to answer with cheek. The being may not know all, but she knew enough. If Lidan wanted help or answers, she had to show some humility. Was this the force her mother had offended? Was it the being Thanie had sent the craw-spirit message to? If this was one of the Dead Sisters who had granted power to Sellan all those years ago, then this was the hand that could prevent the bloodshed that would surely follow.

'I'm not with her, though she is my mother.' Their eyes met and Lidan flinched. It was like staring at the heart of a star. 'I came to warn you, Sister. She means to beg your power again and she means to bring war and death to the world.'

The being sighed. A sad, resigned sound that turned Lidan's blood to dust. She knew.

'Your mother's people know me as Macha, and try as your mother might, she cannot bring war to the world. I alone hold that power, though it has run wild so long amongst mortals it is hardly mine to command anymore. I call warriors to their weapons and grant them entry to the halls of their forebears when they fall upon them, but I am not the Mistress of Fate. That is my sister, Urda. Urda weaves the threads of lives, knowing just how they end and how they begin. Urda alone has the power to grant the boon your mother seeks.'

'No... You can't...' Horror rippled through Lidan. This was the wrong god? She'd managed to fall into the clutches of the sister who couldn't aid her? 'Urda has to stop her. Please! Whatever she asks, whatever price she's willing to pay, whatever she promises you—it's a lie! You can't let her do this. You're the final hurdle in her way and if you fail, she'll destroy...'

Expressionless, Macha watched Lidan crash against the immovable force of a god's will, her energy failing, her heart breaking. This had been her last hope at stopping it all before it began; her failsafe, her point of no return. Until now, a sliver of hope remained that her mother's plans would come to nothing simply because she hadn't been granted the power to make them bear fruit.

Those massive violet eyes continued to watch as Lidan's shoulders sagged and her eyes burned hot with tears. 'I have to speak with Urda. Please. Thousands will die. You have to help me, before it's too late.'

'Ah small one, it is already too late.'

Lidan grew still. 'What?'

'The price has been paid. Urda made her bargain, though it galls me. And the price was paid. We shall yet see if what was promised will be delivered. We will yet see if the souls your mother pledges will come our way.'

'But you want her dead, don't you? As punishment for failing last time!'

Macha shrugged. 'I might, if only to repay the slight against me and to heal the wound her failures wrought upon my power and standing. But she pledges souls to my sisters and I, so perhaps I should want her to succeed? Perhaps I want the change her actions will bring? Wanting her dead is not enough. I cannot see or change Sellan's fate. Why do you think her cousin sought to send her here? While she remains on the mortal plane, she is beyond my reach. I cannot touch her there. What happens while she breathes is in the hands of mortals such as yourself. Should she fall into my realm… Well, her fate would no longer be my sister's domain.'

Lidan baulked. It made less sense than Thanie's riddles but somewhere in the tangle, she understood. Macha may well seek revenge, but it wasn't in the god's power to deliver. Lidan's chin trembled, and she slammed her teeth down on the back of her lip, a distraction from the flaming pit of hate igniting in her core. 'It's done then. You've doomed us all.'

The edges of Macha's eyes crinkled as the corners of her mouth lifted. 'No, I have not.'

'You fucking have! You gave her the deadliest weapon she could ever ask for!' Rage boiled over and Lidan thrashed against Macha's grip. Vain punches landed with no more force than Lidan might feel from an insect bite, the being's expression neutral, her ageless face watching the tiny mortal fight an inevitable truth.

'Lidan Tolak, daughter of the South Lands, once and true heir to the Tolak clan and the lands of the Jagga River, are you so easily defeated?'

The words froze Lidan, slowing her heart, chilling her bones. She'd never thought to hear those titles again, least of all this far from home. She never thought she had the right to carry them beyond those borders.

'I know the wound that made that awful scar, and it was not the loss of friends or a lover. I may not be the Mistress of Fate, and I may not know what lies in your path, but I have seen the road you walked to get here. I have seen the blood you spilled, the stones you crawled across, the mountains you have climbed and the oceans of grief you have swum.' Macha leaned in, looming over Lidan. Her face began to change.

Blazing tongues of fiery hair became thick black curls, torrents of obsidian falling beyond the being's immense shoulders. Her nose broadened, her lips filling out as her skin darkened. Lines of white and yellow emerged across her forehead, her cheekbones adorned with the symbols of the river and the snake. Tolak symbols. *Lidan's* symbols.

Lidan watched in slack-jawed astonishment as Macha became the true embodiment of her ancestors; a fierce warrior woman from stories as old as the Malapa. A grandmother she'd never known, the source of the life-force that thundered through her veins.

'I have seen the weapons you wield and not all of them are steel or stone. There is loyalty and love in you as powerful as any axe, as true as any arrow. You are a warrior, small one. Fast and strong, sharp and deadly as a blade. I *know* warriors and you are one down to your bones. You are the decedent of greatness, of the fathers and mothers of nations. You are glory and you are not broken or defeated until you choose to surrender. Do you surrender?'

'No,' Lidan breathed in a harsh whisper.

Macha's iridescent eyes gleamed with violent joy. 'Are you afraid of this path and its destination, Blade of the South?'

'Yes,' Lidan replied with a shiver.

'Good.' The goddess-ancestor brought her lips to Lidan's ear. 'Then fight.'

With a roar and the searing heat of a thousand suns, Lidan punched back into the night around the camp. Flying backward through a tear in space, she crashed to the ground, skidding through grass and thumping across patches of gravel. The thin sleeve of her shirt tore, the fabric parting with a screech until finally she came to an abrupt stop at the base of the small rise. With a wordless groan she rolled onto her back and stared into the fathomless sky, the stars watching in mute amusement.

'Fuck that…'

'What did you do?' Thanie asked coolly. It wasn't quite a scold, but it held enough judgement for Lidan to know she'd been weighed and found wanting.

'I went,' she grunted, hauling her aching body to its feet, 'to get answers.'

Silhouetted by the campfire's glow, Thanie sat at the top of the rise. Lidan couldn't see the older woman's eyes, but their scrutiny burned through walls she hurried to build.

'Oh, did you now?' Thanie wondered. 'Did you get them?'

Struggling for breath, Lidan rolled her shoulder and found it intact, albeit bruised. Thank small mercies she'd landed on the opposite side to her fragile collarbone. She nodded and squinted into the light. 'I did.'

Lidan crested the rise and Thanie came to her feet. Those storm-cloud eyes sparkled; a thousand questions unspoken. 'You went through the veil? To the unseen realm?'

Lidan could only nod. Her ribs ached like she'd been kicked by a horse.

'Why, girl? Why take such a risk?' Thanie's hands grasped Lidan's arms and squeezed. Genuine concern deepened in the lines of her face, real fear in her eyes. 'Did they find you?'

'I found them.'

Thanie's grip slackened, and her hands fell away. Her eyes grew wide, and the colour drained from her already pale face. Horror moved her lips but held her tongue.

Lidan sighed. 'I had to know. They're the only entity strong enough to gift my mother what she needs. I had to know what they were going to do. I had to know if they even cared.' Their eyes met again and Lidan's shoulders dropped. 'Urda has already struck a deal with my mother. The Mistress of Fate set her price for the gift my mother seeks.'

Anguish rippled across Thanie's face. 'Would they reconsider?'

'Macha couldn't help me. The price has been paid.' One hand found Thanie's while the other squeezed the hilt of her knife.

'So she has won…' Thanie's strangled whisper reached Lidan across the hush of the grassland breeze. 'I can't let this happen again. It can't be allowed—I can't let it—' Thanie clutched her stomach as if to hold back a tide of grief. Shaking her head, her eyes darted across the night, and she staggered.

Lidan steadied her. '*I* won't let this happen again. None of us will. You aren't alone this time.' Hope dared to shimmer in Thanie's eyes and Lidan prayed it wasn't misplaced.

Loyalty and love—weapons as strong as steel and stone. That was what her foremother had said. Loyalty and love. Those things she could leverage where Sellan could not. Blade of the South, Macha had called her—a weapon her mother was not expecting, a force she would not think to reckon with.

'She may have won this battle, but she will not win the war. No matter what it takes, she will be stopped.'

CHAPTER THIRTY-ONE

The Ruken, Isord

Though the trees didn't smell the same, and the birds sang to a different warbling chorus, the forests and rivers of Arinnia rushed Lidan with heady memories of the South Lands. The creeks ran cool and clear, flowing to the southwest, desperate to reach the freedom of the sea. Their waters raced on despite the lack of rain-filled storm clouds that never built on the horizon this far north.

The cleared land around Kederen was the first unequivocal sign that Lidan had crossed into another world. Great tracts of bush and plain had been carved up, first by axes, then bladed carts drawn by massive, muscled horses. Homesteads dotted the rolling hills and easy valleys, each little hall hemmed in by a low wall of stones. Uniform squares of waving crops stretched off into the hazy distance, bordered by the dark eaves of what must have once been endless, unbroken woodland. A wide road cut a near straight path through it all, a thoroughfare giving little heed to the arch or dip of the land, forging toward the Arinnian seat of power.

Aelish set an unrelenting pace, leaving no time to explore or absorb. Lidan's news of the bargain struck between Sellan and the goddess of fate had been greeted with stunned silence and violent curses, Ran disappearing into the night to swear at the sky, his native tongue offering no disguise for his rage.

Each day since had been hard riding, often in silence, tasks completed with the utmost economy until an enormous, highly trafficked crossroad appeared somewhere to the northeast of Kederen. There was no time to see that city, Aelish told them. Their efforts were focused on hiking the foothills of the Ruken and making it to Kotja, the largest city in Isord, before the first night of the full moon. They could no longer afford to wander.

Sellan had surely begun her work. If she had the power of the Dead Sisters, why wait?

Eian and Zarad kept mostly to themselves, circling in and out on scouting runs and watching for Arinnian patrols that might seek to stop them for questioning. Brit hung close to Ran, who had all but disappeared under a dark, brooding cloud. What he thought or how he truly felt remained a tightly guarded secret. He threw himself into training with Thanie, speaking to the others only when absolutely necessary. Lidan sensed Iridia at the edges of her awareness but left the ghost alone. She had no desire to kick the hornet's nest any more than her excursion into the unseen realms already had.

Whatever breakthrough Lidan had hoped for in Ran's mood, whatever caution she'd hoped to nudge him toward, vanished that night. His singular focus, his obsession with gaining strength, with travelling as far as they could each day, wore her down until nothing remained but threadbare tolerance and lingering disdain. It was as if a single second of energy wasted on frivolous chatter was one he couldn't spare.

Lidan's relaxed lessons in northern politics quickly became a crashcourse in Isordian customs and Woaden traditions, as if her life depended on remembering that lower-ranking folk must always stand behind their betters. To be sure, not pissing off the Isordian king within the first five minutes of their hopeful audience would be an advantage, but they had to be granted said audience first. That, as it turned out, may yet prove to be their greatest obstacle.

It was more than Lidan could bear to think about as they trudged higher into the Ruken, a well-worn yet well-maintained road winding from the foothills to the deep valleys and sheer mountainsides. The warm woodland of Arinnia fell behind, replaced by wind-swept scree and shivering shrubs.

'Is it always this fucking cold up here?' Lidan muttered through chattering teeth and chapped lips. Balling her gloved hands into fists, her thickest coat hugged close around layers of thinner clothes until the outermost surfaces were lined with fur and oiled leather. Despite the knitted socks, her toes stung with cold and her ears ached as the wind howled past.

'Not in the summer,' Aelish replied, glancing back down the line of horses.

'It *is* summer,' Eian snapped from somewhere behind them, triggering a smirk and a wink from Aelish and a dry snort of laughter from Zarad.

Zarad nudged his partner with an elbow. 'We've had worse at home.'

Eian's glare could have melted the entire mountain. 'Name a day the wind blew its arse out like this at the Keep?'

'The second winter after Sasha and I arrived.' Ran's voice floated from the rear, rare enough these days that the rest of them turned in their saddles to stare. The dark smudges under his eyes had deepened, his mood dragged down with it. For the smallest of moments, the gleam of a happy memory danced in his crystal blue eyes. 'Worst blizzard on record, Collan said. Tore the roof off the infirmary stores and dumped snow inside for days before anyone could do anything about it. I'd never heard your sister swear as much as she did that day.'

Zarad shared his friend's grin before their smiles fell away. Ghosts spun where the light of fond recollection had been. Death and loss stalked them, and Lidan wondered at the weight they carried. Each of them had a burden to haul up this mountain. What waited north of these ragged peaks didn't care for the scars of the past. It had designs on the future alone.

Ahead the road widened, curving around the shoulder of the mountain and disappearing off to the left behind a cliff. The wind tore at their clothes, whipping through their horses' manes as they turned the corner. Exposed again to the bitterness of the northerly gale, the conversation died.

Breath caught in Lidan's throat, and a warm smile spread across Aelish's lips. Nestled at the head of a great valley, carved from the sides of two imposing mountains, Kotja gleamed. White streaks of snow held tight in the shadows, untouched by the sun as it tracked across the sky, barely warm enough to heat Lidan's back as the day turned toward evening.

Behind her, Eian murmured his surprise and she pulled Theus to the side of the track. The others filed past as she drank in her first view of a real city and all its enormous, stone-built glory. Walls and towers, spires and domes, some carved from the very mountain itself, others immense blocks of stone and great timber beams. Glass glittered alongside snow as the sun dropped in the west. A lilac haze of woodsmoke wafted up, too distant to carry the scent of cooking but painting the scene with a softness that warmed her just to look at.

'Have you ever seen anything so incredible?' Lidan whispered to herself. 'I have, but not by much.'

She would have looked at Thanie had she been able to pull her eyes away. She didn't believe the witch for a second. There couldn't really be anything more astounding in all of Coraidin.

At the very west stood the largest of the buildings, a cluster of impressive structures topped with artful domes and needle-thin spires, the rest of the city spreading out below them like a flowing skirt, concentric circular walls marking terraced lines across the face of the mountain. Through the centre, a wide river wore its way toward the lowlands of Arinnia, one of the many heads of the River Arris she'd seen on the northerner's map.

From the base of that valley, still more of the city stretched away, climbing in terraces up the opposing face of a mountain and down along the riverbank. This side of town seemed more haphazard, as if it had long ago outgrown the strong, uniform lines of the city proper and sprawled into the valley in fits and starts. Walls built over the years tried to hem it all in, an attempt at defence as the number of inhabitants and their dwellings continued to grow. When room inside each enclosure ran out, the city jumped the border again, requiring yet another wall and sentry towers. The result looked like a ripple on a great lake of stone, the largest of the buildings at its centre as if some immense being had dropped them there at the beginning of time to watch the rock and gravel shiver and buck at the impact.

'Where are we going?' Lidan murmured. How did anyone find their way through such maze? The forest of buildings soared up two or three storeys, then higher again for the largest of them. Lidan's chest tightened at the thought. How quickly could she get lost in there? Would anyone ever find her again?

Thanie's gloved finger pointed to the largest cluster of buildings rearing over the city. 'The king will keep his counsel there. If the Yordam's are as high up as I believe, they won't live too far from the centre of power.'

'If Aelish comes from such an influential family, why is the audience with the king so uncertain?' Lidan had examined the problem from as many angles as she could imagine, and still it made no sense. How could someone as well known as Aelish struggle to petition the king? Ran had said something about a matching between the two families, then closed back up, falling into his thoughts again. He couldn't be drawn on the topic and Lidan had given up asking. She could only take so much of his moody sulk.

Thanie's rueful smile chilled Lidan to the bone. There was still so much she didn't know about these people and their history, and something old and painful lingered here.

'I wager the king will see Aelish without issue, Liddy.' She tilted her head at Ran's back, his horse trudging down the road as it wound toward the river. 'Whether he will accept his fugitive grandson remains to be seen.'

The city grew to an incomprehensible size as they walked their horses through Kotja's evening bustle. Windows shone with candle and lamplight, folk bundled against the wind but rosy-cheeked and smiling as they met neighbours in the street. Guards at the outer and inner gates greeted Aelish with genuine grins and whoops of joy. She'd been missed, presumed dead some said. Runners hurried to forewarn her family of their daughter's return, a great feast appearing on groaning tables as the Yordam clan celebrated the unexpected arrival of their missing child.

After weeks of meagre pickings, the spread laid before Lidan burst with such bounty she thought she might be sick. Tray upon tray arrived of foods she couldn't name let alone recognise, some meats seemed familiar while a few certainly weren't. Puffy loaves of bread stood proud amongst platters of vegetables, and in the end, she abandoned her plate half finished, her stomach unable to withstand another bite.

No one seemed to notice her reticence as ale and wine flowed freely around the dining hall, just one of the many rooms of the enormous, multi-storeyed building. Unlike her father's hall, with its woven screens and limited anterooms, this place stretched into a warren of chambers and rooms, some as small as cupboards, others so cavernous her voice echoed. The kitchens were vast, pumping out heat and food at such a rate Lidan wondered if it all happened by magic. That notion would have seemed childish a few moons ago. Now, she saw such trickery everywhere.

Sadness laid its hand on the festivities as Aelish recounted the demise of her trading crew. They'd swung west of that ruined camp, the black stain still visible on the horizon though the stink of burnt flesh had long since faded. Ngaru had torn them apart and Lidan had no desire to see the scattered leavings of that slaughter. At the news, Heike Yordam, the pale-haired matriarch, disappeared to another room. It took some hours for her to return, having sent messengers into the night to the families of her deceased employees.

It wasn't until after supper that Lidan managed to corner Ran alone. Ignoring the opulent strangeness of the building, she slipped from the palatial sitting room and followed him along a carpeted hallway. He'd made noises about relieving himself, but she suspected he meant to sneak off.

Their meal, as warming and comforting as it was, sat like a stone in Lidan's stomach, hardened by anxiety. Ran's retreat from his friends worried her more deeply than she cared to admit. He'd toughened against the world, building a wall to conceal himself from her more than anyone else. Her boots silent on the soft rugs, Lidan darted from shadow to shadow. Ran wandered more than hurried, aimless, pausing here to gaze up at a tapestry or there to examine a carving or weapon hanging on the wall.

'You're so starved for company that you'd follow a man to the privy?' The accusation echoed down the corridor and Lidan's face contorted in a scowl.

'Well, if you took five minutes to talk to me, I might not be so worried about you skulking off by yourself all the time.' She stepped from the shadows, arms folded tightly. 'And for what it's worth, I'm not starved for any kind of "company". After a month on the road with you lot, I could do with some alone time.'

'Then you should understand why I go off on my own.' Dismissive and cold, he turned to feign interest in another wall hanging.

'Except you don't want space, do you?' Lidan's challenge rang against the polished timber panels along the walls. Warm red, ochre and umber tones glowed in the lamplight, like something out of a trader's tale she had no time to appreciate. 'You're hiding. Not as much from the others, and certainly not from Thanie, the person you travelled halfway across the world to drag off to her death. You spend more time with her than anyone else. You're hiding from *me*.'

Ran's affected nonchalance faded, his jaw working. On the far side of the hallway, at the hem of a heavy curtain, a bench seat nestled below a window. Kotja glistened beyond the smooth glass and Ran stared through it, thoughts unspoken. She'd never seen such marvels, from its thousands of panes of glass to its many-storeyed buildings defying the pull of the earth. Metal dripped from every home, every corner, every street adorned with the stuff, yet all Lidan saw was Ran—hands rammed into his trouser pockets, shoulders hunched, scuffing the toe of his dusty boot into the rich floor covers.

'There's a truth sitting between us, Lidan, and I'm not sure you've seen it yet.'

That stung. 'What are you talking about?'

'The things I'm going to have to do…' He sighed, seeking wisdom in the silent city beyond the window. Nothing out there would help him, not the lights nor the drifting wood smoke.

Lidan dared take a step, her heart thudding. 'If you think you carry this burden alone, then you're so phenomenally wrong I can't even begin to untangle it. Do you think I came all this way to see the sights? To travel the world? I'm here to see this evil stopped—'

'And how will it be stopped, Lidan?' The retort cracked like the report of a whip. Rage simmered just below the surface, his nostrils flaring as his body trembled. Banked up like a furnace fit to burst, Lidan fought the urge to retreat from the intensity of Ran's anger. He'd held it in for so long it risked boiling over to scald them all. 'This isn't some faceless enemy. This isn't just another monster to fight in the dark. It won't be like the ngaru or dradur we've faced before. It won't be like any battle we've fought against our own kind. This is *different*.'

'Don't you think I know that?' Lidan growled, her own fury unbridled in the face of his. How dare he talk down to her? She knew more than any of them what they were walking into. 'She's my fucking *mother*, Ran. *Mine*. My responsibility. I hardly sleep. I can barely eat. I know *exactly* what this is, *exactly* who we're up against.'

'And that's why this falls to me.'

'Wait, what? No, that's—'

'Listen to me. It falls to me—'

'No, Ranoth, it does not.' The side of her fist slammed into the polished timber wall at her shoulder, a boom cutting his protest from the air, falling into furious silence. Sometimes all men understood was force, a language of aggression. She'd learned to scream just to be heard. 'You might be some big man where you're from but none of that matters here. You came to my lands seeking justice for a wrong against your people, but what about mine? What about the crimes against *my* people, *my* family? You're not our saviour, Ran. You won't end this on your own. You try it, you die. The sooner you accept that this burden rests *between* us—my mother, your fugitive—the sooner we can get on with stopping her. The longer you spend wallowing in your own self-important sorrow, lamenting this great weight you think you bear alone, the longer we waste trying to convince you otherwise.' She closed the space between them. At this range, she couldn't breathe without him feeling it on his skin, and he couldn't ignore her. 'I didn't come all this way to stand aside and watch you throw yourself into the dragon's jaws. We do this together or not at all.'

Ran's anger dissipated with agonising slowness, leaving a pained grimace in its wake. 'Thanie isn't sure I'll be strong enough, even with all the training and the barriers she's torn down. I'm in a storm right now, stuck at the very centre. If I lean one way or the other, even a little, I risk killing myself and all of you. There is a tightrope to be walked here, Lidan. I won't let anyone else get hurt.'

'She's right. You aren't strong enough.'

Ran jerked back, surprise becoming an offended frown.

'None of us are,' Lidan went on, filling the pause with the truth he didn't want to hear. She didn't like it either, but it didn't make it any less of a fact. 'Not on our own.'

'I can't ask this of you.' Ran shook his head, turned back to the city, and retreated into himself again.

'Can't ask what of me?'

'I thought there was another way, but that was before...'

The weight of what he meant hit Lidan and she winced. She'd flinched from the truth as often as she'd dared, ignoring its inevitable footsteps as it followed her day and night. She hadn't admitted it to him or the others, but she knew what this would take, knew what she would have to do when the end came tearing toward her. The Blade of the South had a nice ring to it until she stopped to see what that edge had truly been honed for. 'Before Sellan had the gift?'

Ran nodded.

'I've always known this, Ran. From the moment I realised who she was, I knew.'

Now it was his turn to stare, shock mingling with sorrow. Had he thought to remove this task from her, taking the weight so she could go on without that memory burned into her mind?

'Thanie and I hoped we could draw off Sellan's magic,' he said. 'Without it, she wouldn't be able to cast the spells to create more dradur. But if the goddess speaks true and the gift has been given, it changes everything. There's only one way to stop her once she has what she needs.'

'That's why you were so upset when I told you,' Lidan murmured.

Ran nodded. 'There'll be a horde of those monsters to stop, too many to take out with our bare hands. We won't have an army at our backs, we won't even have reinforcements. We're on our own, which leaves us with one course of action.'

Her view of the city shimmered through the prickling heat of tears she'd held back for weeks. The acceptance of an inescapable loss she didn't feel the right to grieve. 'Cut the head off the snake and the body dies.'

For a moment, Ran didn't speak. Was this as hard for him as it was for her? Surely, he relished the thought of ending the witch who created the dradur? Surely, he hungered for it? Yet he stood at her side, visibly shaken by the recognition of the truth. It had taken them a turning of the moon to come to this point, to admit it to each other that the hope they once held for another path, for a future where they survived beyond this fight, had blown away like mist across a mountaintop.

Lidan eased her aching body onto the window seat and Ran joined her. Finally, they saw the world through the same eyes, saw each other's truth and knew its weight. That unspoken understanding would carry them through if they allowed it.

'Thanie was very clear on this.' His voice shook a little. Lidan couldn't look at him, anxiously picking at the skin around her nails instead. 'Once Sellan has enacted the final part of the spell, the part that gives her complete control of the new dradur, the only way to stop them is to destroy the magic at its source.'

'Sever the spine.' The truth sank a claw through the barely healed scars in Lidan's soul. The woman had hurt her, beat her, but in her own sick way, sought to protect her from a cruel world ruled by even crueller men.

Despite it all—the scars, the humiliation, the emotional wounds she'd carry for the rest of her life—Lidan had lived in vain hope that one day she might see another side to her mother. That the fear and anger would fade, the rage might mellow, and the woman left behind would be the mother she should have had were it not for the torture lurking in her past.

None of that was possible.

None of it was real.

There was only one way to end the destruction looming on the northern horizon and it was with steel and blood.

Slowly, Lidan lifted her gaze to meet Ran's, regret welding with the certain knowledge of what they must do, a shard of steel wedged against the gaping wound left by the truth. 'What would you have me do?'

'What you do best. Keep the fuckers off my back until the deed is done.'

CHAPTER THIRTY-TWO

Eddark quickly found their new lair with the help of his underground contacts, a suitably opulent establishment that could easily play the part of the temporary abode for a visiting noble. Just in time too. The house-keeper had returned to the Parben house, interrupting Sellan boiling a pot of water. It hadn't ended well for the man, though she'd kept the details to herself.

For the first week Eddark swanned through town with their ill-gotten coin, posturing and smiling at the right people until their story began to spread. Clothes in the latest fashion arrived in carefully wrapped parcels, tailored just so, a well-fitted ceremonial breastplate among them should he wish to play military man and wear it to the games area.

He sent fine robes and a stola of layered fabrics for Sellan, the best any mage-resident could hope to have from her apparent employer, yet not so fine that she out-stripped the glory of her patron. He also sent the chemics she ordered—the pungent liquid for her hair, an acid for her eyes. Sellan stared at the eye drops with daily dread as time ran down until she would have to use them.

Eddark's adjustments were more subtle and less permanent—a slight powder for his face to lighten his bronzed skin, kohl for lining his eyes, a fermented fruit balm to add a little shine to his lips. He trimmed his hair and combed it the way the lords of the Assembly liked to wear it these days. Sellan found herself mourning the fall of his locks as they dropped to the floor—one of the many sacrifices he'd made to break through the invisible barriers of court and find acceptance.

And find it they would. It all hinged on that.

While Eddark played the games of court and society, Sellan wandered the streets. She'd never experienced unfettered access to the maze of plazas and avenues, roads and laneways. Always she'd been escorted, hemmed in by expectation, cornered by what was right and proper. Such restrictions no longer applied, her time her own while Eddark spent long hours laying the foundation of their ruse.

Late into the night she walked, day after day watching the sun set through the haze of the city, sharp scents clashing against her senses, brilliant colours still a little shocking after the muted, organic tones of the south. She searched the alleys and the lanes, the slums and the dark corners of market squares, ignoring hawkers and tea shop owners begging her for custom. She didn't have time to dine or drink.

She needed a body.

By the second week, Sellan was convinced Eddark was a lying bastard. These unclaimed dead he'd told her about were non-existent—a fact she simply refused to accept. Nowhere as brutal and as violent as the capital of the continent's most ruthless nation could have streets as safe as these. Nowhere as polluted and diseased and corrupt as Wodurin had gutters free of the freshly murdered, the recently mugged, or the terminally drunk.

Something else was at play here, and within days of realising, she'd caught a lead on exactly what. Well after dark, disguised in shapeless rags instead of her fashionably elaborate stola, Sellan crept away from the back entrance of the rented house. The few servants Eddark had on staff were already on their way home for the night. He was at a gambling hall, working a kind of magic Sellan would never master—the kind that required her to understand people and what made them tick. She'd watched him one night, awed by the ease with which he played the imperial game alongside his cards. The way he flattered and joked, dropping careful hints and small suggestions. Awe quickly became fear, a side of him shining through—one she'd never seen. He had the instincts of a political animal that could only have come from his father.

After that night, Sellan left Eddark to his own devices, a part of her unwilling to watch him change, even if it was only an affectation for the benefit of others. Her goals lay elsewhere, and she hurried into the night, pulling her veil over her tightly bound hair.

Summer abandoned the north with the setting sun these days, leaving a biting chill unlike any she'd weathered in decades. Layers of fabric huddled under her clothes and still it never seemed enough. Tonight it would have to do. She couldn't risk the attention a well-made cloak or shawl might draw in the grottier parts of town.

Sellan left the upper city behind, crossing the bridge, the fetid water of the Ullis slopping against the piers in the darkness below, unseen but always smelt. The docks of the market district were her best bet, a haven for foreign types too quick to trust a pimp and their whores, too drunk to see an ambush in a shadow. Someone would be dying down there tonight, and either she'd get to the body first, or find the person stealing them from under her nose.

Somewhere in the back of her mind, in the hazy parts she'd tried to blacken from her childhood, she recalled a law against interference with a body. City officials had jurisdiction, as Eddark had mentioned in Myrtford, and anyone seeking a cadaver for medical reasons paid a premium for the privilege. This left two possibilities: either Wodurin had suddenly and inexplicably developed a crack policing force taking care of crime and any resulting bodies, or someone was scooping up the corpses of the lost and unfortunate then spiriting them away. From the rumours on the quayside, it was the latter rather than the former.

The docks came into sight along the quay, reasonably quiet for this time of night, the change in weather keeping folk indoors. A few taverns clanged with badly played instruments and overly loud laughter, women of negotiable affection glancing up then losing interest at the sight of Sellan's rags. Seemed they weren't quite so desperate to fuck a coin out of a beggar's purse, even in this part of town. Someone down here would have a hook in the illegal trade of corpses. Someone in these parts always did.

A lone working girl leaned against a lamp post, staying put as Sellan approached, heavily painted eyes shadowed in the dim light. 'Fancy a tumble, sailor?' she asked in a sweet, sultry tone.

'Maybe another time, love.' Sellan dropped the education from her voice, taking on the edge of the slums, the twang of the docks and burying her hand in her pocket. A single coin caught the light and the girl's eye. She didn't seem at all put off by the feminine pitch of her mark's reply. 'Pay you for what you've seen though.'

'Double or nothing if you just wanna talk.' The coins multiplied and the girl lifted her chin, unfurling her hand to receive payment. 'What you wanna know?'

'Corpse-catchers. Any about?' It was a term Sellan had heard whispered while searching the city. If caught, such folk were fed to the beasts in the arena, a monthly spectacle suffered by any petty criminals who couldn't afford bail or a half-decent lawyer. But a corpse-catcher worth their salt charged well and bribed wisely enough to slip through the clutches of Wodurin's porous law.

The girl's brow rose in silent question. 'Maybe.' Another coin clacked into her hand, gone before the light could reveal it to anyone else on the street. 'They're moving, not staying in one place too long. City watch caught wind of them a few nights back. Tirus had them down here to take a dead mark away and someone reported them.'

'Know where they are now?'

She tilted her head, gesturing southward along the river with her chin. 'Try up on Sabura. The edge of the Slicks.'

The Slicks—another name heard in her fruitless search. Those who lived in slums rarely referred to them as such and the residents of Wodurin's poorest district were no different. Apparently, the name referred to the state of the streets in the rain; no cobbles or laughing drains to keep them dry, only dirt that quickly turned to slurry as soon as the skies opened.

With a nod of thanks, Sellan hurried into the night and tried not the think of what might await in the gloomy shambles of the Slicks. If she got her hands on just one body, it would be a start. She might be able to use the creature she made to bring more to her flock. It would reduce the direct danger to herself if a marhain stalked the streets at night, silencing the rasping snores of the city's less fortunate.

A small part of her wondered at the morality of it. A younger version of herself, more reckless and consumed with white hot rage, didn't care who or what it took to make her army. An entire town hadn't been enough. Her plans had stretched beyond Lackmah, ambling over the Disputed Territory and through Visorcrest and Lativa and a hundred other villages between that fateful settlement and the target of her ire.

Those plans had never come to fruition, which was perhaps for the best. She'd learned her lesson since. It was harder for people to sympathise with a psychopath, harder for them to understand what motivated someone to do what she'd done, especially if that person felt no compunction at the deaths of innocents. To win this fight, she had to do things the right way, a better way. Murdering homeless people wasn't that way. Better to find them dead already. Better to use what would otherwise be wasted. It wasn't right, it was just less wrong. That, at least, she could explain to Eddark without risking his complete and utter revulsion.

The Sabura Way came into sight, the last substantial road before the city became slums. It was a poorly lit, badly maintained thoroughfare, just as likely to be as slick as the rest of the district in the rain and no safer for its size. Taverns and brothels stood cheek by jowl with butchers and pawn brokers, a sparse smattering of shuttered shops spread between. At this time of night, most were dark, with only a sliver of light peeking from between a few threadbare curtains in the apartments above.

A conversation, hissed in whispers, drifted on the breeze blowing from the docks. Sellan gagged on the stench as she turned toward the sound. Where the Sabura met the quay, in the dense black abyss that was the mouth of an alley, a horse stood silently between the shafts of a two-wheel dray, hunched figures arguing beside it. Sellan lingered at the edge of the light, keeping to her side of the street, straining to listen. The wind blew their words away, scattering them along the road and out of hearing. One of the figures waved a dismissive hand and left, muttering something uncomplimentary under their breath.

Unwilling to risk losing them again, Sellan darted across the Sabura and crept around the horse as the remaining figure climbed to the driver's seat of the dray. His face obscured by a hooded coat, he settled down and sucked at a pipe, a ruddy glow doing little to illuminate his features.

'What can I do you for?' His question rattled, smoke billowing into the night.

'Looking to buy,' she replied. The horse snuffled her fingers with its velvet muzzle, hot breath clouding. She absently scratched its nose, oddly comforted by its calm bulk. Steady. Predictable. Was this what Lidan saw in the beasts? For a split second she glimpsed a small part of her daughter's mind, a quiet corner of her heart wishing she'd known the girl better.

'Oh?' The shadow cracked with a slow smile. 'Any preference.'

'Anything tall or broad,' she said, glancing down the street. 'Muscles.'

He paused, sucking at his teeth, no doubt looking her up and down. He saw the baggy, ratty clothes, homespun and dull. He saw the hunch, a ruse to divert anyone who might give a description to the watch. Feigning a look over his shoulder, the corpse-catcher grunted. 'Not sure I've got anything you can afford.'

Two steps took Sellan past the driver's seat and within view of the tray, the cloying stink of rot wafting from a lumpy mass under a cover sheet. 'Really? In all that?' There had to be at least three or four bodies in there, perhaps more. They couldn't be too old either—no more than a day and a night—or else the stench would have been unbearable. Fresh enough for her purposes and an excellent start to her work. 'I'll take them all.'

The man scoffed. 'Not bloody like—'

His dismissal ended in a strangled gasp, his words garbled as an invisible force crushed his windpipe and snapped his neck. Sellan hadn't even looked in his direction. She hadn't needed to do more than lift her hand and clench. A gentle wave brought his corpse tumbling backward into the dray; twitching, limp fingers unwound from the reins and left them to dangle beside the steady horse's flanks.

Hitching her skirts, Sellan climbed into the seat and flicked the reins, driving the cart out into the Sabura. The man, his horse, his cart and his cargo had solved four distinct problems with one simple solution. As long as she made it back to the house, her work would begin tonight.

Skull-dragging five corpses from the back of a badly parked dray and into the laundry building behind the house took longer and a good deal more effort than Sellan anticipated. The corpse-catcher had barely begun to cool, but he was heavier than the rest. At least two were stiff as boards, while the others had begun to relax into death. A blessing, really. Breaking bones to get them into the right positions was a task she didn't relish.

The horse was stabled by the early hours, silence settling in the streets as much as it ever would in a city such as this. It was the time when babes were born and the frail rasped their last breaths. It would not be until these fated souls were interred or burned that they would fully break the bonds of their mortal shells and turn to embrace Ortus in the place beyond. Until then, their spirits remained caught, right where Sellan wanted them.

Reasoning that no one would be using it to actually cook anything, she hauled an old table from the kitchen, draining what little strength remained in her shoulders and arms. The great benefit of faking life as a courtier was spending the entire season eating out and dining on the invitations of others without ever firing up the kitchen hearth in your own home. Eddark's staff were there to tidy and fetch—even the linens were washed elsewhere.

Standing over the five bodies lined up on the cold floor, Sellan perched her hands on her hips, breathless at the effort to get everything in place. Youthful strength had made this so much easier last time. She'd also had help; a luxury unavailable to her now.

The corpse-catcher gaped at the ceiling, his neck at a sick angle and a dark stain gathering where his skin touched the floor. He was the freshest and largest; the rest a collection of two haggard beggars with no obvious cause of death beyond the cold, a woman of middle years who looked to have been strangled, and a short man with soft pale skin who'd taken a knife to the belly in what may have been a robbery.

The corpse-catcher would be the easiest to bring back and control, especially since she was severely out of practise and lacking the focus to pull on a soul already wandering the unseen realms. It had been an age since she'd animated anything of size, and she'd never reached the point of fully imposing her will on the marhain she created. Such a mistake would not happen again.

A trunk by the far wall whispered a summons for her ears alone and the lid creaked open on stiff hinges. A collection of illegally obtained weapons gleamed in the light of her lamp, begging to be chosen. He would do well to carry something hefty—a sword or an axe—something with an air of authority. First impressions were everything, and he would be her lieutenant. The heavy beard of a battle-axe peered from the shadowy depths, an etching across its cheek in a language she couldn't read. She could only guess where Eddark had found these, but they looked to be the bounty of a war won in the far north, weapons of the barbarian hordes of the High Tund. A skull splitter without doubt. She grunted with the effort of lifting the axe free and it dropped with ringing thunk onto the table.

With a weary sigh, she glanced at the corpse. There was no way to get that thing onto the table without help. This part would have to be done on the ground, in the dust and the grime, right where she belonged. Hefting the axe, she went to her knees beside what remained of the man, his corporeal form stiffening the longer it lay between the stone-carved troughs and big-bellied coppers.

From her apron pocket, she took a small purse, plucking a thick, curved needle and heavy thread, more suited to leather work than anything Marrit would use to stitch a wound. A little knife, not dissimilar one used to peal an apple, sliced through the palm of his hand, skin parting and thick, dark blood oozing from within. Somehow this helped them hold their weapons, as if they became part of a greater whole, an extension of being in this mummery of life.

Stiff fingers curled around the haft, resistant to her touch but giving way in the end, grasping the timber in an iron grip. Thread and needle passed through flesh, hands working in deft silence. Fingers drew together, thick black stitches repeating as she'd done a thousand times before.

The years peeled away until once again Sellan sat small and angry in a darkened Orthian farmhouse. So many of her first attempts had failed, bodies piled high for birds to peck the bones clean. Where once she'd worked by the light of her rage, sustained by her blazing hate for Tamyr, now she worked in numb calm, cold acceptance of what must be done and the path she had to walk. There was no turning back. Once she called that power down, nothing would stand in her way.

In the corner of that room in the farmhouse, Sellan registered a presence. It had come to her then as it did now, hunching over a staff and surveying the damage. She'd turned it away again and again all those years ago.

Not ready, not yet, need more time, need more soldiers…

In the end, that indecision had almost cost her life. This time, she would not be so foolish.

'He will do nicely,' Urda muttered with a satisfied sniff.

'It wasn't like I was spoiled for choice.' Sellan tugged the last of the thread through the corpse-catcher's hand and tied it off, turning the limb against the light to assess the stitching.

'And you're better at that, now.'

'I learned a thing or two in my exile.'

Urda grunted and walked the line of bodies. The butt of her staff knocked against the sole of the soft man's boot. 'Not sure I'd bother with this one. Too flabby.'

She was right, but Sellan wasn't exactly swimming in options. This choice selection of the city's dead was all she had to work with. As it was, she had days of work ahead to bring them back properly. 'He'll make perfectly acceptable fodder for arrows.'

The ancient shrugged and Sellan put her tools aside, laying a hand on the corpse-catcher's chest. A deep breath brought her thoughts to centre, cool and steady, like the flow of a river to the sea. Inevitable as the night, breath moving with the force of the tides.

Magic began to pool, a web of blue light spinning from her fingertips to weave a chrysalis of energy around the corpse. Wan light reflected eerily in his eyes, throbbing and oscillating, seemingly alive once more.

'Are you sure you're ready?' Urda asked, moving to stand at Sellan's back, her hands mere inches from Sellan's nape.

'I won't make the same mistake twice,' Sellan told her, teeth clenched to maintain the cocoon of magic, the weave tightening, the bands thickening until hardly anything of the man could be seen.

'Say the words,' Urda said.

Sellan swallowed a lump of fear from her tightening throat. 'I pledge the souls of the marhain to the Morritae, sisters of fertility and life, of war, of fate and the lives of all who have ever and will ever walk across this mortal plane. Winged death, onyx messengers, carry these souls to the embrace of the goddess; to Neuna, to Macha, and to Urda. Give thanks and power to them alone.'

'And…' Urda pressed.

The room warped and twisted, her words distorting across time and space. The ceiling sheered away, stars wheeled overhead, eons passed in the blink of an eye. Time meant nothing to ones such as these, and for the smallest of moments, that weight caught at Sellan and dragged. The pull of the churn, aching to fall into the abyss of that power, turning her heart from all the world's concerns as day and night flashed above. Urda's hand hovered at the back of her neck, a brand poised to scorch.

'I will not fail again, Great One. On pain of death, on the life I breathe, on the sight with which I see, I pledge all of this to you freely and without coercion.'

Fingers of shattered shards of ice caught Sellan's neck and she screamed, her voice torn to rags as the power of a goddess burned through her skin, cracking bones and scoring through muscle.

Bright red light, crimson as blood, vermillion as the setting sun in the southern sky, pierced her spine. Crying out, she arched, bucking away from the agony. Against all instinct Sellan let it come. To resist was death, to pull away now was certain doom.

It pulsed through her, flames licking along her bones, red lightning crackling across her skin and arcing to the cocooned corpse. The web stained a bruised purple, then scarlet as the power of a goddess became that of a mortal, the final act of this long-awaited ritual reaching a terrifying crescendo.

This was what Sellan had run from, what her younger self had cowered from as she'd stitched corpse after corpse, meaning to but never actually committing herself to the moment where the goddess of fate gave her the power to control the dead. The wine-dark flame of this new magic settled in her soul, clenching her stomach and burning out whatever had existed before. Trembling yet unable to move, her eyes flashed open.

In some far-off place she thought she should recognise, her body writhed beside a corpse, the dead man absorbing the pulsing red of this new magic. The new-born marhain seemed to draw breath, its muscles contracting as Sellan seized under the pressure. Life pumped through its veins once more, but it was *her* life—her soul, her magic. Nothing of the old remained.

It took a moment to realise Urda no longer held her neck, the ancient stepping away to watch in silence. Sellan's hand flexed and the chrysalis collapsed, the sleeping marhain remaining on the floor, silent and unmoved, awaiting command.

A handful of wicked claws had grown from fingernails, its teeth grotesquely enlarged, its jaw straining to fit what could only be described as fangs. The hand around the haft of the axe had thickened to a club, welding permanently over the timber. Leg and arm muscles bulged until the man's clothes shredded down the seams, limbs elongating, torso lengthening, adding a foot or more in height. Thick slabs of skin melted into the fabric to form a sort of armour across its back and chest. Deformities that had taken years to manifest in her first army of marhain had appeared in seconds under the force of Urda's power, but at what cost?

Her back screamed in protest as Sellan came to her feet, staggering sideways and catching at a windowsill with her scorched hands. Blisters swelled and burst along the pads of her fingers. A red, globular substance, like molten magic, dripped from her fingertips into hissing puddles on the floor. Her back ached with the pressure, heat coiling in her gut, a rope of fiery pain pulled taut inside her spine.

'How long will it last?' Sellan gasped between shallow breaths, barely able to form words. Her voice sounded like she shouted underwater, her mind retreating from the agony of consequences.

'Until your death.'

She met the goddess' eyes and saw no lie. 'I must do this with each of them?'

'Every single one,' Urda said. With a sigh, she stepped forward and put a hand on Sellan's shoulder. The younger woman cried out and twisted away as if stabbed. Heat tore up her back, the seat of her pelvis grinding painfully as she turned to face the aged spirit. 'It was the only way, little wasp. You have your weapons now. Use them wisely.'

'It fucking *hurts*!' Sellan ground out, stunned to her core. She'd expected pain, but not this much and not all at once.

The goddess straightened and held out her staff. Sellan snatched it away greedily, leaning into its strength, savouring the minute relief offered by such a simple device. A pitiless smile stretched Urda's lips. 'Anything worth doing comes at a price. You want him dead, this is—'

A boot scuffed on stone and Urda vanished, a rift opening in space, sucking the air from Sellan's already screaming lungs. Her hand clawed at her churning stomach while the other strangled the staff, and Sellan lurched around so fast she thought her spine might shatter.

Eddark's wide, horrified eyes darted between the corpses and the crimson magic leaking from her fingers. Sellan's heart fell to the floor.

'What the actual ever-loving *fuck* are you doing?'

Chapter Thirty-three

'What must be done,' Sellan replied with a pained grunt. Skin stinging with the fire of an enraged wasp's nest, it stretched as if freshly scarred beneath her tattered clothes. 'I told you making this weapon would be ugly.'

'*This* is your weapon?' Eddark's incredulous voice echoed from the door. 'A pile of bodies? Where did they come from?'

She glanced at the marhain, seemingly asleep beside the other corpses. 'I found them.'

Eddark appeared in her field of vision, stalking slowly, anger brewing in his eyes. She'd told him sacrifices would have to be made. The disgust in his glare, the way his top lip curled told her he hadn't quite understood just what that meant. With a deep breath, Sellan pulled the leaking crimson magic away from her fingertips and pooled it in her belly, rather than adding to the sizzling puddle on the floor. She had to get a handle on this power if she wanted to get anywhere near court without attracting unwanted scrutiny.

'Were they already like this?' An accusing finger unfurled, pointing at her morbid collection.

'What? Dead?'

Eddark nodded stiffly.

Sellan almost laughed. She might have if her entire body wasn't on fire. 'Yes, of course. Do I look like I've been on a killing spree?' She leaned away from the staff and indicated the front of her ratty clothes and stained apron. On second thought, she did look like she'd just walked out of a slaughter-house, the corpse-catcher's blood smeared down the front of the apron. It didn't matter. Eddark's gossamer thin regard for her had already been torn away. What difference did it make if she'd killed these people or not?

'Are there more?' he asked. Spinning, he searched the dark corners of the repurposed laundry, peering into the shadows beside abandoned coppers and beneath empty washing lines. The trick with this venture would be storing the marhain somewhere out of sight and keeping them from rotting while she recruited more to her cause.

'There will be, just not yet.'

Eddark spun back. 'How many?'

'A dozen.'

'You need a *dozen* bodies?'

'For this phase, yes.'

He leaned forward, palms flat on the table, ignoring the undead corpse-catcher with his newly sewn axe and morbidly deformed body. 'You're *not* taking innocent people off the street for this!'

Sellan's eyes narrowed. 'Who said any of them were innocent? *He* was selling bodies on the black market for gods only know what reasons. I've no idea what you medics get up to with a cadaver, but these folk weren't going anywhere that involved a proper burial and the words said to send them to Ortus. People die in this city all the time—you told me as much yourself. They freeze to death, they drink themselves to death. They get fucking stabbed to death. I could build an army from the corpses lying in the gutters and no one would even notice until it was too late. These were waste, the leavings of a world that cares nothing for them. I merely re-purposed what remained of their mortal forms.'

That wasn't entirely true but there was no way she was telling Eddark that. If he knew the depth of the magic at work here, if he knew the souls of these walking dead would weld to Sellan's, he'd never have agreed. Best to let him think they were nothing but empty shells, nothing but a sad by-product of an inevitable end.

She stabbed a finger at him, regretting the sharp movement as pain bit into her lower back. 'You swore you'd do whatever it took. You said the price was worth paying to see Tamyr fall. Has that changed?'

'I...' His mouth opened and closed, his hands flexing in exasperation toward the bodies on the floor. 'I want the man dead, but this?'

'This is how he falls, Eddark. This is the only weapon he can't defeat, the one he'll see as a deliverance from his enemies. If you can't stomach that, then tell me now.' So she could what? Kill him? Cut out his tongue? Sellan hadn't thought that far simply because she couldn't bring herself to. He *had* to see. He *had* to understand this was the only way.

'How does this get you what you want?' Confusion creased Eddark's brow in a brief anguished frown. 'I don't—'

Sellan took a deep breath and snapped her fingers.

The eyes of the corpse-catcher flashed open, deep vermillion glowing with the heat of a banked fire. She caught a glimpse of her reflection in a window and flinched away, the same red glow oscillating in her own eyes. Urda's magic throbbed through Sellan, channelled across invisible threads in space. An unknowable connection between a magic-weaver and her marhain flared to life as commands rippled from her mind to his. Eddark recoiled as the monstrous corpse climbed to its feet to stand at ease, the head of the axe scraping ominously across the stone floor. A deep growl rattled in its throat, grunting useless breath in and out of stiff lungs. It didn't need air to survive—Sellan provided that power—it needed it to communicate with its subordinate marhain, the creatures it would lead into battle against Tamyr.

'You needn't fear it,' she told Eddark calmly. His expression of terror shifted to curiosity, and he stepped forward, scanning the creature. 'I control it.'

'The weapon is one thing. The method?' Eddark shook his head. Fascination danced in his eyes and Sellan wondered at it. Had she triggered something innate in him, the same instinct that drove him to heal the sick and explore the body? Had she awoken the inquirer beneath the healer, one who'd no doubt wondered just how far magic could extend the life of a human body? 'The method is something else.'

'Have you got a better idea?' Part threat, part genuine question, she needed to know. He folded his arms. This was it. This was where he'd walk away, straight out the door and abandon her when they were so close—

'I might.'

Sellan blinked, stunned. 'I'm sorry?'

'There are few who deserve this fate, Sel; very few indeed. But there are those who deserve much worse. I've heard where they like to serve their needs. I've met people who've escaped their clutches. Of late, I've even met some of the perpetrators. I've sat across card tables from more than a few. If anyone deserves to become an instrument of Tamyr's demise, it's *them.*'

'Who?' Her fear of rejection forgotten, Sellan studied his face. Was he going stay? Was he going to help? Their eyes met and she shivered.

'People just like him.'

She followed Eddark through the darkest part of the dawn, back to the docks, limping with her staff into the stench of the fetid water. He'd eyed the staff, watched her limp and grimace. He'd offered his arm and she'd refused it, still too painfully proud. She answered his unspoken questions about the power throbbing through her body as they crossed the river, excusing the red glow as a symptom of the spell she'd used. The slow look of misgiving made her wonder if he believed any of it, but he pressed on through the city in silence despite his doubt.

The sounds of taverns wafted with the stink. The more reputable establishments kept their stoops clean, their doorways inviting, the walls whitewashed and their merchandise away from peeping eyes. As they drew closer to the docks, the quality dropped—working girls and boys wandering freely, more than a few attempting to catch the eye of anyone passing with their hood drawn up.

Sellan glanced around, then back at Eddark, just to make sure he hadn't taken a wrong turn. Had he known all along where to find the unclaimed dead? Or was he after a live sample? He didn't strike her as that kind of man, and his assertion in the workroom hadn't set her to thinking they'd be targeting anyone on the street.

Ducking into an alley and ignoring the ache throbbing in her back, they shuffled past a young man knee-deep in his work with a suitably distracted client. She followed Eddark into the gloomiest, murkiest part of Wodurin even she hadn't dared to search. Now she knew why.

Ahead a lamp swung above a doorway, a weathered sign creaking beside it. The paint had once upon a time shown a rooster crowing beside a hen, or perhaps on top of it. It was hard to tell in the darkness, as faded and worn as it was.

'Used to be a tavern. *The Crowing Cock,*' Eddark said, adjusting his hood and indicating at the sign. 'Now it's known as the Nest.' He knocked three times, then another two after a pause, scanning the alley in nervous anticipation. He wanted to be here as much as she did, and that was next to not at all, but he'd come all this way on her account. Whatever waited behind that door had to be worth it.

Eventually it swung open, a scrawny girl with straw-coloured hair cocked her hip as she leaned against the doorjamb. 'Got an appointment?'

Eddark gave her a warm smile. 'Not today. Is Irennie around?'

The girl's attempt at a seductive gaze slipped. She stood straighter, leaning away. 'Who's asking?'

'Tell her Ed's in town and needs to speak with her, please.'

She looked him up and down, then jerked her head, indicating the room beyond the door. 'Wait in here. I'll see if she's taking visitors.'

Candles lit the tight space that had indeed been a tavern in a time long since passed into myth. Now couches, day beds and gleaming plant pots almost as tall as Sellan's shoulder crammed the room. Diaphanous curtains clung to the walls, cascaded from doorways and draped over furniture. The rosy glow of the cheap lights, their greasy scent aside, did well to hide the true nature of the place. Sellan had to focus carefully to see it for what it was.

The furniture was haggard and sagging, threadbare and losing its stuffing, the planting pots made of brass not bronze. The hanging fabrics covered holes in the plaster while night workers idled in the corners, turning to stare as Sellan and Eddark waited awkwardly for this mysterious Irennie. This wasn't a bawdy house, but an attempt at a home. No one was working here, no customers pawed over their prizes, no one plied fake laughs or suggestively placed their hands on someone else's thigh. This was a refuge from the street when the cold or fatigue drove them inside and away from the chance at another coin.

'Eddy?' A woman's voice asked from a doorway.

Eddark turned with a smile and opened his arms. 'Told you I'd come back!'

'Took you long enough,' Irennie scowled, trying to hide the hint of a smile. She had prominent cheekbones, a husky timbre to her voice and a lump at her throat that Sellan commonly associated with a man. Her hair fell in a long, well-tended curtain, her clothes neat and tidy despite the poverty around her. She was a tall thing, with a proud nose and laughing eyes. There were scars too, peaking from under the folds of her stola, ropey lines that looked like they had hurt going in as much as they had healing up.

'How is everyone?' Eddark asked, shrugging off his cloak as the straw-haired girl held out her hands to take it.

Irennie raised a brow and turned down the hall, gesturing for them to follow with a gentle flick of her hand. 'Been better. Have you *any* idea how hard it is to get someone decent to give them check-ups? Most of the proper medics won't come this close to the river and those who do want payment we can't afford.' She glanced over her shoulder as she led them into the depths of the building. 'How long you staying?'

'Ah.' Eddark caught Sellan's eye but she looked away, surveying the rooms as they passed. 'Not sure yet. I could come by in a few days' time, just to make sure everyone's healthy.'

'I'd appreciate that, Eddy. So would Caro. You know how much he misses you!'

'Caro's still here? Excellent. He owes me for that last game of cards he cheated...'

Their conversation faded, Sellan's attention on the glimpses of a life she'd never thought to see. Was this anything like the establishments her mother owned and her father frequented? Or were they more like those farther up the hill, the ones with the pretty doors and ornate colonnades? Did it matter? Someone somewhere was getting rich off the trade these poor wretches were plying, and it wasn't the wretches themselves.

There was a sense of happiness here though, of safety. Little groups lounged together, playing cards or chatting over a drink. Others were reading, poring over books stacked on tiny tables in the corners of their rooms. The majority were sleeping while the other rooms stood empty or closed. Eddark followed Irennie into a room much like the others, if only a little larger, which held a pair of lounges and a low table offset from the bed sequestered behind a curtain.

'Please, have a seat,' Irennie offered, reclining on a lounge while Sellan sank gratefully onto the other with Eddark perched beside her. 'Now, what brings you to this stretch of river, and with a friend no less?' The woman's eyes roved over Sellan but not in the leering way she'd become so accustomed to. It was a curious study, a wandering assessment that asked more questions than she could answer.

'Who's running the dark edges of things these days? Is it still Kadek's crew?' Eddark might as well have been speaking another language for all the sense it made to Sellan.

'Kadek still holds the southern docks, but there's a new crew trying to snatch up more streets at the northern end. We're steering clear as much as we can.' Irennie lit the bowl of a long pipe and took a draw, smoke coiling from her lips in tendrils. 'What could you possibly want with that kind of scum? Surely *they* aren't why you've come to see your loves after so long?'

Eddark didn't share her smile. 'Are they still as bad as they used to be?'

A pregnant silence weighed on the room, knowing looks passing between Eddark and Irennie that Sellan couldn't read.

The woman carefully put down her pipe. 'They haven't stopped scooping kids off the streets, if that's what you mean. We still get the leavings coming through here, but most are kept locked up nice and tight on Tanner's Lane.'

A curse hissed through Eddark's teeth and Sellan's heart gave an uncomfortable thud. 'They use Tanner's as their base then?'

'Yes, they do. What's this about, Eddark Parben?' Irennie sat up in a blur of frustration and fixed Eddark with a glare that would have turned men twice her size to water. Eddark didn't so much as flinch as she flicked her ringed fingers at the door. 'Kadek is bad air, always has been. He's offered what he's offered for years, no questions asked, discounts for the loyal and the discreet.'

'What does he sell?' Sellan broke in, drawing Irennie's ire.

'Local girl, huh? Not from down here though. Too well spoken to be one of us,' she finished with a sneer.

'You're not so uneducated yourself,' Sellan pointed out a little too sharply, magic flaring beneath her skin, heat scoring along her bones. 'High-born at least, but not trained in the household etiquette of hosting guests. If you had been, you'd have offered us wine, or at least water, and bread with oil. You weren't trained in such things because that's the sort of menial shit the high-born reserve for their breeding stock. Their daughters.'

'Oh, she's quick this one.' Irennie's sneer turned to an impressed smirk, and she winked at Eddark. 'No, honey cup, they tried to teach this petal swords and politics instead, until who I was on the inside broke through the shell they forced on me. We both know how well *that* kind of defiance goes down in the northern hills.'

Her smile flattened and Sellan's mouth ran dry. She did indeed know what fate held for the aristocratic sons and daughters of the Empire who didn't abide the expectations of their sex. It was one thing to indulge one's truth in private, as long as one's public duties were performed without complaint. But to refuse to remain under the yoke placed at birth, was a death sentence. It was a miracle Irennie had lived to adulthood. Children were left to the elements for less.

There was something in that suffering Sellan could understand. She'd been ignored by her parents, her cries for help falling on deaf ears, utterly denied by her family when it came to choosing between her and loyalty to the Crown. Sellan inclined her head. 'I'm sorry for what you must have endured.' It was a pathetic offering, but it was all she had.

'Endure it, I did.' A small smile danced on Irennie's lips. 'And with the scars to prove it. Much like those few who manage to outgrow Tanner's Lane. To answer your question, Kadek sells children. It's still, thank the gods, illegal to keep body slaves who haven't come of age, so the miscreants and deviants of this wonderful city have to get their rocks off somewhere else. Tanner's Lane is that somewhere.'

Sellan's heart beat a little faster as she looked at Eddark. *This* was his solution? A den of monsters for her to harvest? He gave a slight nod in answer to her silent question.

'Eddy?' Irennie ventured. 'What are you up to?'

'Oh, nothing much,' he replied with a swift smile that didn't reach his eyes. 'A friend of ours might have a solution to the Kadek problem. We just had to be sure his operations were still in the old warehouse.'

Standing, he brushed himself off as if making ready to leave, Sellan and Irennie hurrying to follow. His arms enveloped Irennie, planting kisses on her cheeks before he made for the door.

'Wait, ah...' Sellan began. That couldn't be all of it. There had to be more, something they didn't know, something they were missing. 'How many? Our friend will need to know how many?'

Eddark's broad shoulders filled the entry, holding back the door and waiting, shifting his feet in the worst attempt to feign patience she'd ever seen, while Irennie gave Sellan a sympathetic look. 'At least two dozen. It really depends on whether the Assembly is in session or not.'

A brief frown creased Sellan's brow. 'Only two dozen children?'

Irennie's features crumpled into a mask of anguish. 'No, sweetness. Two dozen *men*. Kadek has a few working the Lane. The rest will be patrons—his precious customers. There's double that number of children in that nightmare of a place at any one time.' The gleam in her eye was not one of joy. Had those scars been earned in the fight to escape her home, the place that had rejected her true self? Or, were they left by an altogether different kind of childhood?

'Oh,' was all Sellan could manage. The certain knowledge she was about to vomit clenched her throat before she could say more.

Irennie caught Sellan's arm as she ducked her head and turned for the door. 'You tell this friend of yours to put a taper to the place when he's done. Light a fucking fire under it, the likes this city hasn't seen since the Academy. Tell him to lock them in and burn the fuckers in their beds.'

'We may need your help when the time comes,' Eddark said quietly from the door. 'To get the children out.'

A vengeful glimmer sparkled in Irennie's eyes then. 'Just say the word and we'll be there.'

Sellan could only nod her farewell and follow Eddark into the pre-dawn chill. The tight heat of the old tavern finally let go as she broke into the street, turning to hurl the remains of her dinner into a gutter. No one paid her any mind, taking her for another corner girl who couldn't hold her liquor.

Her mind spun, memories of the cruelty she'd thoughtlessly, uncontrollably inflicted on Lidan. Her hard hands—hands that should have protected—had turned to hurt, all because she didn't know any better, didn't know how to *be* better. Her crimes against her daughter were unforgivable, she knew this. Had known it even as she'd done it and still, she hadn't known how to stop. The thought of her children—of *any* of the Tolak or clan children—falling prey to the likes of Kadek and his ilk turned her stomach.

She'd felt a wrench deep inside at the look on Farah's face the night Erlon had almost sworn Lidan to match to Yorrell's son. The knowledge in her eyes that if Lidan stayed, the girl she was would die, leaving only a husk. They'd shared a moment as Farah tore the bandages off old wounds that would never heal. Sellan felt it again now—that same ache in the pit of her stomach. That same relentless churn.

'Will two dozen be enough?' Eddark asked from the mouth of the alley.

Straightening, Sellan wiped her hand across her lips, vomit streaking up her sleeve. 'More than enough.'

'Then we can take the weapon to the emperor and this will be over?' Expectation weighed heavy in those words. No needless bloodshed—she'd promised herself that and she'd promised him. This time, she'd be better. Revenge, but at the lowest price.

She nodded and hollow hunger ignited in her belly.

A weapon forged of the very same thing it would in turn kill. There was poetic justice in it. She could live with that. An awful excuse for a human being she may be, but she'd pay for that in time. Sellan probably wouldn't live to see the aftermath of her actions, but this time, she'd take as many of the sick motherfuckers with her as she could.

CHAPTER THIRTY-FOUR

Kotja, Isord

Aelish begged time of Ran. More than he had to give, more than he could bear to allow, but he gave it anyway. Two days, she asked of him. Two days to send messages to her contacts in the palace and the parliament, two days to arrange the proper meetings through the proper channels without alerting the broader political apparatus of Kotja to his arrival. By the third morning he couldn't sit still a moment longer.

Breakfast was a casual affair, a long table set with breads, pastries, spreads, cold cuts of meat and smoked river fish. Folk in the Yordam house wandered through, making themselves a light meal to be eaten by hand as they went off to some task or another, while others lingered over steaming mugs of dark roast or tea. Unlike Orthia, there was little in the way of hot food. Ran stared into his drink, craving something more substantial to distract his fidgeting fingers.

Lidan sat to his left, her plate arranged with at least one sample of each item from the buffet. 'What's this?' she muttered, lifting something on the end of a knife.

'Cheese,' he said, glancing away as quickly as he'd looked over. He didn't have time for this.

'That's not cheese. It might have been once, but it's gone bad.'

Her sceptical frown was enough to elicit a snort of laughter, despite his state of mind. 'It's *meant* to have mould on it. The locals cure it in caves and cellars. It adds flavour.'

'Letting milk go off adds flavour too. Bad flavour.'

'We call that yoghurt.'

The cheese slipped off the knife and hit the plate with a *splot*. Lidan carefully slid it clear of the rest of her meal before picking up a slice of meat she clearly thought was safer. 'You people need to rethink what you class as food.'

Leaning back in his chair, he willed his shoulders to relax. How long had it been since he'd let himself smile at a bout of friendly banter?

Weeks... Iridia said before edging away. She'd been within him, holding tight since the news of Sellan's bargain with the Dead Sisters—the deity his people called the White Woman—reduced to a distant murmur in the storm. His effort to bring Iridia into the realm of the living now replaced by Thanie's relentless pressure to train and prepare.

His magic never really settled anymore. At a thought he warmed his mug in his hand, the liquid simmering up to a gentle boil. Steam coiled against his face and for a moment he imagined the caress of Iridia's hand before reality reminded him that he was alone. Instinct drove him to look for her and logic quashed the notion. She wasn't there. Perhaps if he left the room, found somewhere quiet and secluded, they could talk and—

No, stay here, she whispered against the gale force of his power. *You need this...*

Ran hunched around the uncomfortable emptiness when Iridia vanished, his attention returning to Lidan. He pointed to a pot of fermented milk topped with nuts and seeds. 'People pay a lot of money for this stuff.'

'People are stupid,' Lidan insisted, chewing a strip of thick, dark bread before sitting back to watch the dining room.

The flow of people continued, all manner of folk from house staff to Heike Yordam herself coming through to eat. There was no standing on ceremony with her, the same straight forward manner he'd come to know in Aelish evident in her mother. She nodded politely at Lidan, tapping two fingers to the left of her chest in a sign of respect for an equal, then studied Ran with the precise gaze of a raptor.

'You tap your foot any harder on that floor and you will drill through it,' Heike said, popping a morsel of bread and cheese into her mouth.

Ran crossed his legs a little too quickly. It did nothing to stop the nervous bouncing of his foot. 'I've never been good at waiting.'

'She will have news soon. You are too young to remember the times your mother brought you here, otherwise you would know the political machine that runs this city operates at a glacial pace. Nothing worth doing is done with haste.' Heike's knowing look was enough to quiet his restless heart. There was a deep history between the Yordam clan and his mother's family. If anyone could get through King Harroe's door, it was Aelish.

'I trust Aelish. She'll see us right. She hasn't turned me wrong since I met her and though I'm not patient, I've learned when to heed the advice of those who know better.' Ran risked a glance at Lidan and she arched a disbelieving brow, the ripple of Iridia's laugh stroking the edge of his awareness. 'Mostly.'

His admission was hard won, but enough to satisfy Heike. She moved to leave, pausing beside his chair and leaning down to his ear. 'Then you are a wiser man than your father.'

With a squeeze of his shoulder, she left them, Lidan's dubious look burning through his skin as she chewed slowly at her bread.

'What?' he snapped, his nerves in tatters.

'You're so full of shit,' she replied flatly. It was a statement of fact, nothing more.

'Well, I'm hardly going to tell her I'd punch my own kin to get some answers right now!'

Wiping her hands on a napkin, Lidan settled in. Now would come the slow and inevitable dismantling of his argument before he conceded she was right. Again. He braced for the scorn.

'How long are you going to wait before you do something?'

'We have no choice—'

She lurched forward, stabbing a finger into the table. 'We always have a choice. We have to do things our way, or we'll be here for months. Do we have months? No. Aelish is a good woman but she's limited by her people's customs. We need to speak to your grandfather or leave. Waiting isn't an option.'

Muttering and hissing between themselves, staff cleared away the food unnoticed and the bustle drained from the room as the sun inched above the mountains beyond the windows. As the morning grew old, they drew no closer to a solution that didn't end in them making friends with the gaolers in the local watch house, or worse, the palace dungeons.

A commotion shot down the corridor beyond, the sound of running feet and hurried voices echoing against the timber panelling and smooth glass. Ran was halfway out of his seat, magic crackling up his arms before Zarad barrelled in with Eian at his heels, coats flapping and leaving muddy boot prints on the carpet.

'Good, you're both here,' Zarad puffed, racing past Ran to a window on the far side of the room.

'What in the—' Ran didn't get to finish. Eian caught him by the arm and turned him out of his chair, motioning for Lidan to follow them to the wall. There was no arguing with Eian's muscle or bulk.

'We were coming back up from the market when we saw them.'

Ran tried to catch Eian's eye. 'You went into the city?'

'Of course—the rain cleared.'

'You didn't get lost?' Despite their skill at tracking magic and surviving in the wilds, they'd spent the best part of their lives in the confines of the Hidden Keep. Neither, as far as Ran knew, had ever been anywhere more built-up than Tingalla. He failed dismally to hide his surprise that they'd managed to get into town and back, unescorted and unscathed.

The first time he'd snuck out of the palace and into the streets of Usmein, he'd ended up blind drunk, robbed, and kicked into a gutter only to be found by a duke's guard on her way to start the early shift. His demise had been their little secret, so long as he gave her a glowing endorsement to the commander, which he made sure to do once his black eye had faded.

Eian ignored Ran's confusion. 'Excellent pastries down there, by the way. There's this little tea shop—'

'Later, my love.' Zarad rushed back to the door, easing it closed and pressing his hand to the timber. He traced the grain as if feeling for something and Ran's senses tingled. Zarad was listening to the frequencies shifting through the air beyond the threshold.

'Yes, right.' With a nod, Eian bustled Ran and Lidan into the farthest corner of the dining room, wedging them between a sideboard and a row of spare chairs under the windowsill. 'Soldiers, a whole troop of them, just pulled up out the front. The courtyard is rammed. We got around through the kitchen entrance. Something's happening and by all the sharp, stabby steel, we guessed it wasn't good.'

'So we're hiding in here with the chairs and paring knives?' Lidan asked, her brow cocked in a sceptical frown.

'I'd wager they won't search the whole house,' Zarad whispered from the door. 'But if they've come for our criminal prince, we might have to fight our way out.'

The absurdity of the moment caught Ran and he lost control of a laugh. 'You can't be serious?'

Zarad's sober gaze met his across the empty dining table. 'We haven't come this far to fail now.'

'We need to call for Aelish. She'll know what to do,' Lidan put in. Her knives slid free of their sheaths, as natural a reaction to danger as Ran's magic swarming through his arms.

Without question he was the most powerful of the magic-weavers here, but if they could escape without blasting his power all over the place, he'd be grateful. The last thing he needed was a repeat of the accusations that followed him to Usmein's dungeon. The Isordian government would be loath to help a fugitive who'd just blown up a good portion of their merchant district and taken out half the financial quarter with it, be he the king's grandson or not.

'Shit, shit, shit, no such luck.' Zarad slid back from the door, hands raised to confront whatever threat might break through.

Heart racing, Ran tightened like a bow string, clamping down hard on his magic as it soared from the depths of his abdomen and forced its way out along his limbs. Heat swirled behind his eyes, a faint blue-white sheen falling over the room as time slipped and his vision fractured. Eian and Zarad moved with painful slowness, their voices warped into deep, resounding roars as they called warnings to each other and Lidan. She pressed down, preparing to pounce, every fibre singing to Ran as her face contorted into a mask of determination.

The door cracked open.

Ran's heart leapt.

Iridia appeared and behind her, *through* her, two women emerged from the hallway, faces lit with laughter. *Stop!* The arms of his ghost cocooned him, sapping away the heat and drawing off the anger before she vanished in a savage crackle of air.

Ran's sense of time sprang back with a hard smack and the room sizzled as though struck by lightning. Everyone froze, the newcomers rigid with shock, staring at the room's occupants; weapons drawn, magic fading, energy dissipating, a metallic tang lingering like invisible smoke. Iridia wavered at the edge of Ran's perception, ever watchful, ever cautious, huddled as if scalded by the power she'd stolen.

'Have we interrupted something?' A woman with a curtain of straight brown hair surveyed the room, the casual humour in her voice belied by the tightness of her smile and the tense lines around her eyes. Her hand hovered inches from her waist, where no doubt a knife hid in a fold of her heavy, elaborately embroidered skirt.

Ran straightened but the others didn't move, ignorant of the withering glare of disappointment Aelish levelled from the doorway. 'Villia?'

It took a breath, but Villia Kortson—his cousin, granddaughter to King Harroe and niece to his mother—shifted her gaze from the two young men poised between them and settled on Ran. She didn't even register Lidan, her gaze passing over the woman as if she wasn't there. He swallowed a growl. Any money Villia thought the southerner no more than a mercenary knife for hire, or worse, the help. Her forced smile melted into something more genuine. 'My, you did get tall.'

'What are you—' He paused, realising how ridiculous the question sounded, but he pressed on, already committed to making a fool of himself. 'What brings you here?'

'My dear sister-in-law has sent a good number of desperate letters these past few days. I thought I should show my face to see if she truly had returned to us.' Villia turned her smile on Aelish, who relented and stepped into the room. 'Though I had thought to speak in private…'

It was a statement rather than a question—one artfully ignored by Aelish as she pretended not to hear it. 'Our staff will have refreshments delivered shortly. Such a wonderful opportunity for you to reacquaint yourselves.'

When it became clear Aelish wouldn't dismiss the others from the room, Villia relented with a stiff nod, her eyes lingering on Lidan's blade. A moment of silent communication passed between Aelish and Lidan that Ran almost missed before the southerner sheathed her knives and straightened from her frankly terrifying fight-ready stance.

Aelish *had* been sending letters, but to whom exactly he couldn't say. He hadn't expected Villia Kortson to show up in personal reply. Had she caught wind of Aelish's return in court gossip? Had the news travelled so far so fast?

'It took some digging to discover just why Aelish so urgently requested an audience with the king,' Villia went on. A subtle, almost unnoticed motion of her hand caught Ran's eye before the door shut behind her. Again, his senses tingled, magic brushing over his raw nerves. 'Imagine my surprise to find my baby cousin was in town?'

Magic warmed his fingers as the scent of a threat bled into the room. This time, neither he nor Iridia moved to quell it. Zarad shifted, sensing a change in the air, while Eian remained stoically motionless, his imposing frame unmoved by the apparent high status of this woman. He never did give a shit about protocol.

Again, came the tight smile. 'I thought I had better deliver the news myself.'

'News?' Ran ventured.

'Your request for an audience has been denied,' Villia said with all the warmth of a bitter northerly wind, talking over Aelish's sharp intake of breath. 'I know you'd hoped for something in the next few days, but it simply can't be arranged.'

Confusion morphed into concern and Aelish took a slight step back. 'A decision has already been made? I'd thought the king might take a few more days to consider—'

Villia waved her words away. 'Such a low-level request doesn't fall within the remit of the king. Harroe's days are quite heavily scheduled and frankly, taking up his time with this kind of trivia just can't be justified.'

Aelish's scowl mirrored Ran's, suspicion sparkling in her eyes. Villia might be a daughter of the crown prince, but she was not his heir. She was almost as far as a princess could get from the line of succession, so what was she doing delivering news like this?

'I'd appreciate hearing this from my grandfather, if you wouldn't mind,' Ran countered, his tone as even as he could manage given the warring emotions banking up inside him. To have come this far and be denied? This couldn't be the end of the road. This was *not* where his story ended and it certainly wouldn't happen as his cousin, some five years senior, gazed at him down her straight, pale nose.

Villia shrugged. 'You won't, I'm afraid. There isn't anything that can be done.' Her tone was friendly enough, almost jovial, but there was a double-edge to her words as she swung them gracefully through the air, perhaps not aiming to wound but cutting anyway.

'On whose authority?' Ran snapped. Aelish glared a silent warning he didn't heed.

'Mine,' Villia shot back.

The word sucked the air from the room, a vacuum of stunned silence remaining as the minor princess glared at her younger cousin, his insolence unlikely to find equal. Ran was beyond caring. Did family mean nothing to these people?

'You're a fugitive, Ranoth Olseta. Or did you forget that in all the years you've been missing? Disliking your father may be King Harroe's favourite pastime, but his councillors and ministers are there for a *reason*. Preventing him from inciting an international diplomatic incident is one of them.' With a sharp sigh, Villia straightened and clasped her hands together. 'As Minister for Foreign Affairs—'

'I'm sorry, *what*?' Ran's derisive laugh echoed across the room. 'You have to stand for election to become a minister.'

Villia's hands squeezed together until the knuckles paled. 'I did.'

This time Aelish blinked in disbelief. Eian and Zarad shrugged at each other and Lidan leaned against the wall, arms folded, content for now to watch. 'You're an elected representative of the people?'

'Yes,' Villia lifted her chin and Ran began to sift the thousand pieces of distorted information.

His cousin held very little power as a minor royal, a long way down the pecking order from her father, her two elder siblings and any children they had from ever getting her hands on the crown. So instead of eking out an existence at the fringes of the court, she'd made a play for the heart of the machine that sat *beneath* the crown—the Isordian parliament. Long rumoured to be as corrupt as it was slow and bureaucratic, the ministers holding portfolios likened themselves to puppet masters. The king however, quietly kept the true reins of power where they could neither be seen nor touched. The Isordian ministers who thought they held all the cards did nothing but play the house by its own rules, and as any gambler knows, the house always wins.

It seemed no one had told Villia just how the game really worked.

Duchess Merideth had spent many a blizzard-blown night drilling her son on the politics of what they thought would become his closest and most important ally, after his ascension to Duke Ronart's throne. That future had died on the vine many years ago, but his mother's lessons rang true for him today. If his cousin wanted to bet against him, that was her mistake. Ran had nothing left to lose.

'So selfless to give yourself to public office like that.' If his affected praise reached his eyes, Ran would have been stunned.

Villia blinked, fighting a flattered smile as she smoothed her hands down the front of her gown. 'Well, we were born to serve, were we not?'

He gave her a silky nod, not meaning a fucking word of what he was about to say. 'Of course. And I understand wholly why you must protect our grandfather. Decisions made for emotional reasons are, after all, where society comes apart.'

'I—thank you,' she replied, her gaze darting to the others as her composure resurrected itself. Rebuilding her sense of importance was the key to the next step, reasserting her dominance coming in a close second. 'Aelish didn't mention what it was you wished to discuss. Perhaps it's something I could assist with?'

Before Aelish could speak, Ran caught her eye. Weeks on the road had built a silent, unquestioning trust between them, and while he knew Eian and Zarad wouldn't jump in, he hoped Aelish knew when to follow rather than lead. He waved a hand dismissively, clicking his tongue.

'It was but a trifle. I merely wished to share an ale with the old man before I made my way to the coast. I would never seek to disrupt the balance of an entire alliance over something so trivial.'

'The coast?' Villia's question thinly veiled her immediately waning interest. He was nothing more than a liability now, no threat posed beyond someone discovering that she knew he was here. 'That does sound nice. I do hope you have a pleasant journey.'

'Oh, I'm sure we will. Another day's rest and we'll be on our way.' His fist came to rest over his heart, right where his family crest should have been, and he gave Villia, Minister of Foreign Affairs, a slight bow. Her status should have demanded a deeper obeisance, but as the first son of a duke, he had every right to withhold whatever airs and graces he chose.

If she noticed, she made no indication, merely turning and giving Aelish a dazzlingly fake smile. It wouldn't have convinced the simplest drunkard to part with his coins for a moment of affection, let alone a wily trader like Aelish, but she returned it with gusto, extending her hand to open the door.

'Your highness, I must thank you for coming to us in person. You honour my family and our house.' Formal platitudes rolled off Aelish's tongue with practised ease and Villia took the woman's invitation to leave. Sister-in-law or not, Villia lapped up honeyed words as greedily as the next noble, reminding her of her tenuous royal status a master stroke. A split-second glance from Aelish received a slight nod of understanding from Ran before she stepped out after the minister, a couple of guards thudding along the corridor after them until silence regained dominion over the dining room.

'So we're going to the coast after all?' Eian ventured, turning a wry smile on Ran. 'Brit will be pleased.'

'I've never seen the coast.' Lidan peeled herself away from the wall and stood across the table from Zarad. 'We could go two for two on the list of things neither of us have done?'

Tapping his finger on his lip, feigning deep and meaningful thought, Zarad nodded. 'I hear the weather is lovely this time of year.'

Ran glared at the door, his glower burning a hole where his cousin had been. Galled by her dismissal, fuelled by her outright rejection, he'd never been one to wear such refusal. It was the same vice that landed him in command of his own troops in the Disputed Territory, powered by the same hubris that had seen most dead within days. He only hoped this time his friends would escape his terrible decisions with their lives.

'We're not going to the coast,' Ran said dryly.

'Oh?' Eian's brows rose, his disappointment stage-craft perfect. He'd have made a great actor if he'd been able to hold a tune. 'Why not?'

'Because we're breaking into the palace.' Then he shot Eian a wicked, knowing grin. 'And I fucking hate sand.'

CHAPTER THIRTY-FIVE

Kotja, Isord

Night fell over the city, Villia's visit shrugged off as a family affair as the household went about its day. At dinner Ran made sure to wave away any concerns that the king's refusal might hamper his plans, though he held back from mentioning exactly what those plans were. If their objectives could have been achieved without the king's help, he'd have merely resupplied in Kotja and moved on. But he and his companions weren't getting across the northern Isordian border and into the Empire without catching the eye of either country's troops. The permission and assistance of the crown were critical to that end, but he couldn't admit any of that as they dined on pink river fish and some sort of creamy lemon sauce Brit tried to drink straight from the jug when no one was looking.

Further than needing permission to cross out of Isord, crucial intelligence had to be gathered that could only be provided by the king's agents, fed back from behind enemy lines to the governments of the Free Nations. Everyone knew the Woaden kept agents in Kotja, Kederen and Usmein, all of them playing at passing misleading information at every possible chance; a far less time-consuming task than actually weeding out the spies in the first place. Such information was unattainable while Villia controlled the foreign ministry, her fingers firmly on the strings of the Agency, locking up any information they might have on the Empire, the emperor, and recent events in the capital.

Unless Ran managed to convince the king to reveal his own security briefings, he and the others faced an attempt at the impossible—an illegal, clandestine border crossing, smuggling themselves across country in enemy territory and walking blind into Wodurin and its snake-pit of a court. They couldn't even know for sure if Sellan was in the city, though Thanie assured them this would be her first step, taken long before she attempted to treat with the Dead Sisters.

As the evening wore on and the household headed for bed, Ran glanced across the sitting room and caught Lidan's eye. The slightest nod was all she needed.

Dressed in warm, comfortable trousers and boots, pleading no resistance to the cold, she'd hidden her coat by the back kitchen door, along with one for Ran. Summer it might be, but once the sun set and the north wind rose through the heights of the peaks, it might as well have been a mild winter night. A yawn broke Lidan's drowsy silence and she reached over to squeeze Aelish's shoulder. The trader barely glanced up from where she sat curled in the crook of Brit's arm. There was a mutter Ran didn't catch, then Lidan was gone.

He gave her a few minutes, wary of rushing to make his own excuses and leaving too quickly in her wake. Gods forbid someone get the wrong idea, assuming there was something else afoot other than break and enter against the state. Eian and Zarad slipped out moments later, professing a need to take some air before turning in, fascinated as they were with the city.

Their host vaguely acknowledged them, her eyes trained on the fire, her spirit quashed by her sister-in-law's denial of their request. Aelish's protocols and procedures had failed her in a way she couldn't process, her distress evident in her faraway stare and short temper. Ran wished he could soothe that hurt, but it was better she knew nothing of his plan.

She couldn't tell what she didn't know. If they were caught, Aelish could reasonably deny any knowledge of the break-in. She could disavow them, salvage her reputation and business, and carry on without the shameful weight of his indiscretions on her conscience. But it meant going forward without her help. Ran just had to hope his memory of Kotja's history held true.

Lidan waited in the lee of a wall some distance up the street from the Yordam compound, bundled against the bite of the wind; Eian and Zarad wandering calmly ahead, arm in arm, as if they had nothing to do with the young man and woman meeting in the shadows behind them. To any onlooker, this was nothing more than a tryst—young well-to-do people out for some fun.

'You better be right about this,' Lidan muttered through chattering teeth, reaching for the front of Ran's coat and playing into the role of star-crossed lover.

'The quicker we get to the wall, the sooner we'll know, won't we?' He wrapped an arm around her back and made a show of steering her along the street in the same direction Eian and Zarad had gone moments before. The magic-weavers had spent the afternoon scoping the upper rings of the city for just this reason, returning with news that a market or festival had been set up in the plaza near the palace. It was the best cover they were likely to get and Ran kept pace, following in his friends' path as they wandered through two successive wall gates to the palace precinct.

The plaza before the main gate buzzed with activity, a night market lining the central gardens. Stalls hawked hot food and trinkets shone in the light of torches and lamps, tiny things for citizens to buy and leave at the temples of the spirits of the seasons. It was a time for thanksgiving, something his mother would do for weeks after midsummer, blessing the coming month. They strolled closer to the wall and for the length of a heartbeat, it struck Ran how much Isord reminded him of home.

It wasn't just that the language of the milling populace sung to a place in his heart where only his mother could touch, it was the motifs on the walls, carvings in stone and timber, on the lintels above doors. Each block of houses or street of merchant buildings bore the mark of a religion the Orthian people, absorbed as they were by war, had forgotten even existed.

The temples in Usmein went untended for the most part, fit men and women enlisting rather than pledging to a priesthood. With the passing of time and the wise, the old stories were lost to distraction—the rituals of the seasons and their gods paid naught but lip service if anything at all. The festivals that remained were shells of their former selves. Perce, his unrelenting tutor, hadn't agreed that Orthia had greater worries than the proper observances of the gods and spirits. He'd argued at length, at first with the duke and then with Ran, that the country's ill fortune might just be the result of poor adherence to the old ways.

At the time, Ran thought it the tired ranting of a crotchety old man, bitter to his bones. So what if no one actually went to the temple on the White Lady's day, instead giving each other the gifts customarily reserved for the goddess of the harvest? So what if the darkest day of the year no longer warranted hours of meditation on the meaning of life and the weight of death, a time usually dedicated to the Dark Rider, instead playing host to the biggest piss-up of the Orthian calendar?

It mattered, because as Ran and Lidan feigned their casual ramble through the streets of Kotja, he realised just how far Orthia's people had fallen from their own culture. Their connection to the land, to the heartbeat of the mountains, to the soul of the Stonemason and the song of the Ice Maiden, had been severed by a singular focus—eradicating the Woaden. In seeking the Empire's downfall, they'd slipped their mooring, bobbing helpless in the torrent of violence tearing their country apart, without any purpose other than killing.

'Has she ever told you why my mother wants this so badly?' Lidan's question cut across his musings and drew him to a pause.

'Who, Thanie? Something about toppling the Empire, I believe.'

Lidan nodded. 'There's trauma, I know that much. There's hurt. In Tingalla, Thanie made it sound like a grab for power, as if Sellan wants to rule the north.'

'You don't think that's the case?' He hadn't thought much of it beyond the need to stop Sellan creating more dradur. Her reasons hadn't been his primary concern. To be honest, he didn't actually care. But he hadn't considered Lidan's feelings about Sellan's reasons.

She chewed her lip as they ambled through the crowd, crossing the plaza toward the palace wall. 'My mother is a lot of things but she… Never really struck me as the power-hungry type.'

They came to a stop behind a hot food vendor, sheltering from the flow of the crowd in the lee of the stall. It was a possibility Ran hadn't entertained. He'd taken Thanie's version of the story at face value, never questioning, never doubting. He'd shoved any lingering hesitation away, unwilling to be distracted from his goal of saving Iridia. As much as that went against his better judgement, trusting Thanie was the price he had to pay.

In any case, why would Thanie feed them a falsehood? Why wouldn't Sellan want power? Why wouldn't she want to rule? He found Iridia at the edges of his mind. Her presence shrugged, as uncertain as he was. She knew nothing of the woman's motivations either, and why would she? It wasn't like Sellan divulged her plans to everyone she plunged a knife into. Lidan's doubt shimmered in her green eyes, leaving him wondering if perhaps there was something else behind it all.

'What brought this on?' he asked.

'I just… I've been trying to understand why ever since I went to the unseen realms. Why go to all this effort? Why work so hard to bring down an empire? She risked the ire of gods and failed the first time, then built a new life for herself. Why return after all these years?' Lidan shook her head and folded her arms against the cold. Understanding crept up his spine. She was right. It didn't make sense when he examined it from this angle. 'She was frightened, Ran. Whenever our place in the clan was threatened, whenever she thought I was in danger, fear forced her hand, not greed. I'm not sure this is about power. I'm not even sure this is about the Empire. This is personal.'

He had nothing to say to that. The hubbub of the market coursed around them, the ebb and flow of people and conversation filling their silence like an empty cup. 'We could ask Thanie. If anyone knows, it's her.'

Even as he said it, he knew it a fool's errand. Thanie would take her secrets to the grave. If she wanted them to know, she'd have told them already. And was he willing to risk her wrath if he probed to deeply, too close to old pain? More likely, Lidan's misgivings grew from her own doubt, her own unwillingness to accept of what her mother meant to do and why. 'If it is personal, does that change anything?'

'Perhaps it doesn't.' Lidan shrugged. 'Whatever her motivation, she needs to be stopped. It just doesn't sit right.' She nodded at the Isordian palace, its wall looming at the end of the plaza. 'We still have a job to do. How are we getting in there?'

Ran leaned into Lidan's ear, maintaining the ruse of a couple in love. 'This part of the wall burned down a few centuries back. A rebel group sympathetic to the Empire attacked it while it was still mostly a timber structure.'

Lidan nodded, painting on a smile as if he'd said something incredibly witty before she turned and ran her gaze along the top of the wall. 'It's not timber now, though.'

'No, but in the drawings my tutor showed me years ago, it looked much the same as the walls around Hummel and Tingalla.'

She met his eyes then. 'There's always more than one exit in a wall like that, should someone set the main gate on fire.'

'Exactly. My mother told me stories. When she was young, she'd escape into the city through a trap door in the base of the old wall—a hidden hatch engineered by her forebears.' Turning Lidan in the circle of his arms, Ran made his best attempt to hold her back to his chest while keeping a safe distance. She had knives under that coat. If she even suspected him of trying something fresh, she'd feed him his balls. 'The old wall's stone footing still exists down there, where it meets the mountainside.'

'Surely they've corrected that by now?' Lidan asked, sounding as dubious as she did hopeful.

'It's our only chance. We aren't getting through there.' He indicated the main gate bristling with guards dressed in green, white and grey overcoats. The palace might permit a festival market in the plaza, but they weren't throwing open the doors to the public. 'Shall we?'

A quick glance at Eian and Zarad found them disappearing into the darkness at the base of the wall. Scouting ahead, he listened for a whistled signal that all was clear. Lidan jogged silently along the foot of the wall and Ran dropped his veils, his Sight opening to the possibility of magic-weaving sentries hiding in the shadows. Lamps swung on the ramparts high above, metal on metal shrieking in the breeze, but the residential compounds to their left stood in darkness, only their gateways and interiors lit. For a country at war, Isord was making the exact same mistakes as Orthia before the Woaden attacked.

Their border garrisons were likely so well-manned that the need to maintain proper security in this mountain city seemed overzealous, possibly even wasteful. Why burn precious fuel lighting the street at the foot of the palace wall when a dozen fortified gates stood between any invading force and the royal family? Why bother a street occupied by the wealthy and noble with patrols? This wouldn't be a district known for crime, and the complacency showed.

Your grandfather could learn a thing or two from you, Iridia muttered, floating beside him as he hurried after Lidan. Her footsteps whispered on the pavers, her fingers tracing the ancient footing of the wall.

I'll make sure to mention it when we see him, shall I? Ran gave his ghost a sardonic smile. If Harroe was as gruff and stoic as rumour suggested, he wouldn't take kindly to a young, upstart prince giving him advice on palace defence.

What will you do if he won't help?

Ran slowed, mirroring Lidan's pace as she paused and felt at the stones, her fingertips following a line he couldn't see. Glad for the darkness to hide his creeping anxiety, he raked his hair back from his eyes. Iridia didn't leave. She stared and waited; not going anywhere without an answer.

We'll go our own way, Ran told her, repeating Lidan's sentiment from the breakfast table.

If we're allowed to leave at all...

That really isn't helpful.

Iridia sighed heavily. *Can you at least try not to get caught this time?* This time?

She eyed him. *As fond as your memories of home might be, the palace dungeons were vile. I'd rather not repeat the experience, if it's all the same to you.*

A shudder rolled through him; the cold and the damp, the pain of his wounds, the terrifying weight of uncertainty. He hadn't known what waited for him in the Usmein dungeon, but capture in Kotja meant certain death, and certain death meant failure. Lidan might doubt her mother's motivations, but that didn't alter the path ahead. Failure wasn't a luxury he could afford. He'd prevent another massacre like Lackmah or die trying.

'I need some light,' Lidan whispered. A blue-white glow bloomed in Ran's hand, just enough to illuminate the wall, and Lidan shoved her shoulder against the stone.

Deep within the wall, something shifted with a heavy *thunk*, reverberating through the mortar. By the light of his magic, four stones not much higher than his hip sank into the wall as one.

'Wait, you found it *that* quickly?' he asked, astonished.

Lidan waved for Eian and Zarad. 'The seams in the wall change where the tunnels open. That's one block carved to look like four. The pattern changes from an overlap to a quadrant. It's hard to see unless you know what to look for.' She shuffled back, giving Zarad room to press his hands to the stone. A tang of discharging energy touched Ran's tongue and Zarad forced the block inward with a jolt of frequency magic.

Ran's eyes narrowed in a sceptical scowl. 'And your walls are exactly the same, all the way down in the South Lands?'

'Where do you think we got the design?' She clapped him on the shoulder. 'Isordian traders.'

The tunnel wasn't more than a crawl space, stretching on forever, its winding turns twisting Ran around on himself. By the time the ceiling lifted and the four of them stood straight, he had no idea where they were beneath the foundations of the palace. Memories of his escape from Usmein flashed through his mind, dread curdling in his stomach as he realised he'd willingly put his head in the jaws of a dragon, all the while hoping it wasn't hungry.

Not your smartest move, but here we are, Iridia said, looking up at the roof as if she could see right through the stone above. *No going back now.*

As the others crawled out of the tunnel and into the space behind him, Ran pressed his magic against the walls. *Can you make yourself useful and find an exit, or are you just going to stand here and point out my inadequacies?*

Of course I can't! I'm fused to you. You're stuck with me until that witch helps you free me.

He grunted something vulgar under his breath and pushed his hand to the ceiling.

'She's giving you shit again, isn't she?' Lidan asked, brushing slime and muck from the knees of her trousers then stretching her back.

'Every fucking day,' Ran muttered. Iridia's invisible gaze dug knives into his back and he allowed himself a small smile. She often forgot Lidan could sense their conversations. 'I've got no idea where we're going to come up, but if it's anything like my home, it'll be somewhere down in the cellars or some ancillary rooms.'

'As long as it isn't into a prison cell, I don't care,' Eian quipped. His broad shoulders filled the tunnel behind Zarad's leaner frame. It was a certified miracle Eian had made it through the crawl space without protest. 'I'd like to make it out of this alive if we can manage it.'

'No promises,' Ran replied. He levelled a finger at Lidan. 'No killing people. I don't want to give them another reason to gaol us.'

She rolled her eyes and gave him a mocking bow. 'As you wish.'

Silence greeted them in the cellar. Barrels of ale, stacked one upon the next, stood guard as they crept into the room. Light filtered down from a staircase at the far end, the landing lit by a murky glow that could only be a fatty oil lamp. They weren't wasting good oil on the servants, even if it stopped them breaking their necks on the stairs. A deep earthy scent clung to his nose, the sharp odour of barrel timbers mingling with the scattering of straw on the floor and the racks of vegetables shoved against the back wall. Booze and roots—the staples of any highland diet.

'At this time of night, I imagine we're looking for the sleeping quarters,' Ran whispered. He led the three of them to the doorway and blinked up the stairs. 'It'll be guarded, so we'll need a distraction.'

A grin spread across Eian's face at the possibilities and Ran pinned his friend with a knowing look. 'Nothing too dramatic. Don't burn the place down or get yourselves arrested. Just make some noise then get out of here.'

'What about you two?' Zarad narrowed his eyes, pulling the ever-increasing length of his curls back into a tail high on his head, their bright red sheen darkened by shadow to the colour of old blood. Ran hadn't told him this part because it wasn't up for negotiation. If he could make it to the royal quarters and back again without Lidan's help, he would have. He certainly wasn't taking the others any further into harm's way than he absolutely had to.

'We'll find our own way out. Don't wait for us. Go back to the house and if we aren't there by sunrise, tell Aelish where we went and get her back-channelling. She'll be able to find out.'

Zarad shook his head. 'She's gonna skin you alive.'

'Worth the risk, mate. We need this or it's all for nothing.'

They shared a moment of silent acknowledgement, a squeeze of an arm, then they were gone. Up and out of the cellar, the two magic-weavers left Ran and Lidan in silence.

'What we needed was better disguises.' She looked down, her knees damp and soiled from crawling through the tunnel, her hair a dusty mess of wildly complicated braids. Her eyes shone though, as if the very act of taking action, the very thought of doing something toward their mutual goal set a fire in her soul. Under her dirty outdoor coat, she wore the simple shirt and tunic of a household servant stolen from the Yordam's laundry room. A matching indoor jacket, long in the hem, covered the bulge of the knives strapped to her thighs.

'I'm the most likely to go unnoticed,' Ran said as he shrugged off his coat and bundled it into a dark corner with Lidan's. His jerkin bore a faint household crest, pale green and grey similar enough to blend in with the staff and guards they saw near the gate. 'Stay one step behind my shoulder, keep your eyes down and we'll be fine.'

You hope, Iridia put in.

That's enough out of you.

His sketchy memory of this part of the palace served him well enough, leading them past the kitchens and storerooms. They swiped an armload of linen each, hurrying along as though they had somewhere very important to be and no time to waste. Not a single guard or servant turned a second glance on them as they wove through hallways and up stairs, not pausing for more than a breath before forging onward. Even if he lost his way, Ran couldn't afford to look it. Palace staff knew every corridor and niche, every doorway and unused room. If he seemed uncertain for even a second, their cover was blown.

The halls became more opulent as they reached the third floor and Ran led them quickly but calmly down a gallery lined with busts and portraits. At one point the corridor split, one arm turning back toward the centre of the palace while another kept on straight ahead.

It looked familiar. So many of them did. The faces of distant relatives watched him in silence, some he'd met, others who had passed long before his time. He thought he knew the pattern of a rug or tapestry, the angle of this window seat perhaps a little more than another. He'd been so young when he'd been here last, so overwhelmed, so out of his depth he couldn't be entirely sure—

'Ran?'

A voice caught his thoughts mid-spiral and he jolted to a stop. Eyes down just like he'd told her, Lidan slammed into his back, tipping both piles of folded linen from their hands to tumble all over the floor. Whirling to help her, he realised his mistake and swung back, hands up, fire igniting beneath his magic.

They stood at the junction of the hallways, a lone figure no more than a foot or so away, a lamp illuminating crinkled bedclothes and bleary eyes.

A mug coiled an unfurling tendril of steam into the cool air. It tipped, slipped from trembling fingers, the contents swirling out and down in a scalding cascade. The delicate crockery followed, smashing on the exposed boards beyond the protection of the rugs.

A fragile silence pressed in, fit to shatter at any moment, stealing away whatever warmth Ran had in his limbs. A knife emerged from a sheath behind him, the faint song of steel on leather announcing Lidan's readiness to fight her way out of this and hang the consequences. Ran's hand caught her wrist, the rest of him frozen in place, rigid as he scrambled to understand what he saw.

Dark hair. A slight frame. Wide, terrified blue eyes. Streaks of silver at the temples. Thin, pale lips quivering as they gasped. A tear streaking down the planes of a fine, fair face. 'Ran? It can't...'

The voice trailed off, Ran choking on the same disbelief that stole their words.

This wasn't possible. And yet, it was.

The slightest hint of a smile broke through the shock, his vision blurring as he lowered his hands. 'Hiya, Ma.'

CHAPTER THIRTY-SIX

The Malapa

The thing about returning from the dead was that day by day, one could feel again. Not just a vague flutter of emotion in the chest or the faint echo of conscience questioning a decision. Actual sensations. Cold, it appeared, felt worse north of the Malapa, and no matter how often Marrit assured Loge that it was in fact summer, he refused to believe her.

He blamed Dennawal for it all. Since their encounter in the cave, Loge's perception of the world had shifted dramatically from one of vague indifference to a relentless assault on his senses. Nearly every thought or feeling Marrit had shone in a blinding aura of emotion and intent, blasting his blackened eye. It took days to suppress it, pushing back on the lights until she merely shimmered in his perception.

As far as he could gather, the ancestors didn't speak with words in the realm beyond. They communicated through thought alone, something an eye such as his would be useful for if he'd actually managed to die as he was supposed to. What Loge's eye was never meant to see was the realm of the living, forcing him to witness an unmitigated onslaught of human conscience that at times was more than he could bear.

Travelling alone with Marrit, he was spared the worst of it. They crept through the Pass, gaping at the corpse of an immense ngaru left to rot beside a subterranean lake. The detritus of battle lay silent in the cavern, untouched by Loge or Marrit. He refused to give voice to his fears, holding close his silence. Daylight broke at the end of the Pass and fresh air once again caressed their skin, a weight lifting as they continued northward.

Within the borders of Arinnia they shared the road with other travellers, whose presence forced Loge to take control of his curse, stamping down on the sensation and pushing back on the light. Thank small mercies, he couldn't quite hear people's thoughts as much as feel them; what they wanted, needed, desired. The busier roads had been a waking nightmare, teeming with life and a stream of thought he could barely control. Marrit suggested an eye patch, fashioned of items in her endless pockets and pouches. She'd reasoned his onyx eye would draw unwanted attention from anyone they might encounter on the road. He'd reasoned that he'd just kill anyone who stuck their attention where it wasn't wanted, and that was the end of that.

The irritating auras faded after a few days and the internal mutterings of travellers grew quiet. It wasn't until they climbed out of the foothills of northern Arinnia and into the peaks of another mountain range that the eye's power no longer hung like a mill stone around his neck.

The ascent into the mountains, while frigid and exhausting, at least gave him some respite as the crowds lessened and the path ahead grew increasingly empty. As the road wound through valleys and up the sides of sheer slopes, Marrit clung to the map, trembling under her layers. The parchment held tight in her gloved hand, she checked her bearings on the sun by the hour. He didn't question her obsession. He didn't fancy losing his way in this wilderness.

They were in the right place, she assured him. This was the way to Lidan.

Lidan might have come here, but was she *still* here? That fear burrowed in deep, claws embedded in his mind. If Lidan had moved on and left Kotja in her wake, then the trail turned as cold as the stones beneath their horses' hooves. They'd be stranded in unknown territory at the edge of the world.

Evening inched through the peaks and the first sight of the city stole Loge's breath, his vision swimming as he tried to comprehend its size. The hard-won control of his sight failed, abandoning him just as he needed it most. So many people, so much life, all burning his weird eye. He scrunched up his face, turning from the onslaught and pushing hard against the unwanted side effect of an interrupted death.

The streets glowed like a web in the falling darkness, bodies throbbing with purpose. Pain lanced through his skull, a stinging ache piercing from the crown down through the orbit of his eye and into his cheek. Rubbing at it did little to ease the agony and as Marrit turned in her saddle, he found he couldn't hear a word she said over the garbled noise of the population.

She met his confusion with a frown then waved, pointing to a guard posted at the gatehouse. Was she asking directions? She didn't dismount, instead leaning to shout at the man lazily watching the flow of traffic.

'...Yordam...' was all Loge heard, Marrit's words caught on a wind only he could feel.

The guard lifted his hand, three fingers held up, then pointed to where the road inside the wall vanished between a shambles of houses and shop-fronts. With a nod of thanks, Marrit urged her horse back into the crush. Loge shoved hard against the bright shimmer of the populace, squeezing his eyes shut as Striker moved to follow.

Loge's ears popped.

The sounds of life and living rushed in like a torrent, crashing over him as he followed Marrit up the street. Gasping, relief washed over him, the world returning to rights. The gleam of an entire city's intentions faded away. He relaxed for the first time in weeks, his grip on the reins slackening.

They'd made it.

Torturously over-crowded and crammed with impossibly tall buildings, they'd crossed half the world to find this place.

Lidan was here somewhere. Dennawal would be pleased.

Night fell and cold seeped through his coat, folk lighting their homes against the dark. Metal flashed in more forms than he'd ever thought to see, paved roads winding through markets and past open green spaces that reminded him of Hummel's common. This place was nothing like the Tolak villages he vaguely recalled from the time before his death. This place should have set his heart pounding and his hair standing on end, but he registered little more than dull surprise.

The places he'd once thought of as home no longer mattered. This place, with its strange smells and sprawling pathways and glaring colours, meant little. It was no more than a passing curiosity. Room remained for one sensation alone, and that was direction and purpose and need all in one.

Lidan was here.

They crossed beneath wall after wall, Marrit exuding a confident aura that they belonged here, a thin disguise to the fact that they very much did not. It kept them from notice, for the most part; three gatehouses giving them no more than a cursory glance.

It was in the streets of the fourth city terrace that their luck fled.

Loge sensed them before he saw them. A cluster of shadows peeled themselves from walls and laneways, slipping along behind them as the thoroughfares emptied and people hurried inside for their evening meals. The buildings here leaned in, looming up a few storeys, reaching for each other across the street. Timber and stone, they blocked or caught the wind as they thought fit, funnelling it into gusts that whipped along the cobbles.

Gentle pressure applied to his flanks gave Striker a nudge and he closed on Marrit's horse, just close enough for Loge to whisper, 'We have company.'

'Guards?' she replied without looking over her shoulder.

'Something more sinister.'

A casual glance up at the eaves of a building gave her a chance for a subtle look back. 'Probably marked us as strangers. Easy pickings.'

'Not their smartest move,' Loge grumbled under his breath. An ache in his head scratched again, triggered by the mere thought of a delay. The day wouldn't end well for anyone who stood in his way.

'We could outrun them, but not without attracting more unwanted attention.' She was right. Their only advantage left them open to scrutiny by authorities he didn't have the time nor desire to negotiate with.

'Down here,' he muttered. Urging Striker forward, he shepherded Marrit's horse to the left and into a side street. Need and urgency pulled him toward the largest buildings in town, at the height of the valley. This way was less direct, but it would take them to the right place.

He opened his mouth to suggest picking up the pace when another group of figures crept into their path, blocking the gloomy, narrow street. Suddenly this route looked like a less than ideal choice. Each of these little side streets probably teemed with miscreants just waiting for prey to step into their trap.

And trapped they were.

Throwing stealth to the wind, Loge twisted and glared back down the street, encouraging his deformed eye to reveal the intent of those prowling in their wake. Deep red and swirling black marked them, an oily smoke churning around the figures keeping to the shadows yet growing bolder with each step.

'They're not ngaru,' Marrit said. Loge turned, catching the worry creasing her brow for the briefest moment. 'And I *can* fight them, but not in a saddle.'

'Too narrow for horses,' he muttered. 'We stand here.' *These fucks*, he snarled to himself, swinging down and stomping cold feet on the cobbles. *If these fucks are the reason I miss my chance, I'll fucking flay them all.*

Calm as the night deepened, he drew his axe from the loops on his saddle and clicked at Striker, giving him a light smack on the rump. He'd find him once these obstacles no longer stood in their way. It wouldn't take long. He just had to be careful not to catch Marrit in the fray. He needed her still—his compass until he found his way home.

The figures closed in, chuckles echoing up the sides of the buildings, wary glances shared between comrades seeking guidance from their leaders. Did they wonder at these confident strangers who turned to face them rather than running? Did they think them foolish?

'You are either very smart or very dumb,' a man's sing-song voice spoke from the darkness. 'I will make it simple for you. You aren't from here, so it is polite that I help you understand.' He rolled the common tongue uncomfortably in his mouth, his accent catching on words and adding emphasis where it didn't belong. 'You give us the shiny coin and we let you pass on, yes?'

He emerged at the head of the gathered figures, stepping into a dim sliver of light from beyond a curtained window. Tall and pale, his narrow chin seemed at odds with the broad cheekbones underlining flinty eyes. His lips twisted in a permanent smirk, he folded his hands and examined the travellers.

Loge opened his arms in a welcoming gesture that meant anything but friendship. Axe in hand, he tilted the head to catch the light. 'I can give you shiny, but I have no coins.'

The man sighed and shook his head, overwrought disappointment hunching his shoulders. 'No one comes to Kotja without a little coin. How do you pay for a room or something warm for your woman's belly? You give us the coin and we make sure she has both, yes?'

'Not his fucking woman, arsehole.' Marrit's snarl drew a look of amusement from the man and sniggers from his faceless friends.

'No? Then let me show you hospitality, Isord style.' He grabbed at his crotch and grinned, brilliant teeth, sharp like a wild dog's fangs, shining through the dark stubble on his face.

Marrit snorted a laugh and pulled her knife. 'No worries, dickless. Come try it.'

The grin flattened into a scowl. 'Last chance to make a wise decision.'

Someone moved behind Loge and he whirled, axe swinging. Metal met flesh, the business end of his weapon carving meat from bone. Blood sprayed in a rooster tail, black ink in the darkness of the alley, the night shattering into splintered screams. Gore painted the houses, splattering across windows and slopping onto the cobbles. Heat flared in the place of cold, fire where there had been emptiness, a death song in the silence of his heart as he danced to its tune. Marrit followed her own steps, scything through the attackers. She kept them from his back and he from hers, their violence in tandem without need to speak.

Around them bodies fell like trees in a wood; collapsing, slipping in rivers of blood seeping down the slope of the street, a slick of cooling life congealing beneath their feet. The alley stood silent but for the rasp of heavy breath and the drip of crimson on stone.

One of the wounded grunted and Marrit ended their garbled plea for aid with calm efficiency, her blade wiped clean on the thigh of her trousers as she straightened beside Loge. His axe hung loose in his grip, his stance wide, the blood on his face cooling to a crust that pulled at his skin.

He watched the dead and dying. Ngaru they were not, but they'd made the mistake of getting in his way. It wasn't a safe place to stand. He would have told them that if they'd given him a chance. Now none of them stood at all and his path was clear once more.

CHAPTER THIRTY-SEVEN

Kotja, Isord

'Ma?' Lidan repeated in the silent gallery.

Oh shit, Iridia whispered, breaking cover from behind a heavy curtain and staring in open shock.

Merideth blinked slowly but Ran didn't let her speak again. He rushed her, the embrace tight with overworked muscles, crushing his mother against his chest until he thought she might snap. Her free hand clutched at the back of his jacket, bunching the soft weave in a shaking fist that refused to let go, her face turning to burrow into the side of his neck. A long inhalation ended in a sigh, and she sagged against him, if only for a minute.

Beneath her bedclothes, she was thin—bony even—the ridges of her ribs and the planes of her shoulder blades protruding through the fine nightdress. Ran released her and leaned back, studying her face. A brief frown creased his brow. Gaunt hollows drew her once bright eyes into deep wells of shadow, her cheeks sunken rather than plump, her skin sallow rather than the healthy sheen he remembered.

Merideth slapped him. 'Dark Rider damn you, boy! What are you doing here?'

'Ma!' Ran hissed, rubbing his cheek. She looked sick enough to crumble before his eyes, yet her strike stung like a whip.

'Did that watcher ever find you? Obviously not, or you'd be on the coast or in the Archipelago like a proper fugitive.' Merideth searched the hallway, her scowl settling for a moment on Lidan before returning to scrutinise her son. 'How did you get in here? Are those *servant's* clothes?'

Iridia giggled maniacally in a corner somewhere and Lidan snorted. 'The watcher found him all right, but he's not one for listening.'

Ran rounded on her and she shrugged, smirking behind the pile of bedsheets and pillowcases she'd scooped from the floor.

'Well? Did you listen to Brit?' Lidan pressed.

'No!' Ran snapped. 'There was a small matter of a pair of witches to resolve.'

A hand caught his wrist and yanked him around in a circle, dragging him down the hall. Candles lit the way, dancing with the darkness. Merideth limped along, his arm in her iron grasp, her face a picture of frustrated lines and fire-forged determination. 'I'm sure that seemed very pressing at the time. Doesn't change the fact that you ignored a direct instruction from me.'

'Wait, aren't you at least happy to see me?' His heart raced, throat tightening uncomfortably beneath the high collar of the servant's jacket. Reality shivered in place of waning shock and elation. His mother was in Kotja? The how and why he couldn't reconcile, especially given the state she was in.

Was something wrong with his grandfather? Was Harroe ill, his children attending his bedside to ensure a smooth transition of power? It had to be something serious to bring Merideth all the way from Usmein, especially in the summer. She'd never leave the city unattended while Duke Ronart was in the Disputed Territory.

His mother's presence in the palace should have at least warranted a mention from Villia or Heike Yordam, but neither woman had even indicated Merideth was in town. Surely such a thing would be the talk of the city? Ronart wasn't here, that much was certain. There was no way to keep a man as brash and self-centred as his father quiet for long enough to sneak him into anywhere. So what in the names of all the gods was the Orthian duchess doing here?

Merideth paused at a nondescript doorway. The lantern landed in Ran's trembling hands and she put her shoulder to the door, easing it open before ushering them both inside.

'Happy to see you? Happy to see you are alive, yes...' Her pause sent apprehension crawling across Ran's skin. The door shut behind them, trapping the heat from the crackling fire inside the spacious royal apartment. Ran watched his mother lean against the door, her lips pressed together in thought. 'But am I happy to see you *here*? That I cannot say. What's going on, Ran? Why are you here, of all places?'

This room wasn't the abode of a traveller or temporary resident. There were no trunks or bags, everything tucked away in its place. Dust had settled on some books on the mantle, a collection of papers and quills forming a nest on the desk in the far corner. A side table by the sofa presented a small, framed portrait he thought he recognised from his childhood—three little figures with stern faces lined up in front of a taller, regal beauty with deep blue eyes. What remained of that beauty stood before him, her spirit undiminished by whatever ravaged her body.

'Why are *you* here, Mother?'

'She asked first,' Lidan put in, dumping the armload of linens on a chair and straightening her clothes. She ignored his scowl, scanning the room instead. Probably looking for something to stab.

Merideth pointed a carefully manicured finger at the southerner. 'I don't know her, but I like her.'

The heels of Lidan's boots snapped together and her head dropped in a bow. 'I am Lidan of the Tolak Clan and the lands of the Jagga River, south of the Malapa. Eldest daughter of Daari Erlon. I travelled here with your son to seek aid from the king.'

Merideth's brows rose in suggestion and Ran groaned. 'No, Ma. We're friends.'

'She's a girl and she's a friend. Of course.'

'It's not like that!' he hissed again.

Her hands came up, warding off his offence. 'You could do exceptionally worse.'

'Oh, for fuck's—can we get back to the matter at hand? Has something happened to Harroe? We back-channelled through the parliament and got nowhere with our request for an audience.'

Merideth made her way to a sofa and eased down. He could have sworn he heard her joints creak, and the wave of sickening worry returned. 'Ah, you got caught in the barbs of Villia's vicious political machine.'

With an exasperated shrug, Ran nodded. 'She refused our requests and made no mention of you.'

'That's because she doesn't have clearance to know I'm here. And she's a nasty piece of work.' Merideth winked at her son. 'So, you broke into the palace in the hope of speaking to the king? What could be so important that you'd to go to *all* this trouble?'

'We...' He sighed, relented, and flopped down opposite his mother. Her eyes darkened to black in the shadows of the dimly lit room, night cocooning the city outside. Somewhere out there, Eian and Zarad prepared to set off a distraction. If it worked the palace guards would rush to investigate, opening an opportunity to speak with the king. Time was a luxury they didn't have. 'I wish I could tell you everything, and one day I hope I can, but for now this will have to be enough. We need to cross the northern border.'

Merideth's stare didn't waver as one of her thin brows arched. 'Have you ever just walked away from danger, Ran? Just once?'

Iridia slipped from the shadows behind the duchess. *If only she knew... Best she doesn't.*

'You know me, Ma,' he said with a crooked smile.

'What under all the stars could you possibly need north of the border?' Merideth asked, undeterred by the boyish charm that had worked on her so well before.

'A criminal,' Lidan said from the window. She watched the twinkle and shine of the city through the glass, her breath fogging the pane. 'Someone who doesn't care for borders on maps, who'll tear this world apart to get what they want. Someone only Ran and I can stop.'

'And they're in the Empire?'

'We think they're in Wodurin,' Ran said. 'We had hoped the king could help us cross the border and provide us with any recent knowledge about the capital. We need to know what's going on up there.'

Merideth shook her head. 'He can't help you, Ran. And you know why.'

His heart sank. It was one thing to hear it from Villia, but it was quite another to hear it from his own mother. Hope leaked away, time slipping with it. Elbows on his knees, he rubbed the bridge of his nose and sighed into the cup of his hands. Iridia's silence spoke volumes, her presence fading with her optimism while Lidan remained still as stone by the window.

'But I know someone who might,' Merideth offered.

Ran stared at her. 'What?'

'I can't help you cross the border and, as much as he might like to, neither can my father. But I know someone who has been in Wodurin. They recently returned and might know something at least useful.' The duchess shrugged. 'Whether he can or will help is another matter.'

'Who?' Ran demanded, more forcefully than he'd intended. Some small spark of hope still burned, illuminating the tiny chance that they might just make it to their destination.

'An Arinnian king's agent,' she replied.

Brows drawn together, Ran leaned forward, his voice dropping low. 'What are you doing making friends with Arinnian agents, Ma?'

A wan little smile cracked Merideth's lips and she steepled her fingers, leaning back into her seat with the languid grace of a cat. 'Planning a coup.'

Loge and Marrit walked the horses through the darkened streets, past night markets and glowing storefronts. Patrons drank and dined inside, safe from the nip of the wind or the threat of lurking trouble in the shadows. No one paid them any mind, steering clear of anywhere well-lit to disguise the state of their clothes. Covered in blood as they were, Loge and Marrit must have looked a sight.

'For a healer, you seem comfortable with killing,' Loge muttered.

'What can I say? I'm good with a knife.'

No shit. Glancing up, he let his thoughts wander with the thin clouds scudding across the face of the brilliant full moon. He'd seen two such moons since his return and each time the weight of watching fell upon him as he laboured to find Lidan beneath its gaze. It wasn't just the moon that watched. It was the trees and the rocks, the water in the gutters and the fountains, in the creeks and streams. The birds too; craws and eagles, long-legged scribe birds and yellow crested screamers banking across the sky in the apron of an approaching storm. The lizards and the little dragons watched him too, their reptilian eyes following his steps, passing word from one to another then back to the ancestors, reporting his progress to Dennawal and anyone else who would listen. Would they stop when he found her? Would he stop?

His sole purpose was to return the sword on his back and then… What? Die again?

Loge shook the moment of self-awareness away and focused on Marrit and the city streets. 'I only meant that you finished off that survivor back there, rather than healing him. Seemed odd.'

She glanced over and cocked a brow. 'Says the man who returned from the dead.'

'Point taken,' he muttered. Marrit might have been joking. He still couldn't quite tell, his sense for such things still in a tangle.

'Look, I didn't *like* it. I've had to end more misery with death than I've been able to with healing hands. No one could have saved that thug from his injuries, so I gave him what he needed.' The brilliance of her sincerity bloomed in Loge's mutant eye, stinging beauty, the deep blue of sorrow marbling the gleam of silver throbbing in Marrit's chest as she spoke. Eyes on the cobbled streets, hooves clopping calmly beside them, truth fell from her like rain.

'I was probably thirteen the first time I had to do it on my own. Only a little older than Lidan was when our sister died. You learn very quickly what it is to give mercy with the edge of knife, what it means when someone is down and not getting up again. You learn how to make it quick and how to make it painless. You harden against it. You build a little safe place inside no one can reach, and you keep yourself there, where they can't see you for what you are.'

Their eyes met and for the first time Loge saw Marrit—not as a sister, not as a healer, not as the forgotten daughter of a spiteful daari and dana— as herself.

'When Lidan taught me how to fight, she did it in secret. She knew one day I'd be taken from my home to a place where the only person I could rely on was myself, and that the mercy I gave with the knife might be the only thing that would save me. I kept my true self hidden. None of them knew me. All they saw was a quiet, clever girl who kept her head down and did her job. I am those things, but I was always more.' She sucked at her teeth, glancing at the sky, the brilliance of her light fading from his eye. 'I don't see death like other people do. I don't see it as an end. I see freedom and mercy and a release from pain. I see justice and honour and the glory of a worthy end. Dignity in death. That's what I see.'

'You are mercy,' Loge murmured.

'I'm what?'

Her question skittered off the edge of his thoughts, the sounds of the city bleeding into his mind as they trudged on. Dennawal had made him into something beyond a man—pain and anger channelled into purpose, the brute force of an axe made flesh for reasons he didn't understand. He was fury incarnate; an unrelenting drive held back only by the frailty of the body he found himself in. But he'd fallen into the company of mercy—precise, careful, considered, as inevitable as death itself. Marrit was the counterweight to his aggression, the balance on the other end of the scale. She dealt death with purpose. Loge just wanted to watch the world burn until only he and Lidan stood in the ash.

And then what?

That question echoed against the walls of buildings and skipped across the inky darkness of his gaping soul. At the end of this thing he'd come to do, then what?

'Anyway...' Marrit said slowly, looking at him dubiously as they came around another switchback street and angled toward yet another gate house. 'I don't kill because I like it, I kill because it has to be done and I know I can do it well. Any healer too proud to give a good death is a waste of space.'

A guard stomped into their path and Striker snorted hard. Marrit lurched to a halt, her horse thumping into Striker's flank. Loge stumbled sideways, their forward motion cut by a figure blocking the gateway ahead. 'Passes?'

'Excuse me?' Marrit recoiled with a scowl. None of the other guards had asked this. No one had challenged them, except to ask where they were heading.

'Passes? It's well after ten. You need passes to get into the third terrace after ten.' The man had a long, narrow face that reminded Loge of the bouncers in the grasslands at home. Twitchy, as though ready to dart off at any moment, his lips pinched beneath his sharp nose as if someone had sewn them together. He studied them, taking in their filthy appearance as they lingered at the edge of the lamplight.

'No one said anything about passes,' Marrit countered. Fatigue sharpened the edge of her voice, the sound of the last fuck she had to give echoing into the night.

'Well no one cares who's in the other terraces after ten, but up *here*, they do. Passes or you stay down in the lower city with the rest of the riff-raff.'

Loge handed his reins to Marrit and melted back into the shadows. The guard might think he searched his bags for their papers, or that Loge rifled through their belongings for a bribe, a fat purse of coins or a family heirloom carried across unmeasured distance to finance their endeavours.

What he didn't expect was the head of Loge's axe rammed up under his chin, a hair's breadth between the killing edge and the soft skin of his throat.

Loge slammed the guard back against the wall of the gatehouse, the lamp by the door swinging in protest as they hit. Light strobed under the gate, arcing and flaring, dimming and fading as the lamp careened back and forth on its hook.

'See this?' Loge leered over his axe at the guard. His finger stabbed at his own face, at the caked blood and clumps of gore. 'This is what's left of the last dickhead who stood in our way. We've been on the road for the best part of a moon. We've barely slept, hardly eaten, never bathed and I can tell you with all sincerity, neither of us has had a fuck in a *very* long time. A friend of ours is waiting, just through there. They need something we have. Would you like to be the next idiot I paint my face with? Or would you like to let us pass?'

Something wet splattered on the cobbles at his feet and Loge sneered, a sharp, acidic stink burning his nose.

'Thought so.'

This fool was on his own, outnumbered and outclassed. The rules keeping this city together were no more than piss in the wind when tested, as evidenced by the guard's evacuation on the street.

'How far to the Yordam house?' Marrit asked casually from over Loge's shoulder.

'Ju—just follow the main road. Fourth compound back from the next gate.'

'Much obliged,' came her reply, the razor's edge softened by the slightest hint of amusement. She might not enjoy killing, but she wasn't above a bit of humiliation.

'A *what*?' Ran blinked rapidly as his mother's smile broadened.

'A coup.' Merideth nodded as if that was explanation enough and picked up a little covered dish from her side table. A pinch of white powder emerged on the end of her finger and she rubbed it into the flesh of her gums. The only thing anyone took like that was poppy-ash, and even then they did it sparingly. He'd seen Sasha use it in the infirmary, always wary of giving too much, always keeping her small stock under heavy lock and key. The amount

Merideth had just taken would have knocked a grown man on his arse.

Ran watched in horror, breath caught in his chest.

Ranoth... Iridia's worry reflected his own in painful magnification. *That's... She must be in quite some pain...*

I... What's going on? His mind whirled, his heart hammered. Lidan retreated from the window to stand beside him, her eyes on the wall behind the duchess, right where Iridia had emerged. She didn't ask what the ghost had said. Instead, she placed a gentle hand on his shoulder and squeezed. She'd seen the powder. Did they have anything like that in the South Lands? Anything that could take away pain in the same tiny increments it ate at the very spark of life?

Look at her, Iridia insisted. *Really look at her.*

He was and he wasn't. He wasn't because he couldn't. His vision blurred and he swallowed a choking lump of terror from his throat. 'Against who, Ma? Harroe?'

'Oh no.' She scoffed, the corners of her eyes crinkling. 'Against your father.'

His heart almost stopped completely. 'You're plotting to depose Ronart?'

Her expression carried more pity than anything else, her smile falling as a gleam of weary calm bloomed in her eyes, the powder taking hold. 'Your father is mad, Ran. Wild and insane and lashing out at enemies that don't exist. Someone has to right the ship before he smashes what's left of our people to splinters.' For a moment she searched for words, a sigh caressing the silence alongside the pop and hiss of the fire and the moan of the wind beyond the window. 'It began not long after you escaped, perhaps to compensate for never finding you. I managed to get Eboni out before anyone noticed her magic, but I couldn't help the thousands more caught in his web of fear. It was an easy decision in the end. Nerola is the only one of you I can put in his place until a proper government can be elected. I have to do that before he arranges a marriage for the poor girl.'

Ran's world spun, tilting on its axis. He scrambled to make sense of the words coming from his mother's mouth. 'Eboni?'

'One day it might be safe for the two of you to come home, but while your father is chopping heads off children in village squares and burning families in their homes, I can't take that chance.' Merideth leaned forward. The gaunt features faded, the force of her will pressing against him. 'I must make things right before it's too late, Ran.'

He ignored her implication, shoving straight past the truth she'd offered. 'What has any of this got to do with an Arinnian agent?'

'He's helping to establish a network of informants in Usmein and across the Free Nations. There are a few Isordian agents too, but we can't trust anyone from within Orthia.' She waved her hand and sat back, her gaze caught by the fire. 'Ronart thinks we're here to plan your sister's marriage while he does his best to waste another generation of young Orthians on a scorched field.'

'Where... Where does he think Eboni is?'

'Dead in an avalanche while on a visit to Marlow. A tragic hiking accident.'

'And where *is* she?' Had she arrived at the Keep just after he'd left? Had he missed his sister by days?

Merideth's expression darkened, lips pressed into a hard line, the muscles of her jaw tightening. 'While that man draws breath, I will take that information to my grave.' Somewhere in the distance a boom echoed in the night, the concussion rattling the windows and shaking the floor, glasses on a nearby service tray clinking together before falling silent. His mother glanced up, not at all surprised. 'That sounds like your cue.'

Pushing to her feet, wavering as she found them, the duchess turned and glided to the door. Ran rushed after her. His foot snagged a table and he stumbled, arms wheeling as he came to a stop, catching himself in his mother's grasp.

For a moment he froze. Had he hurt her?

Their eyes met and she smiled weakly. 'I won't always be here to catch you, but while I still can, I will.' She reached to lift a lock of untamed curls from his face. 'I don't know what you're doing in the Empire but do it quickly and come home. Your sisters need you, even if it's from afar.'

'Ma, I—'

'No, baby. Not now. There isn't time.' Another boom shook the walls. Beyond the doors the sound of running boots raced past, disappearing into the distance. 'Remember your lessons. Follow your heart. Listen to your head. They have kept you well and brought you this far.'

'The agent?' was all he could manage.

Lidan had the door open before he knew what was happening, her hand on his elbow, pulling against the feather light weight of his mother. How could someone so slight anchor him so firmly? How did she have such gravity when hardly anything of her remained to hold?

'He'll find you. Soon. Get going, before they come to check on me.'

Merideth let him go.

The place her hands had been, bone thin and cold, burned like a brand. The last thing he saw was her smile. Lidan dragged him away, his vision blurred by tears. His mother, as immutable and eternal as the mountains, slipped away as if she were naught but sand.

CHAPTER THIRTY-EIGHT

Kotja, Isord

The palace blurred as they ran. Household staff and other folk raced along beside them, panicked by the thunderous explosions nearby. Lidan dragged Ran, their arms linked tightly, his gait a stumbling, inconsistent stagger that almost toppled them in the rush. He didn't speak; he would when he was ready. She couldn't be sure what words would come, but she doubted they'd be anything but grief-soaked anger and despair.

Unable to recognise one hallway or corridor from another, Lidan found a set of stairs and started down, throwing herself to the side as a troop of guards clattered past in their moulded metal armour. It seemed an odd choice of material. It couldn't be easy to run in, but who was she to judge? The guards shouted orders in a mixed-up collection of languages; something about an attack, something else about searching for intruders, another about locking down levels of the palace. Heart pounding, she steered Ran back into the flow of people, holding him closely so they weren't pulled apart by the tide.

'They seem sure it's attackers,' she whispered.

'Rebels or Woaden operatives,' Ran muttered, glancing lazily backward. 'That's what they'll think.'

She hoped Eian and Zarad were already out or had at least escaped notice. 'Where do we go?' Once they reached the floor below, she had no idea what to do next. Were they close to the kitchens and the cellars? Could they get there without being noticed or questioned?

'I don't...' Ran scanned the hall and they stepped quickly away from the foot of the stairs. Lidan pulled him to the right with the crowd. Palace staff streamed past in uniforms much like theirs, anxious whispered questions shot between them.

Ahead, the flow slowed and split at the junction of two corridors. People paused for a moment before racing away, as if given purpose or direction. Somewhere in the middle of it all, a man stood rigid, his hair a riot of silver and black, cut into severe, spiky tufts. A pair of gleaming lenses perched on his nose, thin lengths of metal hooking behind his ears to hold them in place. He looked through them to read a book clutched tightly in his hands, then glared hawkishly over the lenses and screeched orders.

'Fuck,' Ran breathed.

'What?'

He almost slipped from her grip as he tugged her back in the direction they'd come. 'We can't go that way.'

'We can't go back!' Lidan hissed. Someone shoved her in the shoulder, and she staggered.

'You two!' A shrill voice cut across the cacophony of desperation and confusion and the muscles of Ran's jaw jumped. 'Report!'

Lidan turned slowly, deliberately glancing down the hallway behind the man, then off to the left and right. People swarmed through the intersection like a nest of pissed-off ants. Did he mean them?

'Yes, you! Girl! Department and name?' The man's hawkish eyes pinned her over the rim of his glass lenses, his greying brows lifting with such expectation that she found herself unable to ignore his demands.

Lidan stepped closer and cleared her throat, leaning forward and indicating at her ear as if she hadn't heard him. 'Sorry,' she replied in common, hoping her accent wouldn't send up any flags. 'I didn't quite catch that.'

Sharp brown eyes narrowed and the man grew still, despite the chaos in the corridor. Beside him, other officials with books and quills went on asking the same question. Upon receiving an answer, they issued a direction and the person darted off to wherever they were meant to be. 'Department and name, for the roll,' the man repeated.

'I, ah,' Lidan began. She glanced at her uniform for the slightest second and Ran's hand tightened above her elbow. Her mind scrambled. She weaponised a disarming grin. 'Laundry.'

'What are you wearing?' The man demanded. Lidan baulked, her hands instinctively pulling her jacket closed over her stolen clothes. 'Those aren't current issue to laundry staff.'

Quick as a snake strike he grabbed at her lapel, pulling it away to expose the crest over her heart.

'That's not a—'

Her fist cracked his nose. Blood spurted in a bright fountain, the book toppling from his hands. Lidan followed the punch with a kick to the knee, dropping the official like a sack of potatoes. He went down screaming, obscenities echoing through the hallway.

People froze but Ran and Lidan didn't wait for him to hit the floor. Spinning into the stunned crowd, they bolted. The threat of discovery seemed enough to break Ran from his grief-stricken trance, his broad shoulders barging a path through the throng. Within a few dozen feet they melted into the stream of people moving away from the man with the bloody nose.

Bellowed orders rose in their wake and the crowd split, thinning to let clanking guards catch up. The shift gave Lidan just enough space to break away from the crush and launch into an all-out sprint after Ran. No point trying to keep track of the doors they passed, no point counting the junctions of hallways and galleries. Ran darted up another set of stairs, taking them two at a time and she bolted after him, careening into a stunned guard on the landing. Dropping her shoulder into his belly, she shunted him from her path.

He slammed into the handrail and flailed, arms whirling as his balance tipped. There was nothing to do but watch him fall, the horror in his eyes reflected in her gasp as she reached out a desperate hand. Instead of catching the falling man, Ran snatched her wrist and pulled her up the stairs, hurrying away from the crunch of bodily impact and the roars of enraged guards.

The stairs ended at a largely abandoned hallway, but they didn't stop moving.

They *had* to survive this.

They had to get out.

Help wasn't coming. Running hard, Lidan kept pace. A swift sidestep avoided a stunned palace resident who unexpectedly stepped into their path from a concealed doorway.

'Ran!' Lidan called, puffed and throwing a glance backward, regretting it as soon as she did. A troop of warriors rushed the hallway behind them. 'Fuck!'

Without a word, Ran darted to the left and a flare of light blasted the dim corridor. A door exploded in a shower of splinters and embers, the solid barrier of timber reduced to nothing by the force of his magic. A biting wind gusted through the void and Ran turned to heave Lidan through the gap.

Cold cut through the thin weave of her clothes, skin flushed with heat now burning as she stumbled onto a parapet and looked down. Gut-wrenching terror reefed her back from the edge. The height of the palace wall fell away beneath her feet, all fifty feet of it dropping into the dark streets below.

Staggering to a stop, she whirled to check on Ran. Were they *meant* to be here? Did he realise they'd gone in the absolute opposite fucking direction to the cellar?

He stood several feet away, weaving a barrier from magic, blocking the door and shunting guards back into the hallway rather than blasting them to pieces. Noble as it was to preserve their lives, he was wasting time.

'Ran! Where are we?' she screamed over the sizzling screech of his magic, brilliant blue cords of throbbing power coursing up the side of the building like the web of a great luminescent spider.

'The wall!' he shouted, turning as he finished the ward.

Grinding her teeth in frustration, Lidan swallowed her mouthful of unhelpful retorts. 'No shit! How do we get down?'

If he says jump, I'll kill him. Right here and now. I'll gut him like a fish.

Her heart in her mouth, they turned to the mess that was the remains of the palace gate. The timbers were fully ablaze, furious flames grasping hungrily at the night. The heat of it reached them even at this distance, drying her skin and stinging her eyes. The stink of oil and wood choked the air, the sharp wind doing nothing to dispel the thick, greasy smoke. Embers caught the wind, sailing off into the city and onto roofs but didn't ignite as they fell. An ember attack could take a whole village in the south, especially in a dry summer. Not much chance of that here. She was pretty sure she'd seen moss growing on at least half the houses.

'I told them *not* to do that,' Ran growled.

'It's still a diversion,' Lidan reminded him. 'You weren't exactly specific!'

Ranoth rounded on her. 'If we get caught, we're dead.'

She returned his scowl as the magic web bulged, guards railing against it with swords and axes. 'That was fairly obvious from the beginning. How are we getting out of here?'

A door slammed and Lidan turned to confront the sound. A darkened tower stood at some distance along the parapet, silhouetted by the brilliance of the flames. Something detached from it, a shadow with its weapon drawn, armour shining. With a shout it broke into a run, more rushing after them, a host of guards come to capture the would-be invaders who dared to wear the wrong uniform.

Ran caught Lidan by the shoulders and spun her to face him. 'Trust me.'

'What?'

He wasn't asking. He was telling.

This wasn't a choice; it was a command.

He turned her to the city, the wind so cold her ears ached, wayward tendrils of her hair whipped from their braids. With a shove she was at the edge of the rampart and lifted awkwardly onto the lip of the wall. A foot or two thick under her boots, it seemed hardly any space at all as she stood teetering on the edge of a gaping abyss.

'Go!' Ran shouted into the wind. 'Jump!'

Heart battering against her ribs, Lidan tried to turn, tried to refuse, tried to throw herself back. Every instinct shrieked at her to run, to freeze, to collapse against the hands holding her at the edge. Her bone deep fear of heights reared hard and Lidan screamed.

Ran appeared at her side, leaping onto the rampart as the guards closed the gap at a weighted sprint. The magical barrier cracked like an egg as the weapons of the soldiers tore at it with fist and blade. 'Jump or die! Trust me!'

The desperation in his eyes almost stopped her heart, her breath catching in her throat.

He took his chance, spun her and pushed.

The pull of gravity took hold. Her boots slipped from the edge, legs pumping frantically as she ran through the free fall. Something else caught her too—a blue blur that solidified under her feet. It was just enough to spring from and Lidan stamped down.

Her mind spun with panic, limbs tingling with icy fire. Somehow, she managed to propel herself forward, launching off the weird blue forcefield toward the nearest roof. Slate tiles came up to meet her faster than she could react and she hit with a hollow crack, tumbling forward, skidding across the sharp edges. Clothing tore into ribbons, no protection from the scales of the roof, her skin parting beneath them with no resistance at all.

Sliding down the roof, arms useless to arrest her descent, Lidan pumped her legs again. Her boots caught the stone sheets, a handful sailing off the edge of the gutter to smash on the street below.

She'd be next if she didn't stop.

With a hard kick, she flipped from her side to her back and dug her heels in, the friction just enough to slow her before her boots hit the eave. The impact jolted through her bones. Her jaw snapped shut and her teeth crunched against her tongue, her pained cry muffled as she bit down.

A boom thundered above, and she glanced up.

A blue-black fireball exploded at the top of the wall, blocks of stone cracking and toppling into the courtyard on the other side. Ethereal fire lit the night, a brilliant flash lighting up the face of the palace. A concussion wave ripped out across the city, shattering windows and rattling shutters in a violent storm of sound and motion. Lidan shrank against the roof, watching the explosion mushroom into the sky over the crook of her arm.

Anyone on the rampart had either been incinerated or blasted down into the yard or the road. No one had survived that.

She glanced at the rooftop above her, expecting to see Ran. Her heart stopped.

Where was he? Surely he'd jumped?

From the blue flames and the smoke, a dark form launched, seeming to run in the air. It hurtled across the gap between the wall and the roof and slammed into the tiles above Lidan's head.

The figure's winded grunt sounded like Ran. Shoulders hunched, head flopping, he bounced across the unforgiving slate then slid swiftly down the incline. Unlike her, his legs didn't flail and his hands didn't grab for a purchase. He just fell unhindered toward the edge and certain, blunt death waiting on the road below. Lidan snatched her knife and jammed it between two tiles, ignorant of the damage to the blade. Steel screeched as it bit between the tiles, and she rolled, knife held in the talon-grip of one hand while the other reached desperate fingers for Ran's falling body.

Her hand caught at the front of his jacket and his arm flicked up as he rushed past. Limp fingers brushed her wrist and she clamped down, her nails biting through fabric and flesh. The cuff of the jacket in hand, his wrist caught in the desperate claw of her fingers, she watched him bounce heavily over the edge of the roof and keep going. It took less than a second for his motion to drag her with him, his weight yanking hard against the knife anchored between the tiles.

Time stretched as Lidan reached the extent of her reach and Ran jolted to a stop, swinging back against the building, spinning awkwardly in Lidan's grip. She grunted wordlessly as blinding hot pain ripped along both arms.

Old injuries in her shoulder and wrist—the former barely more than a moon old—screamed in furious protest as the dead weight of a grown man swung from them some twenty feet above the cold stones of the cobbled road. There was nothing she could do for it. They stayed as they were, Lidan on her belly at the edge of the eave, Ran swinging below with his head bowed, his clothes in tatters.

Now what?

She had to get him up, but how? Ran was out cold, useless and unable to come to his own rescue. He could have reached his free hand for the gutter and helped pull himself back to the roof. As it was, he was about as helpful as a headless chicken.

Voices echoed along the road, somewhere around the corner near the palace wall.

'They're coming.'

Lidan started and spat out a curse-laden cry. If she could have run, she would have bolted backward. Trapped and losing her grip on her knife about as rapidly as she was Ran's wrist, she dared a glance at the source of the voice.

Iridia crouched on the edge of the roof, no more than a foot away from Lidan's head. Blood trickled down Lidan's arm, cooling in the wind, lubricating her grasp around Ran's wrist, but that didn't seem as important as the ghost who'd just materialised in front of her.

'How?'

'He's not exactly using his power right now, is he?' Iridia looked at her like she was an imbecile.

'So, you're what? Stealing it to make yourself whole?' Lidan could barely breathe let alone talk. What was Iridia playing at? Did she *want* to watch them both die?

'You look like you could use some help.' Iridia shuffled closer and dropped onto her belly. Her face inches from Lidan's, the slightest waft of lavender and musk perfumed the air between them.

Stunned, unable to speak for the pain tearing through her shoulders, Lidan watched as the ghost solidified. Her skin shifted from translucent to opaque, her torn shift draping across the tiles. The black wound at the ghost's throat gaped as she inched closer and stretched out an impossibly pale arm, long delicate fingers reaching for Ran's collar, catching, pulling it taut against his arms and shoulders.

'Pull him up,' Iridia instructed. 'I'll get under his other arm.'

With the last of her strength Lidan heaved against the weight of Ran's swinging body. Somehow, the ghost of the girl Lidan's mother had murdered pulled with her, the power she'd syphoned off Ran strengthening her dead muscles and fortifying her hollowed bones. Together they dragged, inch by agonising inch until Iridia shifted her grip to loop an arm under Ran's shoulder. A final heave, punctuated by cries of effort, brought the man up and over the eave, the three of them flopping against the tiles.

Lidan sucked in desperate lungfuls of air, her arms afire, her hands torn to bloody ruins. Blood seeped from a hundred cuts, her mouth parchment dry as her heart raced. The adrenaline of the moment bled away almost as quickly as it had come, leaving her trembling. She turned to thank Iridia.

On the other side of Ran's unconscious body, the ghost was already fading. The strength she'd taken from Ran lasted no more than a few moments, her form evaporating into a wisp of cloud. Her hand disappeared last, cupped around Ran's jaw, her eyes closed as if she'd fallen asleep beside him.

Lidan managed to drag Ran to the ridgeline of the roof, huddling in the shadow of an enormous stone chimney rather than under the glare of the full moon. Voices called in the distance. It wouldn't be long before someone came this way, checking the roofs nearest the wall. Someone had to have seen them jump. Someone had to have seen where they'd fallen. Surely someone had heard her stomping all over the roof even if they hadn't noticed the unconscious man hanging from the gutter.

But no one came.

Apparently, there were greater problems to deal with, like the burning gate and the great rent blasted into the top of the wall.

By the time Ran groaned and opened his eyes, it was at least midnight, the moon riding high behind thin cloud. Lidan shivered violently in what remained of her paper-thin clothes. If any of them had been made to keep someone warm, she would eat her boots.

'Finally,' she croaked through chattering teeth. 'I was beginning to think I'd have to leave you here.'

'What happened?' Ran looked around through slitted eyes.

'You pushed me off the wall and threw yourself down after me. You almost ended up as a wet stain on the road, but we caught you.' With a weary smile she crawled to her hands and knees. Her muscles and joints creaked and moaned, protesting in the icy wind. 'Don't worry. I'll get you back for *that* little stunt.'

'We?' A frown scrunched up his face as if he were looking into a bright light and Lidan reached to help him stand.

'Iridia and I. She's quite handy in a pinch.'

He paused a moment, eyes clearing, his expression flat. 'Iridia?'

Lidan nodded then waved for him to follow, clambering down to a lower storey then onto a wall and to the ground. Time didn't give her the opportunity to explain. He'd have to carry his questions until they were safely behind the walls of the Yordam house.

The streets angling away from the palace were clear, folk either staying indoors or congregating at the gate to watch it burn. Those who chose the latter found themselves subject to the ire of Kotja's authorities, a useful distraction that drew attention away from Lidan and Ran. Staggering together along laneways and roads, they were no more interesting than a couple of drunks trying to find their way home after a little too much fun.

At the two gatehouses between the palace and the house, they slipped through as other citizens argued with the guards, demanding to know what had happened in the palace precinct and refusing to return to their homes. This city, so well defended by its walls and gates, knew little of how to cope when under attack. Its people were in a flat spin, openly ignoring authorities who shouted to be heard in the squares and plazas. If their incursion into the palace had been a legitimate assault, Lidan wagered they could have done significant and irreparable damage. It had only been their encounter with Ran's mother that had stopped them finding the king.

'Do you think he'll come,' Lidan asked, shuffling through the final gate before turning onto the street of the Yordam compound.

'Who? The agent?' More alert now, limping but speaking clearly, Ran had directed her through the maze of streets to safety. He shrugged painfully. 'We can only hope. We can't wait forever. If Villia has even an inkling this was our doing, she'll be on us like a dog on a bone.'

Lidan glanced down as they came into the light of the lamps outside the house. 'We don't exactly look innocent, do we?' They'd have to burn their clothes. She made to turn up the laneway to the staff entrance, wondering if they'd get through unnoticed, when her attention caught on something in the street.

The figure banged a fist against the Yordam's front door, ignoring the knocker and the bell hanging from a thick rope under a lamp. They hammered again and again, leaning back and scowling up at the darkness. 'Open *up!*'

There was a twang to the accent, a clipped sharpness to the vowels that turned the words into knives. It was a sound she hadn't heard in over a month and had reconciled to never hear again.

Lidan stopped at the mouth of the alley and stared. The figure kicked the door and staggered back, a picture of fury as their attempts to elicit a response went unanswered.

'Fucks...' they muttered, sighing heavily. 'We should—'

A stone kicked away from the toe of Lidan's boot as she stepped forward. The figure turned. Light caught their face and Ran straightened beside her.

He saw it too. It wasn't her eyes playing tricks.

He saw. He wouldn't react like that if he didn't.

The figure crouched, reaching for a weapon, ready for a fight. Shivering, too cold to do more than limp, Lidan moved into the light around the doorway. The weapon remained hidden, a moment's hesitation staying that hand. Recognition shone in the figure's eyes and a smile spread across their face.

'Liddy? Is that you?'

'What are you—' The words caught in Lidan's throat. Her vision blurred, heat prickling her eyes. She was wrong, surely? She'd bashed her skull so hard she was seeing things. That voice… She knew that voice. 'Marri?'

Her sister rushed her with open arms. Ran relinquished Lidan to the embrace of a sister she had thought lost forever. She'd left behind her entire world, resolved to put it in her past and think only of the path ahead. Yet here Marrit stood, in the shadows of an Isordian trader's household compound. Shivers wracked the bodies of both young women until a sob broke from Lidan's tightening throat and she buried her face in the shoulder of Marrit's much warmer, much more sensible coat.

'What are you doing here, you insane girl?' Lidan demanded. With great reluctance, she broke away just long enough to take in the younger woman's face. 'How did you even find me?'

'I stole a map.' Marrit gave her a crooked smile. Tears glimmered in the wells of her shining green eyes, framed by the unblemished brown of her skin and the irrepressible curls of her dark hair.

'But… Why, Marri? It must have taken you weeks.' Fear dug hard, bony claws into Lidan's heart. Any tighter it would stop beating altogether. Were her family under attack? Was Marrit the sole survivor of some battle with Yorrell? Had their clan been swept from the South Lands by the malice of such a man? 'Has something happened? Is everything all right at home?'

'Yes and no…' The answer hung in the frigid air and Marrit grew still.

Behind her, something moved in the shadows.

Instinct fired and Lidan moved without thinking, shoving Marrit aside and drawing her knives; blades singing, steel hungry for blood. Whatever it was shifted along the edge of the light, hesitant to step within range of her blades.

'Show yourself!' Lidan snarled, anger boiling over. 'I am sick to the back teeth of all this skulking around and running from shadows. Fight me or fuck off.'

'Liddy, wait!' Marrit cried and someone stepped into the light.

This time, Lidan's heart did stop.

Time stopped.

The world tilted and the stars wheeled. Her blood turned to ice, every fibre paralysed by disbelief.

Loge's tawny hazel eye watched her from beneath a lock of dark hair. He bowed his head. 'Hello, Lidan.'

CHAPTER THIRTY-NINE

Kotja, Isord

Ran's curses broke through the thud of Lidan's pulse. Marrit's reply spooled out into muffled babble, her explanation a nonsensical riot of inexplicable impossibilities.

Loge took a single step forward and Lidan's knife came up, the savage point aimed somewhere at his throat. The gleaming length of metal shivered with uncertainty, the intensity of his gaze faltering as he shoved a thick lock of hair from his eyes. Caked in blood spray from head to toe, he might have stepped from a slaughter yard as easily as he'd stepped from the shadows. Dark rivulets of dried crimson lined his face, the only thing animating his blank expression, a single hazel eye watching her down the curve of the knife. The other eye watched too, a black orb, smooth as a river stone, reflecting the orange of the house lamps.

A jolt of shock twisted her stomach.

The Loge she'd seen in the seconds before the rock fall was not the Loge standing before her now.

Something irrevocable had shifted in him, something crucial left behind under the weight of all that sharp stone. That black void was the eye of the dead—the stuff of tale-keeper's stories and fireside warnings. It didn't belong amongst the living. Lidan knew enough of her people's fables to understand that.

Still, she recognised him. This was no imposter. The curls of that dark, unruly hair. The broad planes of those muscled shoulders, hunched under layers. The sharp line of his stubbled jaw. She'd know him any-where, even if her eyes were plucked out and touch was the last sense she had to her name.

'You're dead,' Lidan choked out. Half-buried grief twitched beneath the skin of her face, tugging painfully at a mask of bruises. Behind her shoulder, Marrit fought to be heard over Ran's shouted denials and demands for answers, pushing him away, his voice receding, leaving Lidan alone in the cold.

'I was,' Loge agreed. His nod was a solemn thing, heavy, considered. The thought seemed to turn in him, a moment taken to wonder at the paradox before he let it fall into the wind. 'I'm not now.'

'I saw you *die!*' Her grip on the knife tightened until the hilt leather squeaked, stabbing it forward to emphasise each disbelieving word. The truth echoed up the street, tearing the soft, thin skin over scars that hadn't healed. Trembling in the marrow of her bones, horror and denial and the unrelenting need to touch him slammed together in a great crashing wave, threatening to drown her, choke her, squeeze the very blood from her veins. Furious tears fell unhindered and she coughed out a sob.

How dare he...?

How dare he leave?

How dare he come back like nothing had happened? How dare he make her cry... again? How dare he remind her of how much that hurt, right down deep where no salve or bandage could ever reach? How dare he look at her with those eyes?

Lidan's vision blurred, and her face flushed hot. 'I *saw* it. I watched you fall. I had to leave you there because you're *dead!*'

'I know,' Loge replied in that coarse, throaty voice of his. Her skin tingled and she shuddered. 'I had to come back. There were things to do.' He took another step, a hand reaching, eyes pleading.

'Don't you fucking touch her!' Ran's warning cracked against the houses and Marrit hushed him, bitter words shared in hissed whispers as she begged silence and time.

'Just let him explain. Just let him do this. There's more at stake here than just—'

'What?' Lidan's question startled Loge. His brow creased, the one familiar eye darting in confusion. 'Why did you come back? Who sent you?'

This isn't real. None of this is real. It can't be. No...

He was a trick, somehow sent to thwart her resolve. Was he the tool of the Morritae? Was he the puppet of Urda, the one allied with her mother?

347

Lidan hurried to erect a wall between them, a rushed structure of thin sticks and wet mud to protect her already shattered heart, his mere presence dismantling it as quickly as she could throw it together. She lifted her chin in defiance of the hope swelling in her heart, ignoring the rush of yearning.

He's not real.

'Dennawal sent me. I had to bring you the hope you left behind.' He offered her the answer as if it were the most common thing in the world, as normal and as unexceptional as the sun rising in the morning and setting before the fall of night.

Silence swept the street. Nothing but the beat of her heart remained. Nothing but the weight of the knife and the certain knowledge that something deep within called for her to believe.

His reaching hand moved again, grasping at something in the gloom behind his shoulder. A long steel blade hissed from the confines of a scabbard. Polished metal caught the light, his calloused hands cradling the battered edges and the blood-soaked leather at the handle, the swirl of the horse-head motif glinting at the pommel.

My blade... the sword of a witness of the blood... a blade of the south...

She knew that weapon, knew the softness of the leather and the balance of the steel. She'd lost it in the bush, torn from Aelish's hands before their headlong escape into the trees. Macha's voice echoed and Lidan's fingers twitched, eager to touch but wary. Accepting the sword meant accepting the truth, didn't it? Loge had brought it back. He'd crossed half the world and the realms of death to bring it back.

Something sparked in a place so deep within Lidan's soul she'd forgotten it was even there. A gasp escaped as a guttering flame flared painfully to life, illuminating buried things, forgotten things. Things that got her out of bed each day after Abbi died, when the hordes of ngaru seemed unending. Things she held close when Yorrell's raiders cut into her clan lands, when her father's refusal to acknowledge her place in their family and her mother's never-ending need for supremacy pressed down, suffocating all that their daughter was and might have been. Things she clung to when all seemed lost and uncertain.

Despite the odds, she'd dragged herself through, across clawing stones and the biting thorns, because beyond stood a future worth having—a place where the darkness receded and hope burned bright. She'd carried on. Tenacious. Surviving because *something* waited past the edge of her fear. The reason to outlast the corruption eating at her world and remain standing at the end.

It had all died with Loge. Falling from her grasp as she left him alone under the stones and the dirt, etching his memory in her flesh as she mourned his loss.

From that moment the light within tarnished, her determination waned, cracking beneath the weight of an inevitable destiny. Lidan *knew* she had to prevail. Known it the moment her mother vanished from Tingalla. What no longer mattered was whether she lived to see the other side of that victory.

A surge of goosebumps rushed down her arms.

In the cycle of the moon since Loge's death, in the time it took to understand who her mother was and what had to be done, Lidan had ceased to care if the world continued to turn once Sellan was vanquished. Her gaze hadn't dared to linger on the emptiness yawning beyond the resolution of that aim. That was a place Lidan didn't want to go, a place where peace pressed in with all-consuming silence. Where a lifetime alone was a sentence worse than death.

She winced as Loge lifted the sword. Acknowledgement passed between them—there was more to be done. Her fight wasn't over. The threat had simply followed her mother north, awaiting with untold nightmares in that wind-scoured desolation.

Lidan wasn't done.

Her reason to triumph rekindled.

'You're real?' Hope dared to build, banking hot in the hearth of her heart.

The corner of Loge's mouth lifted in the tiniest hint of a smile. 'I think so...'

Her hand snatched the sword and tossed it away, meaningless steel clattering against cobbles and screeching into the darkness. Loge jerked back and Lidan darted forward, engulfing him in an embrace that she swore would never surrender.

'You were dead,' Lidan murmured into his neck. Hands trembled, clutching tight at the depths of his coat, ignorant of bruises and cuts, seeping wounds and the aching cold.

'I know,' Loge replied.

Warmth bloomed in her chest for the first time in a month. 'If you ever do that again, I'll kill you myself.'

Aelish and Brit stared in bleary eyed confusion as Ran and Lidan led a blood-soaked Marrit and Loge into the house. By all accounts, the profusely apologetic staff had ignored the banging on the door, thinking it a drunken prank. Instead of answering, they'd sent for the gatehouse guards. The guards never arrived though, occupied as they were with the demands of less cooperative residents.

'Have you seen Eian and Zarad?' Ran asked in a low murmur.

Lidan continued past them, dazed and exhausted, fingers tracing the smooth timber wall panels, the aches and bruises of her fall muted by the presence of the man walking beside her. She couldn't touch him again. She could hardly stand to look at him for longer than a glance. To catch his eye, to meet his gaze, was like lightning in her chest. Disbelief ran riot, a storm of pain and elation, crashing together in a whirlwind of possibility.

How could it be real? It couldn't be real…

She risked a glance. He was there, right where she left him. Perhaps…

'Yes, they got back a while ago. I…' Aelish trailed off into stunned silence. 'Where have you been? What's going on—'

'I'll fill you in at breakfast,' Ran silenced her questions gently. 'I'll know more by morning.'

They muttered between themselves as Lidan drifted down the corridor. Someone suggested calling Thanie from her bed. Ran turned the idea away. If the woman got her teeth into the problem none of them would see the cool sides of their pillows before sun-up. Best to leave it until morning.

The trader and the watcher returned to bed, luring Marrit away with the promise of a warm meal and a wash, leaving Ran, Lidan and Loge to stand awkwardly in the sitting room. Weary house staff brought a platter of food and steaming bowls of water draped with soft cloths, eager that the three of them clean themselves before staining the fresh bed-sheets. Lidan washed in numb silence, the sword glaring from a nearby table. She watched apprehensively as Loge made some attempt to work the blood from his face. The rush of elation she'd allowed herself in the street leeched away as the strangeness of it settled heavy in her chest.

It wasn't that she was unhappy to see him. She'd dreamed of a day such as this, begged for it when she'd curled around her grief, fighting her loss for the briefest instant of peace. But this moment should not have been possible, should not have existed in any version of reality. Yet here she was, living it, breathing it, watching it unfold as if it had always been.

Joy warred with fear—fear of what lingered in the mind of a man returned from the dark side of death, fear of what he'd left behind in the unseen realms, where only Dennawal and the ancestors were ever meant to tread. Mortals did not belong there, for all her intrusions on the place. And things that went there to die were not supposed to come back.

Caught in the middle, his features drawn with exhausted confusion, Ran splashed his face, leaning over the bowl to let the water drip loudly in the silence. 'Can't say this is how I saw this evening turning out.'

Lidan might have replied with a witty quip if her tongue wasn't suddenly three times too big for her mouth. Words failed her, shallow breath insufficient to form anything like a coherent sentence. At risk of uttering total nonsense, she clamped her jaw shut and stared at the fire.

'There are answers you need that I can't give,' Loge said with a shrug. It wasn't a dismissive gesture, but a defeated one. 'I understand your suspicion.'

Lidan glanced up, watching his face, his one good eye. Anguish wormed beneath his skin, thoughts whirling within. Part of him wanted to answer everything, to tell the whole truth. The rest knew it wasn't possible. There wasn't a sliver of deception in him, just missing pieces.

'Why?' she managed to ask. This was too much. It made no sense. Why him? Why her? What possible use could Dennawal, the drover of the dead, have for any of them? Her head pounded with the absurdity of it all.

She *should* have been overjoyed. Instead, she held back. Wary. Once bitten, twice shy; unwilling to place her heart where it might once again be torn apart. If her reluctance and reticence offended Loge, he kept it well hidden, seemingly unfazed. Had she not seen the conflicting emotions dancing across his face, she might have thought he didn't care at all. But the crease of his brow and the hard line of his lips, the genuine weight of not knowing that settled in his sigh—these things told her differently. He railed against the gaps, frustrated by the inadequacy of his explanations.

Loge shrugged a shoulder and her heart skipped as the corner of his mouth twitched up into that lopsided smile she knew so well. 'Because you have to win, Liddy. There's more at stake than the lives of mortals. This is a fight we can't lose.'

Understanding came in an icy flood, her eyes widening. Recollections of her conversation with Macha danced, and the enormity of what must be at stake for such a being as Dennawal to intervene struck a cold spear through her chest.

'All of this… to stop *my* mother?'

'She allies herself with those who seek to unseat the balance of the world. They strive for power and control. They seek worship and sacrifice and for what should be shared amongst many to rest in the grip of only a few.' Loge spoke as if from a great distance, across immeasurable time. These were not his words, though they came clothed in his voice. They were the will of a world-spirit more powerful than any force mortals could know. Chills coursed across Lidan's skin and she caught Ran's eye, shared apprehension passing between them.

'Sellan acts of her own free will, for reasons only she knows or understands. She is under no duress or influence. To those ends, she seeks a power that only a god can give. She has received it in exchange for a promise—the souls she takes from this world will be dedicated to the Morritae, the Dead Sisters. These cursed souls will not be taken to the Other Place. Such an act upsets a delicate balance that cannot be reset once it is undone.' Loge tilted his head as if listening, then blinked hard, the black eye twitching. 'Your need to defeat her for the safety of the mortal realm is aligned with Dennawal's need to secure the balance beyond. He cannot influence your choices or force your hand. Your minds and hearts are your own. He asks only that you try.' Loge's gaze settled on them both in turn, certainty heavy in his tone. 'He wishes you to understand however, that failure will cost more than human lives. This is crucial. *This* is why you must win.'

'Fuck,' Ran muttered.

Lidan tended to agree. She'd known something was amiss when stories of deities and spirits and gods began to slip from Thanie's lips. The Morritae was a name she hadn't heard before, least of all in tandem to the Dead

Sisters. Was that another omission on Thanie's part? The witch almost certainly knew the extent of Sellan's scheme. The why behind the how, a piece of the puzzle she kept to herself. Lidan's suspicions about her mother's reasons reared again, murky and unexplored. There was no doubt in her mind now. This was so much more than a power grab.

They were all game pieces, standing on a board they hadn't seen clearly until tonight. They'd moved and positioned themselves, their motivations weaponised for purposes they hadn't perceived. Their choices remained their own, though the consequences would echo down time to determine the outcome of a battle much larger than any of them could have understood until now.

Lidan ignored the tightening of her stomach, smoothing clammy palms down the front of her dusty trousers. 'We need to leave. We can't wait any longer.'

Desperation must have been written all over her face. Ran's expression turned sympathetic, and he reached to squeeze her arm. 'As much as we want to, we can't leave tonight. A few days. That's all. The Arinnian agent will find us in a day or so. We need their help to cross the border. Until then, we'll ready provisions.'

'It's not soon enough,' Lidan growled, blinking away fresh tears. 'How much damage could she do in that time? How many lives will she take between now and then?'

'We can't save them all, Lidan. We knew that when she made her bargain with Urda. We can stop her. We *will* stop her, but we need to be ready. Try and get some sleep.' He glanced warily at Loge and gave him a stiff nod. 'We'll discuss this with Thanie in the morning. Do you remember her?'

Loge cocked his head, his gaze wandering. 'The Crone.'

'Aye,' Ran said. 'She'll be able to give us more insight into the other side of this. She was allied with these Morritae last time Sellan went on a murderous rampage.' He gave Lidan's arm a final squeeze of reassurance that did nothing to dispel her anxiety. 'Thank you for tonight. We didn't exactly find what we sought, but...'

Sorrow creased Ran's brow and he looked away, clearly retreating from the memory of his mother. Lidan tried on a comforting smile and found it didn't fit. 'You'll see her again, I'm sure of it.'

The look he gave her—mournful blue eyes bordered by a heavy frown—reflected her own badly disguised doubt. She let him go without protest, leaving her in the charged silence of the sitting room.

Lidan licked her lips and sighed in a vain attempt to slow her racing heart. Her gaze tracked to Loge, sitting quietly on the arm of a lounge chair, his expression as blank as a sheet of paper yet burning with the intensity of a forge.

'I don't think there are any other rooms made up, so if you want to, um—'

'I'll sleep on the floor,' he said, cutting her off mid-ramble.

'Where?'

His hand opened to the rug in front of the fire. 'Here.'

Lidan blinked at the ridiculousness of the notion. 'That's not happening.'

Without another word she turned and left, trusting he followed her through the maze of corridors up to the silent guest rooms where her companions had long since retired. Trust was all she had, for the hammer of her pulse drummed over the thud of his footsteps and the rustle of his coat.

Her door opened with a whisper, a fire crackling in the hearth, a few sweet-scented candles throwing faint reddish light across the room. The bed wasn't huge—ample room for one to spread out but not much more—but there were spare blankets somewhere. She stripped off her ruined jacket and tossed it in the fire, rolling up the sleeves of her shirt.

'What's that?' Loge asked from the doorway.

Lidan froze in the centre of the room. His finger came up to point at her wrist. She looked down, her gaze tracing the black bands etched in her lower arm. 'Mourning tattana.'

It didn't hurt anymore. It had healed, itching as the scabs formed and crusted away. Her physical wounds from that day were gone now, her tattana the last remaining marker of the day her entire world cracked down the middle.

Loge looked at the bands as if he'd never seen anything so fascinating. 'Those are for loved ones?'

A frown drew her brows together. 'Yes.'

'Who are they for?' Innocence and ignorance shone where knowledge and understanding should have been. How could he not know?

'It's...' She lifted her arm, studying the black ink needled into her skin. 'One is for my sister. One is...' Why was this so fucking hard? Why did this hurt so much? She'd fallen asleep at night dreaming of the things she'd say to him if she just had the chance. Now she couldn't force the words out of her mouth. 'This one is for you.'

Loge blinked. He didn't understand. He couldn't remember. 'You did that for me?'

'Yes.' She turned away before he saw the tears blurring her vision, distracting her hands in search of a chest of blankets and furs under the debris of her belongings. 'There's a trunk around here—'

'You don't have to do this,' Loge said suddenly.

'Do what?' Lidan couldn't look at him. She couldn't actually see him through the pain. Did he remember anything? Or was it just this one thing he'd lost—the memory of why she might count him among her loved ones?

'This isn't... I know I'm not...' He sighed and Lidan dropped the bundle of clothes she'd scooped from the top of the blanket box. Heart battering against the inside of her ribs, her memory tore open.

Once again Loge faced her across a muddy path in Tingalla, rain-soaked and miserable. Miserable but alive, limping on his ruined knee, her heart aching to see his pain. They'd known what was coming. Her inevitable departure from Hummel, her eventual matching to some unknown man in some far-flung place. They'd known then what the future held. Despite it, they'd clung to hope of a different path rising before them. They'd stolen one night from fate, one night for themselves, and held onto each other, ignorant of everyone and everything beyond.

'You're different,' Lidan said, finishing his sentence.

'Yes.' He nodded slowly. 'I'm not who I was. Not all of him, anyway. I don't know what was left behind, how much of me didn't came back. I know there are things we did, things we felt. Things I've forgotten. I've been gone a while and I'm not the same and I need you to know I don't expect anything.'

'I don't...' She raked her teeth across her bottom lip, staring at the fire until her eyes stung. 'There's...' Her voice caught again, tearing painfully on the barbs of unspoken truth. The sensation of Macha's fingers tracing her scars tingled across her skin and her shoulders dropped, collapsing under a wave of defeated acceptance.

There was no use holding it in anymore, no use holding it back. Might as well tear herself open and flay herself bare. What if there wasn't another chance? What if this was all she'd be given? Her last opportunity to show him the size of her loss, the magnitude of the wounds she carried, and the lengths she'd go to for even a chance at healing?

She'd held it together for so long, pretended to be all right, worn a mask of grim determination for as long as she could. But standing in this room, alone with this man, it all fell away, because none of it mattered. He saw through her even before his eye had turned black enough to see the spirit world. There was no point trying to paste on a brave face for Loge. It would simply wash away the moment he looked at her.

Ugh, fuck it...

'There's a wound in me that won't ever heal, Loge. It's big enough to swallow me whole. For weeks I've stood at the edge, hoping for a reason not to throw myself in.' Her vision swam and she looked at him. Raw and weeping. That's what he'd see. Not beauty or strength or courage, but raw, weeping agony. 'I wanted you back so badly. There was so much I hadn't said, so much we hadn't done. I wanted you back so that hole would be filled again, so that ache would just stop throbbing. So I could stop looking into the abyss wondering how long until it takes me, how long until it consumes all of the person you would have recognised, leaving nothing but a husk.'

Her strangled words forced their way out past barely controlled sobs. 'I don't *care* if you've changed. I don't care if you're not the same. *I'm* not. No part of me is the same. The girl you knew died when those rocks fell. Not one fibre of my being *wasn't* consumed by sorrow and rage and burned to fucking ashes. *Everything* about me has changed, except one thing.'

'What's that?' His whisper scarcely made it through the raging storm crashing in Lidan's heart. He knew the answer. Surely he hadn't forgotten this?

'You.' Throat tight, Lidan's fist slammed into the centre of her chest. 'I need you. Here. With me.'

'I'm not all here, Liddy. I might not ever be.'

She shook her head. 'Neither am I.'

Loge looked at his hands, dark with bloodstains she no longer saw. 'What if I'm too broken?'

Two steps closed the space between them and Lidan put her hand on his chest. At her touch, he shivered, then grew still. Beneath her palm, a steady beat hammered, a gentle thud that but for some fell magic should not have been there. Truth be told, Lidan didn't care *how* Loge's heart was beating, only that it did.

'This shouldn't be real. It shouldn't be possible, and yet it is.' Her finger pressed against the hard muscle of his chest. '*This* isn't broken. This works just fine. And as long as this works, the rest will follow.' A tear slipped unhindered down her cheek. 'That will have to be enough for both of us. Because I can't do this on my own.'

Time folded into itself, night stretching out before them.

Sleep came, curled together on the bed, filthy and fully clothed, wrapped in a tangle of limbs. Lidan held tight for as long as she remained conscious, unable to let go in case he vanished with the dawn like a lucid, taunting dream.

The gaping wound closed as she slept, skin stitching together, broken parts welding into place. She'd always see the lines, the cracks through which she'd once glimpsed the person she'd been. She'd shed the skin of a past self once before, too damaged, too heavy with sorrow and pain to hold on to. She'd left that version of herself behind in the bush when Abbi died, let it slip and fall. As the night deepened and her breath caught the rhythm of the rise and fall of Loge's chest, pressed to her back, his arm flung over her shoulder and draped lazily down the covers, she let the wounded, hopeless young woman go.

A future waited beyond the darkness. A future worth fighting for. A future she would not face alone.

CHAPTER FORTY

The Slicks, Wodurin, the Woaden Empire

The creaking of the dray's axles fell silent, only an echo remaining in the seemingly empty lane. The creature under the canvas cover didn't move, nor did Sellan command it to. She'd only use it if her prey required a heavier hand than she had to wield. She hoped not to need it at all. Prying eyes lingered all around, newcomers known only to Eddark waited in the shadows, watching a dimly lit building down the alley.

The windows were tightly shuttered, leaking pale light into the street between the cracks of the rotting timbers. The door stood unguarded, though Irennie assured them muscle waited on the other side. It was in Kadek's interest to draw as little attention to this establishment as possible. Advertising what went on behind that door was suicide. Being covert kept his patrons happy, their detractors silent and the authorities off his back.

Her gaze traced the height of the building's dull facade to the second storey and back into the shadowy compound. The lane reeked of shit, piss and rot, a sickly stink that burned her nose until she gagged and forced herself to breathe through her mouth.

Invariably there'd be men inside, though among them would be a smattering of women—there always were—rare but just as disgusting. These people deserved to serve Sellan's ends. Like her, they didn't deserve a quiet, painless death. They deserved all the suffering they were about to get. She knew what she was, but did they? Her top lip twitched and Eddark shifted uncomfortably on the driver's seat, glancing back at the small group hiding in the lee of the moonlight.

He climbed down beside Irennie, nodding back at Sellan. 'She'll come in with me. We'll send out anyone we find. Get them out of here and don't come back.'

'No argument there. Use the windows if you have to. I have people waiting on all sides.' Irennie's clandestine contacts from the Nest spread out along the Lane, poised to whisk away the children Eddark would extract from the chaos Sellan planned to unleash. They might miss some, others might be caught in the crossfire, a small few might be too broken or weak to move fast enough. She'd do her best to avoid innocents. She promised herself she would. This time would be different. This time she wouldn't take with impunity.

Eddark adjusted his long, heavy cloak—another of his high-born costume pieces—and smoothed a hand through his hair. Their eyes met and he nodded. It was time.

Grinding her teeth against the pain, Sellan climbed down after him. Urda's staff gave her some semblance of dignity, even as the throbbing magic twisted her spine. Her veil up, her height disguised by a feigned hunch, she followed him toward the door, one aching step at a time.

Irennie and Eddark had set the stage for the attack on Kadek's lair in just three days. City watch officers had been paid-off or lured away with the promise of cheap affection with the Slicks' best, the local homeless warned to keep to other lanes and streets. Whispers spread between the workers of the night that Kadek might be on his last legs, and other criminal emperors eagerly moved into position to fall upon the carcass of his empire. It seemed no one would miss Kadek. He was as friendless as he was morally bereft. Even in a city as reprehensible as Wodurin, what he did for a living was a step too far.

The chances of anyone recognising Sellan were low, the chances of anyone escaping to describe her even less. Still, doubt curdled in her stomach in the days preceding the attack. She had doused her hair in chemics—the smell alone should have woken the five dead things on the floor of her work room. The deep auburn burned away to a silver blonde. Her scream as the acid tore through her eyes, bleaching out the green to a pearlescent pale blue had sent the birds in the garden screeching into the evening. Eddark had come running, though there was little he could do but watch her torture herself, all to stop anyone discovering her identity before her work was done.

'You ready?' he muttered, wrenching Sellan from that painful memory.

'As I ever will be,' she whispered.

'Will it take long to, you know... Change them? Once they're dead?'

Sellan shook her head and suppressed a wince. 'No. Last time—'

'Last time?' His eyes narrowed.

She waved his incredulous judgement away. 'It didn't work as expected because I delayed too long. I let them wander while I made more, instead of keeping them close and at rest until I was ready. I won't make the same mistake twice.'

A long pause drew out as they stopped just beyond the reach of the grotty door lamp. Eddark pursed his lips, sighed. 'Good.'

Sellan twitched around to frown at him, questions in her gaze. That wasn't the response she'd expected.

'I had a note from the palace today.'

Sellan's heart kicked into a gallop.

'Tamyr has caught wind of the rumours I let loose in the court and granted us, well *me*, an invitation to a court audience. You're to attend as my mage-resident.'

Their eyes met, Sellan's mouth suddenly as dry as sand. 'When?'

'Tomorrow afternoon.' Eddark shrugged his cloak closer. 'You need to pitch the proposal, introduce him to the idea of the weapon. Once he grants us a private audience, we can bring *them* with us, but not before.'

'Tomorrow?' Sellan's voice was hardly more than a strained squeak. She would see Tamyr tomorrow? After twenty years, tomorrow was the day?

Eddark nodded solemnly. 'By all accounts he's desperate, willing to listen to just about any crackpot scheme that might give him the upper hand on the Free Nations. He's been burying virgins alive, under the temple to Ortus.'

Sellan stared at Eddark, her jaw falling open. 'He *what*?'

'Like I said—desperate.'

'It's been centuries since anyone thought that ridiculous superstition was anything but a waste of perfectly good virgins, not to mention the sacrilege of burying dead inside the city walls!'

'He slips past that law because they aren't dead when they go into the ground.' Even the dark couldn't hide his shudder of revulsion.

360

She had no idea why she was surprised. Tamyr always had a grotesque obsession with the archaic rituals of their ancestors; worship that required not just blood, but the blood of particular people given in particular ways. This specific brand of idiocy had been the last resort of desperate emperors many generations ago, when the newly founded city came under constant attack from lawless northern tribes. And it was the sole domain of Ortus, nemesis of the Morritae.

Writers of old said it appeased the god through the sacrifice of the same women who invariably swore their allegiance to Ortus' adversaries. If the Rider appreciated the sentiment, he kept it to himself, and the practice fell from favour an age ago. That Tamyr had turned to such acts of wanton barbarity revealed a more catastrophic break in his mind than Sellan had dared hope. If he was frantic enough to sacrifice virgins within the city bounds, he was surely reckless enough to consider her offer of a weapon, no matter how mad it sounded.

Eddark stepped forward, his balled fist hovering over the door, ready to knock. 'Play the long game, Sel. We'll get him where we want him, then we'll close the trap. We just need to hold our nerve.' His knuckles rapped on the timber, the knocking boom deafening in the oppressive, unnatural silence of Tanner's Lane.

The door opened a crack, the broad face of a stout man peering through the gap. 'Yes?' he asked, drawing out the vowel and raising his brows.

'I've, ah, I hope I've come to the right place.' Eddark feigned awkwardness to perfection and Sellan realised he wasn't playing. He glanced nervously down the street, figures inching back into the shadows as he did, minuscule movements in the stillness of the lane. 'I came on a recommendation of a good friend. A lord…'

'Your name?' the man asked smoothly. His beady eyes traced Eddark's height then settled on Sellan. Recoiling as if struck, he registered her weird eyes and the cascade of pale hair beneath her veil, the disgust on his face not entirely deserved. *He* was the one working in an under-age brothel, not her. Sellan cocked a brow but said nothing, biting back a smirk as the man collected himself and returned his attention to Eddark.

'Lord Aedrick. I'm new to town. I've an audience with the emperor tomorrow and I have a frightful need to let off some steam.' He let that statement hang, eyeing the door man. 'If you know what I mean.'

The man's smile was slick and mirthless, his eyes pits of cool calculation. 'Of course, my lord. Do come in. Will your companion also be partaking this evening? Should you require two rooms I am sure we can accommodate both of your—'

'No,' Eddark said, lifting his chin with a sniff and pushing past the man. 'She'll stay with me.'

If the door man thought that odd, he made no mention of it, bowing and simpering as he trotted ahead down the corridor. There was indeed security inside of the door and the stout little man wasn't it. Two huge man-mountains waited in small alcoves just off the hallway, their presence overflowing the tiny spaces in a way Sellan hadn't thought any man but Erlon ever could. She held back from gaping as she limped past, noting the burnished brown sheen to their skin and the ebony black of their hair. They could have been her husband's kinsmen for all she could see of them. As long as she could dismiss the glaring similarities, both would make excellent additions to her troop of marhain.

She set her teeth and followed Eddark into the building.

An atrium opened at the centre, largely empty but for a sparse smattering of potted plants and a fountain. Sellan slowed, scanning the colonnade, the many doorways all shut tight, faint light seeping under the timber panels as they passed. Water chattered across the carved stone, dark in the silver of the full moon. It waned now, soon to diminish toward last crescent, but for now it blazed in the abyss above, illuminating knots of cloud racing across the sky.

What Irennie had described as a warehouse or perhaps a singular building, turned out to be a maze of rooms and chambers, not unlike the houses in the upper city. Someone had gone to great lengths to conceal a domestic abode behind the facade of commercial premises, someone with a lot of money, an abundance of time and a need to appease a selective and pampered clientele.

From beyond the doors came muffled voices, and every now and then, a higher pitched sound that she blocked out, unwilling to think of who or what it might be. The stout man hurried along in front of Eddark like an over-excited goat, nattering on about this and that, asking probing questions about "preferences" and "tastes" that his lordship might wish to indulge. Eddark, for all her wonder, managed to keep his head, answering with aloof, noncommittal statements that one might expect from a lord of the realm wary of giving too much away. He didn't so much as glance back at her when they passed a door, open just wide enough to hear clearly what was going on inside.

The goat-man didn't even flinch, nodding and gesticulating toward another corridor and a set of stairs to an upper floor. 'We have a variety on our menu for the first-time customer. Some prefer to view an assortment on their initial visit—' He ushered them inside an empty, spacious sitting room adorned with day lounges and woven rugs.

They will burn nicely, Sellan thought.

'—and it is not uncommon for a discerning client to take their time over many days, if not weeks, choosing their preferred experience. My lord, I do recommend—'

'Sel, shut him up.'

Her hand came up, fingers splayed wide. Her vision shifted, the world shunting sideways, polarising until Eddark and the goaty man became entities of energy in the form of human bodies. Walls no longer existed, the floor seemed to vanish though it remained solid under her soft leather boots. The faint flicker of the man's spine called to Sellan's power, a gentle pulse of light indicating his life force in the column of bone.

In a split second her eyes flared red-hot, the intensity of her magic building to the point of bursting, a deep throbbing sound stretching beyond mortal hearing. She snapped her hand shut, twisting her wrist in a sharp motion that crushed the goat-man's spine and windpipe from across the room.

He flopped, limp as a dead man's dick, twitching on the floor, eyes bulging as his mind caught up with his body.

'Are you going to use him?' Eddark darted to a window and peered through the shutters along the corridor outside to see if anyone had noticed the thud of the man's falling body.

Sellan tilted her head and slipped her veil back from her face. He wasn't dead yet, but he would be soon. There wasn't much time before his brain shut down, starved of air, desperate signals ignored by the rest of his body. 'No, I don't think so. He can burn.'

His face purpled, lips puffy, dribbling frothy spittle as his body entered the final stages of panic. A slight smile danced on her lips. She'd felt such immense guilt in a moment like this, shame at her fascination in those last seconds when a life left a body and tipped from one realm to the next. It wasn't the same sick, perverted sexual pleasure maggots like the goat-man got from ruining young lives. It was a morbid curiosity she'd always been ashamed of.

Until today.

Fire licked up drapes and raced across carpets, a roar of conflagration raging in her wake. She left the goat-man's corpse to burn, slipping out after Eddark as he hurried from room to room on the second storey, throwing open doors to interrupt whatever vile act might be underway.

At first, they found children huddled in clusters, dressed in the gods only knew what scant outfits, staring wide-eyed as a man burst in and spirited them away. Irennie had people on the roof, scuttling across the tiles to hoist stunned youngsters up and away from the chaos Sellan swept through Kadek's establishment.

She didn't take everyone she found. Didn't have time. There were too many.

But she didn't leave a single one alive.

With each room she snapped necks and lay a hand on the twitching corpses, drawing the remaining soul to her own, cocooning the body in her magic and sewing it to her will.

They followed her, macabre little puppets on invisible little strings. Eddark worked in silence, the protests of each offender cut short by Sellan as she tore out throats and hearts. The fire behind her was the loudest thing in the house, crackling merrily as she fed it a body here, a corpse there, taking only those she wanted and leaving the rest to melt. Children teemed out through side doors and windows, collected by Irennie's friends, vanishing into the night in a dance of silent coordination so magnificent Sellan might have shed a tear had she a shred of humanity left.

With each marhain she made, a small part of her died. With each creature she welded to her will, she gave up a sliver of herself, surrendering what little magnanimity she still had in some final act of sacrifice for her greater good. Whether anyone else agreed that her ends justified her means was none of her concern. This was what she had to do to make things right, to stop Tamyr.

In the end the heavies came, flanking a weedy, rake of a man as pale as the moon and dressed in the latest finery. Dark eyes scowled at her, blades levelled across the atrium as the house burned.

'The *fuck* have you done!' the waspish man screamed. 'My fucking business! You have any idea how long this took to build?' Rage flared his nostrils, the tendons in his neck tight as he snarled. So this was Kadek, the whoremaster.

'I have set things to rights,' Sellan replied, her voice distorted by fire and magic. 'Undone your many wrongs and recycled the pain you caused into something useful.'

She hoped Eddark was out. She hoped he'd found them all and taken them far away from here, where monsters like this man couldn't hurt them anymore. Liquid power dripped from her fingertips, great crimson globs of magic sizzling on the flagstones, corroding it on contact, her body trembling with the overflowing force of the goddess' gifts.

Behind her the marhain waited, some stomping through ember and ash, others slipping behind the curling fronds of palms and the withering branches of apple trees. Leaves blackened in their presence, life sucked from the very ground at their feet as they closed in on Kadek and his guards. He blinked at them, cold shock blanching his already sickly white face to a pallid green.

He recognised his patrons and his guards. He saw their wounds and the signs of their mortality, saw that they were undead, walking amongst the living without a care for flame or cold, for food or water, rest or love. They hissed and growled like beasts, gnarled and distorted by her magic into something less than human, something closer to the distilled evil they had been in life. She hadn't the time to arm them, but she gave them claws and wicked teeth. These weapons would do for her audience with the emperor, when she'd present him with his death disguised as his salvation. She might have time to do more.

Kadek did not.

She caught the eyes of the guards, Kadek's foreign muscle. Likely the sons of slaves, the sons of women taken by Sellan's imperialist family in their unrelenting ravenous conquest. She could give them a chance, the benefit of the doubt. Did they want to be here? Had they chosen this path?

One charged and she braced, a foot sliding back, her hand outstretched. A torrent of fire burst from her palm and tore straight through the chest of the running guard. It cut his breastbone clean in half, slicing through his ribs and the upper lobe of his lung. It cooked his heart in its cavity and he tumbled, carried by his own momentum, sliding across the stones to stop at her feet. Sellan's gaze found the other man.

He put his blade through the back of Kadek's neck before she had a chance to shift her weight.

Blood fountained from the whoremaster's mouth, a great bright gush that slopped to the pavers. He gasped, shuddering as the cord to his brain frayed at the edges of the guard's short sword. The guard let him fall, another for Sellan's army, and she urged a pause to the chaos. Her soldiers grew still, despite the encroaching fire and the scorching heat.

They waited. It would take but a single command, a breath of thought and they would fall on the man, tearing him apart.

'Why did you do that?'

Through her fractured vision, she watched him glance at Kadek and his fallen comrade, then the slavering dead. 'I weren't gonna die for the likes of them. He didn't deserve any better.'

'And them?' She tilted her head at the marhain. 'What do they deserve?'

'No better than that.' He spat at their feet but none of them flinched.

'Your name?'

'Faeon Saworth.'

'Will you serve, Faeon?' Sellan asked, a picture of calm in the eye of a storm. She wondered what he must see—white hair, pale eyes, a long thin staff held lightly in one hand, her magic enough to stave off the pain for now. It would return with a vengeance, but for now she stood straight and tall, fortified by her gift.

'Not like that,' he replied, nodding at the marhain. His accent spoke of the coast, of Eddark's people, of a place where the edges of the Empire bled into the Archipelago and law lost all meaning.

'Fair enough.' Why not give him a chance? Why not prove herself merciful, if only to show herself that she could. 'You fuck up a single time, you betray me or mine and our cause, and I will have you flayed and fed to the dogs. Are we clear?'

He nodded and sheathed his sword.

It took mere moments for her to finish the work of consuming Kadek and his deceased guard. She had her soldiers now, her weapon of mass destruction built for a single target. Sellan would be ready when Tamyr called, when her whispered promises became too much to resist, when he begged her to show him the magnificence she'd created. As long as she survived until then, undetected and beyond his reach, she'd see this through to the end.

They left the house to devour itself, Irennie's throng of helpers long gone from the lane. Eddark waited outside with the dray, his face twisted in stunned fascination as she led a dozen marhain from the house and into the abandoned alley. They climbed into the dray without protest, laying down and appearing to fall asleep at her command. Faeon tossed the canvas sheet over the pile and tied down the edges, Sellan catching a questioning look from Eddark.

'Who's he?' he asked as she dragged herself onto the seat beside him. Already her limbs ached like lead had been poured into her bones, her muscles screaming as her skin tightened at the heat of the blazing building.

In the roar of the fire storm, she shrugged. 'Back up. For tomorrow.'

Eddark nodded, dubious but accepting. So utterly accepting. A flash of guilt hit her, that last shred of humanity clinging tightly. She hoped he survived what was coming. He deserved to see the other side, a world without Tamyr.

Faeon leapt onto the tailgate of the dray and without another word Eddark cracked the reins, leaving the horror of Tanner's Lane to burn.

Chapter Forty-one

Kotja, Isord

Ran knocked on Thanie's door as early as he dared. Scrunched between his cold fingers was a note written in a hand he'd recognise anywhere. His mother had sent her agent, disguised as a fixer who could take them safely to the coast.

Have you seen him yet? Iridia hissed in an excited whisper, almost as if she enjoyed the idea of meeting a real-life king's agent.

No, of course I haven't.

Why not?

He turned with a scowl, and she held up her hands in surrender. *If I'd had time to go down to the kitchen and spy on him, you would know about it. As it is, I need to forewarn Thanie—*

The door opened, the bleary-eyed witch standing on the other side, blinking against the light streaming through the curtains across the room. 'This had better be worth leaving my covers for.'

'Loge isn't dead anymore.'

Her eyes widened so far he thought they might bulge out of her head. 'Loge? Lidan's Loge? Big, tall, puppy dog eyes with an axe?'

'Yep,' Ran replied, rocking on his heels and glancing down the hallway, wary of eavesdroppers.

'But he was...' Thanie made a squashing motion with her hands and Ran grimaced, glad Lidan wasn't nearby to see it.

'He was and now he's not. Apparently, the Dark Rider decided he was more useful here than in the afterlife.' He didn't press the point further, but watched, Lidan's cautious suspicion echoing from the previous evening. Thanie hadn't told them everything. But just how much was she hiding?

Thanie grew very still then leaned slowly away from the door, her grip on the threshold slipping as she stepped heavily back into the room. Ran followed her through. Like a tug on a stitch, he felt Iridia draw away a little magic, materialising by the window, just solid enough to see but still so transparent that the morning sunlight lanced through her form.

'He knows then...' Thanie muttered to herself. 'He knows what she's doing...'

'Knows what?' Ran screwed up his face. Already a headache hammered in the orbit of his eye, a sure sign today was destined to be a chore.

'Ortus. He knows of the Dead Sister's plot to undercut him.'

'That's the thrust of it, yes.' He resisted the urge to vent his frustration. Resisted the urge to demand clarity around Sellan's motives and answers to questions he knew Thanie wouldn't answer. Lidan's doubt sat heavy now, more convinced by the minute that she was right—this was a personal vendetta rather than an attempted coup.

He'd hoped, for the most part, to keep Lidan out of the fight with her mother. Hoped to spare her the sight of her mother dying at his hand, or worse, forcing her into a situation where she might have to do it herself. He'd wanted to turn her focus to the dradur and steer her clear of the grisly reality that Sellan had to die before this would end. 'Lidan has some pivotal role to play in preventing that from happening. It's not the result I'd hoped for, but it seems the gods have other plans.'

Thanie whisked a vaguely dismissive hand, as if she'd only just heard him through the howl of her thoughts. 'They might have plans but the power to enact them is beyond their reach. The gods can't directly influence the actions of mortals. If they could, why wait? If Ortus could wield such power, wouldn't he stop Sellan himself? Smite her from on high? No, they wait for us to ask their favour. Wait for us to seek them out. They can put us on a path, show us the way, but the steps are ours to take. If Ortus wants Sellan stopped, he needs mortal hands to do it. I just never thought he'd go so far.' She turned from slowly pacing across the room and met Ran's gaze. 'He's serious if he's sent Loge back. This is war.'

Ran sighed. 'I certainly got that impression.'

'He's not all there,' Iridia put in. 'Loge, I mean. I remember him from before and he's *different*. He was more dead than I ever was. His eye...' She touched her cheek. 'The eye of the dead is the mark of a place further beyond than I've ever been.'

Thanie's interest piqued, her eyes narrowing. 'Not all there? As in, he seems a bit…'

'Broken,' Iridia finished for her. 'He's come back in pieces, as far as I can sense.'

'I'd be surprised if your kin would recognise the person you are now,' Thanie told her. 'Death changes you. More than just losing a body, you break apart on the inside. You let go the things you had in this life. You recall them, but they aren't as present, as heavy.' She squinted at the dawning day and scratched at her dark bed-tousled hair. 'How else can you leave if you're bolted down to all the things that kept you here in the first place?'

Iridia fell silent, frowning and withdrawing into herself, pale hands rubbing at her bare shoulders. It hadn't occurred to Ran that the Iridia he knew, the woman who'd haunted his steps, might not be the entire person she'd been before her death. Loge seemed colder, harder. He had a sharper edge to him and not just in Ran's presence. He'd always regarded Ran with cool scrutiny, but now Loge looked at him as though he couldn't quite be sure if he mattered or not. A predator assessing prey. Was Ran worth keeping alive? Was he important to the Dark Rider's ends or simply another meat-suit that might get in his way?

Ran resolved not to cross the southern ranger, to not put himself in any position that might make the man doubt his usefulness. Because of all the things Ran might question about his current situation, Loge's blind and absolute devotion to Lidan was not one of them. The man would crush anyone or anything that stood in her way, friend or foe.

'There's something else,' Ran said, trying and failing to keep the trepidation from his tone. He'd wanted to avoid this conversation, but his encounter with his mother forced his hand. Thanie watched him in silent expectation, and he realised she was still in her bedclothes.

Clothed only in a light sleeping shirt, her bare legs were much longer than the skirts of her dresses had hinted at. She certainly wasn't the Crone he'd first met in Tingalla, her almost black hair an unbound mess framing her angular face.

With a flinch he glanced out the window. 'Last night Lidan and I broke into the palace.'

Thanie snorted a laugh, and he heard her settle into a seat. 'This should be good.'

Ran ignored her quip and pressed on. 'We'd intended to petition the king but instead came across my mother. She spoke of an Arinnian agent who could give us information on the Woaden capital—perhaps how to avoid any authorities, the best way to uncover Sellan's whereabouts, some contacts on the ground.' He held the paper toward her. 'He's here, waiting for me to receive him.'

Thanie held her own counsel for much longer than Ran thought polite, chewing her thumbnail and watching a fat wood-pigeon strut along the windowsill outside. 'Can he smuggle us across the border?'

'I fucking hope so. I don't like our chances of evading two sides of a war without help.'

'Fetch Lidan. And Loge, I suppose. He's not going to stay behind. I'll dress, then bring the agent up.'

Without thinking he stepped toward the door, then paused. 'What about the others?'

Thanie's expression was one of pity but also judgement. She thought him a fool, naive at best. 'For now, we play this close to our chests. You and Lidan know this agent for what he is—knowledge *his* life depends on. Until we know whether he can help us, we need to protect his identity or he'll be in the wind faster than a leaf in a gale. Including the wider group would be folly until we have a plan.'

He nodded reluctantly and only once he'd sifted through the possibilities and accepted, against his better judgement, that Thanie was right. Plotting anything without the others seemed underhanded. They each had a strength to contribute, a skill or a perspective he sorely needed. It was only when he couldn't turn to Brit or Aelish, Eian or Zarad, that he realised how heavily he'd leaned on them since their crossing of the Altipa. Moving any piece on the board without their counsel seemed wrong, yet here he was about to step beyond the circle of their advice. He only hoped he wouldn't live to regret it.

Lidan offered no protest at his whispered request to meet in Thanie's chamber, making an excuse about the witch asking to see Loge. He pressed the note into Lidan's hand before he left, hoping to give her a quiet hint that this was in fact, a ruse. She hardly needed it, offering her apology to the breakfast table with a flawless smile.

By the time Ran got to the kitchen, his empty stomach growled at the smell of fresh pastries and baked ham. A pot of dark roast steamed on the scrubbed table in the centre of the bustling room, a man sitting before it with as stunning a smile as Ran had ever seen. His skin the same light brown as Lidan's, the man's close-cropped dark hair stood up at angles that Ran's own floppy curls defied. Deep brown eyes sparkled as he grinned at the cook, the two of them sharing the aftermath of a joke as his drink went untouched on the tabletop.

Those quick eyes snapped around at Ran's entrance and the recognition was instant. Ran wasn't surprised. You didn't make it as a king's agent without a few skills in your back pocket, and one of them was recognising familial traits. Ran might be built like his father, but he had his mother's features. The agent came to his feet and held out a hand in greeting. 'Sir.'

Ran grasped the offered hand with a nod. 'Well met. What should I call you?'

'Soren, sir. Soren Shavar.'

They left the din of the kitchen and strolled the corridor. It took all Ran's effort not to stalk down the hall as quickly as his feet would carry him, eagerness at war with good sense and plain old manners. 'Is that your real name?'

'I'd have to kill you if I told you.' Soren smiled again and Ran didn't doubt for a minute that he would. He glanced at the agent's hands. How many final breaths had he felt with those?

'My mother says you might be of aid to us...' He let the words drift as a servant girl hurried past with a tray of dirty dishes.

'In your trip to the coast?'

Their mutual code established, Ran nodded enthusiastically. 'Yes. As I'm sure you understand, we must leave as soon as possible. The journey promises to be something of a challenge but there isn't a choice to be had, I'm afraid.'

Soren stroked his neatly trimmed, jet-black beard. Where Lidan and Loge's people had a slightly broader nose, Soren's was as sharp and angular as Ran's. 'It's a difficult time of year to travel, if I'm honest.'

They reached the top of the stairs and turned toward the living quarters, Ran's heart plummeting into his boots. That wasn't the news he'd hoped for. 'How so?'

Soren leaned close. 'Just as Orthia has its killing season, so does Isord. Summer is the time for fighting, so the border is a mess of soldiers, supply trains and hyper-vigilance. Doesn't mean it can't be crossed, but it'll be about as fun as bathing a cat.'

As quickly as he could, without attracting attention, Ran ushered Soren into Thanie's room, greeted on the other side with an uneasy silence. Unanswered questions lingered awkwardly between Thanie and Loge. Evidently, there were words to be said between the two and his entrance had cut them short. If Soren sensed the tension, he didn't let it show, bowing graciously and receiving nods of greeting in return. Iridia kept to herself, perched on Thanie's bed, visible only to Ran as the king's agent found himself the centre of attention.

'This is Soren, the man I spoke of at breakfast.' Ran did his best at introductions, then sighed. 'I'm not sure how much my mother told you, but there's little point standing on ceremony. What are the chances? Can we get to Wodurin or not?'

Soren settled on the arm of a small sofa by a cold hearth, lacing his fingers together in his lap. Lithe and athletic, he moved with the elegance of a well-honed blade. Gods only knew what kinds of weapons the agent had hidden on his person. 'I spoke at length with the duchess this morning, and she told me what she could of your needs. I have to say it's a tall ask, my friends. Crossing the border is one thing. Surviving the countryside between there and the city is another. To find who you're looking for *in* the city itself, that's a whole other thing.'

'What's changed?' Thanie cut in. Hurriedly dressed, her hair tamed in a twisted topknot, she looked marginally more awake. 'It always was a labyrinth of chaos.'

Soren paused, recognising Thanie's distinctly imperial accent. 'If anything, it's gotten worse in the past few years. Emperor Tamyr is, well, unhinged. And that's putting it nicely. There never was much in the way of authorities on the streets, even less so now the Assembly of Lords vie constantly with the Congress for power. The emperor is no help to anyone in striking a balance. He's so easily steered from one cause to another he can spend the morning railing at the mages on behalf of the lords, then by afternoon bells he's flipped completely and wants to tear the Assembly to the ground and exile the lords in favour of the Congress.'

Thanie's brows arched with amusement. 'Another day in paradise.'

'If only.' Soren shared her wry smile and shrugged. 'If it weren't for all the infighting in Wodurin, Tamyr might have some clue what's going on in the rest of the Empire. As it is, the regions are fending for themselves, lords running their own agendas outside the remit of the Assembly or the Congress. From one town to the next you can't tell who's in charge—the local lord or the Congress mages.

'Look, you don't have much time, so I'll give it to you straight. This is at once the worst and the best time to attempt your goal. You might just make it. If you use skirmishes as cover, crossing the border is possible. You might dance through the melee unnoticed. But you might as easily get snatched up in the first town you come to by some over-zealous loon with a point to prove.'

Ran and Lidan glanced at each other. They couldn't fail at this. They had to find her mother and stop her, no matter the cost.

'What are the chances of the emperor granting an audience?' Lidan asked. 'If someone were to petition him? Someone he didn't know, for example?'

'A stranger? From outside the court?' Soren chewed his lip. 'It really depends on what they're asking.'

'What if they weren't *asking*, but making an offer? A gift.'

The agent's eyes narrowed. 'What kind of gift?'

'It doesn't matter. Would he see them, or would he turn them away?'

'I'm not sure I understand... This person you're looking for, they're on the run, aren't they?' Soren found his feet in a smooth motion, his stance angled, as if preparing to counter an attack.

'In a manner of speaking,' Lidan replied, her face an expressionless mask. For a moment Soren and Lidan watched each other, silently assessing while the rest of the room waited on a knife's edge, wondering which way the conversation would turn. 'They're fleeing us, though they might seek the protection of the emperor, if only briefly.'

'And the gift?' He wasn't about to let that go. Ran didn't blame him. What Lidan had suggested could have enormous ramifications for the Free Nations, even if none of them knew what Sellan had to offer. If she succeeded in luring the emperor into her web, even just to kill him, the power dynamic of Coraidin would shift. If Lidan was wrong and her mother had designs on ruling, an army of dradur on any field of battle would decimate the Free Nations.

'If we stop them before it's too late, it won't matter what the gift is.' Thanie stepped in beside Lidan, her arms crossed. 'If we don't, it still won't matter, because there won't be any of us left to care.'

Ran couldn't disagree on that score. 'This is bigger than just apprehending a fugitive.'

The look Soren levelled at him was one part horror, nine parts disgust. 'If this reaches beyond the borders of the Empire, if this threatens the people who have held it at bay for generations—'

'It won't, but only if you help us get to Wodurin,' Ran pressed. 'We understand the risks. We knew them at the start of our journey and we knew them breaching the walls of the palace to beg the help of a king deaf to our plight. We'll face this threat, despite it, because we know what the alternative is.'

Spurred, suddenly alight to the depth of the danger, Soren's eyes darted as he thought. 'I may have a way, contacts I can lean on. I'll have to send a few birds and call in favours. It's going to be an uncomfortable ride. I can't promise anything more than a creaky cart and weeks on the road but there isn't time to—'

The crash of distant shattering glass sliced through the conversation and bellowed shouts echoed up the corridor outside.

'For fuck's sake—' Ran snarled.

'Not again,' Lidan groaned over the top of him.

Loge and Thanie looked at each other with questioning glances.

Soren froze. 'You have company. A lot of it.'

Ran met his eyes and he nodded. 'We'll be ready when you are. Just say the word.'

The door burst open and Lidan went for her knives, pulling up short at the sight of her sister stumbling into the room, panting and pointing. 'City guard. Followed us. From last night. Looking for you.' She stabbed a finger at Loge, and Soren took the moment to dart away, slipping out the door and into the rabbit warren of the house.

'They *what*?' Loge came to his feet. He had hatchets at his belt, a choice Ran had thought odd at breakfast time, but now he found himself reaching for a sword that wasn't there.

Ran's blood slowed to the pace of an ice floe, the frigid heat of his magic rolling down his arms and into his fingertips. 'What did you do?'

Marrit sucked in another lungful of air and threw her arms wide in exasperation. 'We pissed off a gate guard. He must have reported us or something. Now someone's in the yard screaming about an attack on the palace? I don't fucking know.'

They weren't getting out of this with diplomatic smiles and smoothly delivered platitudes. Not this time. If the guard tried to pin the palace attack on Loge and Marrit, it would take Villia all of half a second to implicate Ran. The coincidence was too neat, too convenient. What were the chances of a fugitive prince sharing the same accommodation as a foreigner who had, that very night, made enemies with city authorities? It was a clusterfuck of such epic proportions even Aelish's silver tongue couldn't talk them out of it.

Ran glanced at Thanie and she grimaced. 'We need to go.'

'We can't! Soren said—' Lidan began but Ran held up his hand. Into the silence came the raging sound of guards smashing through the house.

'*Without* Soren,' Ran said.

Thanie's eyes went wide. She knew what he was asking. 'No, I can't. I'm not even close to strong enough.'

'Use my power, like she did yours. I'm stronger now than Sellan ever was. Use me.' He looked at where Iridia shimmered near the bed, her form literally vibrating with fear. 'Use us.'

'I can't move all of you, not with Brit and the others.' Thanie shook her head vigorously, stepping back as if he might lurch forward and strike her. 'It'll kill me.'

'Then just us four. We can do this but we need to go *now*!' Ran stabbed a finger at Loge. 'If he ends up in prison, if they catch Lidan and I, we're so magnificently fucked we might as well be dead. If we don't go, we have no chance and this was all for nothing.'

'Oh shit,' Lidan murmured. She understood. She sheathed her blades and grabbed for Loge's hand, dragging him closer to Ran than he seemed comfortable. 'Marri, get out of here. Hide out somewhere. Track that man. His name is Soren. Find him. He'll help you.'

Terror blanched Marrit's face. 'Wait, where are you going?'

'Go, Marri!' Lidan shouted and reached for Thanie's arm. 'Please, Thanie.'

Marrit's gaze darted across her sister's face, backing toward the door as ordered, reluctance weighing down every step. The witch stared at Lidan as Ran took her other hand and placed it on the back of his neck.

Storming guards thudded down the corridor, boots thunking on the boards, doors flying open to slam against the walls, hinges shrieking in protest.

'Please, do it now,' Ran begged Thanie, his hand grasping Loge's wrist.

'Where?' she whispered. 'Where will we go?'

'Somewhere safe. Anywhere but here.'

Thanie's eyes squeezed shut and Ran let his magic go.

He gave it all, everything he had, willing her to take them far away. Willing her to save Aelish and Brit the indignity of watching them leave in irons. Willing her to save Eian and Zarad from any burden of rescue. Willing her to take them as close as she could to the centre of Sellan's world. To the centre of the fight, to the fate that waited at the end of this road.

Heat exploded around them and reality tore in two.

Chapter Forty-two

The Imperial Palace, Wodurin, the Woaden Empire

Eddark's hired litter-bearers trudged up the last few feet before the palace gate then gently lowered the conveyance to rest on the cobbles. Sellan's fingers curled into a trembling fist, her eyes trained on the buildings visible through the sheer curtains. The Assembly loomed to the north, a behemoth, all ancient stone columns and shit-streaked statues. It might be the seat of the lord's power in the capital, but the birds gave less than three fucks about that. It was a perfectly functional avian privy and Sellan thought that suited it just fine.

At least she'd been spared the sight of the Academy on the way up to the palace fore-gardens and gate. It stood across the river, not far from the Congress—another ugly construction with two soaring domes that vividly reminded her of a pair of obnoxiously perky tits. Someone had a laugh the day that design was approved.

'Ready?' Eddark pressed, fighting with the folds of his tunic and robe ensemble. Grunting against the pain, she reached over and snapped the fabric downward, correcting the angle of the fold and dropping the slack of the robe in his lap.

'That needs to hook over your arm, like you're carrying a basket, or it'll drag in the muck.'

'Why would anyone make clothes like this?' he muttered, looking down in disgust. Evidently their game of "dress-up like the rich and powerful" had begun to grow old.

'It's not supposed to be worn by anyone *doing* anything,' Sellan remarked. The day crept on outside, neither of them particularly eager to leave the litter. Exiting meant crossing under the Sylvian Gate and into the palace compound. 'It's for men who sit around talking all day. The longer that robe, the more important they are and the less they actually do.'

'Give me a tunic and trousers any day.' He sighed and handed her the staff. 'Best get this over with.'

'Can't they take us in further?' Sellan shifted her weight and winced. Her hips ached and the back of her pelvis, right above her tailbone, seemed to have separated in a way that made walking an agony of stabbing pains.

'Court protocol—only the Imperial family are carried inside the compound. The rest of us mere mortals have to walk.' His expression was at least sympathetic as he helped her from the litter and abandoned her to limp alone the rest of the way. It wouldn't do for a lord, even a foreign one, to be seen offering his arm to an employee.

She leaned into the pain and the staff, forcing one foot ahead of the other until her muscles warmed and relaxed. A little magic uncoiled and dulled the pinching in her spine, until almost, just almost, she couldn't feel it anymore. She straightened her back, lifted her chin, rolled her neck with a crack and followed Eddark up the stairs to the main entrance. Doves or pigeons took off in a flurry from a nearby orchard, the afternoon sunlight tinted orange in a hazy sky.

Years in the south had taught her what that sky meant. A fire burned beyond the city, likely in the fields or the grasslands. Not close enough to smell the smoke, but near enough to bleed into the sky and fracture the light. It passed beyond sight as they crossed the palace threshold.

Sellan shivered and not entirely from the chill of the echoing entryway. She was on *his* turf now, in his domain. Prey willingly stepping into the cage with a predator. Outside she could melt into a crowd, disappear amongst the shadows. Here she was an oddity—not simply because of her white-blonde hair and colourless eyes—a foreigner as well, a defector according to Eddark's cover story.

She refreshed her memory and the lies they told themselves to convince others. She was Sabine Tolak, mage-resident to Lord Aedrick, formerly of western Arinnia. Hailing from some tiny pinprick of a town on the coast that no one north of the Ruken had ever, or would ever, hear of. Hardly worth mentioning, too remote from Kederen for the government to care what the minor lord got up to. What would Erlon think of her carrying his name like this, so far away and after so much bad blood? She decided she didn't care. It was the name of her children, of the daughters she would never see again. If this one thing kept them close, then she would scream it from the rooftops and take it to her grave. Erlon could have his name back when he rode up here and took it from her.

A messenger darted ahead of them, murmuring to Eddark, Sellan only catching the edges of the conversation as they were led deeper into the palace. A yawning gallery gave way to a colonnaded portico, and beyond it a gargantuan atrium, three storeys high and stretching off to a distance that could have fit the games arena comfortably in the centre. It took all her effort not to gape. An entire forest could have stood in the space with room to spare.

They crossed it, led by the eager boy, Eddark's straight back twisting to check on her twice as they picked their way through groves of fruiting trees and past lovingly tended shrubs. Slaves and servants made way, vanishing as quickly as they appeared. Trained to be absent and present at the same time, dissent beaten out of them at an early age, devotion welded to their core. They'd throw themselves between the emperor and any threat that came his way, gladly giving what remained of their lives for his. Some of them might just get that privilege sooner rather than later. Sellan eyed them and kept pace with Eddark, their faces downturned but their gazes catching every detail.

'My lord,' the boy stopped and bowed, shuffling to the side of an enormous door. Easily taller than two men but barely wide enough for a pair of guards to enter abreast, Sellan frowned as it swung open on soft hinges. It seemed an odd design, unlike any she'd seen in the palace so far. It was as though the intent was to squeeze the entrance, narrowing it so folk had to pass in single file.

She stepped through after Eddark, an introduction called by a disembodied voice, their presence announced with little fanfare or notice.

The roof soared here, enclosing a chamber with a maze of day beds and mounds of cushions in little clusters for courtiers to lounge upon. Diaphanous fabrics cascaded from the ceiling, billowing in the lazy afternoon breeze, disguising a mezzanine floor above and sheltering the seating from direct view.

There couldn't have been more than fifty courtiers scattered around the room, slaves and attendants outnumbering them two to one. A handful of guards stood stiffly against the walls, a jarring display of angular lines and hard planes, their gleaming breast plates beaten to the shape of a muscular torso with the face of a snarling wolf worked at each shoulder. The sigil of the Ultimii—the ruling tribe of the Woaden. Sellan shuddered and squeezed her staff tighter, resisting the urge to vomit.

The last time she'd seen that uniform was in the corridor outside Tamyr's room at the Academy. The same uniform she'd walked past night after night, the same uniform worn by guards ignorant to her cries and pleas. The same guards who'd hunted her from the city, tracking through the trail of pain and destruction left in her wake.

Eddark threw a brief questioning glance over his shoulder, as if that small, furtive gesture might prevent her from toppling into the waves of suppressed terror welling up from the chasm in her soul. The locks she'd kept it behind were broken now, blurred visions of her past drifting through the numbing smoke to dance bloody steps before her mind's eye. A tang stung her tongue as she set her jaw, steely determination driving her on in Eddark's footsteps.

She almost collided with his back when he stopped to bow.

Only the sound of his voice cutting through the maelstrom of her memories caused her to pause, to glance up from her intent study of the flagstones before she slammed into him and humiliated them both. Staggering to a halt, Sellan clung to the comforting depth of his voice. Her heart rattled against her ribs, but Eddark was her stalwart rock in the torrent. As long as he was here, Tamyr couldn't hurt her. Tamyr *wouldn't* hurt her, not in front of all these people.

Her gaze slowly rose.

A plush throne, more a reclining couch than a chair. A pair of exquisitely made indoor boots, woven of the finest lengths of leather. A bright white robe edged in the deepest midnight blue.

He can't hurt me anymore. He's nothing. He's no one.

A brilliant, charming smile. A shock of blond hair, as golden as ripe wheat, streaked with silver at the temples. An easy, disarming laugh. Blue eyes like chips of ice, mirthless despite the smile, bordered on the left by a grisly scar.

She didn't meet those cold eyes. Instead, she looked beyond them to the ruin of his face. The burn had melted the skin completely and might have rendered him blind had it not been repaired. Someone had worked hard to smooth what she'd so cruelly scorched. Hours upon days upon weeks must have been spent in an effort to return it to its former unblemished glory. Yet despite their best attempts, Sellan's rage had left an indelible, unforgettable mark on Tamyr. That stain wasn't ever washing off.

A flicker of solace warmed Sellan's chest. He'd spent the last twenty years as scarred as her, but his wounds could be gawped at and muttered about. He wore the same burden she'd walked around with ever since he'd set eyes on her.

I am a dana, a queen. I am fury and fate. I am the will of the gods. I gave him that scar and it was the least he deserved.

He'd wear her on his skin until the day he died and that was enough to slow the beat of her heart, the thud of her blood fading to a faint drum, the magic in her bones simmering down to a gentle roll.

'Ah yes, the foreign noble we've heard so much about.' Emperor Tamyr of the Ultimii went on, talking to the fake lord of a perfectly non-existent town, unbothered by Sellan's gaze, his voice a coarse rumble that had matured from the brighter lilt of a young man. He hadn't noticed her at all, gently turning his wine goblet on the arm of his throne. 'Everyone says you've a story to tell. We hardly believed them until old Lord Aelius brought that letter. Anyone who can get Aelius *that* worked up is worth at least a few moments of our time.'

The emperor wore no crown or circlet, instead sporting a thick gold torc about his neck that looked heavy enough to sink a ship. Pale blue tattoos lined his brow, curling around the orbit of his right eye and across his cheek, drawn long before lines of worry and woe creased his skin. Only the high mages knew how to read those ancient symbols, words they assured the faithful idiots came from Ortus himself. Sellan doubted anyone in the Congress of Mages, or the Academy had ever spoken to Ortus, let alone knew his will. What they etched on the faces and arms of the emperor and his family were their own invention, stage-perfect paint to give an otherwise ordinary man the appearance of divinity.

A languid hand lifted to stroke the bare arm of a woman lounging at his elbow but Tamyr didn't glance in her direction, his attention trained on Eddark and the tantalising possibilities of his news. Sellan didn't recognise her, but then why would she? She wore none of the trappings of royalty, none of the tattoos or torcs, and had none of the bearing one would expect from an emperor's wife or consort. The kohl around her eyes was smudged but not enough that anyone would notice unless they knew what to look for, the skin of her throat and face pasty and uneven, painted a shade too pale. Her posture reminded Sellan of a kicked dog—loyal, loving to a fault, simpering before its master, just waiting for the next blow.

Eddark's work in the weeks preceding hadn't been in vain. While Sellan scratched through the city looking for dead bodies, he'd spun the Wodurin aristocracy into such a fizz that they'd dropped his bait right into Tamyr's lap. That the emperor had stepped so readily into their trap was at once marvellous and terrifying. How desperate must he be that he would invite an unknown noble to court on nothing but a letter and a rumour?

'It brings me great joy to know my missive reached you, sire. It is my hope that what I have to tell you will bring excellent tidings for this great Empire.' Eddark bowed again and Sellan shifted her gaze so not to catch the direct notice of the emperor.

Not yet. He can't see me yet.

'And who have you brought with you?'

Sellan froze. *Fuck. Fuck fuck fuck.*

'My mage-resident, Sabine. She is the architect of the marvel we wish to discuss with your Imperial Majesty.' Eddark's voice was like silk across her frayed nerves. Gods only knew what soothing effect it had on Tamyr. She'd have gone anywhere with a man who spoke to her with such soft care, such friendly intent. She only hoped Tamyr shared the same desire. 'This marvel, sire—it is beyond imagining. Beyond even the greatest minds. No other can replicate its ferocity, its awe. I hardly have the words to describe it, but I assure you, as my letter detailed, you will not be disappointed.'

'We should love to hear of it!' Tamyr announced. Nearby courtiers tittered, leaning forward without seeming too interested, straining to hear every word without appearing to do more than glance in their general direction.

Eddark's smile laced his voice. 'Oh, but my lord, this is not for the ears of just anyone...'

Make him want it, Ed. Make him crave the unknown. Make him beg.

Silence swept the chamber, all but the birds calling beyond the windows turning to listen. Eddark's feet shuffled awkwardly. Tamyr straightened. 'Excuse me?'

An encouraging hand brushed Sellan's awareness. Urda was with her, *within* her, some part of the goddess remaining in her gift. Sellan lifted the staff and tapped the butt on the stone floor. A resonant crack echoed through the chamber. The emperor's gaze hit her like a physical blow but she held, inviting his scrutiny, allowing herself to revel in the attention of the mob.

Her free hand unfurled and a crimson flame ignited in her palm. Gasps rippled through the gathered courtiers. Fabric rustled as some came to their feet, jostling to see as Tamyr's eyes widened just a little. This was fell magic, unseen in the recorded history of the Congress of Mages.

Magic was always blue. Never anything but blue. The vermillion stain of her gift marked her as something special, something unlike any other mage to ever train within the bounds of the Empire.

'That is *quite* the trick,' Tamyr murmured, settling back on his throne.

'No trick, sire.' She pushed her reply out through a strangled throat. Somehow, despite all the years, the press of his cousin's hands burned in her skin, the talon grip he'd keep her in while he violated her. It warped her voice now to something more earthy, husky and coarse, something Tamyr would never recognise. 'Just raw power.'

'Is this what you wanted to show me?' Tamyr asked Eddark with an amused smile.

Eddark chuckled. 'No, sire. It is but a taste of what we intend to lay at your feet.'

Tamyr watched Eddark closely, those cool eyes surveying the face of the foreigner. Eddark had enough of his mother in him to hide the heritage they shared; a brother he'd only ever known as a face on the back of a coin. How he kept his composure, Sellan didn't know. She marvelled at him, almost forgetting herself. Eddark had it all; the self-control she lacked, the ability to keep his voice even and his hands from trembling. He was an outward picture of calm, though she expected he was tearing himself apart inside.

'So it's true? You have it?'

Eddark edged closer, drawing Tamyr to mirror the movement, as two men might conspire over a mug of ale in the musty corner of a tavern. 'You have heard true, sire. We bring a weapon to win a war.'

Quick as a whip Tamyr's hand came up and the heels of the guards snapped together. Sellan's heart leapt. They were made. He'd recognised her. He knew what she was, *who* she was. It was over before it had even begun. So many plans, so much time, all that energy—

'Clear the room. I would speak with them alone.'

Courtiers hurried to comply.

Sellan watched them go with an affected calm. Like the warmth of the winter sun, her ease never penetrated beneath the surface. A short, thin man bustled to Tamyr's side, drawing his attention from the lithe young woman drifting away with the departing crowd.

'Sire, this is *most* irregular.' He had plump cheeks yet a sharp chin, his flinty eyes darting over the newcomers with unveiled suspicion. What remained of his sparse brown hair had been cut short and carefully combed, as was the fashion, though the blue edging on his robe was not as wide or as deep in colour as the emperor's.

He was a high-level advisor at best, perhaps a high lord of the Assembly. He didn't wear the badge of a mage, nor did he seem to sense the raw magic throbbing through Sellan's body. It was all she could do to stop it overflowing and dripping from her fingers again, too much for one small mortal body to hold.

Tamyr waved the man away. 'Tulius, please. Can a man not have a little fun once in a while?'

Tulius blanched and glared at Eddark, who gave him a slight mocking bow. 'I beg of you, sire. How many more of these charlatans will you entertain?'

The smile fell from Tamyr like a puppet cut from its strings, his glower fit to freeze the blood in Tulius' veins. Sellan flinched on the man's behalf. He either had a pair on him bigger than a bull, or a death wish. 'I only wish to advise, as is my remit from the Assembled.'

'The Assembled do nothing but fondle their own cocks while the Empire lurches from one—' Tamyr suddenly swept his hand through the air, ending the conversation. In a brief flicker of honesty, his mask slipped, the frustration of a man at his wits end oozing through the crack. Tamyr's eye twitched and he gave them all a tight, pained smile. 'We will not discuss this before our guests. They bring merry tidings and I shall hear them.'

Tulius put his back to Eddark and Sellan, shuffling between the emperor and his petitioners. Those remaining in the room slowed their departure to watch. The atmosphere between the two simmered, honest words kept behind clenched teeth. Evidently, Tulius had grown tired of the emperor grasping at straws. How many like him lurked in the shadows of Wodurin? It was men like Tulius who could make or break a dynasty. The kings and emperors of the world were only ever as powerful as those who chose to prop them up. If Tamyr lost his lords, he lost his army, and all tyrants and despots knew—once you lost the support of the troops, you were dead.

'We should keep to our own, sire. The answers you seek lay not in the hands of these—' He threw a scowl over his shoulder and Sellan bit back a laugh. If only he knew who he really faced. '—outsiders. Our own mages and engineers are the greatest minds in all—'

Sellan let her vision shift and unleashed the magic scouring her bones. Let Tamyr witness real power. Let those who remained see what she had become. Let them wonder.

Tulius froze, locked in a prison of his own muscles and sinews. Sellan turned him from facing Tamyr, rigid as a board, in a complete about-face. Curling her fingers into a gentle fist, she pulled him with painful slowness across the flagstones. His feet dragged awkwardly, his expression a mask of horror and rage. Indignity radiated off his skin, bright as a plump ripe plum, he jerked feebly against her control as Tamyr looked on in slack-jawed awe.

The emperor rose from his seat as Tulius grunted, the space in his windpipe growing ever narrower. Sellan locked eyes with Tamyr, fear seeping away, dread at his regard dissolving as her power grew. She didn't even look at Tulius as she killed him. 'A dissenting voice in a palace such as this? Your tolerance is extraordinary, sire. Men like this bleating malcontent sow nothing but doubt and reap nothing but failure. You, my lord, deserve a better quality of advice. One befitting your station, your grandeur, your *divinity.*'

The words tasted of venom and hate but they came out as sweet as honeyed mead, the depth of their deceit only barely covered by a crust of flattery. If Tamyr had men such as this at his heel, then she'd discovered half his problem. What remained was an uncertain, desperate leader who knew the edges of his empire were crumbling. The Empire needed to grow to stay alive, it needed to consume to sustain itself, or else it fell inward like a fire starved of fuel. What Tamyr craved was a firm hand and a solution, and Sellan would deliver it on a silver platter. He would rue the day he opened his door to her, but until then he would eat poison from her hand and beg for more.

Too stunned to speak, Tamyr watched as she squeezed the air from Tulius' chest, crushing it with the sheer weight of her mind. He jolted, twitching as he suffocated, unable to even fall to the ground and flop like a landed fish. The emperor's gaze changed as she let the older man die, a hunger in his eyes she'd sworn to never see again; a desire to know, to take, to have.

Sellan had a secret and Tamyr wanted it.

'Who are you? *What* are you?' He stepped from his dais, almost tripping over himself in his amazement.

'No one important,' she replied with a casual shrug, ignoring the thud of her heart. 'But I have the answers your advisors have failed to deliver in the decades since you took the throne. Answers your people deserve.'

'Tell me more,' he whispered. She let herself smile just a little. He had no idea. None at all. That was how it would remain, until the final moment came. 'Tell me all, tell me what you need. If it is in my power to give, you shall have it.'

As Tulius died and the final lingering fools decided to make themselves scarce, Tamyr fell hard into Sellan's trap and she quietly closed the gate, letting Tulius drop to the ground. Tamyr stepped past Eddark, wanton fascination in his eyes.

This time would be different.

She would make him beg. She would make him crawl. She would make him burn for the answers before she unleashed them to tear down everything he held dear.

CHAPTER FORTY-THREE

Somewhere south of nowhere

Space split like a melon struck by an axe, cleaving cleanly open then rapidly deteriorating into ragged edges that frayed time itself.

Hard ground came up to meet Ranoth, slamming into his side with the force of a charging bull, punching the air from his chest in an agonised grunt. Blinding pain exploded in his shoulder and ribs, ricocheting down his back and into his leg as he rolled vainly away, seeking escape. Bodies fell around him, thudding to the ground, three distinct grunts, wheezes and cries marking the arrival of his companions to wherever the fuck Thanie had sent them.

Her voice rose above the others in a high-pitched gasping wail, and he squirmed around, prising his eyes open to search for the witch. To his left and right, murky figures writhed, the larger of the three rising and staggering to one of the others, murmurs shared between them that Ran couldn't understand. The other curled into a tight ball, moaning and shivering.

His hand reached across the space, rough stone pavers and loose gravel scraping at his skin. Thanie flinched away and he withdrew as if stung. 'You all right?' he croaked.

He thought he saw her nod but couldn't be sure. Was it dark here? A black abyss stretched above; a gaping chasm set to swallow him whole should he fall. A bright orb shimmered off to one side, a disc of brilliant judgement, offering silent rebuke at his stupidity. What was he thinking? They could be anywhere on the face of Coraidin, anywhere from the wastes of the High Tund to the humid sweat chamber of the Rinay Coast. Thanie could have magicked them into a dungeon in Kederen as easily as the sewers of Wodurin. They were lucky they hadn't emerged deep underground, or inside a wall, shattered into a thousand pieces that couldn't ever be put back together again.

That Thanie, his sworn adversary and mentor, had managed to drop them somewhere other than a rat-riddled dump or an ice-blasted mountainside was nothing short of a gods' given miracle. If he hadn't known better, he might have offered up a prayer of thanks for divine intervention, but he *did* know better. At least about some things, if not many others.

It took a good few minutes for his vision to clear and the twinkling shine of stars to crystallise from the blur of the night. Thanie remained chillingly motionless, her rasping breath proof that she was indeed alive, even though she might wish she weren't. They needed her for their plan to succeed, but he wondered if he'd regret bringing her back to where it all began. They were in her domain now, at *her* mercy. Loge and Lidan huddled nearby, their low voices lapping at the edge of his awareness as he pulled himself up to sit.

The roof of the building he found himself in, was missing, though intentionally so. Around them stood a garden, neatly tended but empty of people, the rest of the structure standing dark and abandoned with no signs of life beyond closed doorways and echoing corridors. Ignoring the lashing sting of the handprint burned into the back of his neck and the deep ache in his bones, Ran gaped. Had Thanie actually managed to land them in Wodurin? Had she actually done it?

'Where are we?' he whispered in a hoarse gasp.

'Home,' Thanie coughed in reply.

'Home *where*?' Lidan asked.

'The only place that ever felt like it.' Thanie's head rolled to look in Lidan's direction. 'Your grandparents' city house in Wodurin.'

Silence washed through on the breeze. Loge sat at Lidan's back, holding her upright, Thanie trembled on the ground. Loge seemed less bothered by their mode of travel, carefully surveying their surrounds. Ran felt as though his insides had been yanked out through his balls and shoved back in through his navel. His stomach churned and his head, jaw and teeth ached. Every few seconds his body shuddered uncontrollably before settling for a few beats then shivering again.

'I have grandparents?' Lidan blinked slowly. Eyes wide in the gloom, from this vantage she looked like someone had slapped her with a wet fish.

'I assume they're still alive.' Thanie moaned and pulled herself up to sit, brushing her hair out of her face. 'Doesn't look much different from the last time I was here. Trees are taller. That fountain is new. No one's home, though.'

'Where are they all?' Ran asked, fear running down his back like a drop of icy rain.

Clutching her stomach as if about to retch, Thanie staggered to the fountain and splashed her face. Gasping with relief, she leaned back on the lip of the stone pool and turned into the breeze. 'They don't live here all year around. It's tended by a housekeeper, so we can't stay long.'

'Why come here?' Lidan's question brought Thanie to a pause, memories flickering in a faraway stare, images no one else could see.

'My parents rarely came to Wodurin… My father would when required by the Assembly, but never my mother. She despised the place. They didn't keep a house, not even for those occasions when Lord Orel was here.' She sighed and threw a glance at the shadowy corridors around the atrium garden. 'I'd stay here with your mother's parents, and your mother of course. My aunt was a warmer woman than my own mother, and that's saying something. Lady Mediia was about as cuddly as a cactus.' Her finger circled the air, pointing at the missing roof. 'This should be closed now the weather is turning toward autumn. Something is amiss.'

Ran's gaze followed Thanie's as the four of them caught their breath. It was quite unlike the building style of Usmein or Kotja and a whole world away from the timber and clay huts and halls of the South Lands. If it felt alien to him, he couldn't imagine Lidan and Loge's disorientation. Any atrium in the mountain cities would have been securely roofed, sealed tight against the wind and snow. Ran doubted anyone with a more menial income could afford such luxury. The cost of heating the place would be extraordinary in the darkest winter months.

All the visible doors were closed tight, except one. Shoving away the insistent ache in his joints, he staggered over to peer through the entry. A darkened sitting room waited silently on the other side.

Ran frowned, narrowing his eyes against the gloom. Thanie was right—something was amiss. Cushions had been tossed in a jumble on a pair of day lounges, a bowl and ewer left on a table beside them, out of step with the general decoration of the room. A musty, acidic odour—like food scraps left moulder—permeated the chill air.

'Someone's been here recently,' he called back to the others.

Thanie shuffled to his side and pushed past, running her finger over the bowl and scanning the tumble of pillows. The seat cushions from the day lounges were skewed and a brazier of cold coals stood beside a fireplace that had been ignored. Thanie disappeared into the shadows for a moment, glass bottles clinking before she re-emerged with an empty vessel in her hand. 'My uncle's favourite. There's the remains of a meal gone mouldy. Someone *has* been here, but not in a few weeks, maybe longer.'

'Your aunt and uncle?' Ran asked. It seemed the only likely answer but it sat wrong. This mess wasn't the leavings of the owners.

Thanie shook her head. 'They would have staff to clean up if they were here. And they would use the underfloor heating, not a brazier. This is someone who needed a place to hide and kept to one room.'

She turned, searching for something Ran couldn't see. Pushing past again, she limped out to the portico and off into the house. Leaving Lidan and Loge to orientate themselves, he followed the witch, glancing down corridors as she tried the latches on a series of doors.

Eventually they found the kitchen and a gut-clenching stink hit him as the door swung open. Biting down on a mouthful of bile, he held onto his stomach through sheer force of will. Thanie put her hand to her mouth and nudged a storeroom door open with her toe. The thick stench of death wafted out, coiling up Ran's nose and scraping down the back of his throat. His stomach heaved again, and he cupped his sleeve over his nose.

A corpse sprawled on the storeroom floor, molested by a cloud of buzzing flies and crawling with a black mass that gave it the illusion of movement despite the decay. It was hard to tell what it was in the half light, the only illumination coming from the moon shining beyond the kitchen windows. The body's mouth gaped in a silent scream, pallid skin sinking back against its bones like thin cloth stretched too tight over the ridges of a frame. The muscles of the hands clenched into gaunt claws, stiff and gnarled in death. Tucked away in here, the dogs and birds hadn't had their turn, leaving the limbs largely intact.

'Lower your veils, Ran,' Thanie said nasally through her hand, blocking her nose against the smell.

He did as asked, and immediately regretted it. A bright aura of thaumalux flared, a steady stream of throbbing multicoloured light weaving through the kitchen and back out again several times over. A bright handprint painted the neck of the corpse, the sure sign a spell had been deployed for murder. Frequency magic vibrated the air until it shimmered, the residue of incredible magic he was certain he'd never seen the like of before.

'There's thaumalux *everywhere*,' he muttered in awe. Whoever left this trail was literally brimming with power. It outstripped Thanie's and his own, more powerful again than Eian and Zarad and half the Hidden Keep's magic-weavers combined. The sheer intensity was almost too much to behold, and he shuddered to think what it must feel like to carry such a force within. He'd struggled for weeks to bear his own growing power, a weight he'd only just now begun to wrangle with ease.

'Recognise it?' The witch turned storm-grey eyes on him and for the first time since they'd arrived, Iridia flickered at the edge of his perception.

'Vaguely.' It had a familiar sheen to it, a rapid pulse rather than the slow steady beat he'd come to know in Thanie.

She was here. I can smell her... Iridia whispered, faint and weakened by his loss of power in their travels.

'It's Sellan.'

Thanie gave a slight nod. 'Stronger than before, or the same?'

He didn't have to plumb his memories of Tingalla to recall the trace of magic Sellan had left behind. As Thanie cut her bonds and let her loose on the world, her thaumalux had surged back to life and with it the unmistakable signature of a mage more powerful than he'd ever encountered. 'Much stronger. She's more powerful than I thought a person could get.'

'That's because she's close to as powerful as any person *can* get without killing themselves.' Thanie pointed the empty liquor bottle at the corpse. 'That's the housekeeper, which explains the mess. They must have stumbled in on her. She's covered her tracks as well as she could. It'd be easy to assume this was the work of squatters. It doesn't explain the two dirty glasses I saw in the sitting room, though.'

'Two?' Ran frowned, his eyes watering from the stench. 'She had company?'

'I wonder...' Thanie left the bottle and the corpse behind, limping back through the house to the upper floor. Rooms stood closed, only moonlight showing the way. A door like any other drew her attention and she pushed it open with a gentle creak, the room beyond as silent as a tomb. Thanie took a careful step inside, her hand hovering above a cabinet that could have been a dresser or an altar, possibly both. Thick candles stood cold amongst a scatter of trinkets and little statuettes he thought he recognised. One he certainly couldn't mistake took pride of place—a horse and rider—carefully placed at the centre of the collection. Thanie lifted it to the pale light from the doorway. 'This has been dusted.'

'What are you? An investigator?'

Thanie scoffed bitterly. 'They teach you a lot at the Academy, but not a lot of skills I had use for in the south.' Her gaze swept the room, picking out details he'd missed without realising. 'I *was* training to be an investigator, actually. I'd only inherit my father's lands and titles on his death. Until then I needed a career, so they had me pegged to lead investigations of derramentis mages.'

Ran's eyes narrowed and he folded his arms. 'But you don't have Sight?'

'Oh dear boy, you don't need Sight to find a derramentis. Their thaumalux is just like everyone else's. What you need is an eye for detail and a sense for human behaviour to predict what they might do in a given circumstance. That came naturally enough to keep me alive and out of harm's way.' She lifted the horse and rider effigy and waggled it at him.

'This belonged to a boy my aunt and uncle owned—a young, favoured slave I believe they purchased from an old friend. That's the story, anyway. Eddark, they called him. This was his statuette to Ortus. If his things are in here, he was elevated to freedman.' Their eyes met and Thanie shrugged at his unspoken question. 'This used to be my room.'

'Ouch,' Ran whispered. 'What's this got to do with the corpse and the bottle?'

'Sellan was here but she wasn't alone. Eddark is, or at least was, with her. He's been in here to take some things and couldn't help tending to his altar. It's the only surface that isn't covered in dust.'

Ran's heart hammered a little harder. 'We found her?'

'Not exactly. They haven't been here in a while. She doesn't fear discovery or else she'd have cleaned up the mess when they left. She's in the city somewhere, just not *here*.' Thanie returned the effigy to the altar and made a quick motion with her fingers, perhaps a sign to discourage the eye of the Rider. 'We should get back to Lidan and find somewhere to sleep for the night.'

'What then?' His mouth was as dry as a paper sheet. Was he ready for what was coming? Was he ready to face what waited beyond the walls of this stranger's house?

'Someone like Sellan can't escape notice in a city like this for long. If she's got the power in gift from the Dead Sisters, she's certainly not going to remain in the shadows. Someone will have seen her. Someone will know where she is and what she's doing. We find them, we find her.'

What remained of the night brought a sleep so heavy Ran wondered if he'd died. If it hadn't been for Iridia curling around his consciousness, he might never have opened his eyes. She sat on the bed, not far from his feet, her legs crossed, her shift tucked in her lap. Her curtain of moon-bright hair fell to her waist, and though she remained with him, her thoughts were far away.

'What is it?' he asked, not daring to move lest she disintegrate.

'Something big is happening here.' She stared out the window, the final night of the full moon slowly chased from the sky by the coming dawn.

'I know. Sellan's power is unlike anything I've ever seen.' He'd tried to explain it to Lidan, only to see her withdraw into herself and disappear into a room with Loge, her thoughts and feelings kept tightly contained. If she worried for her fate or his, he had no idea. He didn't doubt that her anxiety stemmed from wondering if her mother had grown so strong that nothing they threw at her would make a dent. It was certainly a thought that consumed him as sleep pulled him into its embrace.

'It's bigger than her,' Iridia said with a shake of her head. 'Something that could change the course of the continent. I can't see it, stuck here between both worlds, but I can feel it. The weight of it, the pull. There's a vortex that has us all in its grasp and we're too close to veer away now.'

A chill whispered across Ran's skin, the hair at his nape standing on end.

Iridia turned pale blue eyes on him, as cold as winter snow. 'Why come here at all?'

'To follow Sellan?' He frowned. She knew this. They all did.

'Not us; *her*. Lidan's right to question the story Thanie told you. Why come here? She's a fugitive, an enemy of the state. Nothing but death waits for her here. Even if it's a play for the throne, she has to know her chances are miniscule. There's an entire political apparatus in this city that has no interest in being ruled by a derramentis witch with an agenda.' Iridia shook her head again, driving Ran's doubt deeper as her words sank through his skin. 'Even with an army of dradur, who'd stand behind someone *that* unhinged? Who'd risk their lives for an unknown maniac in a coup? Surely it's better to back the mad dog they know than a wild mongrel from the wilderness.'

He'd pushed Lidan's questions away, stowed his own where he couldn't see them. He didn't trust Thanie blindly, but he'd swallowed her story with only the slightest hesitation. He'd trusted her because he thought he had no other choice.

'If she promises them victory...' Even as he said the words, they rang hollow. Thanie told them that with Sellan at the helm, the Woaden would wield a weapon greater than anything the world had yet seen. But Iridia was right. Lidan was right. The woman was a declared criminal. What kind of insane gamble was it to walk straight into the hands of those who'd sentenced her to die?

Ran had thought about it himself, insisting on returning to Usmein, but turned from the idea on better counsel. He hadn't seen it at the time, but it was a fool's errand, one he would never come back from if he ever had a mind to try it. 'Why lie? Why make up this tale about deposing the emperor if it wasn't her plan?'

Iridia gave him a piteous look. 'Would you have agreed to stop Sellan if you knew her goal *wasn't* to become an empress?'

In a whirl of bedsheets and blankets, he kicked his way from under the covers and stumbled to the door. Down the hall he found Thanie's room, bursting through without so much as a knock.

'Why is she really here?' he demanded. He'd spent too long wondering. It was time for answers, even if Thanie thought to keep the truth behind her veils.

The older woman sat by a glowing brazier, the golden light illuminating her face from below, drawing it into a mask of deepening shadow. Had she even been to bed? The covers looked untouched, and he pushed the strangeness of that aside as Iridia drifted into the room behind him.

'Who?' Thanie asked, her voice thick with too little sleep. She didn't turn from her view of the city through the window.

'Sellan.' He sighed heavily and rested his hands on his hips. 'You said she'd come here to unseat the government, to overthrow the emperor and take his place, but she's a criminal. They won't accept her—even as powerful as she is—just as my own people would never accept me in my father's place. Ronart might be a lunatic but he's a lunatic they know. There aren't enough lords in the Assembly who'd dare back a power grab by Sellan. The Congress would descend into open revolt at the mere suggestion. Then there's all this shit about the Dead Sisters, or the Morritae or whatever you call them, and gods know what else—'

'You take that name out of your mouth,' she snapped.

'What? The Morritae?'

'It isn't for the likes of you to speak.'

Ran leaned toward her, stone-faced. 'Don't change the subject. This isn't about a name. It doesn't matter what they're called—they're involved either way. Lidan doesn't think this is about power and neither does Iridia. Why tempt the gods like that? Why wouldn't Sellan just run off to the coast or the far south?'

That bitter laugh echoed against the walls. 'Macha save me, sometimes I wonder if I didn't back the wrong horse... Did it really take you this long? You probably wouldn't have made the leap at all if it weren't for the girls.'

Ran shivered at the darkness in her voice, the savage cruelty of the truth clenching her jaw. Hatred simmered there, carefully contained but only just. 'More fool me for trusting you even a little. What is Sellan here for, if not to take the emperor's place?'

'She's here to take his life, Ran.' Her gaze slid from the window and caught him in the corner of her eye. 'She's here for her revenge. Not simply on the Academy, and the Congress, and the whole fucking machine that tried to have her killed for simply being who and what she is. Not simply on the faceless men who pull the strings. But on the one man who took everything from her.' She lifted a single finger and held it up between them. 'One man, Ranoth. She's come for one man.'

'Tamyr.'

'The one and only.'

'And once she has him? Then what?'

Thanie shrugged. 'I doubt she cares what happens after. I doubt she's thought that far.'

Ran stalked across the room and shoved himself into her face, leering over her chair, hands clutching the armrests, shoulders bunching with thick muscle and too much tension. 'Then why the *fuck* are we here? Fuck the Empire and all the cunts who keep it afloat. Fuck them all. Let her burn them to ash.'

Thanie lifted a hand to cup his face and he froze, suddenly very aware that she was not only powerful, but a far more skilled magic-weaver than he could hope to be. He was a club where she was a razor blade. He was brute force where she was calm, deadly precision. He was hot, unbridled rage and Thanie was emotionless, creeping death.

'Dear boy, we *will* let them burn. We'll let her scorch them from the surface of Coraidin and dance amongst the embers. We aren't here to save them or the emperor. That monster could die a thousand agonising deaths and it still wouldn't repay the debt he owes, the toll for the pleasure he took in other's pain.'

Ran's eyes narrowed and Iridia shrank away. Her fear perfumed the air, the horror she'd felt in her last moments surging through him as though he'd lived it himself. His stomach flipped and he flinched from her suffering and the cold hate in Thanie's eyes. What Iridia felt was somehow a mirror to Sellan's trauma, passed like a baton from one woman to the other in the act of taking a life. Sellan hadn't escaped her pain or the memory of it by murdering everyone in Lackmah—she'd used it as fuel to spark an inferno.

'No punishment can negate what he did to her, Ran. Those wounds run deep. She won't ever recover, not even once he's dead. But she won't leave this world without ensuring he's gone first; sent to the Morritae for eternal torment, his soul sacrificed and offered on a platter for them to pick at for eons.' Thanie lunged and Ran staggered back as she came to her feet, blue fire igniting in her eyes as her magic flared. Was that the shimmer of tears catching the dim light of the brazier? Had that pain so readily handed out by Emperor Tamyr been limited only to Sellan, or had his reach stretched further?

He scrambled for a purchase on the truth. 'Why tell us she wanted him dead only to take his place?'

A dark smile twisted Thanie's lips, laced with so much sorrow it might have been a grimace. 'It doesn't matter *why* she wants it, Ranoth. It matters *how* she gets there. Her motivations don't matter if her methods unleash a reign of terror on this world unlike anything you could imagine in the depths of your worst nightmares.

'Once Tamyr is gone, Sellan has no purpose, no reason to care what happens next, no reason to control the fire she'll set in this city. She'll engulf the world and everyone in it, innocent or otherwise. She doesn't want to rule it, Ran; she wants to watch it *burn*. We're here to stop her destroying what's left after the fall. *You* need to destroy the weapon—the marhain she'll use to kill him, and any like him. *You* need to make sure she can never inflict her agony on anyone else, ever again.' Thanie stabbed a finger into his chest and the force of it lanced through to his core. Here was his purpose, the reason he'd come this far and risked so much. The thing he would stake his life against because it meant more than anything else. 'You're here to ensure no one ever suffers as Iridia and her people suffered. *That's* why we're here. We aren't here to win a hundred tiny battles, we're here to win a war.'

Chapter Forty-four

Wodurin, the Woaden Empire

They hadn't been allowed to leave the palace as darkness swallowed the day. A meal appeared, along with the whispering members of the emperor's court. Had he had his way, Tamyr would have kept Sellan and Eddark in his company all night, asking questions and demanding answers neither were ready to give.

Through a miracle of persuasion and speaking in the vaguest terms, Eddark kept the man satisfied and put him off until morning, discussing any other topic than the one the emperor truly wanted. In the end, and with great reluctance, Tamyr agreed to a private audience the following day to view the weapon Sellan had devised, away from prying eyes and overeager ears.

There was little Tamyr could do to force the issue. They hadn't brought the marhain with them in the tiny litter, and they were hardly something one could describe whilst doing them justice. Eddark swore on pain of death to fetch the weapon to the emperor's court once arrangements were made to view it safely, away from spies and those who meant the Empire ill. Much was made of these unseen eyes; faceless folk who moved in secret against the Crown. Tamyr took that baited hook deeper than Sellan could have hoped, eyes widening as he muttered drunkenly about watchers in the walls. Tamyr couldn't trust anyone. He was alone. Even his daughter plotted against him.

As easy as his madness made him to manipulate, it was alarming to watch it take hold, thrilling and frightening to see how swiftly he could be turned from one imagined foe to the next. He'd been eating out of Eddark's hand by the time they'd retired to bed. But instead of returning to their house in town, slaves herded Sellan and Eddark into a guest room at some unholy hour, the apartment bigger than any she'd seen in her life.

In the half light of a fire, as fatigue devoured the last of Sellan's energy and called her aching body to bed, they settled on a quickly drawn plan. Together they'd return to the house and load the marhain in the dray before driving it to the palace. It seemed an incredible idea, but Sellan could hardly walk them through the streets. If they were fast enough, they'd have Tamyr reduced to a broken ruin before anyone knew what was happening, then make their escape, leaving the marhain to their own devices within the palace walls.

Sellan managed little more than a fitful sleep after that, partly disturbed by worry about the creatures left in the rented house, and partly thanks to a presence emerging at the edge of her perception in the darkest hours of the night. A heart-pounding shift in her magic tore her from her dismal excuse for rest, sweat breaking across her skin.

She sat bolt upright in her bed clothes, shivering and alone. She made it to the window without falling over her own feet, leaned her flushed forehead against the cool glass. The city below carried on, eternal and uncompromising, the quicksilver meander of the Ullis River shimmering amongst the twinkle of lights. The presence at the edge of her mind was impossibly familiar, one she'd missed like a severed limb for more than a moon's turning.

Thanie.

She'd never had a sense for other magic-weavers before, not unless they practised spells within a few feet of her. Yet as she stood alone in the dark, she felt her cousin out there, somewhere in the world. She glanced at her hand, at the cracks forming in the skin of her palm, the red glow leaking from within, and she grimaced.

Urda's gift had a shelf life, a point at which it would outgrow her control, a time when her ability to use and contain the magic would be outstripped by the power itself. It was changing her and with it her perception of the world. Wherever Thanie was, her magic reached across time and space, calling her cousin home, yearning for the safety of her presence. It was a shelter Sellan could no longer rely on, and she dismissed it from her mind.

She turned from the window and attempted sleep. It lurked out of reach until Eddark rushed from the adjoining room, dawn blazing at his back. 'He wants to see you.'

Sellan had missed him in the night, but she wasn't about to tell him. Longing for his calm silence in an unreasonably miserable fashion was childish, even if he was her only anchor in this storm she'd created for herself. 'What is it?'

'Didn't say. Only that he wants to see you at dawn.'

Bundled out of bed and into the same clothes she'd arrived in, Sellan trembled beneath a cloak. She hobbled along behind Eddark, escorted through the palace by another nameless messenger child. At the door of a chamber, the child waved Eddark back.

'Only the lady, sir.' The boy stood between the medic and the entrance, shuffling sideways just enough to allow Sellan to pass. Eddark's expression was one of exasperated sympathy as she stepped beyond his help.

'I've called a Grand Council,' Tamyr announced before the door clicked closed. Sellan paused, glancing at the shadows, drawing her magic in tight.

'Sire?' she ventured, unsure if she'd heard him correctly.

He stood at a window, bathed in grey morning light, dressed in no more than bedclothes and a thick robe that dragged across the floor in a whisper. They were in a sitting room of some sort, lounges and low tables arranged at the centre, a battle scene painted on the ceiling in shades of gold and blue, the same runes as carved in his face decorating the borders. In a whirl Tamyr turned and began to pace. 'I want them all to see it. The weapon that will save us. I want the Assembled and the lords, the Congress and their incompetent mages, all of them—I want them to see what they failed to achieve. The solution they failed to deliver.'

Fuck. Panic tightened Sellan's chest. 'I'm flattered, sire, but I... Would it not be wiser for us to first present the weapon to a small, exclusive audience? Perhaps only your most trusted advisors?' If he made her do this publicly, the risks were so much higher, the chances of failure so much greater.

A wicked grin broke across his face, and he stepped toward her. 'Every proposal we've ever had drew doubt and dissenters. But this time, *this* time, I know you have what we need.'

Sellan let his enthusiasm sink through her exhaustion. She had to play this carefully. He was right where she wanted him, desperate enough to do just about anything... Except, it seemed, view her weapon behind closed doors. In private, she could control the situation, manage the risks and the outcomes. What he suggested meant scores, if not hundreds of observers. It meant more guards, more steel and magic to turn against the relatively small number of marhain. In his haste, Tamyr was steering her plans into territory she hadn't accounted for.

'What makes you so sure?' Sellan turned her voice cold. He was not accustomed to hearing no. Only sycophants and anyone too smart and slippery to pin a charge on survived around a man like this. It was a marvel old Tulius had persisted as long as he had. If she challenged Tamyr, questioned his thinking, she might just pry loose a thread she could tug on, a lead she could pull to bring him back to her.

Tamyr grew still. His breathing slowed as he looked her up and down.

'What makes you so sure *this* is the weapon you need? You haven't seen it. You don't even know what it does and yet you insist on inviting half the city.' Her eyes narrowed as she studied him. 'Why risk humiliation if you're wrong?'

The corner of his mouth twitched. 'Should it fail, the world will see you for the fraud you are, and I shall kill you.'

Sellan's stomach flipped, and she bit down on the urge to flinch away. 'Sire?'

'You left me wanting last night and I've had not a moment's rest since. Your employer is a crafty man, all smooth words but nothing specific. You're powerful beyond measure, I see that. I can feel it on my skin. You're like a blazing sun caught in the body of a woman, and that alone gives me hope that this is the opportunity we've waited for. And yet, I've been deceived before. Many have come offering the world only to deliver sand, hopeless dreams that slip through even the tightest grasp.' Tamyr stalked toward her—a wolf bearing down on its prey. She clenched her teeth, focused on the scar she'd left him with last time he'd made her feel that way. 'But should it succeed, should this weapon truly be the answer we seek—and I feel it is—then every doubter will be silenced, every plotter cut from their strings to fall at my feet.'

He traced a knuckle down her cheek, an intimate gesture laced with malice. His fingers traced her throat and she fought a shudder, crushing down the primal drive to snap his neck where he stood. She'd never manage it. He'd break her in a heartbeat. Even as strong as she was now, she was nothing against his skill and training. She never had been, and never would be, his equal. Brute strength was nothing against the whip-fast precision of an expert. The only thing that would finish him was a swarm of marhain.

'So, you bring this weapon, and you submit it to the scrutiny of the Grand Council.'

Sellan swallowed a hard lump of fear, unable to meet his eyes, instead glaring at the day dawning across the city. 'Where?'

'The games arena.'

She locked eyes with him then, too stunned to speak. For the length of a breath she wondered if he'd uncovered her secret, if he knew who she was under all this pain and self-inflicted mutilation. His gaze held hers, those ice blue eyes dousing the heat of her magic if only for a moment.

'If this weapon is as good as you say, then it deserves a showcase. It deserves to be shared with the world and the grateful public of the Empire.' His smile was a leering thing, dripping with desire barely restrained.

'Do it here,' Sellan said without thinking. Scrambling, she let her mouth run, words racing off with her mind in tow, hope dangling by a thread. She could salvage this. Regain control. 'Invite them to a demonstration in the forecourt. If you host it in the arena, you might as well hand the credit to the Congress or the Assembly. You know what they're like—men in high places with ideas above their stations are all the same. You're stronger than them. Better than them. Why go out to meet them on their turf? Make them come to you.'

His brows rose as he considered her suggestion and for blessed relief he moved away, pondering. 'And my people? What of them? Have they no right to see the victory I offer in their name?'

A snort of derisive laughter threatened to overcome Sellan. He wanted their adoration and nothing more. He hated the unwashed masses. He had no interest in those who lived in the Slicks, or the folk in the far-flung colonial towns. Neither had she until she'd found herself crawling in the mud beside them. There was nothing quite like a fall from grace to show you just how far up your own arse you were.

Sellan offered him a coy smile, an unashamed ego stroke that reached across the room and embraced him with false admiration. It did well to disguise her loathing. 'Invite them to see the glory of their emperor and the triumph he stands to achieve. Own it. *Claim* this strength, keep it close and your people will love you for it. Open the gates, invite them in. Allow them to revel in your supremacy.'

Inspiration flared fever-bright in his eyes, his imagination caught in the snare of her honeyed words. 'They will know it was me who brought this victory. And they will never doubt me again.'

Relief washed through Sellan in a bracing wave of goosebumps. She'd come so close to losing him to his whims. How he hadn't collapsed the Empire around them all, she had no idea, but for now his dysfunction suited her purposes. All she had to do was hold him in place for as long as it took to unleash her soldiers.

'You have until four bells. The court will be arranged.' When he didn't continue, Sellan glanced up, hoping for a dismissal but finding herself locked in the grip of his malicious gaze. 'And you have your warning. Fail me and your life is mine to do with as I will. Is that understood?'

She eased her aching bones into a shallow curtsey and averted her eyes for fear he might see the fresh deceit lingering there. 'As you command, my lord.'

Thanie hurried back through the gates of the house yard, her eyes on the ground, ignoring Lidan and Loge as they stood sharpening their blades by a small stable. It was the kind of yard where Lidan imagined there should be horses and wagons and tines tending the household's needs. Instead it stood empty, a bitter north breeze whistling across the cobbles.

The sun shone, though its light held no warmth, high cloud racing to block out what little relief it did offer from the cold. Lidan shivered into her cloak, her belted tunic and trousers pilfered from the bedrooms of her grandparents' house. Loge watched the witch cross the yard, her veil held tight in one hand to keep it from blowing off. 'What's she up to now? She's been gone all morning without a word.'

Lidan scraped her knife loudly across the whetstone then tested the edge against the pad of her thumb. It felt good to tend her weapons, a simple pleasure found in the calm before the storm. It was a task they'd completed together a thousand times before, but one she'd missed like a vital organ when Loge died. As long as she didn't think too hard on the surreal course of events that had brought him back, Lidan could almost pretend none of it had ever happened.

Almost.

'You won't ever trust her, will you?' Lidan asked, squinting against the glare of the midday sun.

'Do you?' he countered. Lidan watched Thanie disappear inside, ignoring the waft of rot from the wrapped body they'd dumped on the midden for want of anywhere else to put it. 'For all we know, she's led us straight into a trap.' Loge spat dust from his mouth and pointed a hatchet at the kitchen doors. 'She's nothing but secrets and deceit.'

Ran's dawn revelations confirmed her suspicions about Sellan's reasons for coming here. Had Thanie thought Lidan or Ran would turn from the task of stopping Sellan if they knew why she really wanted the emperor dead? Did she think so little of them, that they would agree that Sellan's means justified her ends or reasons? What Lidan still didn't know was the extent of the trauma that lay behind her mother's actions. She wasn't sure she wanted to. But Loge was right to be suspicious of Thanie. They all were. There was no telling what else remained hidden in that woman's heart, but what choice did they have?

'I'm not sure—'

'Lidan!' Ran called from the top of the kitchen steps. 'There's news.'

She glanced at Loge and received a quizzical look in reply. Sheathing their weapons, they followed Ran into the house, the warmth of a fire a welcome relief from the bite of the wind. They'd abandoned any hope of stealth in favour of not freezing, ignited the kitchen hearth-fire and hoped no one would notice the column of smoke drifting from the chimney vent.

Ran gestured to the witch. 'Tell us what you saw.'

Arms folded across her chest, eyes on the flames, Thanie didn't immediately respond. It was only when Lidan caught Ran's eye, wondering if she'd heard him, that the woman sighed heavily. 'Something's going on out there.'

Lidan's brows drew together and the three of them shared a look as Thanie held her own counsel.

'The upper city is in a state. I'd guess something to do with the imperial family, a wedding or the like, but the streets aren't decorated, and the crowds aren't in the right places.' Thanie shook her head. 'Someone said something about an event at the palace this afternoon, but it doesn't make sense. The arena is for public gatherings; the forum the next most suitable place. The palace isn't open to the public. It hasn't ever been...'

'What kind of event?' Lidan asked.

Thanie's confusion and distress were evident in the deep lines of worry around her eyes and mouth, her fingers pale with anxiety as they grasped her elbows tight. 'A display. A show, some are calling it.' Her finger picked at the seam in her robe. 'It doesn't make sense.'

'If nothing else,' Ran ventured, 'it might give us a chance to eyeball this emperor, get the lay of the land.' He glanced at Lidan and she found herself nodding.

'If he's my mother's target, there's a chance she might make an appearance, if only for the same reason.'

'Would she risk making a move?' Ran asked as Loge perched on the edge of the table and began cleaning under his nails with his hatchet.

Lidan shrugged when Thanie didn't answer. 'She might. It depends if she's ready.'

As one they fell silent and watched Thanie, waiting for something, anything. Instead, she stared at the fire. 'She'll be there. If he's opening the gates to the public, she'll be in the crowd.' She looked at them each in turn. 'I can feel her. She's been here and she's still in the city. I just can't *find* her.'

Lidan frowned again. 'Can't Ran find her with his magic eyes or whatever?'

Loge snorted but the northern prince ignored him. 'There are too many thaumalux trails in the city. I already tried. Her mark is swallowed up as soon as she steps beyond the gate. If it were that simple, we'd have her already. I'm not the only one with magic eyes though.'

The statement dropped like a hot rock between them. Loge glanced around, his hands falling still. '*I* can't find her. I can only see intent, emotion. She'd have to walk right past me and even then there's a chance I wouldn't see her in a crowd.'

'So we're looking for a pin in the grass,' Lidan concluded, her heart sinking a little. She'd known this wouldn't be easy but held out some hope that between two magic-users and a man with an eye of the dead, they might have some advantage. As it was, they were rolling their dice and hoping for a better hand than their opponents.

Ran's chin lifted in a show of confidence Lidan couldn't quite match. Dread squirmed in her stomach like a basket of writhing snakes. 'This event is our ticket into the palace grounds at least. She obviously hasn't made a move yet, or they wouldn't be hosting anything up there. The city would be in an uproar if the emperor had been attacked. We might have made it in time to stop her.'

'Step carefully now, Ranoth,' Thanie warned, turning from the fire and pinning him with a glare. 'If we're doing this, you need to listen to every instruction I give you and follow it precisely. One wrong move and we end up in Tamyr's prisons, and once you're in there, you aren't ever getting out.'

CHAPTER FORTY-FIVE

Wodurin, the Woaden Empire

The four of them trudged up the paved road, the thoroughfare teeming with people as the sun began to dip toward evening. Three bells had chimed in the south of the city and Thanie's face had blanched before she'd bustled them out the gate and past ever-grander houses to the top of a ridge.

The size of the buildings struck Lidan the hardest. Only in Kotja had she seen anything so massive. How the stones managed to stay upright without toppling to the side, she had no idea. Some seemed unfeasibly old, as ancient and weatherworn as the tablelands and the Malapa, as timeless as the rivers and creeks and the Caine. Cooing birds with bobbing heads and lilac-grey feathers made themselves comfortable on the heads of statues, watching folk hurry past, garish colours painted on the faces of long dead leaders and famous rulers she couldn't name.

Her mother hadn't passed on anything of her culture or language or homeland to her daughters. Hadn't told the stories of Woaden history or mentioned anything of her family. What little Lidan knew, she'd leaned from Ran and Thanie and Aelish. Sellan hadn't even taught her to read the angular script etched on every wall and street corner, carved into plinths on the roadside and on signs above shopfronts. It was as if Sellan cut that part of her life off like a diseased limb, making her escape south and leaving the past to shrivel and die in her wake.

But the past hadn't shrivelled or died.

It had kept on living, just as it always would, and Lidan had followed her mother back to the centre of it, feeling as out of place and overwhelmed as she ever had. Lidan gripped the hilt of her knife for comfort, concealed beneath the fold of the cloak. She was jostled this way and that by folk in robes and tunics, women with their hair beneath veils and tines hauling curtained litters from one side of the city to the other. The noise and the smell were enough to level her, an all-out assault on her senses as they passed eateries and shops, everything from whole pigs roasting on spits to dainty collections of tables and chairs where people sat sipping wine from impossibly delicate glasses.

Her sword hung in a scabbard at her belt, one of the few concessions Thanie had allowed before unleashing them on the city. She'd bullied Lidan into a veil—a piece of fabric covering her hair that was long enough to wrap around her shoulders as a cloak—stating in no uncertain terms that they would attract all the wrong kinds of attention if she went about with her ebony braids exposed for the world to see. Lidan had asked why when her protests came to nothing and received a brusque retort about behaving like a woman of high birth and not a wildling from the bush.

Loge had a hatchet or two hidden on his person, and Ran had found a sword in a storage room, claiming it with a raised brow and remarking on how the blade's slight curve reminded him of Lidan's knives. Thanie, increasingly anxious, chewed her nails and snapped at anyone diverging from her plan, eyeing them like a batch of unsatisfactory cakes fresh from the oven. She'd sighed so heavily Lidan thought she might faint, then nodded with a grunt and led them into the heaving crowds.

Her silent judgement screamed an awkward truth Lidan tried to ignore— none of them were ready and they were unlikely to survive what they were about to attempt. Thanie's frustration was borne of not simply being forced to accept that knowledge, but the realisation she had no time to change it. This was what she had to work with: a barely trained mage prince, a knife-wielding, monster-killing southerner, and a once-dead ranger. Their prospects, when faced with the reality of what Sellan had become since leaving Tingalla, were low.

Very low indeed.

And yet, Lidan set her jaw and walked on.

At the top of the ridge, the slope flattened to a gentle rise, angling toward a structure so enormous it defied the mountains themselves. Open commons full of gardens and cultivated copses of trees and chattering fountains brimmed with people moving to the palace gate, a steady stream of humanity abuzz with the mystery of what had prompted this apparently unprecedented invitation.

'The crowd seems reasonably happy,' Lidan commented to Loge, keeping her voice low and holding her veil between her fingers. It acted like a sail, catching every breath of wind across the open space and pulling at her neck.

Loge glanced around, tucking a stray lock of dark curls behind his ear. Sunlight reflected in the smooth obsidian of his dead eye and she marvelled at it, affronted and fascinated at the same time. 'There's little malcontent here. Just excitement and wonder.' He turned to glance at Thanie, stalking ahead of them. 'Except for her. She's a gibbering mess.'

'And Ran?' Lidan asked, not daring more than a whisper.

'Steady. Alert. His ghost is a bundle of nerves.'

Lidan baulked and stopped dead in her tracks. 'His ghost? You can *see* her?'

His expression flat, he nodded. 'Of course. She's nothing *but* energy and intent. And magic. She's held here by his power. It's like a thread through space. It's thin though, tenuous, like it's been held too long under tension. She hasn't got long.'

Lidan reached for his arm and stepped closer, her mouth running dry. He spoke as though he were commenting on the weather, as if what he saw should have been obvious to her already. It wasn't condescension, just a simple statement of fact. 'Long before what, Loge?'

'The thread snaps.'

Her heart gave an uncomfortable thud and kicked the breath from her chest. Thanie had said Iridia would have to choose between this world and the next. She'd never said why. Perhaps she hadn't known. Lidan threw a worried glance at Ran's back and not for the first time wished she could see what he saw. Did *he* know? Did he have any idea his constant companion was at near risk of being ripped from her threadbare existence on the mortal plane? Perhaps *this* was what weighed on his mind on their journey from Tingalla.

'How long? she asked in a hoarse whisper. She hadn't exactly enjoyed Ran's company in the few days before Loge's death, and he'd tried her patience and trust more than once. Despite it, they'd become closer friends than she could have hoped. He'd saved her life more than she could count, and she'd done the same in return. She loathed to think what losing Iridia might do to him.

Loge shrugged and sucked at his teeth. 'Days, I'd say. Maybe less. He's strong and she's clinging to that. Dennawal will come for her soon. He's left it alone to keep Ran on task until this is over. He won't leave it for long after.'

'Fuck this fucking shit…' Sorrow and anger welled in Lidan. Just as she thought to find her feet, something else swung through to knock away her toehold on hope. 'Why? Why can't any of us just have something small for ourselves, something we can keep safe without fear the world will come and snatch it away?'

Loge's expression shifted and he tilted his head to one side, jostled again by a passer-by. It was a curious, perplexed look. Had he left behind the part of him that understood why such things might matter to people like her, people who still had most of their soul intact? 'Because that's what life is, Liddy. A fight. Anything worth having is worth fighting for.'

'No,' she replied, adjusting her cloak with an aggressive tug and wishing to all the ancestors she could burn this infernal veil. 'That's just horse shit peddled to make suffering seem like an acceptable way through life. People deserve better than that. They deserve peace and happiness and safety they don't have to bleed for. They deserve a life without fear of monsters or cruelty. That's why we're here, isn't it? To preserve the balance? To stop *exactly* that?'

She thought she saw the twitch of a knowing smile as she turned to hurry after Ran and Thanie, their backs almost lost in the distance and the crowd. She thought she saw his amber-hazel eye gleam with triumph and she ignored it, revelling in the rage, bathing in the deluge of determination.

They would prevail today and every day after because they'd *earned* it, and no fucking god or spirit or puffed up, self-important deity was going to take that from them.

Not while she still drew breath.

The gate to the palace stood open, folk bustling through to find a place on the tiered seating. Shoved against the internal walls, the hastily erected stands creaked and moaned, the press of bodies almost too much for the timbers to hold. Someone had gone all-in on the preparations—banners snapping in the wind beside flags of many colours, strips of fabric and pennants whipping with the breeze.

Most prominent among them was a banner of dark blue, the stylised face of a snarling dog picked out in moonlight thread on a midnight field. There were others: greens, yellows, deep russet reds, all emblazoned with a distinct emblem.

Thanie pointed at one with a snake coiled on black. 'I'm surprised he still shows ours. Protocol dictates, I suppose. Though I don't doubt he wishes he could shred it after what Sellan did to him.'

'Ours?' Lidan asked, raising her voice over the thrum of the crowd as they wove toward the western wall.

'House Corvent is my father's family,' Thanie said over her shoulder. Ran shunted through the throng ahead of her, looking for a better vantage. 'Your mother's uncle sits at its head. We're some of the few still left of the Burikanii tribe. Many died or left the country after the Unity Wars. Many more are too embarrassed to claim the name of a once great tribe brought low. The rest of us wear it like a badge.' She said the last with a smirk and a wink, a twinkle of pride in her eye.

Though she'd been separated from her people for decades, there was an air of homecoming to Thanie. She moved with confidence, not hiding her face or shying from notice as she had in her role as the Crone. She didn't have to conceal her magic either, and Lidan wondered if Ran felt the same freedom. Had he even realised that no one here cared?

An archway appeared in the base of the wall, tucked behind a stand of seating, and Ran ushered them into the icy shadows beneath the tiers. 'There should be steps to take us up to the parapet. There'll be a better view up there. We aren't getting into any of those stands.'

The structure above Lidan groaned ominously and she flinched away. 'Not sure I'd want to. Looks like a disaster waiting to happen. Didn't anyone check how many they could safely—'

'Tamyr doesn't care much for the common folk or their safety,' Thanie put in. 'You haven't seen the Ullis River yet. It's about as hygienic as a privy pit and has about the same viscosity.'

Lidan's throat clenched at the thought, and she screwed up her nose. 'Lovely.'

Ran snorted a dry laugh and led them into the archway, then down a corridor to the base of a stairwell. They weren't alone in seeking a higher vantage and they shuffled and jostled up and out onto the top of the west-facing wall, right above the gatehouse. Lidan's breath caught as the immense courtyard stretched out below. Crowds ebbed and flowed like water, crammed in to get the best view, straining to see over each other's heads.

On the far side of the courtyard, a dais stood near the palace steps, a fabric canopy sheltering a collection of plush seats. The chairs were empty, guards standing at attention between the crowd and the stage. Much closer to the dais than the wall, an empty area stood cordoned off by even more guards.

The mob maintained a respectful distance from the guards and the cordon despite the crush. In their eagerness, the atmosphere lifted to something like a festival or feast, not so different to when Isordian traders had arrived at Hummel in Lidan's childhood. The nearest thing she could offer in comparison was the Corron, where hundreds of clansfolk had come together in one place. It was such a rare thing they couldn't help their excitement, despite the grim reasons for calling it in the first place.

In the centre of the space, surrounded by stern-faced guards in muscular chest armour, a large dual-axle wagon stood abandoned. There was no horse, and a dirty grey canvas lay over whatever was in the tray.

Lidan glanced at the others, their position against the rampart wall secure as people shuffled past them. 'I don't get it. There's nothing to see.'

'Yet,' Thanie replied. Lidan followed the witch's gaze to the top of the palace steps. 'He'll wait until they're screaming his name before he comes out. He'll whip them into a frenzy before he gives them what he's invited them to see.'

Apprehension settled hard in Lidan's belly. 'He risks a riot?'

The crowd below were already on edge, primed by rumour and the unexpected thrill of entering a space they'd never been permitted to see. Rousing them further seemed folly of the worst kind.

Thanie leaned close to Lidan's ear. 'Because he likes to watch them bleed. Turn around.' She did as commanded, dreading looking out over the sprawl that was Wodurin. 'See those circular structures over the river, near the building that looks like it has tits on its roof? Those are the games arenas. The killing fields. The bloody pitches where Tamyr and every emperor since the first have watched criminals and innocents fight for their lives and the entertainment of the masses.'

A chill shivered through Lidan, her hands itching for weapons she knew she couldn't draw lest she risk an arrow in the eye from a well-placed guard.

'I need you to bite this idea and hold it, girlie. This is a man who would swim through the blood of nations if it made his dick hard. He'd burn us all in our sleep if it made his morning more agreeable. He'll turn this mob on itself and drink to the sound of its screams just because he's bored. He doesn't give a fuck about anyone but himself. Never has, never will. You watch him and tell me I'm wrong.'

By the time someone appeared at the top of the palace steps, the mob were singing, cries and cheers rising from their ranks as a figure stepped from the shadows and into the cool sunlight. He was a tall man, reasonably lean, with bright blond hair. That was about all Lidan could see from this distance as he waved and swept down to the dais.

Lidan's feet and back ached but the crowd seemed to forget any discomfort at the sight of the man and his entourage making their way gracefully to the sheltered seats, accepting beverages from offered trays. There was a young woman—not much older than Lidan—and a collection of men, all in variations of the same white robe with blue edging. The blond man's outfit was by far the most extravagant, his throat adorned with a thick, yellow-metal band that caught the light like a mirror. Beside her, Thanie stiffened. That sharp intake of breath could only mean one thing.

Emperor Tamyr had arrived.

A group of a dozen men, bound by leather straps at their wrists, were led into the empty space between the wagon and the dais. Each bowed to the emperor and the young woman, radiant with apathy. Lidan wondered if she was even aware of where she was as the men had their bonds cut and arranged themselves in pairs.

Cheers became jeers and a horn sounded. Drums beat steadily behind the stands as the men turned on each other, hands clenched and teeth bared. Lidan jerked back and stared at Thanie, who rolled her eyes.

'Is this it?' Lidan asked, incredulous. 'We came all this way to watch prisoners fight each other?'

'No,' the older woman said with a shake of her head, a pair of ornate earrings clinking. She'd done her best to dress like someone who was meant to be here. 'This is just a warm-up to the main event. Whatever it is has something to do with that cart.'

The fighting didn't last long, a man from each pair falling quickly to his opponent and the victor kneeling before the emperor. Silence swept the gathering as a guard approached Tamyr, who turned from a conversation with a man at his shoulder. The guard's words were lost in the wind, but Tamyr came to his feet and surveyed the kneeling group, turning to converse with the guard again. He nodded, pouting a little as he considered.

As quick as he'd stood, he waved a hand and the guard gave a signal. As one the men sprang to their feet and fell upon each other, an all-out brawl erupting. Wild in its violence, the men tore at one another with their bare hands, rending skin from muscle, throttling and kicking, biting and thrashing.

One man, bigger than the rest, loomed over the group and started snapping necks, dropping his opponents in shuddering heaps of twitching flesh. His cold progression continued until but one foe remained, a wiry prisoner who looked barely strong enough to lift his own weight. His hands dripped with the blood of another, their windpipe and major arteries laying in a bright puddle at his feet. The thin man looked for a moment like he might try to flee, but the crowd surged against the cordon, and he flinched away.

With a scream of desperation, he flew at the big man and leapt at his head, tackling him to the ground and tearing him apart with the savagery of a starving ngaru. Had Lidan not seen the man walk calmly from the palace, she could have mistaken him for one of the creatures her mother made so many years ago. The mob roared their appreciation and Lidan fought the urge to throw up. The emperor grinned, perfect white teeth flashing as he laughed at a joke from his followers. He nudged the young woman but she didn't glance up, examining her nails as if they'd only just grown out for the first time.

The thinner prisoner eventually stood panting and bloody over the corpse of the other man, stumbling to kneel at the foot of the dais again.

'Does he win something?' Loge asked in a low voice.

'Wouldn't bet on it,' Ran replied. He nodded at the mob and a chant sprang spontaneously from within. 'My Woaden is a little rusty but I think they're calling for Ortus?'

Thanie nodded, lips a grim line of disdain as the emperor stood again and examined the victor. 'They believe the emperor a god, in communication with the lord of the dead. They think Tamyr speaks for him.'

'And does he?' Weirder shit was possible, and no one even blinked at Lidan's suggestion.

The witch nudged Loge. 'You've met him. Does Ortus strike you as someone who would bother with a pissant little dictator like Tamyr?'

'Not on his worst day.' Loge's top lip twitched. Tamyr made a signal with his hand again and the guard's short sword ended the prisoner where he knelt. Evidently the gods had decided he was not worth saving.

The roar of the crowd only died when Tamyr lifted his hands, standing at the edge of the dais and waiting for calm. He got it. The mob fell to a silence Lidan would never have believed so many people were capable of.

'My people...' Tamyr began, letting the subsequent ripple of reply fade away. 'You are so very welcome in my home. I'm sure you're all wondering why I chose today to open the gates of this divine temple, and you are right to do so!'

Another ripple, some cheers, an appreciative smile and a gentle wave. There wasn't even a trace of the joy in that smile, not even a shimmer of genuine mirth. Hot panic washed through Lidan and she gripped the edge of the rampart. As one the crowd leaned in.

'I bring glad tidings on this most auspicious day. I bring news of a great hope. A gods'-given gift has been sent to us, one that will wipe the Rebel Nations from our glorious continent and bestow upon us the rights and honours we have long been denied!' Tamyr's declaration echoed, and another cheer roared forth, quickly silenced. They wanted more, *needed* more. The anticipation, the genuine excitement for what was coming seeped through Lidan's skin, her heart rate rising, pulse thudding uncomfortably.

No one moved to clear away the bodies of the prisoners. No one seemed to notice a man emerge from the group on the dais, an elderly woman limping at his heels. He had dark blond hair and skin kissed by the sun. He dressed in a manner not unlike the rest of them, but he stood out as foreign, not of their milk-white breeding.

Thanie leaned forward, her crossed arms on the rampart. 'What's this now?'

The woman with him had long pale hair that cascaded from beneath her veil, her skin as white as the full moon, her back hunched and her limp as painful as Lidan had ever seen. She relied almost completely on a staff for support as the emperor stepped aside and swept his arm to encompass the newcomers.

'Defectors from the Rebel Nations!'

A whisper of wonder rolled through the gathering and people jockeyed to see. The woman stepped from the shade of the dais and Ran hissed a breath through his teeth.

'What?' Lidan and Thanie demanded in unison.

'Not even my veils can block out *that* much thaumalux,' he grunted, shielding his eyes. Somehow Lidan doubted that would help. 'That's—' He groaned and doubled over, coughing loudly enough to draw the attention of nearby spectators. Instinct took over and Lidan reached past Thanie to help, her hands on his shoulders as he leaned his forehead on the cold stone of the wall.

'What's wrong with him?' she hissed at Thanie.

'I have no idea!' she snarled through clenched teeth. 'I've never seen—'

'Lidan.' Loge's voice sliced through the confusion though he barely raised it above a murmur. She straightened, glancing up, reluctant to turn away from Ran's suffering.

'What?'

That same gleam flashed in his obsidian eye, narrowing as he glared at the space before the dais. He'd seen something with that dead eye and she followed his gaze to the woman stepping down to walk amongst the corpses. He didn't have to point because she saw it.

He didn't even have to speak.

He was wrong. It couldn't be.

The hair was wrong, the limp, the hunch...

Even as her mind clutched at denial, her heart recoiled, the truth as plain as the sun in the sky.

Their eyes met.

Paralysed, Lidan couldn't even swallow her fear. 'We found her.'

CHAPTER FORTY-SIX

The Imperial Palace, Wodurin, the Woaden Empire

'What can you see?' Thanie demanded of Loge, her voice heard across the chasm of Lidan's panic.

He had no chance to answer. Lidan lifted her arm to point, her free hand grasping Thanie's elbow. 'Look…'

Below, silence rushed through the crowd, curious onlookers turning to watch the pale woman move amongst the bodies of the fallen. She crouched slowly, painfully, and laid a hand on each in turn. Ran groaned when she did, heaving his meagre breakfast up to splatter on the masonry. Without turning to look, Lidan reached for his hand. Thanie shoved past to stand nearer to Loge.

'It's Sellan,' Loge muttered. 'She's altered her appearance, but she can't hide the intent beneath.'

'It can't be!' Thanie protested in a hiss of denial. 'It doesn't look any-thing—'

'It's her,' Ran said with another pained groan. He crouched tight against the wall, eyes shut, hand clutching his stomach as Lidan gripped the other. 'It has to be. She's doing something vile with that magic.'

He wasn't the only one reacting. Across the forecourt, scattered like game pieces thrown by a child, a handful of folk clutched at their heads and folded over their bellies. Magic-users like Ran, as powerful and as sensitive as he was, crippled by whatever Sellan was unleashing. Ran hurled again and Lidan gave his hand a squeeze of reassurance, tearing her eyes away to look at Loge. 'What's she doing to him?'

'What's she doing to *them,* more like.' He tilted his head, indicating the tumble of bleeding corpses.

Lidan watched, horror tracing up her back like the claws of a namorra come to steal her soul. 'No...'

A web of magic wriggled out from the woman's hand, crimson threads weaving into a cocoon around each body. The corpses gave a small jerk as the woman released her grip, then lay still again. A dream flooded Lidan's mind, swamping her vision. A body on a table, knives sewn into the hands, magic forced into the corpse until it shuddered back to life. It was an image sent to her a lifetime ago; an attempted revelation of the truth, a warning screamed in a language she hadn't understood.

She blinked it away, unwilling to witness the animation of that monster again, and licked at dry lips. Her gaze darted around the courtyard—the emperor looking on with rapt attention, the young woman beside him glancing up and realising something interesting was indeed about to happen. Courtiers and attendants shuffled forward on the dais, huddling behind the man with dark blond hair. He watched the pale woman with cool expectation, his anxiety betrayed only by the way he chewed at the side of his thumb, his stance slightly off-centre, as if preparing to move.

'Is that Eddark?' Lidan whispered to Thanie, the crowd around them hushed into transfixed silence.

For a moment, the witch didn't reply and Lidan turned from the scene unfolding below, inevitable and unstoppable from this distance, a disaster they were powerless to prevent now it had begun. Thanie stared, her grey-green complexion not much healthier than Ran's, tears gleaming in her eyes.

'Yes,' she replied, her voice thick enough to choke on.

'That's my *mother* down there?' Lidan demanded without a need for an answer. What had Sellan done to herself? Her hair and eyes had so changed that her own daughter would have walked past her in the street. Lidan's stomach churned, and she gasped as her heart skipped out of time, the moment tearing away from them.

They were too late.

Thanie offered her a sad grimace of a smile. 'I'd hoped it wouldn't come to this.' A tear slipped down her pallid cheek and a ripple of surprise washed through the crowd. At the centre of the corpse-strewn courtyard, Sellan turned to the dais and rammed the butt of her staff into the cobbles with an echoing crack.

'Your majesty,' Sellan called, her voice ringing against the walls. The air pressure shifted, popping Lidan's ears. She winced and Ran dragged himself to standing as the emperor took a tentative step forward. 'I promised you a weapon, and a weapon I have provided.'

Sellan's arm came up and the air began to buzz as though a swarm of bees had descended on the yard. The hunch in her back straightened with a hollow snap, the diminished stature vanished as the corpses began to twitch. A red glow bloomed in her hand and Ran groaned again. This time Thanie flinched too, clutching her temple. The only one who didn't recoil was Loge, his gaze locked on the witch as her power grew.

Lidan registered the change, pressure settling on her chest, breathless as the magic pooled in her mother unlike anything she had ever seen. The red glow expanded to a hot ball of furious fire barely contained within the cage of the woman's tense fingers.

'Ah fuck, get *down!*' Loge shouted. He tackled Lidan before she could move, knocking the others to the ground with her. An explosive boom thundered across the courtyard, the wall shuddering dangerously beneath them as they huddled behind the parapet. Screams rent the air, folk toppling from the rampart and down to the gardens below, their terror cut short by grisly snapping sounds that echoed in Lidan's ears. Some atop the wall managed to duck, just in time to escape the blast wave that threw dozens to their deaths.

Below in the yard, the sound of horror unleashed and Lidan scrambled back to her feet. The scene of devastation turned her stomach. Loge rose beside her with a grunt, taking in the destruction with a slack jaw and wide eyes.

The tiered seating had all but collapsed, crushing hundreds under the weight of a hundred more. Timbers splintered as the structures gave way, shrieking as the strain increased far beyond what they could stand. Folk rushed for the gates, wailing and bellowing, a stampede of thousands hurrying to escape whatever the fuck had just happened in the middle of the yard.

A single standing figure drew Lidan's eye—her mother—alone amongst the debris, arms outstretched. Blood red magic dripped from her hands, leaking from her fingers like the molten metal in Rick's forge. She didn't need Loge's dead eye to see Sellan's intent, to know her heart, to understand what she was about to do.

People scurried past behind Lidan, shoving wildly at each other. Several tipped over the edge in their hurry, screaming all the way down. More were crushed underfoot as the horde scrambled to escape.

Tamyr, to Lidan's surprise, stood petrified. He stared as his courtiers either fought to extricate themselves from the ruin of the dais or took the palace steps two at a time in a race to the doors. A few guards dragged the young woman free of the wreckage and bundled her away from the crowd, putting their bodies between her and the attacker they hadn't seen coming.

'What can we do?' Lidan gasped as Loge got an arm around her, using the other to heave Ran to his feet.

He didn't get a chance to answer before the first corpse shuddered to life. The reed-thin prisoner peeled himself from the cobbles and lurched to standing. Just waiting. Two more. Then another three. The largest amongst them thudded to his feet and loomed at Sellan's back. The dozen dead men leered at the emperor, arrayed around Sellan like some morbid guard of honour—a troop of ngaru.

They were nothing like the rotting monsters Lidan had fought so furiously in her homeland. These were a different breed—fresh, strong, under control. Their muscles bulged, their limbs elongated and weaponised by claws grown from the very bones of their hands. Their eyes glowed a sickly vermillion red, saliva dripping from savage fangs in their mutated jaws. They didn't sprint off into the crowd, and instead remained steadfast and silent, waiting on their mistress for instructions.

The cover on the wagon twitched back and a huge ngaru crawled out from beneath it, followed by at least a dozen more. They looked worse for wear—their skin the blotchy, mismatched colour of the unburied dead. Limping and crawling, the state of decay increased until Sellan stood with a veritable platoon at her back.

A broad-shouldered male from within the wagon swung a massive axe as an extension of his arm, the only one equipped with a weapon not of its own body parts. The axe head dropped to the pavement, ringing loud in the wind-blown forecourt. The others faced the emperor with only their deformed hands and teeth for weapons. Lidan didn't doubt for a second these were as deadly as any made of steel or stone.

Tamyr gaped, fear and wonder igniting his features. Was he smiling? 'This? *This* is the weapon?'

Lidan couldn't quite believe it. He wasn't afraid because he thought the ngaru were a gift? 'He has no idea...' she said to no one in particular. 'He thinks she's brought him a gift.'

'Oh yes,' Sellan replied over the terror of citizens still in the courtyard. They renewed their retreat with unbridled panic, screaming and scrambling over each other to the gate. 'Though, I fear you've misunderstood its purpose. Perhaps I was remiss. Perhaps I was *unclear.*'

Tamyr blanched, the first twitch of confusion creasing his brow.

Lidan's stomach lurched. 'We have to move!' Her heart raced but the others didn't seem to hear her. There was nothing to be done from here. The way was blocked by so many frightened people they might be killed in the crush themselves.

Eddark, nearer the emperor than Sellan, drew a knife and tucked it behind his forearm. Another man at his shoulder, in the simpler garb of a guard or servant, glanced around frantically before shit-bolting into the crowd. If he'd intended on assisting Sellan, he'd now changed his mind.

'What have you—' Tamyr dropped his question as the ngaru took a single co-ordinated step forward. Lidan's heart almost stopped completely. The emperor jerked back, a step closer to Eddark and his blade, still glaring at Sellan and the dead. The man's eyes narrowed. 'Who *are* you?'

'You're so fucking thick when you don't want to see the truth.' Sellan's voice rang with a smirk. Loge pulled at Lidan, drawing her toward the entrance to the stairwell. The parapet was almost empty now, deserted but for a few trampled wrecks that had once been people. 'Even when it stares you in the face.'

Tamyr retraced his steps and came to the edge of the dais, glowering at Sellan. 'Who the fuck are you to speak to me like this?'

'I am vengeance, Tamyr. I am the red dawn of your ruin. I am the blade that will bring your reign of incompetence and malcontent to an end. I am your worst fucking nightmare.'

Silence suffocated the courtyard.

Those still with a handle on their senses paused, trapped in the moment as Sellan drew magic to her again, shifting the air, tugging on the minds of all still remaining in the circle of her influence. She wanted them to hear this. She wanted witnesses. She wanted them to know, to see, to never, *ever* forget.

'I was always coming back, Tamyr. Always,' Sellan purred. 'I only gave you that scar to remember me by in the meantime.'

'*You?*' he spat. 'You dare come here, to my home? You *dare* stand in my presence?!'

Lidan's mother laughed—a hard, brittle sound, like the shatter of ice—the last of the thin veneer between who she'd been and who she'd become cracking away. 'Yes, it's me. Finally, you see. It took you long enough.'

At the door to the stairwell, Lidan resisted the pull of Loge's hand, drawing him to a stop with the others. They watched, paralysed by the expression of pure, unadulterated malice etched on Sellan's profile.

'You're supposed to be dead!' Tamyr screamed. Lidan thought he might have run if his legs would carry him, but he remained fixed on the dais, sneering with hateful venom at her mother.

'Oh, my love. I am.' The moans of the dying barely reached Lidan over the whistle of the north wind and the hypnotic sound of her mother's voice, distorted by distance and magic. 'I've been dead since the moment you laid eyes on me. Now I've come to return the favour.'

Sellan's long pale finger came up to point, a claw of strained fingers fighting the force of the magic blazing within.

She didn't speak.

The courtyard exploded into chaos.

The ngaru pitched forward and Eddark lunged with his knife. Tamyr didn't see it coming, only turning in time to deflect the strike into his side. He roared as the knife plunged into the soft skin above his hip. A blast of blinding blue light erupted from the dais and Eddark was thrown back into what remained of the crowd. The man vanished beneath the surge of folk rushing to flee, and Loge shoved Lidan down the stairwell.

'Go! Go now!'

Needing no more encouragement, she ripped off the veil and flung the length of cloth at the bottom of the stairs. Ran and Thanie hurried at her heels, their magic tugging on her senses as it pooled.

They burst from the ground floor archway into a maelstrom of suffering. Human screams punctuated the cries and yowls of the ngaru, and Lidan wove through the remains of the tiered seating to stand dumbfounded in the chill of the court.

Tamyr bolted, staggering with his hand clutching the knife wound, the few remaining guards hurrying with him toward the palace. There was no way he'd make it to the door in time to shut it with ngaru and Sellan at his heels.

By the time Lidan reached the empty wagon, Sellan and her monsters were halfway up the steps. 'Mother!' she cried, throwing her voice into the wind.

Sellan lurched to a stop, confusion twitching across her face. She looked half dead, gaunt and drained, red veins of power throbbing down her arms. Her eyes were pale, none of the verdant green remained, her auburn hair turned a shimmering white, closer to Iridia's. Had her new-found magic eaten away at her so ravenously or had she chosen this change; an elaborate, deliberate disguise? Two of the monsters stopped at her side while the others sprinted after Tamyr into the halls of the palace.

Confusion turned to anger and Sellan levelled the staff at her daughter. '*You* do not belong here.'

'I belong between you and whatever evil you think to unleash!' Lidan screamed back. Her knives sung from their sheaths. She would fight to her last breath with these blades. Until every last ngaru lay trembling at her feet. Loge appeared at her side, hatchets hanging ominously in his hands, a look of utter contempt in his eyes.

Sellan baulked, then grinned. 'Oh, he must mean business if he brought *you* back!' She waved at Loge, then Thanie and Ran. 'Kill those three. Bring her to me when you're done.' Sellan turned and vanished into the palace, leaving the two ngaru to stalk down the steps.

Lidan caught Loge's eye, nodding at the approaching undead; a drooling thing that looked like it might have been a man with broad, muscular shoulders and darker skin. A collection of tidy braids now hung loose; languid, grotty hair falling out in clumps from its manky, peeling scalp. It crouched low at the foot of the stairs, scraping bony claws across the cobbles with a threatening screech.

424

'Remember how to do this?' Lidan asked, very sure she'd never forget.

'Always,' Loge replied with a grin. It was the first she'd seen him properly smile since he'd come back, something about it warming and shocking her. He enjoyed this. He was looking forward to this. *This* was what he'd come back for.

Lunging, he took the hatchets to the nearest, biggest ngaru as Ran and Thanie lined up on the other. Ran's blade swung as Thanie drove it toward him. Lidan darted inside the range of Loge's weapons, coming up in the breath after his hatchet failed to connect. The ngaru flinched away, whipping around and snatching a length of lumber from the ruined dais pavilion.

Lidan blanched and staggered back to avoid the timber. Ngaru improvising weapons? What fresh shit was this?

The monster swung it like a club, charging with teeth bared. The muscles of its neck and shoulders bulged and flexed, the make-shift weapon whistling over Lidan's head and careening toward Loge with ferocious accuracy.

He ducked, avoiding the jagged end of the splintered wood, ramming the head of the hatchet into the creature's chest. Lidan took two quick steps onto the stage then launched off the edge, twisting in the air and spearing her knives into the creature's back as it recovered, looming over Loge. The blades caught and the monster arched, clawed hands coming up to grasp at her as the knives scored through its skin and down the edge of the spine.

Claws gained purchase, digging in hard at her shoulder. She screamed and bucked but couldn't escape the monster's grip. Loge swung again, following through with a kick to the creature's stomach that folded it in half. It bellowed and lurched violently, spinning and throwing Lidan off, ripping both knives out as she went.

She hit the cobbles of the courtyard with a crunch, rolling away from the ngaru, stars flaring in her vision as the air punched from her chest. The ghost of her broken collarbone lanced across her throbbing shoulder, an older injury in her hand spearing hot up her arm to her elbow. The grip on her knife faltered as she came to a stop, blinking to dispel the spots from her eyes. With a hungry gasp, she pulled herself upright, vision swimming. The ngaru roared at Loge, who kicked and punched where the hatchet was useless.

She regained her footing, spitting blood, just in time for Loge to bellow a challenge fit to wake the dead. His hatchet swung, sunlight glancing off the blade, then sliced the ngaru's head clean off. A foul, dark-purple liquid spurted from the severed neck, reeking of decay, splattering them both as the headless corpse stumbled and teetered.

It staggered toward them, hand outstretched, clawing uselessly, the club swinging wildly, holding on despite the fatal wound. Loge grabbed her arm and Lidan scrambled back, watching it fight the inevitable as Loge pulled her up the steps. He'd hardly broken a sweat.

Behind the determined, thrashing corpse, Thanie delivered a final blast that turned the scorched and smoking ruin of the other ngaru directly into the path of Ran's sword. He skewered it through the throat—up under its chin and through to the back of its skull. The wet crunch echoed in the silence of the empty yard, followed by a thud as the headless monster finally succumbed to its fate.

Breathless and sweating, Lidan stared at the last of the pair—its eyes glaring and its mouth snapping vainly, tongue lolling in and out as it slid down the sword to the cross guard above Ran's hands.

With grunt of exertion, he twisted into a half turn and wrenched the blade out through the side of the monster's neck, ripping flesh from muscle and spewing more dark-purple fluid over the cobbles.

'Is it just me,' Ran huffed, flicking gore from his sword, 'or were they harder to kill than the last lot?'

Thanie rested her hands on her knees and retched, but nothing came up. She shook her head, wiping a shaking hand across her mouth. 'Harder. Definitely harder.'

'Why?' Lidan demanded. Her legs shook, blood thundering though her head in a deafening drumbeat. 'How is that possible?'

'Fresher corpses,' Loge told them, nudging the closest with his boot. 'More powerful magic. The ones in the south were decaying for years. Could have killed some of them with a soup spoon.'

'These are as fresh as they get, and under her complete control.' Thanie nodded at the gaping palace door. 'The big one with the axe? It will control them if she isn't near. We need to kill them both.'

'This is fucking horse shit.' Lidan spat sour blood from her mouth. 'What is that red shit dripping from her hands?'

'Urda's magic,' Loge and Thanie replied together, glancing at each other then away.

'Great,' Lidan snapped. 'Just fucking great. Shall we find her before she fucks up anyone else's day?'

CHAPTER FORTY-SEVEN

The Imperial Palace, Wodurin, the Woaden Empire

Lidan.
  Lidan is here.
  Why is Lidan here?
  Lidan shouldn't be here…
Confusion tore at Sellan as she hurried in an agonising limp behind her marhain. The singular trail of blood left by Tamyr's wound became a stream left by many, screams of terror echoing through the palace. They rang along porticos and through colonnaded atriums. Doors slammed and weapons clashed in the distance, the final shrieks of the unsuspecting court.

Eddark had wounded Tamyr at the cost of being flung into the stampeding crowd. She had no time to look for him. She had one chance to strike, and she would take it, even if it meant acting for them both. She couldn't afford distractions. Not now. Eddark would never forgive her if she let this opportunity slip by.

She hadn't expected interference from her own daughter. Of all the people to follow her north, she'd never thought it would be Lidan. The insufferable Orthian boy, yes. Even Thanie. But Lidan? And the ranger who'd last been seen making friends with a rockslide? Those two she hadn't expected. They'd thrown her off her game.

The ranger most of all.

That black eye stared right through to her bones. Bored through her disguise to the essence of her being, that little shred telling him more than she wanted him to know. More than she wanted *Ortus* to know.

There was little doubt the god had sent him. No one survived what killed that man. No one came back with an eye of the dead without being properly dead to begin with. Such a gift lay only within the power of Ortus to give. Exactly *why* escaped her, her attention focused on hauling herself up a flight of stairs to the second floor.

Bodies littered the corridor, blood pooling, seeping across boards and into carpets and rugs woven in some far-off colonised province. She paused and glanced at the tangled limbs, the slack-jawed silent screams. She could make more. She *should* make more, but had she the time? Had she the energy, the strength? Sellan glanced ahead, in the direction of the cries. This was the living quarters, the very finest wing of the palace where the emperor kept his family and closest allies. Tamyr was here, cornered, but for how long?

She left the bodies, her thoughts reaching through the realms to Urda. *I will bring them to you. I will give their souls to your glory. I will give them all to you when my work is done. Give me the strength and time to do this final thing and you can have them all.*

Tamyr first.

Then that Orthian nuisance and her traitor cousin. What to do with Lidan, though? She couldn't stay in the city. Sellan would have to send her home, but would the girl go? She doubted it. Trying to make that child do anything she didn't want was like trying to redirect a river with your bare hands.

A snarling, semi-decapitated marhain greeted her at the junction of another corridor, pinned to the wall by a spear through the throat. Thick, indigo blood oozed from the wound. It was the female of her troop, the one she'd recovered from the corpse-snatcher's cart, though her features warped so grotesquely Sellan could hardy tell. Vacant, glassy red eyes glared with primal hunger, its jaw jutting out to accommodate the unnaturally thick teeth. The snapping and snarling eased as Sellan limped closer, eyeing the shaft of the spear. It hadn't severed the spinal column, only pinned the marhain to the wall to bleed and growl.

It whimpered and Sellan glanced up, her magic trembling like a spider sensing a fly caught in her web. The marhain lurched away hard, pulling vainly at the spear. Its eyes fixed down the corridor at Sellan's back, watching the source of footsteps on the floorboards.

Sellan sighed and turned. 'You're a much faster runner than I am a limper.'

The Orthian boy didn't appreciate her quip. Blue fire ignited in his hand and a pale light she knew well flared in his eyes. The shadows of his scowl deepened. 'This stops now, derramentis.'

Rage rushed Sellan. 'I am no such *thing*!'

She rounded on him, hurling her magic down the hallway. The floorboards rippled between them, splintering and shearing. They bucked beneath his feet, rearing up to knock him into a flailing backward tumble. Sellan's hands moved in a blur, lips twitching, words whispered, and wards drawn. She pushed her hands forward and the boy lifted, shoved by the power of her spell and thrown across the carpets like a child's skittle.

He throbbed with power now, more than he ever had in Tingalla. He'd been training too. The eyes gave it away—a side effect of an Academy technique for channelling and controlling one's fast-growing powers that was without equal in the known world. That he'd survived the training in such a short space of time was a testament to his strength and Thanie's insanity. To even attempt it was to risk both their lives.

More's the pity. She limped closer and glared down at the boy. It would be such a waste when she killed him.

Something new growled to her left and Sellan risked a glance away from him. The shimmering presence of a dead girl hovered off to one side, watching and waiting, brilliantly visible to her altered perception.

Sellan pointed her staff at the presence. '*You* aren't meant to be here either.'

The dead girl flew at her, skeletal features emerging from the air to snap at her face. Pure energy and malice, the ghost latched on, digging bony, decayed fingers into Sellan's skin. Sellan screamed and the ghost bit harder, a guttural roar only she and the dead could hear ripping through time and space, piercing her ears until they bled.

Sellan staggered, the clawing, hysterical ghost shoving and slashing from some in-between realm. Blood sprang from the cuts, savage marks slicing down Sellan's face, across her chest, shredding her clothes.

The butt of her staff came up, the shaft spinning. It smacked into the side of the ghost, a pulse of magic bursting down the length and throwing the dead girl across the corridor. Sellan dropped the staff and banked her power, pulling it to the surface and drawing aim on the recoiling presence.

She couldn't kill what was already dead, but she could make it wish it had remained where the dead belonged. A crimson flash ruptured the air, tearing it with a deafening boom. The magic ripped through reality. It collected the dead girl and blasted her far into the aether. Sellan didn't hear or see the crash on the other side. She didn't care to look.

The ghost wouldn't return any time soon.

A spasm of agony gripped Sellan's back. She arched, grunting out curses and sucking air through clenched teeth. Her fingers trembled and spasmed as she reclaimed the staff, leaning hard against it to regain her composure. Slowly, her vision cleared, and she loomed over the boy.

Calling him a child was, of course, an insult. He was in his twenties and taller than she was by at least a head, though he writhed painfully on the floor, fighting to regain his feet. Her magic sizzled across his skin and she called to it, pulling him toward her before dropping him back to the rug with a tortured cry. His hands tensed into claws, his back bowed, and Sellan drew on his strength. Gods knew he had plenty to spare, despite throwing him down the hallway like an unwanted doll.

A thought dug into her mind and she winced. If he was here, did that mean her daughter was dead? 'Are you the only one they didn't kill, little boy?' Sellan released him and he shuddered a breath of relief, groaning.

Then he smiled.

'No,' he muttered, his voice a thick, ragged gasp.

Sellan flinched. 'Then where are your friends?' she purred, hoping it was enough to disguise her surprise. Why face her alone if the others were alive?

He tried to laugh and instead coughed so hard she thought he might dislodge a lung. 'Hunting your monsters.'

'*What*?' she spat.

He hit her with a blast of power before she could recoil. Blue light engulfed her, tossing her straight into a wall. A mirror shattered at her back, a vase followed suit, and she crashed to the floor in a crumpled heap. Her vision stuttered as the Orthian staggered up and began to run, no longer a defeated child, but a mage with barely a scratch on him.

He hadn't come to kill her.

He'd come to distract her.

Somewhere in the palace her marhain began to shriek and Sellan's spine flared into a column of blistering fire, her scream tearing down the corridor in the wake of the running boy.

Ranoth sprinted.

Breath rasping in his ears, the scream of the witch of Lackmah echoed in his footsteps. He tried not to think of Iridia. Her presence was hardly more than a whisper of thought, his insides a chasm of dread as he raced past a struggling dradur and wrenched a spear from its neck. His hands came up as he spun, a sizzling blade of magic slicing through the creature's fleshy, deformed trunk.

It collapsed and he darted away, drawing his power back in as he hurried off at a wobbling run. Whatever the witch's magic had done to these creatures, it was somehow worse than anything he'd seen before. They were so hideously mutated they hardly resembled people. Iridia's corpse had been ruined by time. These had been desecrated by human will.

Ran threw a glance over his shoulder to the dark lump that was Sellan, thrashing painfully amongst ruined floorboards and gleaming shards of glass. He wanted to kill her. He'd thought about it as she stood over him sneering. He wanted it more in that moment than any other, his heart and head screaming for Iridia, calling to her beyond the veils. He wanted to tear Sellan apart.

But he'd promised.

He'd promised Thanie and Lidan he wouldn't try. Because he would fail. On his own, he stood no hope. With them at his side and Sellan weakened by the deaths of her dradur, he could take her.

He'd thought himself strong enough until he'd seen the firestorm of her magic. It'd been enough to turn his bowels to water and collapse him on the wall. The pressure shift, the weight pushing down on his chest, the throbbing pulse in his ears—all triggered when Sellan deployed her power in the courtyard. That was a force he could *not* reckon with—a force no human body should hold. He wasn't stupid enough to try and end her on his own.

He followed the screams, passing the bodies of unfortunate courtiers, servants, slaves and officials littered along the corridors, blood oozing in long, dark slicks. The maze of hallways led him to an atrium, and he raced out onto a mezzanine overlooking an elaborate garden. Trees and hedges obscured his view of the carnage below. It was an enormous space, at least four times the size of the enclosed atrium of the Usmein palace and open to the elements through the roof. What did these people have against perfectly good shelter?

Flashes of magic and cracks of thunder drew him to the southern side. A man and a cluster of terrified soldiers huddled in a loose circle at the edge of an artificial lake, short swords and spears aimed at every shivering shadow and whispering leaf. Three dradur lay twitching at the edge of the carefully cultivated trees, the defenders breathless and dripping with dark-purple gore. That victory had come at the expense of four guards, and others would be watching, concealed by shrubbery and statues.

'I can't believe I'm doing this…' he muttered. If anyone had told him a week ago that he'd be fighting the very things trying to kill the Woaden emperor, he'd have laughed in their face, then punched them in repayment for such an insult. Yet here he was. It was all he could do to stop himself backing away and letting them have at it. If it weren't for the horror that would surely follow, he would have. If it weren't for his need to weaken Sellan by killing the creatures, he'd have helped them in their pursuit of a despot who deserved no more than the grisly death the dradur promised.

Scanning the trees, Ran saw only what should have been there; the dradur too well hidden to be seen from above. The shadows grew longer now, the afternoon drawing closer to night. The north wind swirled down through the roof to bite at his cheeks, the atrium suddenly and eerily quiet, as if time itself took a breath.

Ran blinked away watery tears from stinging eyes and pulled in his power. Thanie, Lidan and Loge were down there somewhere, stalking the dradur through fruit trees and other elaborately shaped greenery. He dropped his veils and the atrium lit up like the sun had exploded. Flinching away, he wrenched the veils up and covered his Sight.

It was useless. Too many trails left by so many mages made the place impossible to read. He couldn't tell Thanie's thaumalux from the rest. Best just to throw himself into the fray.

With a grunt and a little more grace than he'd managed in Kotja, Ran leapt over the balustrade and landed with a soft thud, pulsing his power from his hands to temper the fall.

Silence reigned.

His sword came from its sheath with a sigh. A searching tendril of magic spooled out, hoping to touch Thanie's consciousness.

Instead, he found Tamyr.

Lidan rolled her bleeding shoulder and waved a hand at Thanie, urging her to fan out into the trees.

This place was ridiculous.

A forest had been cultivated indoors for some unknowable reason, fashioned to look wild while maintaining an air of order. Branches reached for the embrace of those nearby, planted in neat little rows many seasons ago, their trunks wreathed in shrubs and the ground carpeted with grasses and moss. Paved and pebbled paths wound through the shadows, glades opening around fountains and garden beds. It was all very pretty, and completely fucking useless.

With a scowl, she crouched at the edge of a small clearing.

Ran was somewhere nearby, the throbbing of his magic so strong even Lidan felt it vibrating the air. Loge picked through the undergrowth to her left, inching ahead. Through the shadows, the ngaru hunted.

Had she not seen it with her own eyes, she wouldn't have believed she could follow such creatures without them turning to attack. Their focus was arrow straight, blinkered, narrowed in on the man her mother meant to kill at all costs. Lidan didn't care whether the emperor lived or died. Her mother probably had a good reason for wanting his guts spilled at her feet, but that didn't change the fact that Sellan had unleashed evil to attain her goal. *That* had to be stopped.

'How many did you get?' she whispered at Loge.

He shrugged. 'Three or four. You?'

'Two.' She glanced in Thanie's direction. She was too far distant to ask without blowing their cover.

'Better catch up then,' Loge replied. He smirked and winked.

'It's not a fucking competition!' Lidan growled under her breath. By her count, there were at least a dozen ngaru, perhaps a few more, roaming the halls and the garden. And as far as she could tell they were under orders to hunt Tamyr.

Tamyr didn't strike Lidan as someone she wanted to save. There was a slimy sheen to him, as if shit just slipped off no matter what he did. Consequences didn't exist for a man like that. The gleam in his eye at the roar of the crowd, the flare of desire when they heaped adoration on him despite the tangible fear of offending him—all these things she'd seen before.

Tamyr had the same greasy, sly demeanour as Yorrell. It was the revolting taint of those who got what they wanted, took what they were denied, and cared nothing for the agony they left behind. That kind of stain never washed out, an internal rot one could smell once they knew what it was. Lidan had no earthly idea why her mother wanted this man dead, but a lingering sense of dread and the wafting stink of corruption gave her some inkling. These two had a past mired in darkness, and Lidan didn't want to expose it to the light.

Loge whistled. Lidan froze.

She saw it.

Hunched beyond the edge of the clearing, behind the bulk of a fountain. It wasn't as big as the others; short and pot-bellied with thickly muscled, stubby legs. The creature might once have lived a good life, without need or want for much beyond what was easy to grab. What remained of its clothes hung in tattered, grimy ribbons over slabs of deformed muscle bunching across thickened bones, clinging to the barest echoes of their stately origins. This had been a rich man before his death, someone who might have stood beside the emperor and not looked out of place. Beady eyes scanned the trees, vacant of humanity, bestial and ravenous, arms too long for the rest of the body, hands clenched in hammer-like fists at the ends.

What a wonderfully unpleasant thing this is. She edged closer to Loge along the border of the clearing.

The ngaru turned whip-fast and stared at where she'd been. Lidan froze again.

It hissed, spittle and dark-purple gunk sprayed into the clearing. It didn't break cover but gnashed its crooked, blackened teeth. Stooped and salivating, it began to stalk. Behind it, unseen in the seeping gloom, something else growled low.

What she wouldn't give for her bow right now. She set her jaw and tightened her grip on her knives. She wouldn't get to pick this one off at a distance. Tried and true methods were all she had. With a grunt, she launched from the shadows and went to work.

What have we here?

The voice slipped into Ran's mind like the cold, clammy hand of an unwanted visitor. He recoiled, turning his attention back to the trees.

Screams burst from the lengthening shadows. Dradur death shrieks and the cries of fighting ripped through the silence of the atrium. Lidan and Loge had found their targets, leaving Ran to linger at the margins, unsure which way to turn.

Without really thinking, he took a step to the right. The voice had come from this way. Tamyr's magic called from this direction. Perhaps he could do them all a favour and end the emperor while no one was look—

Don't be foolish, the voice sneered. *We could be allies, you and I.*

Not fucking likely, Ran snarled. Two more steps brought him to the clearing.

Across carefully trimmed grass and pebble-strewn pathways, Tamyr waited, guarded on all sides. Short swords caught the fading light, turned this way then that, swivelling to confront Ran as he emerged from the eaves. In their plumed helms and contoured breast plates, the emperor's guard looked almost comical, huddled around the man in a loose circle. 'Do you think steel will save you from them?'

'Orthian and all…' Tamyr caught Ran's accent and raised his brows, ignoring the question. What reason did he have to doubt it? Three of the monsters already lay cooling on the grass. It didn't matter how many soldiers he lost subduing them. 'Very interesting… That's an alliance I never expected. What's an Orthian doing fighting with a Woaden derramentis? You know she's a criminal, don't you? Mad as a bag of wet cats.'

Tamyr smirked and raised his hands. Blue lightning crackled between his fingers, a mirror to Ran's power. A few guards took a wary, if not minute, step away.

'I'm not her ally.'

'Then what are you? *My* ally? Have you come to save me from her wicked beasties?' The emperor's smirk deepened and Ran scowled. 'I didn't think so. What did she promise you? Money? Land? Freedom?'

Ran couldn't answer, trapped in a web of words, paralysed by their implications. He wasn't here to save the man, but would he stand by and allow Sellan's dradur to devour him? A power vacuum at the top of the Woaden Empire was the last thing anyone needed.

'I can promise you more than whatever she's offered. *So* much more. You needn't ever go back, you know. You could find a place here, away from that murderous bigot, Ronart, so bent on wiping out our kind.' Sickly sweet pity dripped from the sharp edges of Tamyr's voice. The guards didn't seem to hear him, their attention on the trees, watching for an even greater threat.

Tamyr never stepped from the protective circle, the confidence in his voice betrayed by the angle of his shoulders, turned to present a smaller target, his posture coiled to strike or run. He favoured his side, stained bloody from the knife wound struck by Sellan's accomplice.

His skin seemed paler than it should have been, pallid and wan, his eyes rimmed red, lips a thin, frustrated grimace. He had nowhere to go, and that injury would bring him down if his body didn't begin to heal on its own. The lake at his back had him cornered and by the fever-bright fear in his eyes, the emperor knew it.

A twinge of familiarity tugged at Ran. Here, he was surrounded by people just like him. The place teemed with them. Unlike his homeland where magic-weavers fled for their lives, here they were revered, even celebrated.

'Boy, you are fighting for the wrong side.'

Ran crouched lower, sword in one hand, magic igniting in the other. 'I doubt that.'

Tamyr grinned. 'The last words of a dead man.'

'Better dead than bending the knee to the likes of you.' His magic unfurled into a snaking rope. A hard flick cracked it like a whip across the clearing. It snapped against the legs of two guards, slicing through their shins in a bloodied spray of shattered bone. Screams lanced the twilight, joining the others, a chorus of denial and pain as dradur and guards alike met their match.

The remaining soldiers leapt forward, spurred into action as their comrades fell. Suddenly the young man before them was as dangerous as the monsters in the trees. Blood splattered and wild-eyed, they charged.

Ran didn't hear them coming.

Neither did the guards.

No one heard the calls over the cries of the bleeding guards or the roars of their comrades.

The trees exploded with dradur, and the clearing erupted into mayhem.

Chapter Forty-eight

The Imperial Palace, Wodurin, the Woaden Empire

Sellan made it to the doorway, the cavernous atrium opening as it had when she followed Eddark to meet with the emperor. She wished she knew where he was, wished she could sense him, but he was beyond her reach now.

White hot pain bloomed in the small of her back and she staggered, ramming her teeth against the back of her lip, the metallic tang of blood on her tongue. Another of her creations had been killed. Each one cost her, each time she staggered and gasped, another piece of her threadbare soul stripped away.

Too many to count.

She tried to track them, tried to tally how many she'd lost in the waves of agony; torrents of pain as unrelenting as the storm-whipped sea. Perhaps five, maybe more. She couldn't tell how many remained, her senses scrambled as she hurried into the garden.

They would have to be enough.

They were all she had. There was no time now to make more.

Screams and cries, the barking calls of her marhain in the distance. She sent a command, a directive none of them could fail to heed.

Kill Tamyr. Ignore all others. Kill the emperor.

She sent a vision of his face, hatred burning in her gullet as the pain of loss tore up her spine. The column of bone twisted as each marhain died, deforming in tandem to the sounds of fighting and dying. She was becoming her vengeance, the poison she wished upon Tamyr like a caustic draught she, too, had been forced to drink.

Where is he? she demanded of her second, the monstrous corpse-catcher fitted with the axe at the end of his arm.

Centre. Middle. Water. His size clearly gave no indication of his intelligence, but Sellan saw enough in her mind's eye to make sense of his gibberish. Tamyr was cornered, surrounded by guards and dradur on all sides.

Now. It has to be now.

She pressed her will into that image, sought it in space and shifted. The fabric of reality splinted, and she vanished from the atrium's entry way.

Time stopped, darkness stretched, space re-opened with a screech and Sellan dropped into the clearing. She ducked, magic arcing overhead, dradur swinging wildly at guards as someone of exceptional power fired shot after shot at a single target.

The sound of her arrival drew the melee to a pause.

For a breath, nothing moved.

The Orthian spared her a glance, eyes darting between her and Tamyr. Her marhain waited.

Tamyr recovered first, his guards panting and dripping sweat beneath their ceremonial armour and silly leather kilts. The emperor pointed, blue magic crackling up his arm. 'Deal with them. She is mine.'

Sellan's staff came up as a marhain swatted the Orthian boy from its path. He lifted from the ground and sailed across the clearing, skidding awkwardly into the shadows near the tree line. As one her monsters turned their ire on Tamyr, his guard charged out to meet them. Had they held shields, they might have stood a chance. Instead, their bodies took the brunt of the attack, flesh parting for tooth and claw, armour not nearly enough to forestall the relentsless barrage of club-like fists and scything, overgrown nails and finger bones.

Tamyr came at her like a crazed dog, teeth bared and magic flashing. Bolts screamed past her head, close enough to singe the lengths of her silver hair. Blood seeped from his side, his perfect white robes stained crimson and a dark, foul purple. The stink of burnt hair and flesh mingled with the stench of voided bowels and cloying corpse rot. His blue eyes shone with manic purpose, blond hair frenzied, his being electric with anger and denial and betrayal. How dare she attack him like this. How dare she challenge his supremacy, his *divinity!*

The bloody power of the Morritae rose to meet him and Sellan turned all she had to defending herself. The staff spun, deflecting withering blasts as one might bat away a fly. Her wards fell short though, pinging off into the trees or scoring trenches across the ground, missing Tamyr for the first few seconds.

Until he faltered.

He fired high, arms up, magic rupturing the air above Sellan's head.

She went low, dipping into a crouch, her arm extending, palm out. Crimson lightning caught Tamyr in the mid-section, glancing off his injured hip and spinning him sideways. Staggering, he roared and whirled to correct his stance, shock in his wide-eyes, magic firing in a savage volley with no aim or target. Just destruction. All he ever wanted was destruction.

A flare of blue light—pure, unadulterated energy—illuminated the atrium as night fell. Another marhain fell, victim to the relentless attack of the guards, and Sellan stumbled, gasping for air.

Her grip on the staff slipped.

Her leg collapsed and she followed it down, her knee slamming into the ground. Sharp heat cracked the bone on her thigh, and she screamed in wordless agony.

Tamyr emerged from the chaos, smug and triumphant. He'd absorbed her power, deflecting some, syphoning off the rest to restore his reserves.

Fucking typical. Sellan snarled and lurched up, her staff whirling, the butt connecting with his chin with a snap. Teeth rained from his mouth amidst a fountain of blood, shock warping his features as he struggled to regain his footing, teetering and blinking, clutching his jaw. The staff came around again and punched into his stomach, a pulse of magic ramming into his gut with the force of a draught horse's kick.

Gasping, Tamyr caught himself before he fell, whipping around to glare at Sellan. He hadn't expected this. He hadn't thought she'd last this long, hadn't anticipated she'd put up any kind of worthy fight.

She hadn't last time.

Last time she'd been too afraid. Frightened of what he might say, of the stories he'd tell, of how he might shame her family. She'd frozen, screaming on the inside while her body betrayed her, refusing to fight back, refusing to kick and scratch and rend his flesh with whatever weapon she could find. She'd hated everything about herself in that moment.

But she was not that girl, and she was no longer frightened.

She would fight and she would fucking win.

Tamyr charged and Sellan rose to meet him. Their magic met with earth-shaking thunder, the palace foundations trembling, masonry cracking and tumbling down in a hail of dust and stone chips.

Blasting, deflecting, parrying, shoving.

Another incantation, another chance shot.

The skin of her arms split, paring away from muscle and sinew. There was no more pain, just vengeance. Her spine an incandescent rod of magic burned at her very core. He spun, went to his knee and the heels of his hands met, his palms open toward her.

She couldn't move fast enough to dodge the blast. She didn't have time to ward a defence. It hit her like the collapse of a mountainside and Sellan's world went black.

Lidan shoved the ngaru back, spinning to kick it hard in the chest, cracking ribs as it fell. What would have killed a ngaru in the South Lands didn't come close to making a dent in these monsters.

Quick and muscled like a wrestler, it came back swinging. She went in hard, punching, jabbing her knee into its side, knives slashing and stabbing. Anything to wear it down, anything to create an opening for a head shot. Anything to drive it to a mistake, revealing the soft flesh of its neck.

A death scream tore into the twilight and Loge ended his ngaru with a grunt and flurry of curses.

'Ranger!' Thanie cried behind Lidan. 'Finish this!'

Magic boomed and another scream bid farewell, a wet thud as something heavy and dead hit the ground. There were more. There was no time to stop, no time to look.

Her ngaru turned its head, massive dog-like teeth slick with dark ooze and purple blood. Its head tilted, as if listening and Lidan took her chance. She leapt at the thing, catching it around the neck and swinging around to its back. It went to its knees, unprepared for her weight on its shoulders. Her knife plunged into its nape, parting the skull from the spine with a grisly crunch. A twist and a wrench and the knife came free, the corpse falling forward and face-planting the grass like a tree cut from its roots.

The explosion hit her before she fully found her feet, the concussion wave blasting her backward to skid across the grass. Ears ringing, Lidan gasped, her chest screaming for air. Her skin burned; her muscles trembled.

The world tilted, juddering off its axis.

Torn and bleeding in a thousand places, bruises and cuts welled with fresh blood. There could only be a handful of the creatures left now, but she'd long ago abandoned her count. Lidan pulled herself to her feet, wheezing and shaking. Her tunic was a ruin, her face swelling as the marks of too many hits emerged from beneath her skin. Her shoulder screamed as she worked a knot loose and spat a gob of blood on the grass.

'The fuck was that?' she croaked.

Thanie came to her feet and tore away a ruined sleeve hanging by a thread. Blood ran freely from a gash across the top of her arm and at least one ngaru claw had found purchase in the woman's side. 'Tamyr,' she replied.

Thanie would heal from her wounds as fast as Ran, but —

Ran... Panic tightened around Lidan's chest. 'Where's Ran?'

Thanie pointed in the direction of the explosion.

Lidan was running before she knew where she was going. Loge shouted and his footsteps hurried after her. Breath rasping in her ears, she didn't hear what he called, didn't stop to heed him. Heart pounding, branches whipped her face. She ducked below the limbs of trees and vaulted a carved stone seat.

Lidan broke the edge of the clearing; a gleaming lake stretched off into the lengthening shadows. She'd expected to see Ran fighting for his life against the emperor.

Instead, a man stood over her mother's moaning body.

Sudden rage boiled up; rage she hadn't thought she'd ever feel.

Lidan didn't stop.

He raised his hands, blue magic igniting at the tips of his fingers. He snarled and Lidan did not stop.

Instead, she screamed.

Tamyr glanced up in time to see her slam into him, a body-tackle folding him in half. They fell in a tangle across the grass, thrashing at each other in the churn of ngaru feet and soldier's boots.

She thought she heard Ran call as she staggered upright. She thought she heard Loge spit a furious string of curses as he emerged at the edge of the lake. She thought she felt Thanie unleash all the Underworld's ferocity on the ngaru.

Tamyr came at her before she knew any of it for sure.

His magic rained down and she dodged, weaving and ducking into a clumsy roll. She came up beside his feet, landed a few punches, shoving him back, slashing at his face, his arms, his torso as he blocked and counter attacked.

He disarmed her knives with a swift grab and flick, wrenching them from her gasp as they grappled, punching and snapping and biting like animals.

Lidan would not cede.

She would not see this monster stand over her mother like that. She would not allow it.

As awful as her mother was, she was still *her* mother. *Her* mother, *her* problem. Mistakes had been made and they would be paid for, but not today and not to this fucker.

Lidan drew her sword, the last weapon remaining to her name, slicing it at his head. He battered it away with a swat of magic, the energy burning her forearm to blisters. Lidan cried out and grasped at it, stumbling back.

He was fast—faster than any ngaru she'd ever fought, stronger and nimbler than a man should be after the fight he'd had, bleeding from as many wounds as she. He *should* have been weakened, should have been tiring, but it was as if he had an unlimited reserve, unending magic that boiled over like water from an untended pot.

Tamyr stormed and Lidan faltered beneath the onslaught. More of his hits connected than she could return. Her usual advantages crumbled under the weight of his attacks; her speed cut, her size and swiftness inconsequential as the emperor broke her down with no more than his fists.

No man was this strong, no man was this powerful.

Someone called her name.

She knew that pleading, begging, crying voice.

She'd heard it the day she was born, and she'd loathed the very timbre and cadence on more days than she could count. But it was still the sound of home. She hated it and adored it and she turned.

Sellan regained her feet, hunched, unaided by her staff. The sheer effort drew deep, weary lines in her face, the muscles of her neck taut, the strain shivering her legs, her arm shaking involuntarily.

Terror-wide eyes watched as time slowed. Lidan wondered what her mother saw.

An unruly child? A restless young woman?

A warrior? A fool?

A sharp sting and hot pain exploded in Lidan's stomach.

She doubled over, hands clutching at the agony, her mind spinning.

What?

Her hands came away wet, dripping red.

Sellan started screaming.

The dagger flashed before Sellan could move. Lidan hadn't seen it coming. How could she? She'd turned to look at her mother and missed the threat standing in front of her.

The steel vanished into her daughter's belly and twisted, wrenching out sideways and spraying blood in a sickening arc. Sellan screamed, shredding the falling night. She didn't turn to see if the rest of them saw it. She didn't wait or call to them.

She drew a bead on Tamyr and fired.

Her vision blurred, burying her pain, ignoring her body's protests. Sellan blasted her tormentor. Wards more powerful than she had the strength to maintain streaked across the clearing, syphoning off the magic given to her marhain until they dropped like flies around a corpse.

The battle noise faded.

Nothing mattered but her barrage.

Tamyr staggered, faltering, stumbling back toward the lake. Her breath caught as Lidan fell, hands clutching the ruin of her stomach. Blood vomited from her mouth, bright in the twilight.

Sellan bore down on Tamyr, her marhain crumbling as she drew off every drop of power, every spark she'd pledged to the Morritae, to Urda.

She took it all. Her bones hollowed, gutted by fire, the flames of her rage burning out what was left of her peace, what remained of her patience.

'You took me! You took everything I had, and I fought for every scrap I took back!' She didn't care if he couldn't hear her screams. He tried to deflect, tried to fight back. His blasts hit her, wounding and cutting deep. Blood sprang from the gashes, splattering across the grass.

Sellan didn't care.

She just hit him harder. Harder than he'd ever been hit in his miserable fucking life.

'You could have killed me. I'd have gone knowing it was the way of things. But you come for my fucking *daughter*? Have you any idea what I've done to keep her safe? The things I've fucking subjected myself to? The things I did *to her*?'

Her next shot sent him tumbling into the shallows, cold, dark water splashing as he fell. Bleeding and breathless, Tamyr emerged, ragged and soaked, but still sneering. 'She looked so much like you, Sel. I couldn't help it.'

Fury blind, she threw everything at him, ignorant to the cracks in her bones, the blistered, raw flesh peeling from her hands. Fuelled by rage and anguish, anger at the mistakes she'd made and the time she'd lost, the ignorance and arrogance she'd carried into the world, the wounds she'd passed to her child while running from them herself, the torment she'd sought to save Lidan from but subjected her to all the same. Sellan drove a storm toward Tamyr, one he would never escape. A cyclone of hatred and a maelstrom of self-loathing consumed them both, disembodied voices calling from beyond the tempest.

A man roared in defiance and Sellan felt the power of Ortus surge.

Running footsteps charged the fray.

A blade flashed.

The ranger plunged a sword deep into Tamyr's abdomen and the emperor's magic vanished.

The blue lightning disappeared. The incandescent light in his eyes blinked out.

Tamyr coughed and a gout of blood spewed forth.

Sellan knew that sword. Lidan's sword.

Lidan...

Magic fading, heat dissipating, Sellan collapsed.

In the churned grass and mud, blood and gore, marhain ichor and the detritus of battle strewn around her, Sellan stared.

The ranger, the tool of Ortus, ripped the sword free and Tamyr staggered. His hands clutched vainly at his belly, the purple-grey ropes of his intestines snaking out from between his fingers. Blood spewed from his mouth again and he winced. Their eyes met and he grimaced, lips moving as if to speak.

The ranger swung the sword.

Steel met flesh, a blade of the south spraying a rooster tail of blood across the lake shore. Tamyr's head separated from his body, the two pieces falling like the shards of a shattered glass. The splash echoed through the atrium, silence reigning in the aftermath.

The water darkened. The body bobbed beside the head.

Sellan sighed.

Lidan fell, clutching her stomach, folding in half around the wound and staring in blank horror at her hands.

Ran sprinted, calling out to Thanie as the last of the dradur dropped like discarded toys. A lump of terror rose in his throat, and he dropped to his knees, sliding across slick grass, bright blood bubbling at Lidan's lips.

'No, no, no, stay with me. We're here. We're all here, you'll be fine—'

She coughed and blood splattered his face.

He didn't reach to wipe it, his hands pressed to her wound, desperately pushing torn skin together, willing something of his magic to heal her, begging her insides to go back where they belonged.

The blade lay not a foot distant, the slight curve of the steel shockingly familiar, as though he'd seen it a thousand times before.

He had.

It was an imperial dagger. It had killed more dradur than he could hope to claim. It was Lidan's knife.

Tamyr had used *her* knife.

Bile rose, the only thing that could dislodge the choking horror. Ran bit down hard. He would not break now. Not here. Not when he could save—

A desperate, rasping gurgle drew his gaze from the pumping wound.

Her eyes wide, her hand clung tight to his sleeve. Lidan couldn't speak, though she tried. The colour drained from her face; light faded from her emerald eyes.

'Liddy?'

In the very corner of his vision, Thanie stood paralysed. Her hands trembled, the rest of her frozen in shock.

Ran pressed the wound again. The gush slowed, the bleeding eased. Again, he forced his magic against it and again it did nothing. What use was all this power, all that training, if none of it could save her? What fucking use was he to any of them if he couldn't save her? Ran shook his head, a futile refusal of what he knew to be true. He brushed tangled locks from her eyes.

Adventurous and determined eyes, eyes that saw the good in people and their danger. Eyes that saw hope for something more. They stared past him, as if he wasn't there.

As if he never had been at all. As if she hadn't been those things and so much more.

As if his friend wasn't there anymore.

As if she'd gone and left without saying goodbye.

She wouldn't leave without saying goodbye.

No.

Never.

He bit his lip to stop it shaking, drawing blood. 'Liddy?'

Motionless, blood-flecked lips. A glassy, vacant stare at nothing but the sky above the reaching trees. Her last breath left her, a whisper no one heard in the storm of screaming and dying.

Lidan was gone.

CHAPTER FORTY-NINE

The Imperial Palace, Wodurin, the Woaden Empire

Sellan blinked.

Night had engulfed the sky above the atrium, silence settling like a fog over the garden. In the near distance, cracks rent in the stonework during the battle gave way to gravity, enormous lumps of masonry tumbling from the rim of the atrium, thumping into the soft earth.

She *should* be dead.

By the gods she wished she was.

Her gaze dropped from the sky, following the line of the trees and the pale light of the moon. A few torches burned on the mezzanine. Not many. Most of the slaves were dead or gone. There was no one left to light them.

Within the space of a breath, the ranger crossed her line of sight and crouched. His hands grasped at something, a desperate moan escaping his throat. Wordless yet heavy with meaning, his anguish drew her eye.

Blood.

So much blood.

Small hands, covered in pale little scars.

One hand fell to the side, flopping to the grass and the muck. It didn't twitch or grasp. It didn't move at all.

Little fingers she'd seen curl around her own when they were still so helpless, so vulnerable she'd sworn to burn the world for them. Hands that learned the work of death to defend their people, hands that had tried so hard to please, so hard to do right.

Sellan's gaze traced the length of the motionless arm, the skin above leather braces paling. A slack jaw, soft lips, eyes partly closed.

No...

Others gathered nearby, forms she couldn't discern through the murk of her mind.

'Liddy? Liddy, it's me. You have to come back. Please…' the ranger begged, his voice tiny for a man so tall, cracking at the edges like ice holding more weight than it could carry.

He was wrong.

Sellan knew he was wrong. He couldn't be right.

'It's Loge, please come back.'

Lidan didn't move.

Sellan blinked hard and her heart stopped.

The Orthian boy sat curled around his sorrow, caked in blood and staring. Thanie stood further off, pale as the moon and rigid. Only Loge moved. Everything else was either dead or had fled.

Soldiers' bodies cooled beside marhain, the lapping of the lake against the shore a far-off whisper, the ripples of Tamyr's fall fading as Sellan rolled over.

Her throat contracted and her heart hammered in and out of time, a hard thump knocking the wind from her chest again and again, pumping anxiety and grief and horror to every extremity.

It was all she had left. The only thing that kept her going.

She clenched her jaw until it shook. 'No.'

Loge snapped around, glaring, desperate hands tugging the body closer. Lidan's body. Lidan's blood all over him, soaking his shirt, his trousers, smeared from where he tried to stop the flow that was no longer a pump but more of a seep. 'The fuck did you say?'

There was no sensation below Sellan's waist, not even a twinge as she heaved herself onto her belly, her legs dragging. Everything she should have felt—pain, burning, tingling—all gone, erased in the blink of a star in the darkness above.

Sellan ignored the void and crawled.

'I said, *no*,' she repeated through gritted teeth.

Hadn't he fucking heard her? He was *wrong*. She would prove it. He was so completely wrong. Lidan wasn't coming back because she hadn't gone anywhere.

She couldn't. It wasn't possible.

It simply *was not possible*.

450

Sellan dragged herself by her elbows, her hands bloodied, blistered wreckage. Useless. Her back broken, her spine shattered somewhere above her hips, it was all she could do to move the three feet between where she lay and where her daughter had fallen.

'What?' Loge's eyes gleamed with tears, his chin quivering. They fell, unashamed. He didn't reach to brush them away. Instead, he held Lidan tight, pulled her closer, crushed her against his chest as if the sheer force of his will and the ache of his arms would be enough to wake her.

Thanie didn't move more than to tremble where she stood. Sellan didn't think the Orthian even registered her movement, his eyes fixed on Lidan. What they saw was death. What they saw was the end.

What Sellan saw was impossibility.

She saw something that could not be because she would not allow it. Their grief was real, as real as Tamyr's cooling body in that pretty little lake he'd had made for his own amusement, but what Sellan saw was beyond that.

She saw beyond and refused, point blank, to allow it.

Her tears were ignored. Her pain dismissed. Her sorrow and the rising voice of dissent that whispered she was wrong, that this would not work—all rejected. She had no time for them. Had barely time left at all. What little remained would serve one purpose alone.

Loge watched her crawl with his black eye, lifeless and glistening in the pale light of the rising moon. Sellan glared at it, dragging herself closer, inch by fucking agonising inch.

'You can't have her.' She didn't speak to Loge, the ranger who'd survived death. She looked deep into his eye and spoke to Ortus. That fucker was listening. She knew he was there, watching, waiting for his due. '*You cannot fucking have her!*'

Her arm extended and she grasped the lifeless, outstretched palm of her daughter. Her baby. Her small, innocent girl who'd fought so fucking hard. Sellan's grip tightened, and she screwed her eyes shut.

'You *will not* have her.'

Sellan unleashed it all.

A torrent of power, everything she had left. Her life, her loves, her fears, her doubts, her dreams. Her vengeance and her pride, her joy and her hope. All of it, the small and the colossal, all coursed up her arm and into Lidan.

Red raw and losing blood, losing time, losing strength, she poured all of who she was, had been and could be. Every year she had left to her name and would never use, never see. She gave her daughter the regret and the sorrow, the forgiveness she wished she deserved and knew she did not.

She gave it all up, glancing at the shadows behind Loge's stunned face, ignoring the gasps of shock. Sellan found Ortus. He stood dark and stoic in the evening, surrounded by blood and death and the wreckage of her revenge.

Sellan had done what she'd come here to do. It was over for her. She'd defied gods before, and she grinned at the confusion in his violet eyes. 'You cannot have her. You're taking me instead.'

The night imploded into white, and Sellan vanished.

CHAPTER FIFTY

Beyond the edge of everything...

She saw her mother's face as she fell back into time. Toppling through a thunderstorm, she'd almost missed Sellan. They caught each other for a moment, no longer than a breath held against the force of a racing current, her mother's hand clamped to Lidan's wrist.

Words weren't enough in that split second of aborted time. They couldn't hope to express the pain and regret, the bone-deep yearning to atone for past mistakes. Lidan didn't get to ask why or how. There wasn't the time or the need.

She'd died.

They both had. One before the other. One to save the other. One to bring the other back.

There was sorrow in Sellan, throbbing up Lidan's arm. This was the last thing her mother could do to make things right, the final act within her power to force upon the world. Sellan's intent rushed Lidan, raw thought and emotion crashing in, leaving no doubt about what her mother's actions meant.

Lidan would live.

Lidan would go on living.

She'd have the years Sellan would have squandered on revenge and running and hating and self-loathing. She'd take them and turn them into something worth remembering, her chance to walk her own path returned, permission given to step beyond the bounds of what had been expected or required. There was nothing in the past but shadows and ghosts. Going back there was folly.

Sellan smiled and let go. Lidan tried to scream but the sound died before it left her throat.

The white place collapsed and Lidan lurched, gasping like a fish on a bank, her lungs burning and eyes watering. Arms held her tight, her stomach a ragged mess of pain and pressure. She moved, but not by the power of her own legs. Someone carried her, staggering to a stop as she writhed in their embrace.

She moaned and Loge stopped running.

'What are you—' Ran started.

'She's back, she's alive,' came Loge's breathless reply.

'Took longer than I expected,' Thanie said with a grunt of disapproval. 'You have to keep moving. Get her back to the house. I have things to see to here.'

'Wait, what could you—' Ran began again.

'Just get her the fuck out of here before anything that looks like a guard arrives. If you're caught here, you're dead. Don't think he won't happily take you either. There's no one coming to save *you* from Ortus.'

The jolting of Loge's hampered, limping run rocked Lidan back into the darkness. When her eyes fluttered open again, the lintel of a gate passed overhead, shadowed in the light of the full moon.

Time shifted like quicksand, and she slipped again, this time into the clutches of sleep.

Beyond the compound walls, Wodurin descended into madness, chaos in full reign within an hour of them shutting the gate to the house courtyard. Ranoth hadn't dared do more than watch from a second-storey balcony, his eyes on the alley beside the house, wary of looters and opportunistic thieves looking to take advantage of the murder of an emperor.

Fires peppered the upper city, a ring around the palace in a glowing orange crown of flame and billowing smoke. He'd heard stories, read them in books, been taught the history of the Woaden and their ways, but never had he thought to bear witness to a Purge.

The death of an emperor by natural causes was as rare as an eclipse, most finding their end at the point of a blade, or by poison or war. No matter how the man died, the Purge that came after outshone their final moments by the power of a thousand suns.

Up on that hill, even before Tamyr's body had cooled, the great families vied for position. Some sought the throne for themselves, others would fall in line behind the heir and their factions. Whoever came out on top would ensure those who opposed them didn't see the following dawn. And thus, the new regime began, awash with the blood of the one before.

This far removed from the palace and the powerful houses of the Empire, they were safe enough. No one would come here looking for an ally or a foe. Sellan's family were too far down the food chain to matter. Ran watched for a sign of Thanie in the mayhem, some indication she'd made it out of the palace alive. He couldn't say why he cared. Couldn't explain why he wanted her back behind these walls rather than out there amongst the rabble. Not more than two months ago he'd wanted her dead. What was so important that she'd risk remaining at the palace?

His mind a churn of conflicting images and emotion, he wrestled for control of the trembling waves shuddering through him, triggered one moment to the next by memories of the atrium.

Lidan's last breath, her last gasp for life, her last moment. His desperate hands pressed to her wound. The blood pumping through his fingers, hot and viscous; a sensation so intense he picked and scratched at his skin, trying to scrub it out.

What Ran couldn't reconcile was the magic it took, the sheer power required to bring Lidan back. Sellan had literally shredded herself out of existence. She'd poured every part of her magic and her being into Lidan and winked out like a gale-blown candle.

Nothing left. As though she'd never been there at all.

Ran's hand clenched; broken, bloodied nails biting the flesh of his palm, tears welling. Awful truth weighed on his chest. An incredible magic-weaver—a mage without equal in Coraidin—had sacrificed her life to bring her daughter back from the dead. An act of utter selflessness so violent it had torn Sellan apart.

Even with the power of the gods at her fingertips, it had killed her, and with her all hope for Iridia had died. The thread between him and his ghost was as thin as a spider's web and stretched beyond all recognition. It was a wonder it held at all. It wouldn't last, though. It wouldn't be enough to hold her here.

Iridia had emerged from the void beyond the veils in the hours since returning to the house, but still her voice remained too distant to hear, her face too far off to see. By all the gods and the sky and the world at his feet, Ran needed her now. More than he ever had, more than he ever thought he would, he simply *needed* Iridia; by his side, at his back, leading him to the other side of his fear, peeling back the facade of his bravado and bluster. He needed her like air, and nothing he could do would spring open the locks on her prison.

Loge was upstairs somewhere, welded to Lidan's side for fear she might fall back into the realms of the dead, leaving Ran to tend the hearth and half-heartedly search out some food.

The full depth of night encircled the city by the time Thanie eased back the kitchen door and stepped into the dim light of the hearth fire. A man followed her in, battered and bruised, limping through to the darkness of the house with little more than a nod of recognition for Ran. She'd found Eddark then. Ran didn't have the energy to ask or care how.

'A copper for your thoughts?' Thanie muttered as Eddark disappeared.

'They're worth a weight of gold tonight.' How could he put any of it into words without sounding selfish and entitled? One of his closest friends had quite literally died in his arms and all he could think about was freeing Iridia.

But what else was there to do now?

Sellan was dead, or at least some version of dead. Every one of the new dradur had died with her. She'd killed them in the end, sucking away the power she'd given them like she'd never meant them to have it.

Ran had wanted her dead as much as he needed Iridia to be alive. To bring Iridia back, her killer had to die. In that transaction, all the years the murderer would have lived returned to the victim, all the time they'd stolen returned to the one they'd robbed so grievously.

But Sellan had given those years to Lidan.

Nothing remained for Iridia.

And nothing remained for him.

Was he to return to the Keep? To Sasha and Quaid? Should he go back to Kotja and his mother and sister, to help them launch a rebellion that would invariably end in his father's death or his own? Could he risk their lives with his presence, knowing Villia would turn on him at the earliest opportunity?

'I haven't a weight of gold, but I can carry some of the burden,' Thanie offered. Their eyes met for the briefest moment and every dark thought he'd ever had about her paled into insignificance against what they'd faced together. Thanie had only ever wanted justice. Had Ran wanted anything different for the wrongs done against him? 'If you'll let me.'

'I... I don't know...' he murmured. A plate of cold food sat beside him, untouched. The urn of ale on the table was close to empty. Two more lay drained beside it, the dull warmth of alcohol still not enough to soothe the pain.

Thanie took a seat opposite, grimacing as she lowered into the chair. She'd fought hard today, and it showed in cuts and bruises and blood, dark smudges under her eyes. 'Is it Iridia?'

Ran looked up. *How did she...?*

She tapped her temple. 'She's faint. Barely there at all. I noticed too. I felt what Sellan did to her.' She sighed and laced her fingers together on the table. 'Do you want to know where I've been?'

Ran shrugged, too numb with exhaustion to speak, too heart-sore to form a coherent sentence.

'There's an archive in the palace. A high-level, top-secret kind of place. Only the highest mages in the Academy ever get access to it. My teachers knew of it, so did my class. We were, after all, training to investigate and those records were often needed to form cases. Not one to sneeze at an opportunity, I found it.' She drew a narrow scroll from the pocket of her tattered, bloodied gown and placed it on the table. '*That* is the last remaining record of a spell to return the dead to the realm of the living.'

Ran's breath caught. 'Someone wrote it down?'

Thanie nodded. 'They did, many centuries ago.'

'It's been in an archive this whole time?'

'You'd be surprised what's hidden in the dusty libraries and private collections of this continent.' Thanie's knowing look gave him pause. Memories faltered before his eyes of a scroll once given to him by a tutor.

Ran's hand waved in an exasperated kind of way, fuzzy from drink and not enough sleep. His magic fizzed uselessly at the edge of his consciousness, yet he thought he felt Iridia draw closer. 'If it's as easy as reading a recipe, why isn't everyone doing it?'

'Because no one knew it was there. I had a suspicion but not certain knowledge. As for why it's never used, well...' Thanie unwound a ribbon from the barrel of the parchment, carefully unrolling the paper until it stretched across the table. Slowly, she turned it toward him, weighed down the curling corners with the empty ale urns, then leaned back into her seat.

Ran scanned the length of the scroll. His heart thudded hard in his ears.

Thanie's storm-grey eyes darkened in the shifting shadows of the room. 'I was wrong, Ran. The killer's death doesn't gift the victim the years of their life. It merely opens a door. The scales are tipped then, too heavily toward death with both on the far side, with no retribution on our end. What brings them back is something else entirely.'

A heavy pause filled the night. Ran stared at her, his heart in his throat, his tongue too thick to talk. He couldn't believe the faint, scrawled ink, his unpolished Woaden just enough to translate the text.

'No one uses the spell because the sacrifice required is much more personal than the death of a murderer,' Thanie went on. 'It's something you, the magic-weaver, have to give. The only question is, are you willing to do it?'

He swallowed hard. It was an immense choice, a life changing decision that would alter who and what he was for the rest of his time on this world.

His head twitched in a nod. There was no question. It was not an option. There was only one answer.

'Yes.'

In their rush from the kitchen to the yard, Iridia slipped further, despite her attempts to claw her way back. Her voice faded even now, calling urgently through the veils to him, to Thanie, to anyone. The north wind ripped across the yard at the back of the house and the moon rode high. Ran stood in the dark with Thanie at his back. The teeth of the wind cut through his shirt, bit his skin, numbed him against what he was about to endure.

'Call to her, Ran,' Thanie ordered. 'Do it now or the thread snaps and you lose her forever.'

Ran sent his voice across time and space, silent to the living, a siren call to the dead, his heart pounding, his skin tingling. Exhausted as they both were, their sheer determination drove them on. It had to be done *now*. There was no time to wait, no time to tell Loge or ask after Lidan, no option left but to try and succeed or die in the attempt.

Iridia? he asked the night, pressing against the veils between the realms, searching for a chink in its impregnable armour. There was a break here somewhere, a weak spot he could exploit. His eyes slid shut and he pushed, seeking, searching, asking for a sign, listening for her voice.

She was there. He knew she was there.

A whisper on the wind.

Ran?

It was gone as soon as he clutched after it. Frustration welled in his chest but he forged on, teeth clenched in determined rage.

Come on... He flexed his fingers, magic pooling. He reached again. *Iridia?*

The air pressure changed, and something flew at the membrane between worlds, bulging it toward him. It creaked and moaned, protesting the expansion, fighting the will of another.

Ran snapped out and caught it.

He knew that presence. Knew it like he knew the creases on his hand.

Ran! Iridia cried, her voice distant and muffled, like she was trapped in a storm, parchment thin and fading no matter how hard she pushed back.

'Now!' he called to Thanie. Her hand caught the back of his neck and he collapsed to his knees.

'You have her tight?' she demanded. The wind picked up, dragging her words away like tattered flags in the dark.

'As tight as I'll ever get. Do it!'

'You're sure? I can't undo this!' A gale buffeted them now, jolting them back and forth, whistling through gaps in the gate, smoke from far-off fires stinging his eyes and burning his throat.

'If it kills me, I want her free!' At least then he'd die knowing he'd done something good, that his life had mattered for something other than vengeance. If it killed him, he'd go knowing he'd left something behind that deserved to be there. 'Take it!'

Thanie's hand clenched and Ran roared into the wind. Dust and smoke and debris flicked up, his hair caught by swirling gusts. The witch's voice deepened, dropping off the natural scale and into a distorted snarl as she intoned the words and drew on his power.

Ran let it go.

He released it all to Thanie, holding nothing back, not a single spark or a moment of regret. He let Thanie take it and fell into the bliss of knowing that if he survived, Iridia would be here. That alone was worth the pain. That alone was worth the agonising flames consuming his power.

His grip on Iridia tightened as she grabbed onto him. Cold hands clutched at his, fingers wound in tight around his wrists, the veils peeling back with the reluctance of sinking-sand. Her voice, crying out in pain, grew clearer, closer, nearer. Her hands more solid, her arms now, up to her shoulders.

Thanie pushed harder, spoke faster. Her draw on Ran's magic doubled down and he roared at the pressure in his back, the white-hot burn of the power finally giving over to Thanie's will.

A deafening rip echoed up the walls of the compound, shaking the very foundations of the city, and Iridia materialised from the darkness. She collided with Ran, toppled him backward. They slammed into a stable door with a reverberating crash.

The wind died and Thanie swore through clenched teeth. With a splash he heard her dunk her hand in a rain barrel and hiss as icy water enclosed her arm. A burn in the shape of her hand branded his neck, his lower back a concentration of rippling agony. Something heavy rested on his chest, pressing down, suffocating him. He lurched beneath it, groaning.

The dead weight didn't move.

Ran blinked and turned his head painfully toward it.

Iridia lay diagonally across his chest, clear blue eyes staring at the sky, her silver blonde hair catching the light of the torch by the kitchen door. At her throat, the old gaping wound didn't bleed. Her chest didn't rise or fall.

Was she alive?

Dread gripped Ran, panic rising, his hands shaking. 'Iridia!'

A hard gasp and a jolt. She lurched up and scrambled across the cobbles, crouching in a shadow. Hacking a violent cough, she doubled over, clutching her throat and wheezing for air she hadn't drawn in decades. From the shadows, her eyes gleamed bright, ethereal, unnatural—the eye-shine of a beast rather than a person. Still she coughed, the sound like boiling gravel in her chest.

Ran threw a desperate questioning look at Thanie. The woman sat slumped on a step, holding her stomach as if ready to vomit, no help to anyone even if she had known what to do.

He didn't dare approach Iridia. Didn't dare interrupt the process of return. He'd been warned it was messy, warned it could take weeks if not months for her to feel human again, and yet he lived in blind hope she'd make it.

Ever so slowly, in the smallest increments, the eye-shine diminished, the coughing eased. Her hand fell away and Iridia crawled forward on wary, wobbly limbs. Her shift was torn and bloodied. Her skin milk-pale in the light of the moon. But her throat wound was naught but a scar, the heave of desperate lungs slowing as she caught her breath.

'Ran?' Iridia asked in a ragged, husky whisper.

'Are you really here?' He didn't dare touch her. What if she disappeared into the calming wind? What if she faded with the coming dawn?

Curious, yet hesitant, like a wary cat, she crouched just within reach. She didn't have the eyes of the dead like Loge. She'd never been properly dead, never passed into their realm like he had. She'd remained stuck, caught in-between.

'*Am* I really here?'

His fingers danced across the back of her hand, a touch as light as silken thread. Ran's heart skipped. For the first time, she was warm to the touch. Apart from her scar, Iridia was as normal and human as the rest of them.

'I think so.'

'What did you *do*?' Iridia scowled and Ran would have laughed if his entire body hadn't felt like it was on fire. That accusing frown hadn't changed. It was Iridia down to the ground. When he didn't answer, she smacked his arm.

He pulled himself up to sit on the frigid cobbles, his back aching like he'd been hit by a falling anvil. 'Gave up my magic.'

'What?' Iridia demanded. Silence pressed in like murky water, wonder and panic in her eyes. She scanned down his body as if searching for the spark she'd welded herself to in the house of bones. Eventually her gaze returned to his face. '*All* of it?'

A moment of doubt caught in his throat, and he searched within. Nothing. Not a warm glow, not a glimmer of residue. 'Every last drop.'

Across the yard, Thanie smiled and heaved herself up before stepping back into the house, no doubt looking for a bottle of hard liquor and a bed. Sadness etched itself into the lines of Iridia's face, worry warring with anger at his rash choices and headstrong will.

'Why would you do that?' She shook her head, silver hair falling in a curtain, a shadow descending over her iridescent eyes. 'Why would you waste such a thing on me?'

'Waste?' Ran repeated. 'How could you ever think such a thing a waste? My whole life I've wanted to do something that mattered. Defending my home or protecting my family. I wanted my time here to *matter*. And in all my life, I've never seen a more worthy use for such power than bringing you back. I didn't want it. I *never* wanted it. I told you in Tingalla—whatever the price, I'd pay it. No matter the cost, I was getting you out of there.'

For the length of a heartbeat, a span of time that somehow felt like an eon, Iridia looked down at her hand. Blood pumped through the veins. What had once been cold now warmed despite the chill in the air. A finger twitched out to touch him, tentative but electric, lightning and quicksilver charging through Ran's chest.

Then Iridia smirked. 'You never could leave a thing alone once you got an idea in your head.'

'Not now, not ever.'

CHAPTER FIFTY-ONE

The sun broke the overcast sky, light leaking through the cracks in the clouds, long fingers slicing down to drape across Wodurin. Lidan gingerly inched herself out of bed, Loge's sleepy groan drifting in her wake. Unsteady steps brought her to a mirror and dizziness bloomed black in her vision. She wavered, clutching at her sleeping shirt.

Nausea rolled through her belly, a rush of uncomfortable heat pumping down her limbs. For a moment she thought it might take her to her knees, and she grabbed at the arm of a plush lounge, leaned into the pain, let the agony pulse through and out the other side, releasing it into the brightening day.

Cautious fingers pulled at the shirt until the hem came up above her hips, above her navel and to the base of her ribs.

A ropey scar glared back from her reflection. A proud wound, bordered by mottled bruises, shades of blue-black and purple stretching from her ribs to her groin. Nausea rolled again and her fingers slid across the puckered skin, thick with meaning and memory. Macha would be pleased with this one.

It hurt. By the ancestors it *hurt*, but it wasn't going to kill her. The magic her mother poured into her body hadn't simply brought her back from the brink, it had healed her from the inside out. The tear hadn't been stitched. There was nothing to tend or dress, no need to watch for infection. It was just... done.

A patchwork of bruises and cuts marked Lidan from the crown of her head to the bones of her ankles. Her once-broken collarbone ached and her vision dragged, jumping to catch up with her head when she turned.

The night had been spent lurching in and out of consciousness, asking Loge the same questions over and over.

Where was her mother? Dead, he told her, reciting the tale of the fight again. Lidan recalled seeing Sellan in the white place, along the ragged border between the realm of the living and the place between. She remembered the vivid sensation of hope and grief—her mother's emotions, impressed on her as life passed between them. She still didn't truly understand why her mother sacrificed herself, some part of her remaining in the power she'd forced into Lidan through the raging burn on her lower arm.

Where were the ngaru, she'd asked Loge. Dead, he said, reassuring her that the monsters in her dreams weren't coming for her anymore. How long would it take to believe him? Would she ever not look over her shoulder or watch a shadow for movement that shouldn't be there?

What about Ran? Thanie? Alive. Downstairs. Waiting on his word of her recovery.

She'd collapsed into sleep then, knowing they'd survived. That Ran hadn't torn himself apart to destroy her mother. That Thanie hadn't been forced to murder her cousin and friend. That they'd made it out past the guards and tines and servants and escaped into the city. These things brought Lidan peace through the pain as her body stitched itself back together. It gave her a sense of right, that the world had been set back on its feet despite the gaping holes the fight left in her. The balance between Dennawal and the Morritae had been corrected. The feud between them—if only for now—had been doused by the failure of the Morritae's tool.

A howling wind had kicked up in the darkest part of the night, smoke choking in from beyond the window. Even now as she peered through the shutters, a dense haze settled heavy over the city. Lidan edged through the door and onto a walkway overlooking the atrium of her grandparents' city house, squinting against the hard light of day.

The city beyond the roofline looked like a battleground. Smoke rose in thick grey columns along the ridge around the palace. What looked like a great chunk of the outer wall had collapsed, and even at this distance, blackened smudges marred the otherwise pristine stone facade of the building, the fingerprints of fire and chaos.

In the apron of the palace, many of the enormous, opulent buildings were either actively aflame or smouldering. The citizens beyond the house shouted to one another, their language foreign to Lidan's ears but their tone carried all the meaning she needed.

Take what you can. Give nothing back. Survive. Keep your head.

She blinked in surprise. Had *they* done all this in their battle with Tamyr, or was this the fallout of the emperor's death? She remembered a glimpse of the man doubling over as Loge drove her sword deep into his gut. There was little chance he'd survived, not after stabbing Lidan with her own fucking knife. Loge wouldn't let that stand, even before death had eaten away at his humanity.

Dread and warning crept up her spine. Curious as she might be, she had no desire to wait around and find out who or what had caused the destruction around the palace. Someone would be searching for the emperor's killer. Someone would want to be the hero of the day, bringing either traitor or invader to justice for their attack on the seat of power. Someone had to have seen them leaving the palace too, Loge carrying her back to this house with Ran at his side. It was only a matter of time before a line was drawn between the two.

'You're up early,' a familiar voice said.

Lidan started and turned steadily toward the sound. Her vision wavered and she tried to smile a greeting, bruises protesting even that minute expression. How much worse was the discolouration of her face in the sunlight? 'I've had enough sleep for now.'

Ran stood from a bench—a stone plinth carved from solid marble—outside his room and limped heavily to her side. He was as bruised and battered and mangled as she was—both hands wrapped in bandages, soiled by dark patches where blood seeped through the cloth. His lips were cracked and cut, as was the skin above his eye. At the side of his neck, another gash marked where a ngaru claw had passed just shy of taking his head. None of these injuries should have been a surprise, not after the fight they'd endured. What surprised Lidan was that Ran hadn't healed.

Lidan frowned then wished she hadn't. 'You look awful.'

He paused. 'Thank you?'

'I meant,' she said, scrambling through the mud of her mind, 'you look as wrecked as me. That's not normal. Right? You're usually all healed up. Did you use so much of your magic that you can't?'

The fog settling over Lidan's thoughts made her wonder if she made any sense at all. Little points of light danced in her vision, her words slurring across her tongue, her sentences simple collections of barely connected words that sounded better in her head. Ran gave a little chuckle and turned to look at the city with a deep sigh. Emotion twitched his features. Was it sadness, regret? Sorrow in mourning? There was happiness too, a glimmer of joy at the edge of the pain.

'I gave up my magic last night. A last-ditch attempt to bring Iridia into the world of the living. Not unlike what your mother did for you.'

Lidan's jaw dropped. 'You did *what*? Did it work?'

He grinned, mischief bright in his blue eyes. 'Like a charm.'

'Where is she?' She glanced clumsily behind him as if the girl who once was a ghost might materialise from a doorway at any moment.

'Sleeping. Coming back from the dead is tiring.' A smirk slipped its confines and Lidan narrowed her eyes.

'Yes, I'm sure that's what wore her out.'

He couldn't even hold the mock look of offence and abandoned it in favour of a kind smile and a wink. Silence settled between them, the sounds of the waking city drifting on the wind with the smell of baking bread and suffocating wood smoke. Despite the madness of the night, the day dawned just like any other. Food had to be prepared, life would go on. The struggles on the palace hill were not insignificant but for the vast majority of Wodurin, they were not the end of the world.

In the shadowed colonnade by the atrium, a figure sat obscured, the smallest movement giving them away. Thanie stepped past, handing them a steaming mug before wading out amongst the herb beds.

'Who's that?' Lidan asked, her curiosity and trepidation muted by her weariness.

'Oh him? He came back with Thanie.' One of Ran's brows arched. 'Eddark.'

Lidan gaped in disbelief at the figure in the shadows. 'Surely he died in the crush?'

'These Woaden. Like cockroaches. Just when you think they're dead.' He made a circular gesture toward Lidan's stomach. 'Speaking of dead, how's the... *wound*?'

'Hurts like fuck, but it's healed. I'll live.' Blinking quickly, she scanned the horizon and cursed the stupid tears springing unbidden to her eyes. Her mother would never abide such soft sentiment. Not after everything she'd done to save Lidan from oblivion. She heard that acerbic voice, saw the stern frown and that emerald glare. 'Never thought I'd have Sellan Tolak to thank for that.'

'She actually did love you, in her own way.'

Lidan nodded. For a moment, she had no answer to that.

Sellan *had* loved her. It was that final act of sacrifice that proved it in the end. She'd loved Erlon and Marrit too. Lidan knew this to her bones. But the woman had wounded all of them in ways from which they couldn't recover. Sellan's was a sharp, unforgiving love. And while it *was* love, it was the kind that hurt. 'I wish she'd had a *better* way. Love shouldn't hurt, Ran. No matter how strong it is. But here we are.'

'Here we are indeed.' Ran's gaze tracked to the palace. 'I don't know about you, but I'm not planning on staying here a minute more than I have to. If history holds true, this place is going to eat itself alive for the best part of a year. Tamyr had a daughter, not much older than you. From what I saw yesterday at the demonstration, she's not at all ready to rule. What happens in this city at the end of an emperor's life is chaos at the best of times. I've no clue who or what will be left standing once this is done.'

'Where will you go?' Lidan asked, shielding her eyes from the dawning sun. It was an odd sensation, the thought of him walking away on a diverging path. She couldn't put her finger on why. Hardly more than a month had passed since they'd set out on this journey, though it seemed longer, as if time hadn't moved with the same flow.

'I need to see my mother. There are things happening at home that need seeing to...' He leaned down to rest his elbows on the balustrade and narrowed his eyes at the sunlight. She'd expected to sense peace in him now, fulfilment at the end of a long, hard road. Instead Lidan saw worry and anguish. The weight of seeking justice for Iridia and her people had been replaced by something else, something closer to home. 'A message arrived just before dawn. A bird from Soren, the king's agent.'

'He *found* us?' Lidan asked, unable to disguise her surprise.

'His contacts did. He's frighteningly well connected, though I'm beginning to think we weren't as stealthy as we thought we were.' Ran lifted the tiny slip of parchment between his fingers. 'He says Marrit found him. She's well. Angry at being left behind, but well. Brit and Aelish made our excuses to the Isordians, something about leaving for the coast. Zarad and Eian are with them still. I need to get them home. The wrath of Zarad's sister is not to be tempted.'

The gaping hole in his assertion stared at them both and he looked quickly away. Neither of them wanted to face the deeper question they should have been asking. Neither of them wanted to look out at the world from this new vantage and acknowledge that it was time to let things go. Lidan tilted her head to catch his eye. 'Can *you* go home, after all this?'

Ran shrugged and picked at his nails. 'I might have set my magic aside, but that doesn't change who I am. Unless we force it to, Orthia will never see me as anything but a threat to be eliminated. I can't do magic anymore, but I'm still a magic-weaver. People like me deserve better. I can't reclaim my old titles. And I don't want them. I have more important work to do.'

'Will you be happy with that, Ranoth Olseta of the North?' Her question burst out before she registered the words and immediately wished them back. What business was it of hers?

He took a moment, chewing his thoughts before he let them out. 'As much as I could expect to be, I suppose. There's justice in what we did. Vengeance for those lost, even if it didn't look exactly like we thought it might.'

When she didn't reply, Ran eased back from the handrail and turned to face her. 'What about you?'

Lidan sighed. There had been so much lost.

She looked down at herself and wondered how she'd survived it all. Her hands were scarred, her soul was scarred. Her mind would be forever haunted by the ghosts of the ngaru, of her dying little sister, and her friends. Her dreams would forever replay her mother's face as they whipped past each other in the place between. She'd never truly ease the ache in her repaired shoulder or reconcile that the man in her bed wasn't the Loge she'd known, but a version of him that had survived death. She'd always wonder what her life might have been had her father loved her for who she was, or if her mother hadn't carried the wounds of her past right on into her future.

None of it mattered.

The *what ifs* and the *maybes*. They were in the wind.

All Lidan had was the path she'd forged for herself, the journey she'd chosen beyond her father's needs and her mother's wants.

In the garden below, Thanie moved amongst the herbs, picking at this and sniffing at that. Lidan wondered if the older woman knew those words still echoed, the call to arms she'd issued all those years ago. Something told Lidan she did. Something told her Thanie knew exactly what she'd said and what she'd done, and just how the hard words of an old crone had turned the life of a small girl on its head.

Lidan let herself smile. Just a little, just for that.

'There was a time when I didn't care what happened after the ngaru fell. A time I didn't want to look beyond the things I had to do to stop them. But I can see a path now, a place where I can be… me. My own self. Not the person they wanted me to be.' *Her* journey. *Her* path. She liked the sound of that very much. 'I think it's the same for you, Ran. We're our own masters now. That has to make the fighting and the loss worth something.'

Ran waved his arm at the city beyond the opulence and splendour and the stench of the smoke. 'And where in this vast, untamed world will you go?'

She smiled and raised a suggestive brow. 'I hear the Archipelago is lovely this time of year.'

Epilogue

'So…' Macha began, stepping into time and onto a ledge of a wind-swept mountain. 'You won.'

'So it would seem,' Ortus replied. He turned, a smug smile dancing on his lips.

Macha looked at her nails. He wasn't even trying to hide it.

'No blood on those hands, though.' He said it like there should have been, though they both knew the truth.

'There never is.' She caught his gaze. 'For either of us.'

For a moment they stood together in the pause, the ridge of the mountain falling away in a cliff below, the wind whipping upward to catch the heavy lengths of their cloaks like the wings of an eagle.

'Change is coming,' Ortus said. Hands clasped behind his back, he looked for all the world like those human generals, surveying the field of battle after another good day of dying.

'It's already here,' she replied. He glanced at her, brow raised. 'Urda is dying.'

'As you predicted.'

'Her gamble failed.'

'And you?'

Macha shrugged. She had already rewarded the soldiers and guards who fell in the fight, sent them on to Ortus and the halls of their ancestors to feast and revel in their bravery. She had already seen to the warriors of the countless battles and skirmishes of that short day, a blip in time to her but an eternity to them. 'I had everything to gain should she succeed, and nothing to lose if she failed. She won't move against you again.'

Both brows rose then, and he nodded.

He saw. He knew.

Urda, regressing into the darkness of a forgotten deity, had put her faith and power in the losing side. Macha and their younger sister had not. Urda's mistake, her trust and blind faith, her hunger for power and control, would be her downfall. Fate already spiralled out of her hands; stories written not by the powerful behind the veil but by the actors on the stage. Choice was the door Urda's death would open. Free will was what her demise would herald. Both dangerous, both unknowable, both the source of death and war.

'Where does that leave us?' Ortus asked. Those violet eyes shone, intent and promise barely disguised.

'Even.' In exchange for her neutrality, Ortus had promised her the spoils of her sister's defeat. Macha touched his arm, her skin moon-pale against the dark umber of his. Her fingers traced the lines of the hard muscle beneath, ancient strength disguised by the gentle nature of a sleeping giant. She would not be on the wrong side of the fight should that giant ever wake. Macha allowed herself a smile. 'Urda diminishes. Someone must claim her mantle. It would be irresponsible to leave her duties unattended.'

'Indeed it would.' Ortus held her gaze. Lust evaporated to hard scrutiny. 'And the balance now restored? Does that remain unchallenged, as promised.'

'Of course, my love.' Her smile dazzled, genuine and bright. 'The balance is restored and will remain so. My sister and I have no need or desire to walk our elder's path nor partake in her folly.'

A younger, foolhardy goddess might have seen an opportunity and rushed to exploit it. Macha was many, many things, but stupid was not one of them. You didn't engineer the death of a god by being simple.

You did it by being careful.

Sharp.

Prudent.

Patient.

THE END

ACKNOWLEDGEMENTS

We made it.

It happened.

A whole trilogy, from start to finish.

I couldn't have done it without some very special people. People spread across the globe: new friends and old, family, readers and fans. People too numerous to name here. Every one of you made a difference, every message, every tweet, every positive review. You got me through a pandemic, another surgery on my hand, seven months stranded in Australia, waiting to get back to the UK. Thank you.

Anne & Ian - thank you just doesn't seem enough. Your enthusiasm and support is irreplaceable and immeasurable. I hope you are proud, because none of this was possible without you.

Hadrian - no matter how far I go, no matter how long I'm gone, you have my entire heart from the moment we say "see you later" to the moment I get back.

Graham - what an adventure we've been on? These books wouldn't have seen the light of day without your friendship, love, encouragement and support. I couldn't think of anyone I'd rather spend the apocalypse with.

My production team - Pen Astridge (covers), AJ Spedding (editing) and Clare Davidson (print edition interior design and formatting). You are stars and I'm honoured to work with you.

The SPFBO5 Finalist crew - nine incredible humans without whom I wouldn't have survived the two years from the launch of *Legacy of Ghosts* to the release of *Empire of Shadows*. Your impact on my life can't be overstated.

ABOUT THE AUTHOR

Splitting her time between Central Queensland, Australia and Lancashire, England, Alicia is a writer, a mum, and a cat-herder. There are rumours she may in fact be a quokka in disguise, but these are not to be believed. She began writing in her teens and never grew out of the phase, publishing *Blood of Heirs* in 2018, *Legacy of Ghosts* in 2019, and the final book of The Coraidic Sagas, *Empire of Shadows* in 2022. She is an accomplished editor and holds a Bachelor of Education and has studied a Post Graduate Certificate in Ancient History.

Ingram Content Group UK Ltd.
Milton Keynes UK
UKHW010652130723
425019UK00007B/40/J